The
DRESS

KATE KERRIGAN lives in County
Mayo, Eire, with her husband
and children. Her novels include
Recipes for a Perfect Marriage,
shortlisted for the 2006 Romantic
Novel of the Year Award and *Ellis
Island*, which was a TV Book
Club Summer Read

Also by
Kate Kerrigan

The
DRESS

KATE KERRIGAN

HEAD
of ZEUS

First published in the UK in 2015 by Head of Zeus Ltd

9 7 5 3 1 2 4 6 8

A catalogue record for this book is available from
the British Library.

ISBN (HB): 9781784082383
ISBN (XTPB): 9781784972288
ISBN (E): 9781784082376

Typeset by Adrian McLaughlin

Printed and bound in Germany
by GGP Media GmbH, Pössneck

Head of Zeus Ltd
Clerkenwell House
45-47 Clerkenwell Green
London EC1R 0HT

WWW.HEADOFZEUS.COM

FOR NIALL, LEO AND TOMMO

It is amazing how complete is the delusion that beauty is goodness.

Leo Tolstoy.

The
DRESS

Prologue

Ireland, 1935

The schoolmaster found the boy collapsed against a stone wall at the side of the road. His nose was smashed and bloody and his right eye so swollen that he could barely see out of it.

'Dear God, Francis, what happened to you?'

The boy looked at him and shrugged. His eyes were defiant, angry.

'Your father?'

John Conlon held out his hand to help the child up, but Francis waved him away and forced himself to stand alone. His legs were shaking. He had taken some battering that morning. His father had caught him unawares and dragged him from the bed. To stop himself from crying Francis reminded himself that he had fought back and given his father as good as he got. It was the first time he had stood up to his father, and that was how Francis knew it was time for him to leave.

The last thing Francis wanted was his teacher's pity. He was a man of fifteen, he could look after himself now. John held out a handkerchief and he took it.

'I'm leaving anyway,' he said, wincing slightly as he put the cotton square up to his nose to stem the flow of fresh blood. 'I'm going to America.'

John Conlon leaned against the wall with his pupil. He had taught the Fitzpatrick boy from when he was five, until last year. His mother had died and his younger brother, Joe, had been put in with the nuns, so Francis was left alone in the house, with his brutal pig of a father. The area they belonged to was broad and remote, a vast hinterland of bog and mountain. It was a place where a man could hide his wife and children away from the eyes of the world, but not those of a prying Irish schoolmaster. John Conlon made it his business to know every child in the area and managed to persuade most of the parents to leave them in school, until they could read and write. Francis had been with him until he was thirteen, but had left then to stay at home to nurse his sick mother. Now she was dead and the baby had been taken away, so there was nothing left at home for him. He was a bright young man and John believed he could have had a future. However, with a father like that, he never stood a chance.

'America? That's a long way off,' said John.

Francis glowered at him; he could feel himself starting to crack. He had no idea how he was going to get there, but his mother had a brother in New York and before she died she gave him a letter, saying he would secure Francis a job if he could get himself to America. The only thing Francis knew for certain was that he was never going back home. Not ever.

'Will you come back to the house and have a bite to eat with us, before you head away?'

Francis knew he could not walk another step that day; it would be dark soon and he did not want to sleep on the side of the road, so he followed the teacher to his horse and cart. He hated to take charity from anyone, but John Conlon was different, and Francis felt the teacher genuinely liked him. Maybe John would lend him enough money to get him as far as Dublin, where he could pick up a job and start earning for his passage to America.

They drove to Bangor town in silence. John could see the boy was exhausted, scrawny and weak; he hadn't eaten for days. Francis was five miles from his home when the teacher picked him up. He might have died there and would anyone have cared? Would anyone have even noticed?

When they arrived at the Conlons' terraced townhouse, John's wife Clare made a huge fuss of him at the door.

'Would you look at the state of the child? Mother of God, he should be in a hospital!'

She sat Francis down on the settle, fetched a blanket, draped it over his shoulders, then set about cleaning his face.

'This might hurt a bit,' she said and, before he could object, she twisted his broken nose back into place with a loud crunch, then wiped away the blood with a warm cloth.

Francis leaned his cheek into her hand. Her touch put him in mind of his own mother. When he was very small, he remembered her tending to him like that, but not for a long time now. Clare Conlon was assured and matronly: a strong loving woman. His own mother had been too weak, too afraid to love her sons, for fear of upsetting her husband.

Francis closed his eyes and, as his face reached for the touch of maternal love, he felt tears starting to pour down his cheeks. Clare wiped them away softly, pretending not to have seen, until he opened his eyes and said, 'May I use the toilet?'

'Of course,' she said, laying down the cloth. 'You go out back and I'll fetch you some clean clothes. Then we'll have tea. There's no better medicine than a cup of hot, sweet tea.'

As he left the kitchen to go out into the yard, Francis paused in the scullery and overheard the couple talking about him.

'Surely to God, John, something can be done about that man.'

'I'll go and have a word with him.'

'You'll do no such thing – your interfering will only make things worse. Francis can stay here with us.'

'Clare, be practical. We have the baby now.'

'Well, we can't send him back to that brute, and I'll not see him in one of those industrial schools...'

The boy had heard enough. He had intended to ask John for a loan, but he could tell, now, from the way they were talking, that they thought he was still a child. They could send him to the reform school, which was no better than a prison, and he might never get out of it. No. He had to get away. He knew Clare kept cash in a tin on the second shelf of the dresser, next to where he was standing. He had seen her take it out to pay a turf man, once, when he was studying there, after school. Francis would eat with them, stay overnight on the settle bed in their kitchen and then leave at first light. Clare would not notice the money gone for days, weeks maybe. He wasn't a thief. He would write from America and explain. He would send her a gift – jewellery perhaps, a pair of gloves – he just needed a start.

His heart was thumping as he reached up for the tin. His hands shook. He reached in and took out a handful of notes, but as he was stuffing them in his pocket he heard a noise behind him. He started slightly, then saw that it was the Conlons' baby, who was in a pram just outside the open back door. She was sitting up and looking straight at him, her head, in a frilly bonnet, cocked to one side. She was frowning, as if she knew what he was doing. If she started crying, John and Clare might wonder why he wasn't already outside in the lavatory, in the yard, and guess what he was at. He went over

4

to placate her, but as he moved forward, something in the child's gaze stopped him in his tracks. Her eyes were locked on his. She was not a pretty child. She had a big round face and an almost comical scowl, but her eyes radiated the kind of deep knowing you would expect from a wise old woman. It was as if the baby could see inside his soul. In that moment Francis felt so ashamed that he turned to put the money back in the tin, but, as he was reaching to take it out of his pocket, Clare walked in, so he kept it where it was.

'Ah,' she said, 'you're back. I'll just feed the baby, then I'll put the dinner on. You go and sit by the fire with John and rest yourself.'

As Clare picked up the baby and laid her across her shoulder Francis looked across at the strange child and, as he did, she smiled, a huge toothless grin. All is forgiven, he thought. He pulled a face at her, and the baby giggled.

'She likes you,' Clare said, laughing.

Francis looked at the plainly dressed master's wife and her peculiar looking baby. As they smiled at him, he suddenly had an overwhelming sense of their beauty and a feeling of deep happiness opened up inside him. Francis Fitzpatrick had never felt anything like it before. He did not know that this unfamiliar emotion was simply his birth right, the thing that every child should have: the knowledge that, above all else, they are safe and loved.

One

 *London, 2014*

There it was, exactly what Lily had been looking for: a large 1940s sideboard radio with the original Roberts tag on the front, perfect for the vintage accessories shoot she had booked for the following day. The window of Old Times was the usual messy jumble, but Lily liked it that way. The squinting old mannequin was wearing a wretched fake-fur coat, and the beautiful old radio was almost hidden, tucked behind a stack of 1980s albums and a coffee table piled with mismatched crockery. Gareth, the owner of this place, had a talent for picking up interesting bric-a-brac but a useless one for marketing. Lily smiled. She could tell from where he had placed the radio that he didn't want to sell it. Lily did that all the time, splashed out on an exquisite vintage piece for her online store then hid it in some distant corner of her website in case somebody actually wanted to buy it. While the world was rushing around consuming the next new thing, people like Gareth and Lily stood firmly at the centre of the fray, hanging on to the old stuff, guardians of the cool and the beautiful.

Lily worked from home and had needed to get out of the house today. The shoot tomorrow was kind of a big deal. She'd been invited to style a vintage set for a Sunday supplement but she had hardly given it any thought. Instead she had stayed up half the night researching a blog about the influence of Dior's 'New Look' on the current designer collections.

The door opened with a satisfying 'ping' and Lily got the frisson of excitement she always experienced when she stepped foot inside a second-hand shop. Old Times was one of her favourites. Most of the shop was taken up with huge boxes of records and comics from the 60s to 80s, but there was always some well-chosen bric-a-brac scattered randomly on the shelves, and a few baskets of old clothes just crying out for a rummage. Gareth had a good eye but at the same time he wasn't that interested in anything much apart from his old records, so you could nearly always knock him down in price.

Gareth stuck his head up from behind the counter where he was continuously cataloguing his vast vinyl collection.

Lily ambushed him.

'I'm after the radio,' she said.

'It's not for sale.' He came straight back at her.

'Good, because I can't afford it. I just want the loan of it for a shoot.'

Lily was pure glamour, always done up to the nines with full retro hair and make-up. She was pretty but not full of herself. Gareth had assumed she was just a regular rockabilly-girl until one weekend he had opened his Sunday paper and found she was number forty-three in the Top Fifty Most Influential Fashion Voices 2014. Lily Fitzpatrick had a quarter of a million Twitter followers and even more blog subscribers. You'd never think it to talk to her though. She was really down to earth. Sharp too. Funny. Lily was always haggling with him but the truth was he fancied her so much he'd give her most of the old tat she picked up for free.

'Oh, I don't know. It's really valuable...'

'BS. It's worth about half of my Kelly handbag.'

'It'll ruin my window display.'

Lily raised her eyebrows at him.

'OK, my window-dressing skills aren't great.'

She raised them higher.

'All right. They are atrocious.'

'Tell you what,' she said, 'you loan me the radio for the shoot, and I'll come in later this week and transform your window for you.'

'I don't know...'

'Old Joe won't like you upsetting his little girl.' Lily's ninety-year-old grandfather was a regular customer. 'I know you've got your eye on his Jim Reeves collection...I have pull; I can help you get a good price off him.'

Gareth smiled, then put his head back and groaned. He wasn't bad looking, Lily thought, but he had one of those horrid unkempt hipster beards and he rarely wore anything but geek-logo T-shirts. Lily preferred it when men went to a bit of trouble with themselves.

'Argh, you got me,' he said. 'Actually, I'm half expecting Joe in this morning...'

'...and think how happy he'll be if he knows you've helped out his darling granddaughter?' Lily batted her eyelids theatrically at him.

Gareth registered the curve of her hips in the tight grey day-dress, the high heels, the perfect red lips, the coiffed auburn curls and the eyes that lit up with sunshine every time she smiled. For a moment he allowed himself to dream something might be possible...

'Go on, Gareth, help me out here, be a mate.'

...then it was gone.

'And in return, I am just running out for coffee, would you keep an eye on this place for a minute?'

'Sure,' she said, although she was already on the other side of the shop with her arms elbow deep in a basket of scarves.

'Oh, and get me a chai latte, would you please?'

'For you, Lily? Anything.' He said it quietly so she didn't hear him, not that it would have made any difference if she had.

Lily rooted, digging for treasures in the basket like a child in a lucky dip before pulling out a square of silk with a scene of Rome on it. It wasn't that old but it was stunning, with its muted, dusty shades of pink and blue, depicting the Trevi Fountain in delicate line drawings. She was sorely tempted, even wrapping it briefly over her head and under her chin in 'The Queen Style', before telling herself she already had dozens of scarves just like it at the flat. She passed over the shelves of familiar bric-a-brac that had been there for months; the brass deer figurine which she still might get as a Christmas decoration for her mum and the cute, 1930s ceramic serving dish with gold and white daisies. Folded on a table was a 1960s candlewick bedspread. With rows of soft scallop-shaped tufts in old chenille and crisp white cotton, Lily could barely leave it behind. However, she sensibly reminded herself she had nowhere to put it. Then she saw her find of the day. Over on a shelf under the till counter, lying on her back in a neat blue minidress was Midge, Barbie's best friend in the 1960s. She had the same body as Barbie but she wasn't as pretty. Midge was in good shape, eyeliner intact, with a full head of hair, and sitting next to her was Alan, her boyfriend. He was topless and had been attacked with a biro, but Lily didn't mind. She had been hunting down an Alan doll to complete her Barbie set for years. Lily could not believe her luck, but as she picked up the boy doll and started to rub the pen marks off his chest, she was distracted by an urgent shout from outside that could have been her name. She turned towards the door, then again she heard, 'Lily!'

It was Gareth shouting for her.

On the pavement outside, he was crouching over something. A body on the ground.

'He just collapsed,' Gareth said. 'I was coming back with the coffee and he was waving at me when...'

Lily knelt down, numb and disbelieving.

'You stay with him,' Gareth said. 'I'll call an ambulance.'

Lily gently lifted her grandfather's head and put her arm under it. One of the old man's arms was splayed to the side where he had fallen, his hand still wrapped around a supermarket bag filled with Jim Reeves records. Lily leaned in and put her face right up close to his. She kissed his familiar papery skin saying, 'Hey, Grandad, you'll be all right, come on now, the ambulance is coming, you've just had a fall, you'll be grand...'

His body felt limp and lifeless in her arms. Panic rose up through her chest and she screamed, 'He's not breathing! He's not breathing!'

Then Gareth was there again, trying to resuscitate the old man, pumping his chest, and breathing into his mouth, while Lily looked helplessly on. She put her shaking hands up to her face to disguise her fear. Where was the ambulance? He couldn't be dead, he just couldn't be. Gareth's foot knocked the coffee holder and the liquid spilled across the pavement in a creamy puddle, flowing along the gutter. Lily leaned across and grabbed the bag of records so they wouldn't get spoiled. Grandad Joe would want them when he came around.

But he did not come around, and the paramedics shook their heads as soon as they saw him. One of them put his arm around Lily and she collapsed against the heavy plastic of his jacket, sobbing. Gareth picked up the bag of Jim Reeves records and said, 'Do you want me to come with you?'

She wanted to say yes, but she didn't know how, so she shook her head.

The paramedic closed her grandad's eyes and kept him uncovered in the ambulance so that Lily could sit beside him and say goodbye. Lily rubbed his hands and talked to him. Even though he was gone, she wanted to let him know that he wasn't alone.

'You've had a shock,' said the paramedic, and seeing Lily was shivering, he put a blanket around her shoulders.

'How will I tell my parents?' Lily said. 'I don't think... I don't know how...'

'Give me their number and I'll do it for you, if you like.'

'Can you do that?'

'Of course,' he said, 'it's my job.'

Lily wrapped the blanket tightly around herself and put her hand on her grandfather's cheek. He felt cold now and Lily knew there was no point in talking to him. His spirit was elsewhere. He was truly gone.

Lily's mum, dad and grandmother picked her up from the hospital and took her home with them. It was the first time Lily had experienced grief and she was surprised at how overwhelming it was. Her grandfather had been very old, and she knew he couldn't live forever (although sometimes, with the twinkly eyed old imp, it seemed as if he just might), but even so, the next forty-eight hours passed in a haze of shock. Lily felt as if somebody had scooped her insides out. She kept bursting into involuntary sobs. 'It has to be gone through,' her mother said. 'Cry yourself out, there's a good girl.' Yet Lily could not believe how many tears she had inside her.

Sally Thomas was art directing a catalogue shoot across town when she got the call. She was Lily's best friend and had been getting texts from her all day asking advice about the shoot. The last one was a picture of an old radio and it said, *Urgent opinion! Found this in Old Times. Wotcha think?*

Sally sent one back saying *Perfect!* and when Lily didn't reply straight away she assumed her disorganized friend had just let her battery run low. Now she picked up her iPhone and, as soon as she heard the voice of Lily's mum, she knew something was wrong.

'Holy shite!' was her first reaction to the news of Old Joe's passing. 'Jesus, I mean, sorry, Mary.'

Subtlety was not her strong point, but Mary Fitzpatrick had known her only daughter's best friend since they were children. Sally had a bit of a mouth on her but she also had a good heart.

Sally was there within half an hour. Mary opened the door and brought her into the sitting room, where Lily was curled up on her parents' sofa, with her feet up under her chest. She looked about ten years old. Sally put her arms around her, and said, 'Right, what needs to be done?'

'There's the shoot tomorrow, I can't cancel...'

'You won't have to. I'll take care of it.'

Sally got straight on the phone to *Style* magazine and arranged to take over the shoot for Lily. Then she drove up Kilburn High Road and pulled her car up onto the pavement outside Old Times. She had never met Gareth before, but Lily had mentioned him often enough. Once she had introduced herself, Gareth said, 'How is she?'

His face was creased with worry. A crush? Of course. Everyone fell in love with Lily.

'Fine. Awful. Oh God, I don't know! Her grandad's dead, how do you think she is? Can I take the radio with me now for the shoot tomorrow?'

Gareth looked at her aghast.

'I'm doing it for her,' Sally said, 'and I'm double parked so can we hurry this along, please?'

Reluctantly Gareth carried the radio out and put it in the boot of her two-seater MG while Sally got in and started the engine.

'Send Lily my...' He paused. '...best, um...'

Sally raised her eyes to heaven then nodded goodbye and said, 'Sure, will do,' before speeding off.

That afternoon, Sally moved into Lily's cramped apartment. She slept on a pull-out bed behind a rack of vintage evening wear in the living room and, for the next forty-eight hours, kept Lily sane.

Two

Lily usually blogged daily, and posted her outfit on Instagram each morning, but now she could not face going online.

'You really need to put something up on your blog,' Sally said, with her head full of rollers, on the morning of Joe's funeral, 'just to let people know that you're not dead yourself!'

Lily went to her computer desk and clicked the mouse. Her stomach tightened as she saw it was still open on the page she'd been researching on that terrible day. It showed an old Vogue article about a 1950s evening gown. Lily book-marked the link, then opened her own blog and posted, I'll be offline for a few more days. Back when my heart heals. #LilyLovesHerGrandad, before shutting down her computer and walking over to the enormous gold-framed antique mirror that dominated her tiny apartment, to put the finishing touches to her funeral ensemble.

Lily adjusted the flat feather fascinator to the left of her parting and placed her long, auburn hair, styled into broad Lana Turner waves, neatly across the shoulder of her 1940s fur cape. Then she searched through her collection of red lipsticks for the perfect shade: Dior Dolce Vita. She never left the house without her trademark matte red lipstick. Red hair, red lips – it was against all the rules but when it came to fashion, Lily never followed the rules.

Trends came and went but Lily remained steadfast in her passion for old-school dressing. As her blog said, Lily just loved vintage. She loved that the clothes were made so much better then. Every skirt, every dress had a lining, every jacket had folded seams and double-stitched cuffs. The embroidery and embellishments were all done by hand and not in a sweatshop. Lily loved rummaging for bargains in the vintage market – she even loved the slightly bitter, musty smell because it reminded her that among the un-cleaned clothes could be a priceless piece of old couture waiting to be discovered. She loved imagining the history of each piece; was this tiny white satin shrug part of a wedding trousseau? The woman who owned this scuffed 1950s leather handbag must have only owned one bag because she had worn it down to the bone. That's how things were back then. Women had one bag, one pair of shoes, one 'good' dress, so they had to make them last, they had to make them special. Every bag, every dress, even down to the cheap beads or embroidered handkerchief she picked up from a 50p basket at a charity shop till was cherished by Lily because she knew it had been owned and, at one time, loved by another woman. Fashion wasn't disposable in the past, like it was now. Clothes were important, something to be treasured.

Today Lily was wearing her grandfather's favourite rose-print vintage tea dress. 'My little lady,' he used to call her when she wore it, although he often added, 'you should be dressing for lads your own age – look at those Kardashians. If you dressed like one of them I'd be a great-grandfather ten times over by now.'

Lily did not have the heart to tell him that no one had truly taken her fancy since she had split from her school sweetheart at twenty-two. She had tried playing the field and sleeping around a bit, but she found it a depressing and unsatisfying way to live. She was better off on her own.

Lily was still shocked by Joe's death. Sometimes it felt as if the past few days hadn't happened. It was an unreal feeling, as if part of her was still sitting by the kerb on Kilburn High Road, nursing the old man's head in her lap.

Sally had helped. With no siblings to fall back on, Lily felt incredibly lucky to have a best friend she felt so close to. Of course, they sometimes fought, misunderstood, or simply got bored with each other. But at heart they believed their friendship was unbreakable.

'She's as good as a sister that one,' Joe had often said. 'Friends are as good as family and that's the truth.'

Both girls agreed it was important they get dressed up to the nines in his honour.

'There will be no shirking in the wardrobe department,' Sally said. 'We'll go to town for the old bugger.'

Lily knew that Joe would have wanted her to be looking her very best at his funeral. The old man could never stand to see anyone looking sad, especially not his only granddaughter.

'Let me see that lovely smile, Lily,' he was always saying to her. 'Let me see you're happy.' Then he would draw a bag of sweets out from behind his back and make her grin until her cheeks cushioned up into fat balls.

Lily pulled up a chair and sat in front of the mirror, then painted her lips in a perfect bow. Grief and exhaustion had taken its toll on her eyes but she nonetheless drew herself up and applied two slicks of Benefit eyeliner.

Then, checking that the seams on her stockings were

straight, Lily slid her feet into the original snakeskin stilettos her grandmother had worn on her wedding day. It would make the old lady so happy to see them on her today.

'I'm ready...' Lily shouted.

Sally appeared in the doorway. Her voluptuous curves were poured into a black tube dress with two chunky, full length zips straining down each side.

'I thought we agreed you were wearing vintage?' Lily said.

'This *is* vintage. Gucci, circa 1999.'

'That is *not* vintage.'

'It *so* is,' Sally replied, and grabbing a dictionary from Lily's desk she quoted, '*Vintage*; denotes something from the past of high quality.' She continued, 'And let me tell you, any zip that can keep these curves in shape is *very* high quality indeed.'

'You're a disgrace,' Lily said, jokingly.

Sally was trying to cheer her up but Lily was dreading the funeral. She had never been to one before and all she knew was that she wanted it to be over.

St Agnes Catholic Church on Cricklewood Lane was packed with people. The Fitzpatricks were at the heart of the Kilburn–Cricklewood Irish community. Joe had moved here from Ireland as a young man of fifteen, worked on the buildings then apprenticed as a mechanic and had lived and worked in the area ever since. He never missed Sunday mass, and he never missed his Friday pint in The Bridge Tavern. Lily's grandmother had been a dinner lady in the local primary school, as was Lily's own mother. The whole Catholic community, including the West Indians and Italians, knew the family, but everybody had a special fondness for easy-going, jovial Joe. At ninety he was still walking down to the high street to get his newspaper every day.

Sally sat in the front pew, next to Lily. When she saw Lily fumbling inside her tiny black clutch bag in panic, Sally reached seamlessly into her cavernous Vuitton and emerged with a fresh pack of lavender-scented tissues. Sally's bag was equipped with everything from sewing kits and hosiery to wet wipes. In that moment, Lily felt such a surge of love for her friend that she felt a lump come to her throat again.

When the mass ended, Sally stepped aside to let Lily join her parents, as they walked behind Joe's coffin. Gareth, who was standing at the back of the church, noticed Lily had been crying and wished that he had the right to go and comfort her. Never having been to a funeral before, he had shaved his beard off for the occasion, as a mark of respect. He now realized that was rather a silly thing to do. The suit he had on would have sufficed, lots of men had beards and he felt curiously naked without it. Lily glanced up from her handkerchief and gave him a slightly confused look as if she was trying to figure out who he was. Gareth was mortified. Dramatically altering his appearance before a funeral had clearly been a terrible idea. He left straight after the church so as not to confuse her again.

Lily found the burial extremely painful. Seeing the box being lowered into the dirty, grey clay hole in the ground and knowing that he was inside it was the worst part. Lily's good shoes sank into the soft grass, as she clutched her grandmother's arm and said goodbye.

Afterwards, there was a reception in St Agnes church hall.

'My God, so many men, so much bad tailoring,' Sally said, looking around and grimacing at the crowd of parish mourners.

'Don't be such a bloody snob,' said Lily.

'Ah,' Sally said, grabbing a foil tray of sandwiches from

a passing church lady, 'you can put them down here in front of moi, thank you.'

'Not so snobby when it comes to your food, are you?'

Sally glowered at Lily. 'Ah, good, the bitch returns. I was beginning to wonder if she had been softened permanently under that pile of grief. You know, Old Joe propositioned me once?'

Lily gave a tearful giggle. 'He didn't!'

Sally picked up a sandwich again and stuffed it into her mouth, with a cheeky nod, then said, 'Actually, no, he didn't, but it made you laugh. I got to go, babe. I've got to pick up half a dozen woeful jumpers from a warehouse in Peckham for a night shoot in town. Will you be OK until tomorrow?'

'Of course,' Lily said, even though she wasn't entirely sure that she would be.

The funeral crowd started to dissipate. Old Joe had been waked, prayed for and buried; tea and whisky had been drunk in his honour, sandwiches had been eaten, condolences given and now it was all over. He was gone, taking his past with him. Behind the tea urn were a dozen or so framed pictures from various stages of Joe's life, selected by Lily's mother. They included several of Lily as a child with her grandfather, but there were none of Joe himself as a boy; the earliest picture was one of his wedding day. Her grandmother had had to dig it out from the album; he had hated having old pictures lying about the place. Joe lived by the mantra, 'never look back'. Now, as she looked at the photographs, Lily wondered about that and wished she had asked more questions about his past. Seeing her grandmother, Eileen, sitting on her own for the first time that day, Lily went and sat down next to her.

'You OK, Nan?'

Despite her sadness, Eileen's eyes were warm.

'He went the way he wanted, Lily, no fuss. I'm so sorry you were there when it happened, but I am glad about it too. You were his favourite girl.'

'You'll miss him terribly; we all will.'

'True, but I'm glad he went first. He wouldn't have managed on his own. Your grandfather hated being alone...' She paused as if she had something else to say, so Lily asked, 'Why did he never go back to Mayo?'

The old woman let out a sigh. 'He never wanted to. Too many bad memories. I don't know the half of it myself.'

'What about his parents?'

'They died when he was very small. He had a brother, though.'

'Still alive?'

'I doubt it, he was a good few years older. He went to America just after Joe got sent to the nuns.'

'What was his name?'

'Francis,' she said, 'or Frank.'

'And how old was Frank when he went to America?'

'I don't know, darling, he never said.'

'What year did Grandad go into the orphanage?'

Eileen got agitated and said sharply, 'I don't know, Lily, now for goodness sake will you leave me alone – I'm just after burying my husband!'

Lily didn't like upsetting her grandmother but at the same time she felt there was something else, something the old lady was not telling her.

As Lily walked home she thought about how different the world would be now with no Joe in it. A distant roll of thunder brought rain and as she wandered through the familiar streets of her childhood her stomach jerked with memories. There was the plum tree that had been splattering its fruit on the London pavement since she was a child, there was the corner wall where she used to stop and kiss boyfriends after youth-club discos, there was the broken down garage where her father used to park his old van and where she and Sally had slept one night after forgetting their keys and being afraid to get her parents out of bed. These streets were Lily's comfort zone but they didn't bring her any comfort today. As she reached her flat, the top floor of an old Victorian terrace house owned by her parents, Lily stopped and tugged at the gate. The catch had been tricky to open for as long as she could remember. For a moment it was as if the past had entered the present, as if nothing had changed. Except a lot had changed.

It felt unnatural to know that someone who was so much a part of who she was, and where she had come from, simply wasn't there anymore. Along with that there was a new sensation nagging at her. Talking to her grandmother had only intensified the feeling that she did not know as much about her grandfather, about his life, as she might have done.

Lily had never been to Mayo where her own people were from. She didn't even know if she had 'people' there. For all she knew she might have dozens of cousins all over Ireland. Joe Fitzpatrick had left Mayo as a young boy in the late-1930s and had never returned – not even for a holiday.

How could it be that her grandfather had died, that she had known him for thirty whole years, and yet was left knowing so little about him now? How was it possible that she had never asked? The answer, of course, was that she had never thought that he would die one day and take a part of her with him. Lily had always known she had loved the old man but now that he was gone she felt something more than that, as if a link had been broken.

When Lily got home, she was exhausted. She fell into bed but was too wired to sleep. She decided to go and catch up on some work, hoping it would wear her out. What with the funeral and everything, Lily had fallen way behind on her daily LilyLovesVintage.com posts, so she opened the blog up and resumed the last story she had been working on.

People are making a big deal out of Lucy Houston's new evening wear collection because of the full skirts, but it's been done before. When a certain Mr Christian Dior launched his couture house on 12 February 1947 he became an overnight sensation with a collection of designs featuring sloping shoulders, big busts and tiny wasp waists above full, voluminous skirts. A rival couturier at the time described Dior's 'New Look' as 'a total glorification of the female form' which given those times, could have been either an insult or a compliment...

The text wasn't really flowing so Lily turned to her bookmarked page and pulled up the *Vogue* clipping she had saved earlier for some inspiration.

There was a beautiful picture of a woman in a divine, full-skirted evening gown. She had one of those archetypical haughty, high-cheek-boned faces so familiar from the old Avedon shots which Lily had scattered about the flat. The headline read: *Exquisite Irish Beauty* and the face looked a lot like the model Barbara Mullen who had been around at the time. However, when Lily scrolled down and checked the caption, she got a surprise as she read: *Mrs Joy Fitzpatrick wearing what has become known among the discerning couture clientele of New York as 'The Dress'.*

Gripped by the coincidence of the name she scrolled down further and magnified another, smaller society picture. This caption read: Joy is the wife of dashing Irish-born steel magnate, Frank Fitzpatrick.

Lily sat looking at the screen for a moment, at Frank Fitzpatrick's name, then at his face. He bore a striking resemblance to Grandad Joe.

Three

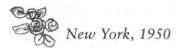 *New York, 1950*

It was New Year's Eve, ten years after he had first arrived in America. Frank Fitzpatrick's journey from the wilds of Bangor to the sophistication of New York society had been short, but hard won.

The beaten boy had left with the Conlons' money at first light as he had planned, taking a pair of his host's dress shoes from the front hall, tying them by the laces around his neck in order to spare them. Then young Francis walked and hitched his way across Ireland, all the way to Dublin. The six-day journey took him ten, because he worked for food along the way so he could save the cash he had stolen. He stacked turf for a widow in Pontoon, in exchange for a loaf of bread and a bottle of tea, that he made last two days. He whitewashed stones at the front of a rich-man's house in Strokestown and they gave him a hot meal of salty bacon and potatoes, which he ate with his hands from a china plate, in their shed. If the weather was dry, he slept in a ditch at the side of the road. When it looked like rain, he would go off route and seek out an old shed or a house that had been long since abandoned by famine or emigration.

When he arrived in the city, Frank went to the first

menswear shop he passed and bought a shirt and tie. On O'Connell Bridge he asked a fellow street traveller where he could find the nearest public baths and the man, weathered, as if he had not bathed himself in some time, put his hand out for money, as he told him, 'Tara Street.' Francis reached into his pocket and handed the man a penny. As he did, he felt a thrill, realizing that he had been in Dublin for less than a day and yet as such already felt he was in a position to give away his cash. Looking at the worn face of the street drunk at his feet, the young boy knew that he had finally escaped the brutality of his childhood and was about to begin his new life. No matter how hard the coming days would be, no matter if he was hungry, or had to work until his hands bled, the worst years of his life, all fifteen of them, were behind him now.

There were only half a dozen men, at most, in the public bath, and an official in a white coat looking down on them from the balcony above. One or two of his fellow bathers nodded a greeting, but he ignored them. He sank his head under the soapy, steaming water and stayed submerged, until his lungs hurt, then flung himself back up in an exploding breath, into his new, clean future.

His father's violence, his mother's death, leaving his baby brother behind, stealing from the Conlons, they were troubles too heavy for the young boy to bear. So Francis washed off his feelings and his conscience. He left his past, bobbing in a trail of soap scum on the tiles, at the side of the public baths in Tara Street, and he told himself he would not stop, he would do whatever it took, to get as far away from his past as he could.

In the changing rooms, he brushed down his dusty trousers and polished John's shoes which, although a size too small, gave him a respectable enough demeanour to secure him an apprenticeship, as a carpenter in a workshop, on the Northside.

When the boss asked him his name, Francis said 'Frank'. It made him sound older and came out so naturally that it didn't feel like a lie. He was somebody else now, somebody new.

Frank worked hard, he was single-minded and diligent, he barely drank, or socialized with the other apprentices. He got the cheapest digs he could find and saved all of his money, so that after five long years, he had his passage to America.

Standing at the front of the ship, the young man watched the Dublin mountains recede. Beyond them were the hills and boglands of Mayo and he was waving goodbye to the whole damn lot of them. With the wind whipping across his face, blowing up under the new coat he'd bought to carry him across the world in style, Frank Fitzpatrick felt free.

As soon as he arrived in Manhattan, Frank went straight to an Irish bar near the docks, which he'd been told about in Dublin. He ordered a whisky and asked the barman, straight out, did he know a Donal Hegarty? From Bangor?

The man behind the bar opened his mouth to laugh, then seeing the serious expression on the young man's face, decided against it. The kid looked like he meant business. Young Francis Fitzpatrick was on a mission now. These were going to be difficult times for him and he would need all the help he could get from his only remaining relative, his mother's brother.

'Would that be Bangor, County Mayo?'

Frank nodded. New York was a big place, but it had the same number of Irishmen in it as Dublin, where everyone seemed to know each other, and if they didn't know where to find a man, they knew a man who would.

'I know a man called Donal from Bangor, all right. You won't find him in any bar in New York, though. He's been banned from all of them.'

Frank found his uncle queuing for soup in the Bronx. A broken man, a useless drunk, he tried to tap his nephew for what he had left of his savings. Frank gave him the price of a meal, then left him where he found him and determined to go it alone.

If Dublin was hard, New York was harder, but Frank came to thrive on the challenge of survival. Already running from the failure of his childhood, he became even more driven by what he did not want to be. All around him, Frank saw disillusioned Irishmen, men who had followed the American dream only to be plunged into the Depression, many of them despairing and turning to drink. Francis was determined that would not happen to him and vowed to be the very opposite. He pushed himself to the top of every employment queue. He saved every penny of the small wages he earned, sleeping rough through the spring, summer and fall, and in homeless hostels during the harsh winters. He foraged food from the garbage bins of the wealthier houses he worked in and stuffed all of his cash in a cushion which he kept next to his face. Frank never feared thieves.

One night a heavy-set, dangerous bum tried to steal his money. Frank had invested so much in his dream of being a success in America that he knew he could kill any man who tried to take it away from him. Enraged, Frank threatened to see him off with a beating like the one he had given his own father. The bum recognized determination and desperation when he saw them, knew the danger they spelt and ran off.

Frank's hard work and talent, as a casual carpenter, eventually got him noticed by a landlord, who put him to work as a building superintendent in a rambling, shabby brownstone in the Bronx. The landlord was a drinker and when he complained to Frank about people not paying their rents and the hard time he was having himself, Frank knew his big moment had come. He invested in a cheap suit, went to the bank and persuaded the manager to give him a small mortgage. The times were changing; there was hope on the horizon. Frank got the landlord drunk and persuaded him to sell him the Bronx brownstone for a song, using his cushion-savings cash as a down payment.

With that single building, Frank's property empire began. Ten years later, the boy from Bangor had a portfolio of rental properties on the Upper East Side of Manhattan and stakes in a Boston hotel and a steel-mining business. He had an office block in town, with a secretary and an accounts department. He lived in an apartment on Fifth Avenue. When he wanted female company, it was easily found in the bars and clubs of Manhattan. The journey from gutter to Fifth had taught Frank how to charm, as well as work, so that the angry Irish schoolboy had become a successful, urbane New York businessman: Frank Fitzpatrick. Frank had created the perfect life for himself. People didn't pity him anymore, they envied him. Although there was still one thing missing...

'You need to get yourself a wife...' Victor Truman had said to him one night. Victor was his main investor, an old-monied hog from the Upper West Side. They were sitting in a booth at the Stork Club, surrounded by the trappings of rich men: a lobster dinner, whisky sours and compliant showgirls.

'No man should be without a wife,' Victor said, quickly shoving his cigar into his mouth and catching it between his teeth, as he reached for the bottom of a passing waitress and gave it a pinch, hard enough to tame a dog. 'Ain't that right, honey?'

'It surely is, Mr Truman,' the girl laughed. Victor, sensing Frank's disapproval, said, 'The problem with all these cheap floozies,' and he swept his hand around to indicate another passing waitress, 'is that they'll bleed you dry and you get nothing in return, except maybe a piece of action, and you've got to ask yourself, Frank: what's a piece of action worth to you?'

Frank nodded, although he was insulted by the implication. He found it impossible to think of women in those crass terms. Many of the women he had been with could arguably have been described as floozies, but he respected them, even though he had not felt inclined to marry any of them. Frank had broken a few hearts, but nobody had ever broken his.

'A good wife can be an asset,' Victor continued. 'She will entertain for you, keep the house nice and believe me, if you're firm from the start, she'll work to a budget. A wife will make you look good, Frank. You should get one. Come to our New Year's Eve bash. Norah knows all the ladies, she'll fix you up.'

And so it was that Frank found himself in a large suite at the Plaza, on New Year's Eve, 1950.

Frank had not been expecting to fall in love that night, even though he had noticed her as soon as he walked into the party. The long white neck seemed too delicate to hold the collar of fat pearls at its base, her hair was caught up in a tightly-wrapped bun, and she was casually waving a lit cigarette. Even from behind she cut a compelling figure. The mere fall of her slim shoulders, the curve of her tiny waist, conveyed a grace and presence that had him walking across the room towards her, until she turned. Then he was stopped in his tracks.

The young woman had an almost frightening beauty. Her high cheek-bones seemed carved from some exquisite alabaster and her painted red lips were shaped in a perfect, symmetrical pout. However, it was her eyes – two dark pools of immeasurable depth – that held him. She had a look of knowing that transcended her sultry beauty. Although she was a complete stranger, her fathomless gaze seemed to say that she recognized him, recognized the vein of sadness which, despite his great success, still ran through the core of Francis Fitzpatrick.

Frank did not seek out an introduction, he would not have presumed, but Victor's wife, Norah, must have noticed him staring because before he knew what was happening, he was being introduced after all.

'This is Joy Rogerson,' Norah said.

Frank took the pale, delicate hand in his and tried his best to retain his composure. But as he looked into the girl's deep, sad eyes, Frank knew that, despite the great distance he had travelled, despite the efforts he had made to chase away the vulnerable boy and become the strong, capable man that he was today, Frank Fitzpatrick had utterly lost himself.

Four

Joy Rogerson knew what a privileged position her family held in the world and yet, even as a small child, she'd always felt somewhat estranged from it.

The Rogersons were an old Protestant family. Joy was their only child and had grown up always feeling nervous of people and uncertain of her place in the world. Her father was distant, always off somewhere doing business, and her mother, Ruth Rogerson, was a plain woman who relied upon jewellery to create her glamour. Her everyday style (always haute couture, *only* Paris) was markedly severe, seeming to draw attention to her plainness rather than camouflage it. At every black-tie occasion out would come the Tiffany diamonds or the antique pearls and the whole room would be agog. Men would flirt with her, women would envy her and, for that night, Ruth Rogerson would sparkle. Before she left the house on these evenings she would call her young daughter in to see her. Joy could smell the Chanel No. 5 and one or two early cocktails. Her mother always held out her hands and asked, 'Am I beautiful, Joy?'

'Yes, Mother,' Joy would say, automatically, not really knowing or understanding what beauty was, unaware that she had it herself in abundance.

Ruth would let out a tight bitter laugh and say, 'No, I am *not* beautiful, Joy, but the diamonds are, and when the eye is dazzled, the heart cannot always see. Beauty and wealth are a woman's *only* assets, Joy. Remember that and be smart with them.'

When her parents left, Joy would run to the window to watch them get into the car, her father waiting, while the chauffeur lifted her mother's long fur cape and tucked it in beside her. Joy came to understand that adult life was an endless round of chauffeured car rides and perfumed parties.

Joy had always been astonishingly beautiful. When she was out with her nanny, even strangers would stop and say, 'What a lovely child.' By the time she came out as a debutante the whole of their social set agreed that Joy Rogerson was the most beautiful girl in New York. Joy came to understand that beauty was her destiny, her gift, yet she could not see it in herself. All she saw, all she had ever seen when she looked in a mirror, was her own fear, the reflection of her large eyes pleading back at her like a beggar looking for money from a stranger. Although she knew it was her greatest, in fact aside from money, her only asset, Joy Rogerson hated her own face.

On the night of New Year's Eve, 1950, Joy was twenty-one and just back from the season in London. After an unremarkable academic career and a stint in a Swiss finishing school, Joy had come into her own during her season in Europe. Ruth had trusted Joy with a substantial clothing allowance and Joy had discovered she had a passion and penchant for commissioning stylish clothes. She was even listed in the *London Times* society pages as one of the best-dressed debutantes in London that year. This gave her confidence its first boost.

The second boost came from the champagne. Joy had

her first drink, a glass of pink sparkling champagne, at her coming out party in The Savoy of London. The moment she felt the bubbles whizz down her throat and fizz through her bloodstream Joy felt herself turn into a better version of herself. Her vision seemed crisper, her words wittier. Activities that had felt awkward in finishing school – dancing, knowing the correct cutlery to use at an English table, offering a compliment to a man – all flowed out of her more easily. With a little champagne inside her, Joy felt relaxed and at ease, as if she had somehow arrived in her body for the first time. The titled boys, known as 'Debs Delights' were positively crawling after Joy that year in London. She had money and beauty and wit and she found the British were more discerning than American boys her age. She could have taken her pick. Instead, she returned to New York and, while her parents were wintering on the West Coast, found herself alone at Norah and Victor Truman's party.

She had not been expecting much of the Trumans' staid, Plaza-suite party. Norah's blunt matchmaking attempts were embarrassingly obvious and invariably off the mark, her tongue constantly acerbic, but only occasionally witty.

'This is Frank Fitzpatrick,' Norah said, adding in a stage whisper, 'He's Irish and a little old for you, but he's also *terribly* rich...and clever, I believe.'

Joy thought she had never seen such a magnificent man. He had thick black hair that was slightly longer than it should have been, barely tamed into a businessman's parting. He had broad shoulders and his jaw was already darkening with tomorrow's shadow. The man's eyes were so blue and piercing that she found them almost impossible to look into.

'Why do you look so sad, when your name is Joy?' His eyes held hers.

Although her knees were shaking, Joy took a deep drag on her cigarette and deliberately stared back before answering, 'How did an Irishman get into *this* party...and in such a cheap suit?'

'Well, perhaps the Trumans just took pity on poor Paddy and embraced me so that I wouldn't have to spend New Year's Eve selling oranges on the streets of New York.'

'You don't look like a man that would inspire pity – despite the atrocious tailoring.'

'I'll have you know this suit was very expensive.'

'Did no one tell you? Money can't buy taste.'

'I thought in America money could buy you everything?'

Joy deliberately paused before answering and arched a perfectly shaped eyebrow. 'Not quite *everything*...'

'I see,' he said, trying not to laugh. 'In which case, aren't you going to ask me how rich I am?'

'I'm not remotely interested in money,' she replied, taking a drag on her cigarette. 'It comes from having too much of it, my father says.'

'I thought Americans believed you could never be too rich.'

'Oh, certainly you can! Overt wealth can be insufferably common if it's not used with taste.'

'And are your family rich?'

'Why? Are you after my money?'

'Absolutely.'

'Well, my mother's string of day-pearls are certainly worth more than the average man earns in a year. However, you are not an average man. You must be very rich indeed, otherwise Norah would certainly never have introduced you to me and you certainly wouldn't be making comments like *that*.'

He laughed, and Joy felt as if she was suddenly filled with sunshine.

'You certainly know your way around these people.'

She smiled. Not just her ordinary smile but the dazzling, from the inside out smile. 'These people? Goodness, I've never heard us called that before.'

'Why, what do us ordinary folk call the upper classes in America?'

'*The* people, Mr...what was your name again?'

He paused and looked at her quizzically. 'You've got a very short memory for such a smart girl.'

Joy found she wanted to reach over and touch his arm, and there was a moment when she wanted to say, 'Ask me again why I look sad?' Instead, she quipped, 'I'm not a girl, I'm a woman. Besides, "smart girls" wear blue, woollen stockings, and as you can see that's not really my style.'

Joy could have stopped the game of verbal cat and mouse but she didn't. This man had noticed the sadness that lay beneath her beautiful veil. Frank Fitzpatrick knew who she was and that was enough for Joy. More than enough.

At the end of the evening, Frank told the Trumans he would accompany Joy home, on the short walk across the park, to her parents' apartment. All the way down in the elevator, walking out through the glittering, holidaying busyness of the Plaza lobby and negotiating the wide car-honking craziness of Park Avenue on New Year's Eve, Frank was the perfect gentleman. He held her slim hand in the wide arm of his cashmere evening coat with the formal care of a benign uncle, but Joy could feel the undertow of passion simmering beneath the surface. She knew he wanted her. Joy met men who wanted her all the time – young, handsome men. She was usually either disinterested or disgusted by their attentions, but tonight she liked being wanted. However, Joy knew Frank would never make a move, so when they had walked a hundred yards into Central Park, fuelled by fresh-air and champagne and the presumption of her beauty and youth, she turned to him and said, 'Kiss me!'

Frank laughed. They were standing under the shelter of a huge oak. The cold, damp air smelt fresh and mossy. Like home.

'What makes you think I want to kiss you?' he said.

'Of course you want to kiss me.'

Although in that moment Joy felt her fragile confidence plummet, she added defiantly, 'What are you afraid of? My parents?'

'I don't know who your parents are,' he said, 'but I'm afraid of no one.'

That was true. Joy felt a shiver run down her spine as he said it. Nonetheless, she could sense he was afraid of her, or rather, afraid of his own desire for her.

Joy let her cape drop from her shoulders and, revealing the bare flesh underneath she moved close enough that she could smell the alcohol and cigar smoke on his breath. Her face reddened, her breath was coming out in white, frosty puffs of air and she said, again, 'Then go ahead and kiss me.'

Frank leaned down but just as Joy closed her eyes he suddenly lifted her slim body up and held her at arm's length, pushing her against the tree.

Frank was determined to get a grip on himself but she was just as determined to stop him. Joy arched her back against the oak until the damp bark seeped through the velvet of her cape and she coquettishly whispered, 'Coward.'

'They call it "gentleman" where I come from.'

His hands on the smooth skin of her arms felt firm. It thrilled her to be held by him, even at bay like this. Joy's eyes flashed triumphantly. But Frank had remembered himself and now he loosened his hold.

As soon as he did so Joy shrugged off her damp cape and let it fall to the ground so that she stood there, brazenly, with nothing but a flimsy evening gown between her bare flesh and the cold night air.

'I'm cold,' she said.

'Put your coat on,' Frank said. 'I'm taking you home.'

Joy shook her head. 'Not until you've kissed me.'

Frank smiled, shaking his head, and picked up her cape from the ground. His hand lingered as he placed it around her shoulders and Joy closed her eyes as she felt the warmth of his breath on her neck. It was more delicious than any kiss.

He held out his arm for Joy to take and as they walked in silence through the park Joy knew she had met the man she wanted to be with for the rest of her life.

Five

 *London, 2014*

Millions of Americans have the name Fitzpatrick and of them many hundreds of thousands must have the forename Frank. Lily knew this and yet when she tried to sleep on the night of her grandfather's funeral the name Frank Fitzpatrick kept dancing around in her brain with a bunch of what-ifs? What if the woman in the *Vogue* picture was married to Old Joe's brother? What if Lily had a whole family in America just waiting to be discovered? The possibilities this shadowy uncle threw up were just so thrilling Lily could not get them out of her head.

She kept telling herself to go to sleep, that it was silly to even think about being related to this random person she had seen in a magazine clipping. Yet the mystery of it was driving her mad.

At 5 a.m. she got out of bed and rang her father's mobile.

'What's wrong?' Patrick said, his voice thick with sleep and shades of panic.

'Nothing's wrong. Oh, sorry, did I wake you, Dad? I just wanted to ask you something…'

'What time is it? Jesus Christ, Lily, it's five o'clock in the morning!'

'Do you know the name of the woman your Uncle Frank married in America?'

'For God's sake, what kind of a question is...' Then Patrick realized he was too exhausted from the grief and drink of the day before even to question his daughter, never mind fight with her. Vaguely a name began to filter through. 'Joyce? Josephine? No...'

'Joy?'

'Joy, yes. Yes, that was it.'

Lily could hardly believe it. 'Are you sure?'

'Yes, yes, I'm sure that was it. When I was a lad, Mam saw something in a magazine and I remember them talking about it. Your grandad went crazy. He and Frank didn't talk. It was the one time his brother was ever mentioned in our house. That's why I remember the name. Joy.'

Lily punched the air.

'Is that it? Can I go back to sleep now?'

'Yes, Dad... Thanks, Dad.'

Straight away Lily switched on her computer. She made herself a pot of strong tea in her favourite art-deco teapot, pulled on her silk 1920s robe to bring her luck and set about finding her family in America.

Lily registered on Ancestry.com, typing in all she knew about him, which was that Frank was from Bangor, County Mayo, Ireland and had left Ireland sometime after 1935, the year her grandfather went into the orphanage. Quickly, she found fifteen Francis Fitzpatricks from Bangor who had sailed to New York City in the years 1935–1945. One of them would have been her great-uncle, but there was no way of telling which one. In any case, apart from the fact that his wife's name was Joy, Lily had no other information about the man. No address, no offspring, no place of work. She googled their names along with some leads from the *Vogue* piece, but nothing came up. Lily was afraid she had reached a dead end and was about to call it a day when, trawling through a heritage chatroom, she discovered a day-old posting from a woman called Maisie Fitzpatrick in Wisconsin: *My aunt, Joy Fitzpatrick, was a wealthy, stylish woman living in New York all through the 1950s. I would love to find out more about this side of my family. Picture on request.*

Lily was beside herself. Wealthy? Stylish? That sounded like her Joy. She replied to the thread and attached her blog email address for them to reply to. This could be it!

Lily was longing just to sit and wait for a reply to pop up on screen but she had an afternoon date with Sally. As a sort of good luck talisman, she printed out the *Vogue* article and put it in her bag. It was the middle of the night in Wisconsin now. The woman would still be in bed, but when she got up and checked her email, Lily would be waiting for her. In the meantime, she would just have to get on with her day.

Sally had persuaded Lily to come along to a fashion show that afternoon. Sally's employer, the high street chain and catalogue retailer, Scott's, was having a glitzy show in a warehouse in Shoreditch, at the other end of London. Sally felt Lily needed to get out of the house and back into the real world after all the upset of the past few weeks. This big event, thrown by her boss, the playboy fashion king Jack Scott, would be the perfect event for Lily to re-launch herself after the funeral.

'Make sure you get dressed up, they'll all be there,' Sally said.

Lily took the bait. As the most popular vintage blogger in the UK, Lily had a reputation to maintain and always went to town on herself for fashion events. Today she opted for a Claire McCardell two-piece in navy and cream. The 1954 wrap-over halter top and full three-quarter length skirt were in mint condition but the design was so fluid, so contemporary, that people always got a surprise when they found out it was 'historical' vintage, aka pre-70s. To further the deception, Lily kept her make-up light, just her trademark red lips, and wore a pair of Orla Kiely Dotty shoes; Orla Kiely was one of the few contemporary designers whose items worked with her authentic look.

While they walked across the busy streets to the warehouse where the show was being held, Sally filled Lily in on the gossip of the day. As somebody who worked at the high end of the retail fashion market, Sally knew all the most influential people in the London fashion business and kept herself bang up-to-date with all the news.

Today was Scott's debut show for the hot young sportswear designer Karl Bundy, who Jack Scott had poached from his arch enemy and rival, David Durane, CEO of PopShop, Britain's biggest fashion retailer. Scott's was number two. The fashion bloggers had gone wild when the Bundy-stealing story broke.

'I don't rate Bundy as a designer, actually,' Sally said, 'but this show is a really big deal. I had to fight to get you a plus-one today.'

'Gee, thanks,' Lily said, beginning to wonder if she was really ready for such a heavy dose of Sally's fashion-drama.

'Would you believe PopShop offered me a job last week? Artistic Director. Full time, freelance contract – good money too.'

'Really?' Lily said, trying to sound interested. Sometimes she got exhausted just listening to Sally talk about her work.

'Oh, yeah. These retail kings are so competitive it hurts. It's like *Next Top Model* but with men in suits. Durane rang me himself. God, he's a sleazebag. Tragic dresser, fifty-plus and kitted out like a rapper – lots of gold. Very sad. I said no. He's only after me because he knows Scott's will never let me go . . .'

'Hmm,' Lily said.

'. . . especially not to work for Durane. Jack *hates* him . . .' she carried on, even as they arrived at the door of the warehouse. Sally flashed her pass at the doorman and, giving the briefest of 'We're A-list' glances, continued, '. . . partly because Durane's a psychopath but then, as I keep telling him, we're selling clothes, Jack darling, not feeding the world or saving kittens. You need to toughen up.'

Even though Lily was only half listening she could not help smiling at the idea of Sally giving advice to one of the most powerful men in the fashion industry.

Fashion was Sally's life. She ate, drank and slept it every week, every day, every minute of every season. Lily didn't care about what was 'in', or 'out', she only cared about the clothes themselves, their quality and fit. As a stylist, Sally would quite happily take a 1950s Robert Piguet cocktail dress and put it under a 70s vintage jacket. It made Lily flinch to see a beautiful piece of couture accessorized with anything outside its original era. It was the only thing the two friends fought about.

'If Dior were alive today,' Sally once said to Lily, 'he would definitely put cowboy boots with that gown.'

'Well,' Lily snapped back, 'he's *not* alive today and he didn't put them with cowboy boots back then so there is no reason to expect he would now!'

The warehouse was a huge white rectangle that had been customized specifically to house this type of promotional event. The interior was basic, just a catwalk with tiered seating crammed along either side. The cool, street-fashion crowd of journalists and stylists and fashion hangers-on were a fairly homogenous bunch, not like the rich starlets and high-end press that came to the seasonal shows. There was nobody over thirty and nobody, Lily noted, wearing anything more than two years old.

A guy in black with a headpiece guided them to their seats. They were six rows back, in the middle.

'Why are we sitting in these crappy seats? Hey!' Sally shouted after the security guy, who was now seating row seven. 'I'm front row baby!'

People were flooding into their seats and the two women would have had to clamber over heads to get to the front row, so Lily sat down in the empty chair and dragged Sally down next to her.

'We can see everything from here,' Lily said. 'They're good seats.'

'Newsflash, Lily,' Sally said, looking at her dumbfounded, 'these are the *worst* seats. The only place to sit in a high-street show is front row with the C-list celebs or right at the very back with the cool crowd who don't want to be seen.'

'Well, I'm fine here,' Lily said, sitting down. 'I don't want to be sitting in the front row with everyone looking at us.'

Sally opened her mouth in mock horror, although actually, in this case, it was genuine. She was wearing skin-tight mock-croc leggings and a pastel tinted sweatshirt with a gold unicorn emblazoned across the front.

'You think I wore this magnificent ensemble,' she said, running her hands down her front in a dramatic sweep, 'to be hidden in the fashion desert of the middle row? Sometimes I wonder if we work in the same business, Lily, honestly I do.'

But she sat down anyway and started to root about in her handbag.

'Tell me you haven't got a sandwich in there, Sally?' Lily said.

'Of course I have sandwiches. You think I'd sit through the tedium of a show like this without proper sustenance? If we're not in the front row at least I can eat my sandwich in peace.'

Lily laughed. She loved Sally. She fingered the picture in her bag and wondered if she should tell her about the cutting. Sally would probably think she was mad. She thought Lily was stuck in the dark ages. 'Vintage is fine but there is so much more you could be doing with it. Forget the past, get with the future.'

Lily decided to leave it until she had heard from the woman in Wisconsin and distracted herself from thinking about it with some people-watching.

Immediately she noticed an almost impossibly handsome square-jawed, sandy-haired dreamboat of a man in the front row. He looked as if he had stepped straight off a yacht and was flanked by two women, one with long shiny black hair and one with long shiny blonde hair – both models. He whispered to one of them, and she threw her head back and laughed, prettily.

'Who's the man with the shiny teeth?'

'That's Jack,' said Sally, 'and urgh, he's got "the twins" with him. He does love matching his girlfriends. So predictable.'

'Rich *and* handsome – just your type,' Lily said. 'He's waving at you.'

'Still-breathing and own-teeth is my type, dear, and he's waving at me but he's *looking* at you...'

He was, too, looking right at her. Lily blushed and turned away.

'…the dirty slut.'

'Gee, thanks.'

'Not you, *him*. Jack's a disgrace. He's probably identified you as the only woman in the room he hasn't slept with.'

'Including you?'

'Not on my own doorstep, dear. Oh God, he's incorrigible – he's *still* looking at you.'

'Don't be silly.' Lily found herself smiling. 'Is he? Really?'

She was trying to be dismissive but he really was extraordinarily handsome in an American celebrity type way. He was so not her type. Nonetheless, his efforts to catch her eye were quite flattering as well as amusing. She let her eyes flick over to him again for a second.

'His teeth are so *white*.'

'You are such a grubby Brit,' Sally said. '*Everyone* has teeth like that in America. It's the law.'

As the show started the house lights went down until it was pitch black in the windowless box, and deafeningly loud dance music travelled down the metal girders of the roof and up the hollow legs of the chairs they were sitting on. As the models pounded up and down the catwalk in their fluorescent sports gear, Lily had a mental flashback to her college show. She had been in her element that night, loving every moment from the hair and make-up marathon beforehand, with Sally helping to peel the models in and out of outfits, to the glorious walk down the catwalk with her girls when it was all over. She remembered looking down from the stage with the other graduates and feeling as if she was shining from the inside out. Lily had believed that night was the beginning of her life as a fashion designer, but then she had got that bad review. The journalist had called her collection 'historically derivative', which, as a selection of 1950s-inspired dresses Lily could see that it absolutely was. Disillusioned, Lily put down her pencil and sketchpad and started indulging her passion for genuine vintage instead. Blogging fame followed. Lily was happy with life the way it was but sometimes, when she was at a show like this, she couldn't help but wonder what would have happened if she had stuck with the designing.

The show itself was average. Scott's had obviously spent a fortune on the lighting and music, and the girls they sent down the runway were a good mixture of alluring and competent. The hair and make-up was superb – gothic, techni-coloured – but the clothes?

'They were rubbish,' Sally said to Jack when they found themselves pressed up beside him in the single-exit crush to get out.

But Jack was looking at Lily and Sally felt a frisson of annoyance as he said, 'Lily Fitzpatrick, the vintage blogger? We're honoured to have you.'

Jack's eyes were fixed on her as if she were the only woman there. Lily guessed it was the kind of thing rich, slick dreamboats like him did to everyone, though she was taken aback that he knew who she was.

'Don't get excited,' Sally butted in now, as if she could read her mind. 'I told him who you were so he could put your name on the door for me. Thanks for the front row seat, buddy...'

'Ah, Sally, you do know how I like to keep my best girl happy but alas, there wasn't room for you both.'

'The clothes were pure pants,' said Sally. 'Day-Glo? 80s slogans revisited? Yawn, that is *so* 2010. We want something different, you know? Not more retro crap. Lily's a much better designer than any of the idiot kids coming out of college these days.'

'You're a designer as well as a blogger?'

'Only the best damn designer of her generation,' Sally said.

'Oh?' said Jack. 'What happened?'

'She got a bad review and gave up...'

'Actually, I discovered I preferred vintage,' Lily said, glowering at Sally.

'I can see that,' Jack said, fixing Lily again with his playboy blue eyes. 'I like it. Do you think those old shoes will walk you across the road for a drink?'

'They are this season Kiely,' Lily said, 'and I'm afraid I have to go home.'

'Ah,' said Jack, with genuine regret in his voice. 'Can't we persuade you?'

Sally looked in astonishment at Lily. 'You're being weird. Are you ok? I know you're still upset over Joe...'

'I'm fine,' Lily said. 'I'll call you tomorrow. Nice to meet you, Jack.'

On the way home Lily sat on the packed tube and wondered if she was fine or if she really was being weird, leaving her best mate and a handsome man so she could go home and check up on a lead to some long lost great-uncle and his wife.

She was still sad after Joe, of course, but she probably could do with a night out. Why was she rushing home?

As if to answer her own question Lily clipped opened her leather purse bag and took out the *Vogue* cutting of Joy Fitzpatrick in her magnificent dress. Even in this black and white computer print-out, the voluminous skirt made Joy look as if she was sitting on a bejewelled cloud. For a moment Lily wondered if it was the rather haughty looking woman she wanted to be related to, or the exquisite gown she was wearing.

With that thought, the seed of an idea planted itself in Lily's head.

Six

 *New York, 1951*

On his first day back at work after their New Year's break, Frank's secretary came into his office and said, 'There is a Miss Rogerson waiting for you in reception, sir.'

Frank had thought of nothing but Joy since New Year's Eve. When he closed his eyes at night he saw her face, her lips parted, waiting for his kiss. However, Frank decided to put her out of his mind. The girl's age, but also her grace, her wit, the sheer audaciousness of her mesmerizing beauty was way beyond him. He told himself, repeatedly, to forget Joy. She was simply a flighty girl who had passed a moment with him. Also, she was from an important family and Frank didn't need that sort of trouble.

'Tell her I'm busy, Nina.'

Nina came back two minutes later and said, 'I am sorry, sir, but she refuses to leave until she has spoken to you. She was adamant.'

Joy was sitting on the long black chaise in an eye-catching cherry-red suit.

'As I told Nina, I intend to sit here, in this lovely reception area, until you agree to take me out to dinner tonight. She told me she'd be kind enough to supply me with coffee for as long as it takes.'

Nina smiled, a little nervously, but Joy had certainly charmed her.

She stood up and held out her hand for Frank to kiss and, like a fool, that's exactly what he did.

He took her to a modest Italian bistro for an early supper, hoping the gauche gesture would put her off. 'I know what you're doing,' she said, 'but you can take me here every night and feed me spaghetti until I am as fat as a house. I'm holding out for my kiss.'

'You'll be waiting a long time,' he said.

'And why is that?' she said. 'Because you're too much of a gentleman?'

Frank leaned across the table and held her eye so intensely she could feel her skin burn. 'No,' he said, 'because I couldn't stop with a kiss.'

She had no reply, only a blushing cheek and a flickering eyelid.

'You, Joy Rogerson, would turn this gentleman into a man.'

They married within five weeks.

Frank wanted to ask her father for Joy's hand. He understood that he was an outsider, older and unknown to her parents, but Frank hoped he could win them around. However, Joy persuaded him that they were not reasonable people, especially when it came to their only daughter. It was better for her to present the engagement to them as a fait accompli, she said. It turned out she was right.

The Rogersons were furious at both her choice of husband and the lack of consultation. However, they also knew that their daughter was a handful and they worried that if they turned this one down, she might never find another, so they conceded.

The wedding was a small affair, unforgivably small for someone of her social standing, but Joy did not care. She was marrying the love of her life. After the church service the bride and groom, along with Ruth and Charles Rogerson and a handful of carefully chosen cousins and great-aunts, went for a discreet wedding breakfast in the Waldorf.

Frank was anxious to impress Joy's parents but they virtually ignored him throughout the meal. Ruth barely acknowledged him, and it became clear that Charles did not even intend on saying the customary few words of congratulation.

Frank was humiliated. There were circles in American society where the Irish were respected: the unions, the judiciary – even politics. However, the old money of the Rogersons did not recognize new respectability. Frank was not entirely unsympathetic. He understood their chagrin at his daughter marrying not just an Irishman but a common Catholic, outside not only their social circle, but also their creed.

Joy was not as forgiving. Ashamed and hurt by her parents' behaviour, Joy did not eat throughout the wedding breakfast but stroked her new husband's hand and gazed into his eyes to let everyone know how she felt about him. As coffee was being served she stood up, held her Martini glass aloft and said, 'I should like to propose a toast to Frank Fitzpatrick and his new wife – me!' While the glasses were raised she added, 'Now, if you'll excuse us, I have a husband to attend to,' and before he could object, she dragged Frank away from the table.

'You are a dreadful and wicked person,' he said as they made their way up to the suite. 'Your parents will never forgive me.'

'My parents will never forgive you anyway.'

When they got up to their suite Joy suddenly felt nervous.

They had both been waiting for this and, while she had kissed boys before, she had little idea of what was ahead of her. Stripped of her flirtatious bravado Joy went over to the drinks cabinet and poured them both a whisky. Frank stood watching her, looking at the pert ladylike way she moved, her lacquered hair caught up in an elaborate swoop at the base of her neck, the demureness of her white, wool suit. Joy handed him the whisky and smiled but there was a glimmer of girlish fear in her eyes. Frank threw the whisky back in one gulp then took the glass from her hand and laid it on a side table. He cupped her face in his hands and kissed her until she thought she would faint, then lifted her onto the bed. Everything became lost to her in the certainty of his touch. Joy was powerless with desire; this was everything she had ever wanted. As she felt the sting of him entering her for the first time, Joy held her husband's eyes. In them she saw a kind, beautiful man who was drunk with love and Joy felt, for the first time in her young life, as if she completely belonged.

Joy was determined to prove to her parents that they had made the right decision in allowing her to marry Frank, and over the coming year she poured everything into becoming the perfect wife, as her beauty, poise and education had prepared her to be. She quickly worked her way into the very heart of her parents' social set and brought Frank with her. Although he would always be something of an outsider, Joy's own background, coupled with her respect for and adoration of him, helped place Frank firmly at the centre of America's oldest banking families. The 'Irishman's' business acumen and charm did the rest.

Within weeks of the wedding Frank bought them a large, two-storey apartment on Fifth Avenue. Joy drafted in the Hollywood interior designer Adele Faulkner to decorate it. Faulkner found the beautiful young socialite both charming and surprisingly discerning. Impressed with her client's good taste, she guided Joy towards the finest young designers and artists of the day. Joy filled the Fitzpatrick home with revolutionary modern design. She took risks, placing Gerrit Rietveld classic Zig Zag Chairs around an Eames plywood table. Clean lines and modern tastes were unusual among the Rogersons' traditional set but Joy was not afraid to stand out. When the Fitzpatrick apartment featured in *Architectural Digest*, the doubters all came to her housewarming cocktail party and cooed over the new, modern look.

Joy became as ruthlessly stylish as her home. She believed it was essential that she be seen to dress perfectly in order to build Frank's profile as a man of affluence and substance. She attended the shows, commissioning couture each season and was rarely seen publicly in the same outfit twice. Frank too underwent a makeover. Joy had new suits made by a Savile Row tailor sent over from London. She insisted that his shirts were all American cotton and laundered daily. His old ties were given away and new ones bought, all in French silk. His comfortable, worn shoes were replaced with Italian leather brogues.

Frank did everything Joy asked of him. He built up his businesses so he could be seen as a wealthy, worthy husband for her. He fraternized with her 'set', enduring endless cocktail parties where he was flirted with and teased by godless, bony socialites. As time went on, he even spent dinners in the company of Joy's parents, although they never bothered to disguise their snobbish loathing for him. Frank loved Joy so much that he was willing to lay everything on the line for her, even his pride. All his life Frank had been hungry to fall in love and now that it had happened it was not only with the most beautiful woman in all of America, but she also loved him back. The glory of his good fortune was all he needed to sustain him.

Privately, however, Frank continued to feel something of an outsider. He wondered at his wife's driven perfectionism. He himself did not really believe in the necessity of being seen to be better than the next man. (Certainly his own business empire had been built on the opposite premise – on an ability to gain the trust and support of every man.) Frank knew Joy had their best interests at heart. The socializing and the decorating and the endless buying of clothes gave her something to focus on. Frank could see that, far from being a shallow socialite, his wife was using all this frivolity to fill the gap in her life. He did it by making money, she did it by spending it. Until the children came along, it was important for her to feel she had a purpose. Even if that purpose was simply making them look like the Big Shots they were. When the children came, everything would change.

Joy had her own idea about extending their family, and when the decorating was complete she set about employing staff. Frank came home from work to his somewhat stark new home and found a tall man in the spotless kitchen preparing an elaborate meal of lobster, steak and French fries.

'Good evening, sir,' he said. 'May I fix you a cocktail before dinner?'

Frank scowled and went in search of his wife. He found her in the bedroom.

'Hurry up and get dressed, darling – the Balforts will be here in an hour.'

'Who the hell is that in our kitchen?'

'Our new butler,' she said, 'and before you complain he is perfectly charming. He's called Jones and comes with a personal recommendation from the Wilsons in Boston.'

'Well, I won't have it, Joy. This is too much. It's not natural, another man living in my house.'

Truthfully, Frank was uncomfortable with the notion of having servants. He had always paid various women to clean and cook for him as necessary, but the idea of somebody living in the house with them was unacceptable.

'He needs to live somewhere, Frank, he's come all the way from Boston.'

'We don't need anyone else. We can get a woman in to clean, send the laundry out, eat in restaurants...'

But Joy was adamant. She had grown up with staff, many of whom had been kinder to her than her own parents, and it was a rite of passage that she employ staff of her own.

They compromised and Frank found Jones a fully functioning separate servants' apartment, with three rooms and a kitchen and bathroom, in their building.

Jones quickly grew fond of Joy. She had a sense of taste and style way beyond her years. She had created a home of such modern elegance that it was a delight to manage, and while her husband was almost embarrassed to give him instruction, Jones' discretion and loyalty soon won him over and Jones learned to respect the honest, charismatic Irishman.

The same could not be said for his in-laws. Ruth Rogerson remained sceptical about her only daughter's choice of partner. It wasn't just that Frank was 'new money' and that he appeared to have no family, rich or poor. Her lack of approval was instinctive, based on a mother's mistrust. Finding herself widowed, less than a year into her daughter's marriage, Ruth transferred her assets into jewellery and gems, which she put in the bank, to be released only to Joy on her death. It was not a moment too soon, for a heart attack claimed her, too, within months.

At her mother's graveside, Joy gripped Frank's arm and wished she could crawl inside his cashmere coat and stay there forever, safe and warm in the shelter of her husband's love. At the reading of her will the lawyer revealed that the jewels were to be kept safe 'in case my daughter ever needs them', which they both knew meant, if she decided to divorce Frank.

Joy did not stop to grieve for her parents. Instead she focused even more intensely on her marriage and Frank. For their first anniversary she booked a romantic trip to Ireland, hoping to learn more about her husband's background. But it ended up being a disaster. They stayed first at The Shelbourne in Dublin for two days. The hotel was nice enough but Joy found the weather inclement and the city frankly rather dull. Frank remained elusive about his family and Joy was left believing that he was ashamed of them. Joy herself was ashamed of how her parents had behaved towards him and of her own inability to protect him, so she did not push the point. With nobody to see and no social engagements to attend they had pointlessly wandered the dreary streets, with Frank becoming increasingly mournful and ill-tempered.

Eventually she whisked him over to London and then to her spiritual home. Paris, with all its galleries and ateliers and nightclubs, was where Joy felt truly at home. They drank champagne and ate oysters and together they went to Chanel's salon and bought her a magnificent gown with a marabou train. Frank allowed himself to get caught up in his young wife's joie de vivre but nonetheless, the miserable trip to Ireland had cast a small shadow. On the way home, as they ate dinner together in the first class lounge of the aeroplane, Joy was making plans to return to Paris for the following season's shows when Frank said, 'I don't think you ought to travel for a while, Joy. I think perhaps it would be better if you rested.'

They both knew what he was trying to say, although it was not something either could openly express. Both had hoped that she would return from their holiday pregnant but she began to bleed on the plane. As she walked up the aisle from the ladies' room she gave Frank the almost imperceptible blink of disappointment that had become their shorthand for 'no'.

She knew her husband was desperate for a child and Joy wanted to give him one. She knew their marriage would never be complete without that. Although, at twenty-two, Joy had no great maternal instincts herself, this did not temper her frustration and disappointment at her failure to conceive for her husband.

As each month passed into the second year of their marriage, Joy could see her husband's sadness building. She watched him nod politely as other men talked about their sons at business dinners, excusing himself when they asked about his progeny.

Joy always covered for him, saying, 'Silly man married a much younger woman, and I am far too busy having fun with *you* lovely people.' Joy charmed her way through every awkward moment, but they could feel the pressure building with each passing month.

They went to see the Rogersons' family doctor who said, 'These things can't be forced.' He added, 'Joy is a healthy young woman.' Frank smarted at the inference and Joy saw, for the first time, that Frank believed this was his fault, his failing.

That night she initiated their lovemaking and afterwards

lay across his chest and assured him she would get pregnant. This was her fault. There were things a woman could do, she said. It was all to do with timing. She would eat more, exercise less. She would look into drugs – there were drugs for everything these days. A woman's body was complex but she would sort things out. Soon, they would be a family.

Frank cheered up as she reassured him and they opened some good wine to celebrate their optimism. Frank got quite drunk and once they had drained the second bottle they started fantasizing about the children they were going to have. Frank had it all worked out. Molly and Jack Fitzpatrick. A pretty girl in a ballerina dress and a scruffy boy who he would teach to play Irish hurling. They would buy a house upstate and Joy could fill it with as many servants and as much fancy furniture as she liked, as long as there was one big bed where the children could come and jump them awake on a Sunday morning before church.

'Church?' Joy cried.

'Of course,' Frank said. 'When we have kids we'll be quite the respectable family!'

Joy laughed, but she didn't know what to say. She was taken aback.

After he had talked out his dream, Frank fell into a deep, drunken sleep and Joy walked across to the bedroom window. She looked out at the city sky and wondered if Frank loved the idea of a family more than he loved her.

The thought that might be true made her feel empty inside; it was a cold, lonely feeling. As if there was a yawning black hole inside her that needed to be filled.

Then the anxiety came. Suppose she couldn't make good on her promise to give him a child. Would Frank leave her? Did he love her at all?

Unable to curb these dark thoughts, Joy went downstairs to the mirrored bar and poured herself a double scotch, just to help her sleep. Then she crawled in next to her husband's strong, warm body and told herself that tomorrow was the day when everything would be perfect in her world again.

Seven

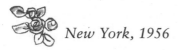 *New York, 1956*

'You will be nice to Minnie, won't you darling?'

It was a Saturday morning and the Fitzpatricks were entertaining that afternoon. Frank had asked his wife to introduce Minnie and T. J. Yewdell, a rich but homey Texan couple, into their New York social scene. Frank had done business with Ted, liked him, and was keen to help the couple settle in New York. Joy had arranged an intimate afternoon drinks gathering, there, at the apartment. Canapés and cocktails. She would even do the hostess thing and mix some of the drinks herself.

'I am *always* nice to our guests, Frank.'

Joy was in bed with a breakfast tray on her lap tucking into her English tea and toast, her only proper meal of the day. Frank was sitting up, enjoying the novelty of watching her eat.

'Yes, but sometimes you can be a bit snobbish...'

'Only if people are vile.'

'Well, Minnie and Ted are not vile. They are very nice but they are from Texas so they don't exactly fit your idea of...'

'Stylish?'

'Exactly.'

She stuffed a piece of toast into her mouth. 'Don't worry,'

she said, raising her eyes to heaven like a scolded child. 'I'll be kind.'

He leaned over the bed and gave her a kiss. This was how he loved Joy. Wearing not a scrap of make-up she looked so sweet and innocent, like an ordinary girl. He felt close to her when she was relaxed like this. When she had finished eating, Joy would get up, shower, dress, then transform herself with clothes and make-up into 'Joy Fitzpatrick', his impeccable, socialite wife. He preferred Joy natural but knew she couldn't go about her life looking, or indeed being, like that. That was not who she was. Frank was the only one allowed the privilege of knowing the real Joy, and so he cherished these early mornings alone with her.

While she was in the bathroom Frank drained his wife's teacup and grimaced at all the sugar.

Five years into their marriage he should know how his wife took her tea. After all, it was still just the two of them and that was a bitter blow for Frank.

Frank had never especially wanted, or intended, to become a rich man; he had certainly never sought the kind of glamorous limelight into which his wife had put him. Frank had been driven forward less by ambition and more by a fear of falling back into the poverty of his childhood, but he had always aspired to an ordinary home life. Children, more than wealth, had been a part of his dreams. The opportunity to make good on his own painful upbringing.

Frank had earned all the money he needed to live life as he wanted it, for the rest of his days, but the other aspect of ordinariness, the sense of family and security, had evaded him. Joy was wonderful in many ways but she was a woman to whom the word 'ordinary' was anathema.

Frank's initial disappointment at not being a father had

given way to a quiet resignation. He had a good life, plenty of money and a beautiful wife, and he tried to focus on that. If he was sad about not being a father, he hid it well from everyone. Even – indeed mostly – from himself.

However, he knew that Joy felt his disappointment as her own failing. Nobody blamed him for their childlessness. Joy was the one they were all looking at and talking about behind her back. That was why, he believed, his wife remained so caught up in proving herself with all the clothes and parties. It was also, Frank believed, why Joy drank too much sometimes. Motherhood had not come to soften the sharp-edged vanity of her youth. Only he knew the Joy that still lay beneath the couture and the make-up.

'Oh, by the way, I ordered another piece of art yesterday, a perfectly ghastly abstract thing by Bauer.'

'Why do you keep buying paintings you don't like?' Frank asked, calling down to Jones to bring them up coffee.

'I know. The poor man's been dead three years but she *keeps* pushing his work on us. She's convinced he was brilliant, it's just that our plebeian tastes aren't refined enough to see it yet. She knows what's she's talking about I suppose. She *is* Guggenheim's eyes after all.'

'I suppose it cost a fortune?'

'I paid for it myself.'

Frank smarted. 'I wish you wouldn't keep buying expensive things without consulting me first.'

Joy's independent wealth bothered Frank. Without a woman's dependence a man could not gain the full respect of his wife or, indeed, exert any authority over her. Joy had her mother's fortune still tucked away somewhere in a bank vault to draw on. She didn't need Frank's money – ergo, she did not need Frank. It wasn't normal.

'Sorry, darling, it was an impulse thing. Don't worry, it's not very big so we can pop it in a corner. Hilla Rebay talked me into it. Honestly, I don't know *how* she keeps selling me her friends' work. She is such a charmless bore, I don't know how Guggenheim puts up with her.'

'It's that sort of talk I don't want inflicted on poor Minnie Yewdell this afternoon.'

'I don't know what you're talking about Frank. You know I am always perfectly charming to your business associates. I shall be the perfect wife.'

Six hours later Minnie Yewdell was perched nervously on the edge of one of their Eileen Gray Bibendum armchairs. She was a small redhead, wearing far too much make-up and way out of her depth. She seemed terrified that the modernist chair with its soft black leather edges might close in and swallow her up.

Frank found himself looking across at the poor woman and realizing his wife's promise to be charming to her might have been optimistic. Joy hated it when her guests looked uncomfortable. She said it interfered with the line of the furniture. Frank knew she was only half-joking.

As Joy got up to fetch more drinks Frank saw the eyes of the three other female guests follow her across the room. Joy was wearing a simple Chanel shift dress with day pearls and low, black stilettos. As she raised her tall, slender frame from the chair he noted each woman self-consciously checking their own outfits, flicking the hem of a skirt or fingering the collar of a blouse, painfully aware they were, inevitably, wearing the wrong thing. They had all made a huge effort to impress his wife and were frothed up in full skirts, wide belts and voluminous blouses, the latest craze. 'Dior,' he had heard one of them say, too loudly. Joy didn't go in for fashion fads;

she liked to carve out her own style. Even walking across her own drawing room, Joy Fitzpatrick was magnificent. His wealth and her beauty, plus her innate sense of style, put her beyond the jealousy of Manhattan's elite wives. She was their queen. If you didn't know Joy Fitzpatrick you were out of the circle and if you were out of the circle in New York society, well then, life just wasn't worth living.

'You're a lucky man,' T. J. said to him. 'She's one beautiful lady.'

Frank smiled and nodded but as he watched his graceful wife wander over to their elegant, mirrored cocktail bar the thought crept up on him, not for the first time, that actually, he didn't give a rat's arse about any of this social-climbing, polite chit-chat nonsense.

However, he liked Ted and was determined to help him and his wife fit in to the exclusive social club in which he had found himself living.

Joy stood over her nervous new guest with the Martini shaker.

'No, really,' Minnie objected, lifting the glass a little higher, 'it's way too early for me.'

'Nonsense,' Joy said smiling.

'Ooh, don't get me tipsy,' Minnie said. 'In South Carolina we ladies don't drink so much as you do here in New York.'

Joy's smile vanished. Frank felt sick. It was going to be one of those afternoons. Despite Joy's composure he knew his wife was always on edge when she had guests. Joy said she needed the Martinis to loosen her up – to loosen them all up. His wife spent her life creating expectation from her peers and exceeding it but Frank knew this was not so much because she wanted to impress them as because she felt she needed to. Ever since she was a child, she had felt the world's eyes judging her. Judging what she was wearing, how she behaved, the way she wore her hair. In the early years it had touched him, and he had comforted her and loved her insecurities away.

Joy tapped the cocktail shaker slightly on the side of her new guest's glass and said, a little sharply, 'If you're feeling unwell, Minnie, I can ask Jones to bring the car around?'

Joy gave Frank a look across the room that clearly said, 'Why am I entertaining this gauche overdressed southerner in my home?' Between the strong cocktails and the tense moment, Frank could see that Ted's wife Minnie was almost in tears.

'Oh no, Joy, I didn't mean to...' As the Martinis kicked in, Frank knew Joy would become even less sympathetic about Minnie's pitiful attempts to ingratiate herself socially.

He looked across at Jones and gave him the secret nod that said they needed to start winding things down.

Within a few minutes Jones announced that cars were outside waiting to take them down to Sardi's. Things were easier when they were out. The atmosphere was less intense and it didn't seem as obvious somehow if Joy got drunk in a crowded restaurant as it did in their own apartment in the company of a handful of people.

'I thought we were eating at home tonight?' Joy said.

There she was, his magnificent Joy, in her perfect dress, in their perfect apartment, holding aloft the shiny cocktail shaker, and in that moment Frank suddenly felt something strange happen. The beautiful bare-faced Joy he had breakfasted with a few hours earlier, the real Joy, was gone. He had lost her. Frank gathered himself together. He was being foolish.

'Oh, sorry darling, did I not say?'

Jones handed Frank Joy's fur cape. He walked across the room, draped it around her shoulder and kissed her tenderly on the cheek.

She closed her eyes and leant against him in sheer, loving bliss. Seeing the other women watching, Frank felt separated from himself, as if he was on a stage, acting in a play he had written, except he had forgotten his lines.

Over dinner at Sardi's Joy was snobbishly verbose, just as she had promised Frank she would not be, talking about artists that nobody had heard of and the poor quality of American couture. She managed to get away with it by ordering copious numbers of cocktails and making everyone drink alongside her. Frank held back, cautious of how things might end if they both got drunk together, something that was happening less and less often. By the time dessert came, poor Minnie was drooling on her husband's shoulder. Finally, Ted Yewdell carried his legless wife out of the restaurant, full of apologies for her sorry state.

'*That* was embarrassing,' Joy said, making a face after them while her friends laughed. Frank felt furious.

After dinner, when all their friends had gone home, Sardi's filled up with a party being held by a theatre impresario Joy knew. She insisted they stay on and socialize with the arty set and while Frank wanted to go home, he was too afraid to leave her there alone. As they worked the room separately, Joy fingered her diamond earrings and looked coyly across at her handsome husband, making sure all the women saw her. Frank kept up his buddy-Irishman thing and was all smiles and handshakes and 'no business talk tonight in front of the ladies' back slapping. They drank champagne and danced and appeared to everyone like the perfect, happy couple. Frank almost believed they were just that, until after midnight when it was time to go and they hit the fresh air. Without an audience Joy's transformation from perfectly groomed lady to belligerent drunk was complete. She stumbled against Frank and started shouting that she wanted to return to the party until he managed to cajole her into their car without anyone seeing. She leant against him murmuring, 'I love you, I love you so much,' until eventually she fell asleep.

Frank carried her across the lobby, into the elevator, in through the door of their apartment and laid her down on their bed.

With her limbs flopping in a dead sleep, Frank easily peeled off Joy's coat and dress and unwound the string of pearls up over her head. Then, he took off his jacket, loosened his tie and sat on the bed next to her looking, just looking, at his lovely wife. Her perfect pouted lips, her large eyes closed, their half mooned lids framed in that trademark black line she painted on so meticulously each morning. He placed his hand on her forehead and pushed the hair back from her face, marvelling at the smooth cream of her skin against the coarse lines of his large, rough hand.

She looked so innocent asleep like this, like his Joy, and he was relieved to have her back. When she was asleep like this, he was able to fall in love with her again.

Frank lay down next to her and realized he was exhausted. He checked his watch. It was not yet 1 a.m., not so late for a Saturday night, yet he felt as if he had been run over by a truck.

He was glad the day was over. Tomorrow was Sunday; Joy could sleep her hangover off, then on Monday he would be back at work and able to resume some semblance of the ordinary life he craved.

Eight

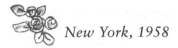 *New York, 1958*

Honor looked out of the window: New York was glistening under the streetlights. From the shabby brownstones of Harlem to the verdant green lawns of Central Park everything was covered in a blanket of thick snow. It was nearly 10 p.m. on Christmas Eve 1958 and Honor Conlon was the last person left at work.

'It's so beautiful,' Rosa, the newest seamstress had said that morning. 'In Mexico we don't have snow. You have snow in Ireland?'

'Yes,' Honor said.

She was tired of all the chatter and gossip in the workshop. Endless exchanges between the dozen women on how their husbands annoyed them, what they cooked for Thanksgiving dinner, and now, 'Look how pretty the snow is!'

Honor was the best seamstress there. She could machine-sew an evening skirt to couture finish in less than two days or embroider the collar and cuff of a blouse so that a socialite would pay a small fortune for it. Even Colette, Monsieur Breton's right hand woman, acknowledged that the young Irish girl had an instinctive way of interpreting the designer's drawings, which baffled the elegant older seamstress, who had been working for the renowned couturier since their early days together in Paris.

'She is the best I have ever seen,' Colette told Breton, after he had admired a piece of crochet work Honor had done overnight.

'The Irish learn to crochet from their mother's breast,' he said. 'They do it to keep their hands warm.'

Nothing could have been further from the truth. Honor had learned to sew and crochet in the workshop of the great Irish designer Sybil Connolly in Dublin, but her teacher parents had made her finish school before she was allowed to take up an apprenticeship. The Conlons were puzzled by their daughter's determination to become a 'humble dressmaker'. Honor's own mother Clare could barely darn a sock.

'Will he ever let me work with him in the design studio?' Honor asked the old French woman.

'Perhaps...' Colette said, elusively, always stopping short of praising Honor to her face.

Barbara, who had been there six years, to Honor's three, said, 'They'll never let you out of here. You're too good.'

Honor's dream of designing clothes, instead of merely making them, was fading with each passing day. Now, here she was, on Christmas Eve, working into the early hours on a finicky white-on-white embroidered panel for some spoilt rich woman's New Year's Eve party dress. It was her own fault she was still here.

'Something pretty, something feminine,' Breton had said, rubbing his long slim fingers with his thumbs, in a soft, fluid motion, like her mother binding fat and flour for pastry.

Honor could have started something simple. She could have done daisies, or snowflakes, in a few hours. Instead, she thought of the fine grey frost on the window of her small cottage bedroom in Ireland and tried to replicate it with the thinnest embroidery thread she could find. Before she knew it, she was making panels of lace that would have taken five Kenmare nuns a full week. She knew it was madness but she could not help herself: once she had an idea she was driven to create it.

The light was fading and her eyes were smarting from the intensity of pulling the thin thread through the taut silk-skin but looking out of the window didn't help. Honor hated the snow. Not the cold, but the way it turned the whole world into white velvet.

'There's no variety.' She once tried explaining her dislike of it to her mother. They were sitting by the fire, back in Ireland, during her last Christmas at home, three years ago, just before she had left for New York.

'I need colour,' she said. 'Look at this...' And she held up a piece of knitting that seemed, even to her mother's untrained eye, to capture perfectly the coppery winter grass and the deep purple heathers on the boglands that surrounded the town of Bangor, County Mayo, where they lived.

'White snow is boring – it makes the earth look like a shroud.'

Her mother smiled and looked across at her eccentric, artistic daughter.

'I want you to make me a dress the colour of a duck's head,' Honor had said when she was seven.

'And what colour would that be?' her bemused mother asked.

'Dark, dark green,' the child answered. 'Although some-times it changes to a blue – like the night sky.'

Seven-year-old Honor could not hide her disappointment at the green cotton dress her mother had had made for her by the local tailor, but years later, when Honor came home on a Christmas holiday, from her apprenticeship with Sybil Connolly in Dublin, she brought with her a Panné Velvet gown, in those exact colours. It skimmed Clare's slim figure perfectly, although she would never have anywhere to wear it.

'I'll send for you, Mam, one day, when I'm a big designer in New York. I'll take you to a party where you can show it off.'

When Honor's father complained to his wife about their only child's obsession with making clothes, she pointed out it was his fault. It had all started with Honor making costumes for the amateur dramatic shows which her father ran in his school hall. It was through John's love of Shakespeare that his daughter had got a taste for velvet capes, puffed medieval sleeves, elaborate beading and gold braiding. Honor spent all her free time embroidering handkerchiefs and making costumes. She would tear up her father's good shirts and remodel them into blouses for herself, then pick apart clothes she had grown out of and patch-work them into skirts and aprons for her mother.

Despite this eccentric hobby, Honor kept up with her schoolwork and when she got top marks in her Leaving Certificate exams at the age of eighteen, her father assumed she would go on to teacher training college. John had a private hope that Honor would then return to Bangor and join him in the school. Classroom numbers were growing and John was confident that he could get funding for another teacher. When Honor announced that she intended to go to Dublin to work as a seamstress, he was furious.

'Have you any idea how few get called for teacher training?' he argued. 'You cannot possibly consider wasting your good brain sewing for a living?'

'But I love sewing,' she said, 'and I don't want to teach – I just want to make things.'

'Well, I love acting,' John said, 'but I'm not about to rush off and try to get a job at the Abbey!'

'Well, maybe you should,' Honor snapped. She was red-faced now. Not just angry, but afraid that her parents were going to stand in the way of her dream.

'I wouldn't be that selfish,' John said. 'I would not abandon my town, my community, my family, to follow a foolish notion.'

'It's not a foolish notion, it's a good job.' But even as she said it, Honor knew that running off to Dublin to become a seamstress would hurt her parents and she could not bear to do that. Her parents were good people. She was a good person. She would have to do what her father wanted, but she was damned if she wouldn't put up a fight first.

In the end they let her go.

Honor had been hoarding fashion magazines under her bed, scouring her father's newspapers every day for news of shows in Paris and London. She had filled a broad, brown scrapbook with cuttings and her own designs. Clare knew where her daughter's heart lay and she showed the stash to John. Knowing it was the right thing to do, he rang the only person he knew connected with clothes. This theatrical fabric supplier in Dublin was a kind man who managed to secure the headmaster's daughter an apprenticeship.

Honor would never forget the moment her parents called her into the kitchen to tell her. Her mother was beaming, as her father handed her the letter, on thick official paper, offering her a place in Sybil Connolly's Dublin studio.

'I don't even know who she is,' John said.

'She is the best designer in the world!' Honor screamed.

'Thank you, Daddy. Oh, thank you.'

'I still think you're making a terrible mistake,' he said, but it didn't matter now.

'You'll lose her,' was what Clare had said, when he had stubbornly declared he would force her into teacher training against her will. 'You can have her body, or her heart, John, but if you push this, you could end up losing both.'

Clare and John continued to dream that their daughter would return to Bangor one day, perhaps marry and be content sewing for the local women and making costumes for her father's productions. In her weekly letters, Clare often jokily asked if her daughter had met any nice men in New York and if she did, to be sure they were from the north-west coast of Mayo.

Yet three years later, here Honor was, still stitching sequins onto hems and no closer to the dream that had brought her so far from home. She had expected to be designing by now. She had done her time. All the other women were happy in the workshop, clocking in the hours, until they could get out, to either find a man or return home to one. Honor was twenty-three and unmarried – a spinster. She didn't care about that. She just cared about creating beautiful clothes, her *own* beautiful clothes, with *her* name on them.

The lace was not going well. Despite using the finest thread, she could see her freehand stitching looked less like delicate frost and more like fat fingers of coral. This had been a mistake – it looked awful – but Honor had done too much of it to start again.

Exhausted and despairing, Honor went to get some coffee. As she walked down the corridor to the staff kitchen she noticed that the light was on in Monsieur Breton's studio. Instinctively she moved towards the door then hesitated when she noticed the maestro was sitting at his desk. He looked up briefly, barely acknowledging her, and then went back to his drawing. The two of them were often the only ones left in the building, but Honor had not expected to see him on Christmas Eve. Why wasn't he at home? Though she knew he had no wife. 'Me? I love only my work,' he often said to the women who left his employ to get married.

Honor's hands were cold and her fingers stiff from the work, as she held them near the stove while the kettle boiled.

As she carried her strong black coffee back to the sewing workshop Honor was careful not to look in at her employer and incur his displeasure. At her worktable she peered down at her lace tentacles with a fresher eye. Perhaps they were not so bad, after all. The shapes were unusual but they were interesting and they reminded her of something. Absorbed in her thoughts, Honor reached for her coffee without looking, and spilled it all over her lace.

She screamed, partly in pain, as the hot liquid splashed her hand, but mostly for her ruined work. She reached out to rescue it when, suddenly, the maestro appeared from behind her, grabbed her arm and dragged her away from the table. At first she thought he was in a fury and was about to throw her from the building, but he simply guided her firmly and quickly into the bathroom, turned on the cold tap and carefully placed her scalded hand under it.

'Hold it there,' he said, 'for at least ten minutes.'

'It's fine, really,' Honor said, taking her hand away, anxious to get back and rescue the lace.

Breton glowered at her and pushed her hand back under the water. 'You are of no use to anyone with a scalded hand, girl. Keep it here for *dix minutes* – I will come back.' Then he went back into the workshop.

Honor started to cry, partly with frustration, but also with fear of what would happen when her boss saw the ruined lace. He would sack her for sure. Then what would she do? Start again, sewing anonymously for another designer? There was no other designer in New York worth working for and in any case, who would have her without a reference from Monsieur? She might as well be back in Ireland, fixing hems for a local tailor, or making simple blue burial gowns for the undertaker.

As each minute passed, Honor became more and more anxious until finally her boss came back, turned off the tap and checked her burnt hand.

'It will be fine,' he said. 'No swelling.'

He was right, her hand was red from the freezing water, but there was no sign of the original burn.

'Leave it tonight,' he said. 'Go home.'

'I can't, Monsieur,' Honor said. 'I have to finish my lace.'

'Pfft,' he replied, flicking his hand up. 'It is done.'

'No,' she said, 'you don't understand, it's just that . . .' Her voice dropped to a terrified whisper. '. . . I haven't finished it, and the coffee . . .'

'Mon dieu,' he said, 'follow, follow.'

She followed him over to her desk and there, hanging above it, on the line she used for his drawings, was her unfinished lace. The frost lines were no longer white but a faint shade of ochre gold.

'Bog grass,' she said.

'Non,' he said. 'I dyed it with the coffee.'

But Honor was lost in rapture at the beautiful copper colours of the field of heathery threads in front of her.

'Bog grass is what we have in Ireland, before the snow comes.'

They stood together in silence for a moment, looking at the lace.

'So now it makes sense,' he said. 'It is finished. You have time to sew it onto the collar after Christmas. Now you can go home.'

Honor did not want to go home. She wanted to stay looking; she wanted to sew it into the white silk gown straight away.

'The heather under the snow.'

'How did you know?' she asked. She had to know. It was amazing, what he had done. 'How did you think of it?'

'You think you are the first person to spill coffee in a sewing studio?' He could see she was disappointed, so he shrugged and added, 'I am a genius.'

'Yes,' she said, 'you are.' Honor felt as if he had looked inside her imagination and unearthed something she had not even known was there herself.

'Also, my mother used to dye things,' he said. 'She sewed. I like to sew sometimes, too, and dye. You think the maestro cannot sew?'

'Well, I . . .' She had never thought about it.

'I can sew! My mother taught me. I stitched my own clothes from the age of eight! I can sew better than any woman in this room. Now? I am too important to sew. Now, I am a genius.'

Then the maestro did something which, in her four years of working for him, she had never seen him do before. He laughed. Then, looking at the lace, he said, 'It looks better, yes?'

'Oh,' Honor said, 'much better.'

The he stood back and said, 'Yes, like heather under snow, I like this. You and me, we think alike.'

Honor felt a kick of excitement in her stomach.

He paused, then added, 'You are good, Irish girl, very, very good...' Then he turned to go and added, '...but you are not a genius yet, Honor, not quite yet.'

He knew her name.

'When?' she asked. He turned at the door, shocked at her cheek, but she had to ask. She had to know.

He paused again, then said, 'When you know there is heather under the snow, then you will be ready to design.'

Honor packed up her things, turned off the lights and walked out into the crisp, snowy night. The sidewalks had turned treacherous from thousands of busy footsteps crunching snow into icy concrete, but Honor smiled, as she realized that on New Year's Eve, there would be a beautiful woman walking these same New York streets, wearing her Irish heather.

Nine

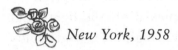 *New York, 1958*

Joy wasn't sure about the collar on her dress. She ran her finger along the rim of the soft chiffon, so fine it was barely there, then scraped the edge of a scarlet nail inside the almost invisible fabric, until it sat, just so against her throat.

Her dark, straight hair had already been styled earlier in the day and was pulled back from her face, ready for her to make up her face. In front of her, on the broad glass-dressing table, was the palette of powders and paints she used to turn herself into the person people recognized and admired, the person she needed to be. She tucked tissue paper in under the collar of her new dress and briefly checked her naked face before smoothing on her foundation.

Joy spent a lot of time tending to her face and what a face it still was. She had high cheekbones, a straight slim nose and her lips formed a perfectly-proportioned bow. Her eyes were broad, slightly slanted almonds, dark brown in colour, speckled with hazel. The *Vanity Fair* columnist who had sat next to her at the Waldorf Astoria Halloween Ball the previous year, had described them as mesmerizing.

She checked the time on the clock above the bed. It was a Gilbert Poillerat Sunburst she'd had shipped across from

France. It was 5.50 p.m. Not quite cocktail hour yet.

She checked the collar again, studying the feathery stain against her skin and still wasn't quite sure whether she liked it or not. Joy had specifically asked for the garment to be pure white, but then the designer, Breton, could be a law unto himself. He rarely followed instructions, even though Joy was always quite clear what she wanted. Nevertheless, he was still the best; the only designer in New York worth going to. She preferred to buy in Paris, of course, but recently Joy had found herself less inclined towards travelling to Europe to shop. She hated leaving Frank, who seemed to be busier and busier at work these days. New York was limited in what it had to offer by way of couture. Breton was virtually unique. Joy had been annoyed when she pushed back the tissue paper on his box and found not only that the collar and cuffs had a strange design which she had not been expecting, but were a different colour from the rest of it. Attention to detail was very important. Without detail a woman was nothing. Without everything in its exact right place, a delicate woman could fall apart.

Joy had certainly considered taking it back and complaining. However, she decided to try it on first and was glad that she had, because in this instance, the designer was right. The golden heathery hue worked against her skin. White would have been too harsh, too unforgiving. She held the matching cuff up to the collar and decided that she liked it after all. It would have been a shame not to have worn this dress tonight, after all the money she had spent on it.

Tonight was the eighth anniversary of the night she and Frank had met. Joy never celebrated their wedding anniversary. It was New Year's Eve that meant everything to her, the night Joy hoped Frank would fall in love with her again.

She snapped the lid of her compact shut and checked the

clock again: 6.15 p.m. It was a quarter into cocktail hour now. Joy wasn't finished getting ready and made a point of never drinking until after she was fully dressed. That was one of Joy's rules, along with no drink in the bedroom, no drink without mixers, no drink on a Wednesday (Thursday was drinks party day), no drink in front of Frank's business partners, and no drink at lunchtime, unless you had your own driver with you. Joy had so many rules, she reasoned, that it was a wonder she ever managed to have a drink at all. Anyway, it was now after six o'clock, which was the time when *all* civilized people had their first cocktail and those silly rules of hers were made to be broken. She walked barefoot out to the drawing room and over to the bar. The small Frigidaire was already stocked with ice and a large cocktail glass, which saved five minutes of messing about. It also prevented the glass from filling with melted ice and diluting the alcohol because, let's face it, Joy thought, there is nothing viler than a watery cocktail.

Joy scooped the ice into the tall mixing glass, measured out three jiggers of gin and two of dry vermouth, gave the mixture a brief stir, poured it to the rim of the frozen triangle and threw it back. Her head was barely upright as she poured the second one, paused briefly to draw breath and drank it back too. She could relax now. She carefully measured out two and a half measures of gin and one of vermouth back into the mixing glass on top of some ice. Then she took out some olives, sticks and peeled off a lemon rind, pushing it around the edge of a fresh glass and arranged all the accessories on a mirrored tray. She took a quick mouthful out of the mixing glass, just to taste, and spilled it down her chin but, as Joy reached for a napkin, she found there were none in the napkin tray.

Pure rage ran through her making her hand shake, as she reached up to dab the bitter gin away from her chin. Too much vermouth. She put in another jig of gin to bring it back. Really, this was not good enough. How many times – how many *times* – had she told Jones that keeping this bar stocked was to be the new housekeeper's first priority (the housekeepers were either useless, or kept leaving and were therefore always new)? Here she was mixing her *own* cocktails like a common barmaid and now she was expected to forage around for napkins, like a forest animal. She checked her watch and saw it was nearly half past six. Frank would be home shortly and she had not finished dressing. This was their big night. Joy needed to be dressed and relaxed when he got in, ready to hand him a Martini. Just how was she expected to do that, when her butler could not even organize some half-witted woman to press and starch half a dozen napkins for her cocktail bar? Was that too much to ask?

Furious, Joy clenched her fists, curled her slim frame into a hunched ball, then opened her mouth and roared Jones's name at the top of her voice.

Just at the very moment that her husband Frank walked into the room.

Ten

 *London, 2014*

There was no email from the woman in Wisconsin whose aunt was Joy Fitzpatrick waiting for Lily when she got home, so she spent that evening and most of that night trying to track down the original dress online. She tapped in the designer's name – 'Honor Conlon' – and hashtagged all the design and finish details she could find in the article: #RoseSilkTaffeta, #CarrickmacrossLace, #ExquisiteBeadwork, #50sDesignersNewYork, and even the ubiquitous #50sEveningGown, but while she trawled through thousands of similar dresses on hundreds of specialist dealer sites, Lily could not find the dress she was looking for.

The following morning Maisie Fitzpatrick sent her an email with a picture of her aunt attached. Lily's hand hesitated to open the file, knowing that the content of it could, literally, change her life. When she did click on the file, Lily ended up staring at the image in disappointed disbelief. It was a portrait studio shot of a woman in an enormous showy fur coat, dripping with probably every piece of jewellery she owned. She had a tight perm and a face like a startled hippopotamus wearing lipstick. This woman was as far removed from the elegant vision in the *Vogue* cutting as it was possible to be. Although Lily tried hard not to judge people by appearances, she was somewhat relieved to find that this terrifying-looking harridan was married to a man called Frederick and that he was from Cork – so they were definitely not related. She politely emailed back and said as much, but nonetheless Lily came away from the computer feeling crushed and stupid for having had such high hopes when the odds were so stacked against her.

It was time to give up, but before she closed down her computer, Lily realized she had been so caught up with finding a family link that she had forgotten to post her original blog featuring The Dress.

She attached the picture, adding the caption, *This lady has the same name as me – Fitzpatrick. Another Irish woman who loves her frocks*, before pressing 'post' and resigning herself to that being the end of her connection to Joy Fitzpatrick and her glorious gown.

After all that emotional excitement, Lily decided she needed a coffee and a hardcore sugar hit to go with it so she picked up her bag and headed down Kilburn High Road towards Costa Coffee.

As she approached Old Times she paused, remembering the awkward look she had exchanged with Gareth at the funeral. She hadn't recognized him without his beard, and was afraid she must have looked straight through him. Now, she wasn't sure that she was ready to see him; being in the shop might bring back the memory of that awful day. Then she saw what was in his window.

Damn, she thought. There, on the shabby, boss-eyed fashion mannequin, looking down on a 1970s record player and a pile of dusty comic books was a genuine 1960s leopard print swing coat. She had to have it.

'I thought you'd be in for that,' Gareth said, nodding at the window as soon as she walked in.

'Take it down,' she said. 'It's mine.'

'Don't you want to know how much it costs?'

'I'll give you a fiver,' she said, moving towards the mannequin to get it herself.

'It cost me more than that to get it cleaned,' he said, smiling.

He looked odd without his beard, more grown-up or something.

Lily unashamedly sniffed the fabric and said, 'Since when did you ever get anything cleaned? I'll give you fifteen.'

'Tell you what,' Gareth was grinning now, 'you can get the chai and croissants for a full month and we're even.'

'You're on,' Lily said, putting the un-cleaned coat over her shoulders, taking her purse out of her bag and running next door.

Ten minutes later they were sitting at the worn Formica 60s table that served as the Old Times counter.

'I'm sorry about rushing off at the funeral,' he said. 'To be honest, I found the whole thing a bit...weird.'

'Yeah,' Lily said, not wanting to go there but trying to be polite, 'funerals are weird.'

'It's not that,' Gareth said. 'It's just that...I'll miss him, you know?'

Lily nodded. She was feeling emotional but trying to hold it in. She knew Gareth, but not well enough to bawl in front of him. And her eyeliner wasn't waterproof.

'I don't know if you knew but Joe used to come in here nearly every day. He was my best customer. If I wasn't busy I'd crank up the gramophone and we could play a few tunes.'

Lily shoved a croissant into her mouth to swallow the tears back.

'The afternoon before he, erm, fell...' Gareth took a bite out of an apple Danish himself before continuing, '...he asked me to play him my John McCormack record. It's really rare – a 1916 recording – worth a fortune.'

'Will you play it for me now?'

'Sure,' Gareth said, reaching down under the counter. The record boxes front of shop had largely 80s *Top of The Pops* albums which nobody seemed to want. If collectors came in Gareth reluctantly took out his most precious finds for them but only if they asked and even then he usually priced them out of range.

No wonder he's always broke, thought Lily, with a vague sense of recognition, he won't part with the good stuff.

Gareth took the preserved record out of its plastic cover and placed it carefully on his record player. In a moment the scratchy, slightly high pitched tones of the old Irish crooner filled the shop.

Dear face that holds so sweet a smile for me,
Were you not mine, how dark the world would be!
I know no light above that could replace
Love's radiant sunshine in your dear, dear face.

It was her grandfather's party piece; he used to sing it to her.

The tears started pouring down her face again, and, as Lily reached into her bag and grabbed a handful of yesterday's tissues, the *Vogue* cutting came floating out of her bag and landed on the ground at Gareth's feet. He picked it up and, more to stop her crying than anything else, looked at the sheet and asked, 'What's this?'

'It's a dress I am thinking of making,' she said, wiping her cheeks.

The words had just come out of her mouth as a sort of excuse for why she had the computer printout in her bag. However, as soon as Lily said it, the idea seemed to claim her as if it was an absolute truth.

Gareth passed the sheet of paper over to her.

'It's beautiful,' he said and as the word 'beautiful' came out of his mouth he leaned down. For a split second Lily panicked, thinking he was going to kiss her. Except she wasn't quite sure if it was panic or that thrilling I'm-about-to-be-kissed feeling, because John McCormack was singing her dead grandfather's theme tune.

'It looks pretty complicated,' he said.

'Not really,' Lily said, a little put out by his tone. 'I'm a trained fashion designer. I made plenty of dresses in college. Plus I'm altering clothes all the time. You know, for my work?'

The problem with Lily was that once she said she was going to do something, she simply had to follow it through. It was a pride thing; she could not let herself fail. As a result of this compulsion in herself, she was very careful about what she let herself take on. Lily kept her ambitions, her expectations of herself, manageable. It was one of the reasons she had never pursued the design career after college. Fashion was a risky business and the risk of failure was too great. The bad review sealed her deal and seemed to point her in a direction where she felt safe and certain, if unchallenged. Lily neatly diverted her ambitions into the world of vintage and succeeded at that. She won blog awards and had industry respect as an expert, but she never went after anything herself. Partly for modesty, but partly because she didn't want to put herself under pressure. Failing made people unhappy and Lily didn't like to be unhappy. However, the longer this conversation with Gareth went on, the deeper she could feel the idea of remaking Joy's dress embedding itself in her. Partly because she felt so emotionally drawn to its beauty but also, and very annoyingly, it felt as if the conversation with Gareth was challenging her. Less than a few minutes ago, making this dress had been a private, if crazy, idea, but now he was drawing words out of her it was making the whole thing real.

'If we can't find the dress though, I can always help you source some materials. There's a fabric dealer I know in Somerset...'

'You think I don't know where to buy antique silks?' Lily snapped.

'OK, OK,' Gareth said, putting his hands up and laughing, somewhat nervously.

'Sorry,' Lily said. 'Still a bit sensitive, you know.'

Gareth had the urge to gather her into his arms and give her a comforting hug again, but it was out of the question.

'No problem, I'm just saying I can keep my eyes open is all. Actually, I was planning to go up to the big antiques fair in Birmingham next weekend.' Then in a moment of pure madness Gareth found himself saying, 'You could come along with me, if you like? There's a place I stay in, it's quite nice, actually. Clean, you know? Not expensive...'

Lily looked slightly taken aback.

'Ah, I would,' she said, 'only I'm *really* broke at the moment...'

Gareth blushed across his beardless face – he had known the beard was there for a reason. What was he thinking? A 'clean' room. Not expensive. How creepy did that sound? Why couldn't he just have kept his stupid mouth shut?

'Of course, of course.'

'Another time?' she said.

'Sure, sure.'

Rendered numb by his own awfulness Gareth then stood up, with a curious air of formality. 'I should get some, you know, work to be done,' he said, desperate to claw back some dignity.

'Thanks for the coat,' Lily said and as she walked out the door he called after her, 'See you around.'

Lily noticed it was not, 'see you tomorrow' but 'see you around'. Ouch. Maybe she had been a bit sharp with Gareth – dismissive of his offers to help.

As she walked home Lily shook her head and said to herself, 'What is *wrong* with you, Lily Fitzpatrick? Why such a *bitch* today?'

The truth was, she was still hurting after Joe.

It was late afternoon when she got in and Lily decided to run herself a hot bath, get into a pair of fleecy pyjamas (her one concession to modern slobbery) and sit reading a book until she could respectably call an end to this rotten day and start again tomorrow.

As the bath was running she gave her social media and blog a quick glance through. She had been neglecting both for a while and there was sure to be a massive backlog.

Sure enough, her blog email was jammed, and the comments on her post about The Dress that morning were already numbering twenty. She skimmed them, and was about to turn away when one of them, sent a couple of hours before, hit her like a hammer: *Joy Fitzpatrick was my grandmother. OMG! We could be cousins!*

Eleven

 *New York, 1958*

'What the hell is going on?'

Even as he said it, Frank Fitzpatrick wondered why he bothered. He knew exactly what was going on. His wife Joy was crouching beside the bar, roaring for Jones, and she was drunk.

'You know what?' he said, loosening his tie and stepping over her as he went to the bar to pour himself a whisky. 'I don't even care that you're drunk. I could use a night in anyway. Just do me a favour, will you, and leave Jones out of it? He's a decent man and he doesn't deserve your screeching histrionics, and now I come to think of it, neither do I.'

Right on cue the butler came in, answering his mistress's feral call.

'Ah, Jones,' Frank said. 'My wife here,' he indicated Joy, who had curled herself up into a small, sobbing dome of designer silk on the floor, 'was just calling you in to say take the night off.'

'Will you not need me to collect you after the party, sir?' the butler said, assiduously avoiding looking at his mistress.

'Indeed not, Jones,' Frank said, downing his whisky and pouring another. 'My wife and I will be having a cosy night in. As you can see,' and he looked down at Joy, 'we're not really fit for company this evening.'

Jones coughed lightly and said, 'Very good, sir, I'll prepare a cold plate for you and leave it in the kitchen before I leave.'

When Jones left the room, Joy stopped sobbing and she began to shudder with sheer rage. She rose up and, flinging her arms out like a swan taking flight, she screamed, 'How *dare* you speak to me like that in front of Jones?!'

Frank poured himself another whisky, then held the bottle out to his wife.

'Here,' he said, 'why don't you drink it from the neck, dear? Be an honest drunk, at least.'

Joy looked at the bottle then focused, haltingly, on his face.

'I am *not* drunk,' she said. 'How dare you speak to me like that? I have had *one* cocktail, Frank, one small cocktail at six o'clock, on New Year's Eve. Is that such a reckless act? Really?' Then she shook her head with a mixture of shock and embarrassment and added, 'Frank, I don't know *why* you do this, but I am really getting sick of you constantly insinuating that I'm drunk.'

She wasn't 'drunk', that was true. She was still lucid and at this stage it was easy for them both to believe that he was exaggerating her faults. But Frank could tell from the almost imperceptible sway of her body, the timbre of her voice, and the softness in her eyes, that she had about four cocktails in her. One of them a double. Even as his mind searched for a clever way to tell her this, he became incensed, with himself as much as with her. Was this the man he was now? A man who counted the number of cocktails his wife had taken?

'Really, this ludicrous fantasy you entertain about me having a drink problem, Frank? I know you've got my interests at heart but, well, it's demeaning, and frankly, darling, a complete and utter *lie*.'

For a long time it had been easier for Frank to go along with Joy. To imagine that what she said was true, that it was all in his mind. Perhaps he was paranoid and all this was just a sly kickback to his childhood. The smell of alcohol on his father's breath as he roared out some insult, the bottle of expensive whisky in his father's pocket while his mother wept over the empty food cupboards. Maybe, Frank told himself, he *was* too sensitive to other people's drinking habits?

He took a deep slug from the neck of the bottle and, as he did so, Joy reached over, put her hand on his arm in a gesture of tender understanding and said, 'You're working too hard, Frank. Look at you, you're so tense. You need to relax. I'll run you a bath; your evening clothes are all laid out for you. Why don't we take our time getting ready tonight? There's no rush. Jones said he's left us some food, so we can eat here then arrive at the Plaza late and just stay for an hour.'

She paused and her eyes pleaded with him. She seemed sober. Maybe he had been wrong about the number of cocktails.

'Please? Darling? Let's not fight, not tonight?'

In his mind Frank conceded that sounded OK. Joy was making sense. He was working too hard. A bath, a cold plate and one hour at a party didn't sound too bad. Frank didn't want to fight either. He had fought growing up, he fought at work; Frank just wanted to relax and be with his wife.

'OK,' he said.

Joy grinned and clapped her hands. When she did that she looked beautiful again. The Joy he had fallen in love with. The mind of a sophisticated woman in the body of an unblemished girl – a glorious contradiction.

She ran and kissed him.

'OK, OK,' he said, reluctantly laughing. He unbuttoned his shirt as he walked towards the bedroom. Joy wouldn't want to get her hair messed up but hey, it was New Year's Eve and she was always a knockout, even when her hair was half-down.

He turned to take her hand and saw she was behind the bar again, fixing up a shaker.

'Be right with you, baby, just mixing us up something special.' There was a little triumphant dance in her step.

Frank was overtaken with thundering rage and he knew he had to get out of the apartment or, so help him God, he would kill her.

He picked up his coat from the chair where he had just put it down.

'Frank?' she called out. 'Where are you—'

'I'm leaving.' The words came out cold and muted, almost under his breath, but they were meant for her to hear.

'Frank! Please...don't leave...don't do this...' she screamed as he walked towards the door. 'Frank, I need you...!'

He stopped, took a step towards her and said, 'You don't need me, Joy, you've got your mother's *fortune. Remember?*'

Joy flinched, partly at the cruelty of his tone and partly because it was true. 'Please, Frank, don't go, I love you...'

'The only thing you love is *this*,' Frank shouted and he drew his arm across the bar, sending the cocktail shaker and glasses crashing to the floor. Then he stormed out.

The whisky bottle survived and as soon as he was gone Joy picked it up, drank deeply from the neck then slid down the side of the bar and sobbed herself out.

Frank had 'left' her many times before but he had always come back. The words were the same but this time it *felt* different. It felt as if he really meant it.

Joy finished the bottle of whisky then passed out on the Eames. When she woke, and Frank was not back, she resolved to stop drinking. She loved Frank more than she loved drink, of course she did.

She went to the glass shelf behind the bar and picked up a bottle of gin, unscrewed the lid and began, reluctantly at first, to pour it down the small bar sink. As the clear liquid glugged out, Joy gained an excited momentum and grabbed another bottle, then another, working two hands at a time, pouring everything away. When the last one was gone, she stood and surveyed the empty bottles with a sense of achievement. This was the answer: no more drinking. The fear that it might be too late was there, but she did not allow herself to entertain it. She could not afford to think like that because life without Frank was unthinkable. Joy knew she could not be alone. She could not.

As she went up and down the stairs, carrying the bottles to the kitchen, leaving them by the scullery door for Jones to deal with, Joy thought about what an excellent idea this was. Aside from the fact that her drinking upset Frank, she was turning thirty this spring, and she had heard that too much alcohol could ruin your looks. Although her face had fewer lines than most women her age, the spidery tendrils at the sides of her eyes were a sign that time was catching up with her. If she did all she could to keep herself beautiful and stopped drinking, then there was every reason her husband would want to stay with her.

As each hour passed, Joy's nerves began to unravel. She tamed the anxiety by keeping busy. First she cleared the bar area of all glasses and cocktail shakers then, as the heart of her living room looked so bare, Joy had the brilliant idea of filling it with the flower arranging paraphernalia she had acquired in an (insufferably boring) home floristry class. She arranged crystal vases on the glass shelves and stacked oasis foam and floristry wire under the counter where the shakers and cocktail sticks had once been. There. She didn't drink anymore. She was a respectable, flower-arranging wife!

Finding she felt hungry Joy went down to the kitchen and made herself an omelette. She even cleaned up her own pans afterwards, and arranged Jones's cold plate of meats and salads for Frank, for when he came back in. Her stomach was still churning with fear so, as she closed the kitchen door, she resolved, in a kind of silent prayer to herself, that the plate would be empty in the morning; Frank *would* come home.

Knowing she was too agitated to sleep, Joy took out the 'medicinal' brandy she kept hidden in her bathroom cabinet and drank back three long slugs. She swallowed two barbital, then, before she could take off her evening gown, fell into bed and into a deep sleep.

The following morning, when she woke, Frank was sitting on the edge of her bed. His back was to her, upright and stiff like a statue. She crawled across the bed and crying with relief, pushed her arms under his and wrapped them around his chest, resting her sobbing head on the back of his shoulder. Joy knew she was being pathetic, but she couldn't help herself.

After a few minutes, when he didn't pull away, Joy felt reassured and said, 'No more drinking, Frank, I promise. Everything is gone, I got rid of it all. Did you see what I've done with the bar?' She moved around on the bed so she was facing him, wiped her face and nose on the sheet like a child, drew herself up and said, 'I am going to arrange flowers, Frank. I shall be the Mistress of my Own Vases!'

Then she noticed his face, stern and disbelieving. Frank pulled away from her, walked over to the bathroom and stood in the doorway accusingly holding up the small bottle of brandy.

Joy laughed; he was being ridiculous. 'You can't be *serious* – that's just brandy, to help me sleep – it's medicinal.'

He smashed the bottle on the bathroom floor then steadied himself by leaning into the sink and said, with a mixture of rage and pity, 'Don't laugh at me, Joy, don't ever laugh at me.'

'I'm sorry, Frank.' She had never seen him like this before. Or rather, she had never seen him like this while she was sober.

Gathering himself he came back out into the bedroom and said, 'Where's the rest of it?'

He reached over and dragged her out of bed. Then he hauled Joy, still in her nightgown, around the apartment rescuing bottles. Two vodka, a small Jack Daniels and three gin jiggers from various places around the house. The small drawer of the Alvar Aalto dressing table in a rarely-used guest room and under the bed in that same room – Frank knew them all. The apartment was large and well-furnished enough for Joy to squirrel away a dozen bottles while still persuading herself they were all in the open drinks cabinet. Frank had been methodically seeking them out for years.

When the final bottle was removed, from behind a bucket under the sink in Jones's scullery, Frank sat down on a chair and put his head in his hands. Joy just stood looking at him and waited. She felt as if her life depended on what he said now.

After a few seconds he lifted his head and, rubbing his cheeks in a gesture of pure exhaustion, said, 'I can't do this anymore, Joy. Really, I just can't.'

She replied quickly and certainly. 'I'll stop, Frank. No more hiding, no more lies. I'm off it for good, I promise.'

He smiled at her wearily. He wanted to believe her. 'How do I know that's true Joy? You've said that so many times before.'

'Because I love you and I don't want to lose you.'

'I've said I'd leave before, but it hasn't made a difference.'

'I've never believed you before. I know you mean it this time. I'll change, I want to change; I want to be a good wife.'

Her face was urgent, pleading with him.

Frank shook his head. 'I don't know.'

'Just think,' she said, 'of all the magnificent flower displays I could make if I put my mind to doing something useful with my life. I'll learn to cook, I'll wear an apron, I'll spend less money on clothes, I'll even gain weight if you want me to.'

'It's not that...' Frank said.

'Good,' she said, 'because you know I could *never* gain weight.'

Frank was smiling now.

'And you know I will always spend *all* of your money on clothes.'

'I know,' he said, unable to stop himself laughing. 'All right. I'll stay.'

Joy ran over and kissed him and danced about the room making plans for dinner and all the wonderful things she was going to do for him.

For better or worse, Frank knew he had to give his wife a chance. He hoped he still loved her enough to see it through.

Twelve

 *New York, 1959*

Honor sat back in her seat and gazed out of the train window. The view along this stretch of line, just outside Hastings-on-Hudson and heading back into the city, was the most beautiful part of the journey. Along here the broad stretch of the Hudson was bordered by forest: the water was a flat grey sheet, the lacy branches of tall trees were mirrored in black shadows along its rim. The sky was a watery blue filter and the winter sun shot through it with shards of pink. Late afternoon was the best time to view this landscape, which was why Honor always made sure that she returned from her day trips out of the city at this time.

'Going out to the sticks again – but you went last week. What the hell do you *do* out there?' Barbara said, in their shared kitchenette, although she knew what Honor did: sketch.

It was all her Irish roommate ever did. Their whole apartment was covered in sketches: small landscapes, bits of flowers, but mostly dresses. Dresses, dresses, dresses, everywhere. She needed Honor to go to an afternoon tea dance in a city hotel with her this Sunday; Barbara simply had to find herself a husband.

'I just like to look around,' Honor said. 'Why don't you

come out with me? It's so beautiful there. There's a forest I go to, and the trees…'

'There are trees in Central Park, and there are also *men*. Please, Honor, stay in the city this weekend.'

Honor gave her an apologetic grimace and Barbara waved her off resentfully. She and Honor were the only two girls in the studio left on the shelf; sometimes it seemed like they were the only two left in the whole of Manhattan. If they didn't pull together, they'd end up as spinsters. Barbara couldn't walk into a hotel dance alone, but equally she knew there was no point in trying to reason with her stubborn roommate.

'Such a plain Jane, it's a shame,' the girls in the workshop said about her behind her back. 'If she spent a bit more time putting lipstick on her face, instead of daubing paint on paper, she might have some chance of meeting a man.'

Honor knew her roommate Barbara was getting fed up with her, but she wasn't too worried about it. She had not come to New York to get dressed up and go dancing and she certainly had not come all the way to America to find a husband: there were any number of dancehalls and dozens of good Mayo men more than willing to marry her, back home in Ireland.

Honor had had a sweetheart back in Dublin. Sean Duffy was a nice young man, only a few years older than herself and a schoolteacher. She had enjoyed Sean's company and she had certainly enjoyed the danger of illicit passion. However, a year into their relationship, after they had crossed all boundaries of Catholic propriety, Honor felt the relationship shift in gear. She would have been happy enough with them enjoying each other and carrying on as things were, but Joe had wanted them to get married and she knew that if her parents got wind of a teacher for a son-in-law, that would have been her future, set. There would have been no hope of ever becoming a designer, so she got herself a ticket and fled. Honor Conlon was in New York to get away from a man and marriage, not to find one.

She came here because she wanted to make it as a fashion designer. Nonetheless, she might have sacrificed today and gone along with Barbara, if she had not believed she could be on the verge of a breakthrough. After their experience with the white dress, Monsieur Breton had come back from the Christmas break and asked to see some of her sketches. The following morning, they had finally arranged for him to look at her drawings and Honor was hoping, beyond hope, that he might be impressed enough to allow her to design some garments for his next collection.

She opened the sketch pad on her lap, then began frantically sketching the landscape and scribbling hasty notes: *Still grey water, mirrored, sequins, slub silk – water-marked velvet.* Under the hastily drawn landscape she wrote: *Reflection of trees, high collar, black lace, satin fabric dipped in black, like branches bleeding? Embroider or lace?*

She outlined the dress with a long sweeping skirt, an ornate high black lace collar and a landscape detail along the hem, to give an illusion that the wearer was emerging from a pool of water.

Honor closed her pad, then opened it again and held it in front of her as if looking at the dress for the first time.

It was a beautiful image, but somehow, Honor knew that it wasn't enough.

In the past few days, Honor had come to feel that her work was not up to scratch. She had always believed the opposite: that she was as good a designer as anyone and better than many. However, since the debacle with the lace collar, her opinion of herself had changed. She thought there was something missing from her work, although she could not quite put her finger on it. She knew she could draw – her sketches were as beautiful and as functional as any design Monsieur Breton put in front of her – and her current work was as good as it had ever been, better, in fact as her drawing had become more skilled. Some might say she was brilliant in both her speed and form. Aside from that were the practical dressmaking skills she had learned from her two-year tenure with Sybil Connolly. She knew everything there was to know about structure, fabric, and the line an outfit should take to fit the various shapes and sizes of a woman's body. Honor believed her work was also unique, in that she drew her inspiration from that greatest of female forces, Mother Nature. Honor knew she had everything she needed to produce extraordinary designs and yet, prolific and skilled as her drawings were, she sensed that they were somehow...lacking.

'When you know there is heather under the snow,' the maestro had said. Now she wasn't even sure she knew what that meant. She had thought he had been alerting her to understand every detail of her work, but now she was not so sure. Perhaps he was just fobbing her off as not good enough? The idea that she might not be a good designer terrified Honor.

Shaking with nerves, she showed her work to the maestro. He leaned over Honor's sketches, which were scattered chaotically across the large mahogany table in his office. One or two of them had fluttered from the smooth surface onto the floor, but Honor was too anxious to rescue them. She had been up all the night before, arranging her sketches in the particular order she wanted Breton to view them, intending to take him through each one, explaining the ideas and inspiration behind it. However, he snatched the pile from her as soon as she walked in, as if he was either in a hurry to get the meeting over with, or anxious to see them; he placed them quickly and haphazardly on the table, then walked around, viewing them as a whole, before lifting them up, one by one, with the tips of his thin fingers, in order to inspect them in more detail. Breton flicked at the edges of the paper as he put each picture down, in a gesture that suggested he thought it worthless; but then, she had seen him display this peculiar tic before, with his own work. Honor felt sick, and when he finally spoke she was bitterly disappointed.

'Yes, this is nice. Very good.'

Nice? Good? Cups of tea are nice, she thought, well-behaved children are good. A well-designed dress is sublime, or beautiful, or even magnificent. He was obviously just being polite – he hated her work.

'Yes, I like this one,' he said, holding up a sketch she had done the day before. 'Slub silk, you say? Yes. Good, I approve this...*and* this two piece...' He handed her another sketch, of a green tweed day suit, with a full skirted dress and tiny cropped jacket. 'This one is good. A black dress, but it needs something more. Trim on the sleeves? Think of something,' he said as he passed across another sketch. 'And a belt on *this*.' He passed across three more designs, with instructions, and it was only when she got the last one that she fully understood Breton was putting six of her designs into his collection.

'Can I just be clear,' Honor said as he waved her away, 'are we going to *sell* my designs?'

'No, *we* are not going to *sell* your designs,' Breton snapped, already back behind his desk and clearly irritated that she was still there. '*You* and the women are going to make samples, and we are going to *show* them and then we will see if people want to buy them...then we will *sell* them.'

Colette had come into the room and, interrupting them rudely, shut the door behind her and said in a hurried whisper, 'Joy Fitzpatrick is here!'

Breton's harshly impassive face was suddenly alight with anxiety. He leapt from his desk, with an almost comical agility, straightened his jacket and ran to the mirror to check his moustache.

'Mon dieu,' he cried. 'I need more time to get ready. I must prepare...'

'It's too late, she's *here*. I couldn't stop her...'

The door opened and a woman walked in. She was tall, elegant, almost impossibly beautiful and was wearing a dark navy dress, with a scoop neck and three-quarter length sleeves; its unadorned simplicity and elegant lines were instantly recognizable as Balmain. Breton was sensitive about Pierre Balmain. He did not like to think that any of his clients bought in Paris ('*Why* would they go to Paris when *I* am here? In New York. For them, *only* for them?'), but if they did go, at least come back with something that was widely copied (Dior) or somebody new and up-and-coming (Givenchy). Breton knew Balmain through the now-retired Paris-based English designer Edward Molyneux – but was deeply jealous of his friend's wildly successful protégé. It hurt him deeply that his most feted client was wearing Balmain, although she would never have turned up in such a dress, had she known. He had dressed her late mother and knew that the Rogerson women, for all their grandiosity, had impeccable manners.

Breton turned his couturier charm up to maximum, which was ebullient if not always entirely convincing.

'Joy!' he exclaimed and held out his arms like an excited Italian bistro chef welcoming a favoured customer. 'And wearing my friend, Balmain. How...*wonderful*.'

The woman gave him a smile so dazzling it was as if somebody had turned a light on in the room. Honor thought she had never seen anyone who possessed such natural glamour.

'It's two seasons old but I just love the line of it. I didn't know you knew Pierre, Mr Breton?'

'Oh, please. Call me Jean. But of course I know Balmain, from Paris, he worked for my old friend Molyneux.'

'Of course,' she insisted. 'How dreadfully silly of me not to remember that. He made quite a point of mentioning it to me the last time we met.'

She is humouring him, Honor thought, and it was working; Breton was almost faint with delight.

'Are these your new designs?' she said, walking over to the table which was still covered in Honor's drawings. She began picking through them.

Colette looked as if she might collapse with anxiety. This woman was like nobody Honor had ever encountered before: beautiful, yes, but there was also a cleverness and an honesty about her that Honor liked. Colette and Breton were clearly overawed by her style and her great wealth but Honor wasn't: she liked her.

'These are good.'

Again, that ordinary word 'good' to describe Honor's work. 'Oh, no, this is exquisite, actually – I *love* this one.'

She held up the sketch of the dress with the black lace collar and 'liquid' hem.

As the woman stood there holding up her sketch Honor felt a little kick in her stomach. In her mind's eye she stripped the woman, Joy, then draped her in steel grey silk and quickly drew an intricate lace around her neck and shoulders. She was, this stranger, this woman, a magnificent canvas waiting for a designer to draw on. In a flash of inspiration Honor suddenly knew what had been missing from her work, and knew too that at last she had found it: a muse.

Joy had woken that morning feeling anxious, for no particular reason. The sun was streaming in through a crack in her bedroom curtains and Frank was already dressed and sitting on the edge of the bed, putting on his shoes.

'Come back to bed,' she said.

'I'm late for work,' he replied.

Joy sighed. She longed for her husband's affection but didn't feel she could just ask for it straight out. So she got out of bed and went over to her dressing table.

'Urgh, I am getting old,' she said, grimacing then patting the side of her eyes with the tips of her fingers.

'You look fine to me,' Frank said without looking over.

'I am going to be thirty soon,' Joy said. 'Will you still love me when I'm old?'

'Of course I will. We're married aren't we?'

'That's not a good enough reason.'

'Well, it will have to do for now.'

Things had improved with Frank since she had been dry. They were making love again and the fighting had stopped, but Joy still felt there was something missing between them. Something she could not put her finger on. A slight cooling of passion. Was he taking her for granted, perhaps? Life was becoming rather humdrum and ordinary and Joy wasn't sure that she liked it.

'I think I'll throw a party. Let's make some plans, darling. Small at the Plaza Palm Court or a huge bash at the Waldorf?' She was bluffing, but if she kept talking, kept charming, he would come around and join in the fun.

'I really don't mind, Joy. I'll go along with whatever you want.' Frank stood behind her and straightened his tie in the mirror. Joy caught sight of her own disappointed expression. Frank did not seem to notice. He barely appeared to notice her at all, these days.

'You'll do whatever you want to do, my darling, so it makes no difference what I think.'

'The Waldorf, then, the biggest party anyone has ever seen.'

Keeping busy was the best way Joy knew of holding her cravings at bay and this party would offer her the perfect excuse.

After Frank had given her a cursory kiss and left, Joy decided to spend the day planning her party. She wandered over to her dressing room and had begun rifling through the cupboards for ideas, when she spotted the white dress she had worn on New Year's Eve.

That terrible night had tainted Breton's dress. She had got drunk and almost lost her husband in it, then she had stayed up all night emptying bottles in it. It was certainly the first couture garment she had cleaned in (possibly the first garment of *any* kind she had cleaned in); she had wept into it, fallen asleep in it, then taken it off in a drugged fumble and left it in a tangled heap on her bedroom floor. Nonetheless, Joy felt drawn to it as if its terrible provenance was revealing some kind of truth to her. Despite the overwhelming drama she had experienced in that dress, the garment itself still sang to her. Not loudly – like her gaudy but magnificent Dior – or with the steady assertive tone of her sturdy Chanel two-piece, but in a gentle, tuneful whisper, like a small bird singing above the traffic beside a slightly opened window. It was in the detail: the lightly stained embroidered collar and cuffs. As Joy gathered the dress up from its hanger she noticed how the delicate fronds of silk were the same as they had been the moment she had put the garment on, fresh from the bag. Despite her vicious treatment of it the lace had not torn, or even weathered. It still looked fragile and delicate – new, untouched by the trauma it had experienced. Underneath the beauty this garment was clearly well built and strong. It was this realization that drove her back to Breton's studio.

Joy did not like the man himself – she thought him a cliché with his thick French accent and his flourishing hand gestures. Worse than that, he was average. Joy believed Breton produced couture for the ladies of New York who didn't know any better. His clientele had never shopped in Europe because they lacked either the resources or the refinement required to do so and so didn't mind that his designs were safe and lacked imagination. But Joy did. She wanted her clothes designed by an artist, not by a glorified dressmaker, and that's why she was always adding instructions and design flourishes of her own. For these reasons, Joy was loath to admit that the dress she had commissioned for that fateful New Year's Eve was the best garment she had seen in a while. In the name of all that was fashion, she had to return to his studio.

When Joy entered Breton's office, her eyes were immediately drawn to a sketch of a long flowing gown with an endless black hem and high collar, and she immediately recognized that it was not Breton's work.

As she picked up the drawings, she noticed a rather plain young woman standing behind the desk.

'Are these yours?' Joy asked.

And it was then that the girl began babbling like a fool.

Thirteen

Honor could see that Mrs Fitzpatrick was the kind of lady used to getting her own way, and not the sort of person she should address directly. However, when Joy picked up Honor's sketch of the black-hemmed gown, she found herself shaking her head emphatically and saying, 'No, that's too dark, black is not right for you. Your frame is too slim, it would make you disappear. Besides, black is too *obvious*, it's elegant I agree but not for you, not for evening. You're already *strikingly beautiful* – you need something to offset your beauty. You could carry something more subtle, perhaps a light grey, maybe tapering down to a dark navy. Oh, emerald green – not many women can carry green but you could...'

Honor trailed off in the face of the deathly silence that had descended on the room. Breton and his assistant were staring at her, open-mouthed, as if she had spoken so *deeply* out of turn that they had not yet figured out how to react.

'What I mean is...ma'am...'

Breton's sense of self-preservation overtook his fear of Joy. He swept across the room and, with a flourish of his arms, said, 'Mrs Fitzpatrick. May I present to you my new protégé, Honor...'

'Conlon,' she said, helping him out.

Honor had been so flustered that she had forgotten to remove her atelier apron. Now she quickly undid the ties and threw the work garment to one side, revealing the wide navy skirt and crisp white blouse she had chosen to impress Breton. Joy took Honor's hand.

'So, these are your drawings?' she said.

Honor nodded. 'Yes, ma'am.'

'And you designed my New Year's Eve dress?'

'Well, I made it, and...' Honor looked across at Breton.

'Yes, indeed, Honor designed and made the dress, under my instruction of course.'

Joy paused, arched her brows and said, 'Of *course*,' before quickly turning to Honor and saying, 'Well, then, I have a very important event coming up and I need a dress, so let's get started, shall we?'

As Joy talked, she picked up Honor's sketches and studied them, before putting them, carefully, respectfully, back down on the desk. 'These are really *very* good, I am sure some of them could be adapted to suit me. Although, I am not so sure about green – *nobody* wears green. You'll have to sell that one to me a bit harder.'

Honor was elated. She looked across at Breton and, smiling, he waved his approval. Even Colette seemed happy, as she helped Honor gather up her sketches and take them across to the private fitting room, next to the atelier, where the client consultations took place.

One wall was mirrored and the others were a light salmon pink; the carpet had a thick white pile and satin drapes lined the changing area. The room was designed to flatter the women and the clothes by throwing a soft light over them both, but in this overtly feminine space Honor felt the woman's beauty fill the room. She could barely believe that she had been commissioned to design a dress for such a tall, slim, perfectly elegant creature and yet, on another level it felt like an inevitability, a piece of fate that this woman, above any other, should be her first client. Honor's head was exploding with ideas. Joy Fitzpatrick was the link she had been missing – her dark hair, the angular, assured beauty, her long neck, slender arms, endless legs and the way she floated across the room. As Joy stood in front of her in Breton's flouncy dressing room, Honor realized this was the woman of her imagination, the woman she had been drawing since she was a child. She was the figure standing in an Irish field, as acres of soft, golden bog grass swayed around her, and she was the silhouette emerging from the black water of the Hudson in early evening. Honor was momentarily dumbstruck.

'First, I should warn you,' Mrs Fitzpatrick said. 'I am a very exacting client. Secondly, I know what suits me and I know what I like. That is not to say that I do not expect a high level of design, because I do. It just means that, when I say I want a change made or something specific done to a garment, I expect it to be done just so. Detail is of the utmost importance to me...'

'I still think you should consider green; only a very deep emerald, in a heavy satin to give it movement, bring it to life.'

Joy looked irritated. 'I specifically said...'

'I know what you said, Mrs Fitzpatrick, but you're not anybody, are you? Most women struggle with it, but I know you could carry it and if you can wear something other women can't, then I think you should.'

For a moment there was an uncomfortable stand-off.

'So what you are saying is, I have a *responsibility* to wear green.'

'Yes,' Honor said, 'most definitely. I can't lie. I can see you in it.'

'And because *you* can see me in it, I should wear it?'

'Absolutely,' Honor said. She had never felt surer of anything in her life so she added, '...because I am the designer,' then appended as an afterthought of respect, 'Mrs Fitzpatrick.'

Joy seemed annoyed and stayed silent. Her face, beautiful and imperious, was impossible to read. Honor realized that she had gone too far. This woman was, after all, not a mannequin, but a monied New York socialite and, by her own admission, a fussy customer. Honor was trying to think how she might reverse what she had said when Joy said, 'Make me a day dress, in green. Nothing fancy, just plain lines, in whatever fabric you prefer. If I like it, we'll consider green for the evening dress, and if I don't...' The implication was clear.

Honor felt sick. She had managed to lose the evening-gown commission. What would Breton say?

Joy briskly picked up her bag and pulled on her gloves, saying, 'Have it sent around on Thursday, please.'

Three days? Was the woman mad?

'But you'll need a fitting.' Honor stood shocked as Joy went to leave.

'Breton has my measurements.' And with that Joy Fitzpatrick swept out, past a confused Colette who was coming in with a complimentary glass of champagne.

Colette drained the glass herself, then, as soon as she was sure Joy had cleared the building, said, 'Don't worry, Breton will understand. Joy Fitzpatrick is the best dressed woman in New York but she is also the most discerning. She's rich and beautiful but she is also exacting. She makes you work for your praise!'

'She wants me to make her a day dress, by Thursday.'

Colette raised her eyes to heaven. 'Jesus! In three days! What did you say?'

'I said I'd do it.'

Actually, she hadn't said anything. Joy had just assumed.

'Honor, you stupid girl. You measured her very quickly...'

'Actually, I didn't. She said you had all her measurements.'

Colette opened her eyes in an exaggerated French look of horror. 'I don't know where her measurements are! We will have to call her and say it's a mistake...'

'No, Colette, please, I can do this. Please, it's my big chance. Let me try and make her the dress.'

Colette looked at her and saw the determination and, yes, the talent in her young Irish seamstress.

'All right,' she said, 'but what will you do about her measurements...?'

'Don't worry Colette,' Honor said, 'leave it to me.'

In the moments since Joy Fitzpatrick had left, Honor had already begun sketching out the shape of a dress in her head, something that would not need precise measurement to look supremely stylish. She knew she could design her something she would love, but Colette was still shaking her head.

'A client like that can ruin a design house. One mistake...'

Honor pulled a pen out of her skirt pocket, grabbed one of her sketches and began drawing on the back of the sheet. As the black page filled with the soft strokes of her pencil she said, 'Mrs Fitzpatrick is a slender woman, and women of that build can wear loose-fitting garments, without appearing oversized. She's tall, but only a few inches taller than me; much of her height comes from the way she carries herself, so it will be easy to make an accurate estimation for the hemline. Look, if we bring the shoulders down like this, straight to the waist, we have a simple shift dress that will fit any woman and then we can simply pull it in with a matching wide belt – maybe a matching squared-off bolero jacket, to make it smarter.'

In the time it took to describe the outfit, Honor had it drawn out.

Colette pursed her lips and nodded tightly. 'Yes, all right. OK, OK, you can make the dress.'

She would have to square it with Breton, but he always took her advice. If Honor failed to produce what Joy Fitzpatrick wanted, she would never come back and neither would her friends. However, if she was told they had lost her measurements she could do the same thing anyway.

If the girl made a success of the outfit Joy would send all of her friends and Breton's name would be refreshed among the fickle couture clientele. Colette privately worried that Breton had become greedy – he wanted to keep the clients at any cost and as a result he was losing his 'flair', his designs were becoming too safe and somewhat mediocre. He was disappointing his discerning clients, the clients who shopped in Paris, clients like Joy Fitzpatrick. This Irish girl had something, Colette could see that and it was only fair to give her a chance.

'You can work exclusively on the dress until it is done.'

'Oh, thank you, thank you, ma'am.'

'But you had better get it *right*...' She nodded towards the fabric catalogues on the glass shelf. '...and you had better get on with it.'

Honor gathered up the heavy books and brought them into the atelier where she piled them on the edge of the cutting table. The girls were all out to lunch, so she would have some peace.

The dress itself would be simple to make: the fabric was the most important thing. It had to be the right texture, but most of all, it had to be the right green. The client was right, green was a difficult colour to wear and the least used in fashion, and yet Honor loved it. Green was organic, the colour of nature, but it was also the colour of Ireland, of home. Her hands flicked over dozens of books and hundreds of pages, before lingering briefly over light green worsted. Tightly woven wool was comfortable and soft, a popular daywear fabric but – no. It was too ordinary, too flat. True, she wanted something understated and not too flashy, but at the same time, this outfit had a point to make. Here was the tweed for the jacket: a deep moss with flecks of heathery purple, perfect, but still nothing for the dress itself.

Honor closed her eyes and asked her imagination to carry her back home, to a place she loved. There was a Protestant church on the outskirts of their town, a tall, grey, imposing building, barely visible from the road. Leading up to it was a short narrow path, lined by high trees, with dense ivy crawling up them, the ground a carpet of moss and twigs, clumps of curling ferns and the thick, glossy leaves of the rhododendron bushes.

Her eyes flicked open and she reached for the satin swatches until she found what she was looking for: a thick duchesse in a deep, leafy shade of green.

Fourteen

 *London, 2014*

Zac Podmore was a twenty-one-year-old fashion student at Parsons in New York City. Like Lily he was an only child, and he was thrilled to discover he had an Irish 'cousin.' Within minutes, they were Skyping.

'I feel like Obama!' he said, jumping up and down in front of the screen in his cramped apartment, which looked even more cluttered with clothes than her own. He had a shock of blond boy-band hair and a pretty face to match. Lily searched for some trace of familiarity but couldn't find anything.

Zac told Lily the little that he knew about his late grandmother. She had been a stylish woman who even in her eighties dressed impeccably and smelt of, in his words, 'Chanel-smoked chiffon'. While going through her things in his mother's attic Zac had found the *Vogue* cutting and some photographs of a beautiful dress she had commissioned in the 1950s. Thrilled to have found she was in *Vogue* he scanned and uploaded the cutting to his Pinterest page, which is where Lily must have sourced it from. The photographs, he still had.

'I didn't put them online. My grandmother was very secretive about her past...'

The same as Old Joe.

'…she never talked about her life before she met my grandfather, so I felt they were private. The *Vogue* cutting, though, I couldn't resist putting that up and now look! It led us to each other!'

'Why do you think she was so cagey about the past?'

'I don't know what the big deal was. I only discovered she was married to this guy Fitzpatrick, your great-uncle, when I found the *Vogue* cutting.'

'My grandfather was the same. I vaguely knew he had an older brother but he was really cagey about his childhood. His family put him in an orphanage after his mother died and he never really forgave them.'

'Wow, I don't blame him!'

Lily hadn't thought about it like that before and realized Zac had a point.

'Except now I regret not asking him, you know? I think he might have told me more about himself if I had bothered to ask.'

'Maybe, but then again, maybe not. Could be he would have lied or got mad at you,' Zac said. 'You'll never know, so let it go. That's what my granny used to say.'

'She was a wise woman.'

'Guess she was. Death sucks. Granny died when I was fourteen and I still miss her like crazy.'

'Joy's dress was so amazing,' Lily said. 'I tried to find the original…'

'Me too,' he said. 'No luck?'

'None.' Then she blurted out, 'I'd love to make a replica of it, though.'

Zac looked at her, then went silent for a moment before saying, 'Oh. My. God. That is an *amazing* idea.'

In that moment, Lily realized that she could not undo this crazy idea of hers. More than that, Lily understood that making The Dress had now grown from the niggling, impulsive notion she had in Gareth's shop into something that she actually wanted to do.

Zac agreed to email across all the pictures he had plus an interview with the designer, Honor Conlon, which his mother had found, published in a 1950s drapery magazine and detailing some of the technical elements involved which he thought Lily might find useful. They arranged to talk again the following week.

After they had hung up, Lily sat by the computer and waited for Zac's photographs. As each file came through Lily opened them one by one, and watched the images of an extraordinarily beautiful woman appear. They were amateur snapshots, taken outdoors in a woodland. Slightly fuzzy and in black and white, the detail was poor, but nonetheless they had an old-world glamour about them. Joy's dark hair was drawn into a high chignon and her face was tilted up in a pose both haughty and demurely feminine. Joy Fitzpatrick was the archetypical 1950s couture beauty.

Lily grabbed a pencil from her desktop and some paper from the printer tray and began to sketch. Although she hadn't done anything like this since her college show, she found that she was as fluid, as fast and as confident a sketcher as she had been as a student. Within a few minutes the floor at her feet was scattered with dozens of drawings. In simple, sweeping lines Lily tried to capture the candy-floss lightness of Joy's voluminous skirt, the neat curve of her torso, the delicate detailing of the lace on the bodice – discarding and re-sketching, over and over again.

When she had a drawing she was more or less satisfied

with, Lily went to the 'untouchable' storage cupboard in her hallway. She pulled out old coats, wellingtons, a broken vacuum cleaner and numerous bags of lightbulbs and cleaning fluids until, finally, at the very back, she found the dressmaker's dummy her parents had bought for her fifteenth birthday. Next to it was an old bag of muslin strips that Lily had used to make a toile in college. Amazed it was still there, she stuck her head into the bag and sniffed. A bit musty – not surprising after nearly ten years – but usable.

Lily took the bag, tucked the dummy under her arm and ran up the stairs. She pushed back some clothes rails, put the dummy in the middle of the room and looked at her drawing. This would be no sew-along-the-seams factory garment, it was going to be like the original, a full couture gown. She would have to make a bodice, and use yards of fabric on the train alone. She would have to learn about beading, appliqué and embroidery – things she had never done before. Before she let the magnitude of it all sink in, Lily reached for the sewing basket she always had to hand. As she picked up her first strip of muslin and pinned it across the torso of the worn, beige dummy a thrill of delight seemed to shoot through her fingers. Like falling in love, the adventurous feeling that something completely new was about to happen.

Lily stood with a mouthful of pins, pasting fabric strips to her dummy and it occurred to her that she was actually pretty broke at the moment. If she wanted to do anything more than simply fiddle around with muslin over the coming days, she knew she would need to get her hands on some extra cash. She could try and sell some of her clothes, but that would take up time, loading pictures up on the website and eBay with no guarantees. The alternative was a lengthy trip to a trade fair. Like a flashlight going off, Lily remembered

Gareth talking about his upcoming trip to Birmingham. She picked up her phone and rang his number.

'How do you fancy selling some frocks for me?'

'Erm...' Gareth sounded taken aback. Maybe this hadn't been such a good idea. 'Well, I don't really have a big market for vintage clothes in the shop, apart from you.'

'Ah, right. I was just thinking, if you were going up to Birmingham anyway, you might take some of my good pieces around to some dealers for me. Only I need the cash...'

'Oh sure, sure. No problem.'

'...And, of course, I'll give you a cut. You just think about how much.'

'No problem, no problem. Just drop them in anytime today.'

Lily spent the rest of the afternoon going through her very best pieces; the ones that would raise her the most cash. The 1950s duchesse satin tulip shape Nina Ricci skirt in perfect condition; a green Donegal tweed suit by Sybil Connolly from the 60s. These were her treasures. She always intended to sell them on but often, too often, she fell in love and clung onto them. Her prize possession was a Chanel LBD dating back to the 1940s. Lily unzipped the bag and looked inside at the delicate silk dress, slightly greying with age but nonetheless, a valuable collector's piece. She loved this dress more than any other. She had found it in a thrift shop in Paris just after she graduated and it had cost Lily her entire savings. However, if she wanted to make this dress, she would have to part with some of her own, so she sat down at her computer and printed out a reserve price list for Gareth.

When she arrived up at the shop with armloads of heavy bags, Gareth came out to help her.

'I've done a reserve price list for the couture stuff,' she said, 'then put in a few smaller pieces that you might sell through the shop? I thought 10 per cent for you…Is that OK?'

Gareth nodded. He wanted to say he would do it for nothing if she'd go out to dinner with him, or to the pictures, or…just where *did* an ordinary bloke like him take a sophisticated goddess like Lily Fitzpatrick? On the plus side, she had reached out and asked for his help. Lily must not think he was a complete loser after all.

As she handed over the Chanel bag she said, 'This one is really special. It feels like I am handing you my life, Gareth. Be gentle with it,' giving him real hope, before adding, 'Thanks – you're a real friend.'

'I'll call you,' she said, running out of the door.

Back in the apartment Lily felt better, freer. Out with the old-old and in with the new-old – although it would take weeks for that sales money to come through and she needed something sooner.

So she rang Sally.

'I need cash.'

'What for?'

'A dress.'

'Of course, because you don't have enough dresses.'

'Ha, ha.'

'Well, it just so happens I need an assistant to press and steam a mountain of cheap, nasty catalogue clothes from Scott's budget range. Although, I should warn you, the last one died of boredom.'

Sally picked Lily up at 7.30 a.m. the next morning and they drove bleary-eyed through the London rush hour traffic picking up six boxes of 'catalogue tat' on their way, from the client's offices in Great Portland Street.

As they drove, Lily told Sally about The Dress and Sally told her she was mad.

'You know, Lily, if you want to get back to designing there are better ways than just copying some old frock.'

'Firstly, I don't want to go back to designing, and secondly, it's not just some old frock. It's an amazing couture vintage gown that belonged to my great-aunt. In America. Have you not been listening to a word I've been telling you?'

'Of course I have. I am delighted you have a dead great-aunt...'

'...and a cousin.'

'...and a live cousin – well done you. I just want to know, what's the point?'

'What do you mean?'

'Why are you making this dress? What are you going to do with it?'

'There is no point. I just want to do it for the sake of it. I see lots of beautiful clothes all the time but now I just want to make something really beautiful myself. Is that so weird?'

'Yes, it is weird. I just wish—'

'Don't say it.'

'I just wish you would stop being so obsessed with dusty old clobber and get back to designing your own stuff.'

'There it is. The Best Friend Nag.'

Sally shook her head. 'You lack ambition, Lily Fitzpatrick.'

'Thank you,' she replied, smiling, 'and you lack soul...'

'...and scruples. Especially when it comes to looking out for my BF.'

'Oh, but Sal, this dress is so special, wait until you see it. The problem is I'm going to need to make some more cash. There's yards of good silk on the train, tonnes of beads and stuff.'

'I'll see if I can get you a bit more work. There's a trip to Miami coming up, I might be able to get you a freelance gig – leave it with me.'

The studio complex was in a large industrial estate in Sutton but once inside the state-of-the-art equipped studio was huge. There was a fully catered canteen area, vast white walls and soft grey sofas with various models and helpers lounging across them. It was as glamorous and airy and as buzzy as a film set.

Fashion styling, Lily knew, was one of the most overrated jobs in the fashion world. Most of it was about planning and administration with occasional bursts of fun but really, like any job, it depended on the people you were working with. Luckily, Sally always pulled together a good team.

'Stick to the beige and the browns today, Justine...' Sally advised the make-up artist. They were having to re-do half of yesterday's shots. They had been so bored that Sally had allowed Justine to do this season's solid Day-Glo eye make-up on the model and the client had freaked.

'Can I grink ni gee yet?'

'Jesus, don't *talk* Sharon,' Justine cried, 'not while I am doing your lips.'

'Can I drink my tea yet?'

Sharon was an Amazonian brunette from Wisconsin, one of America's most successful plus-size models, with full lips, creamy, flawless skin and glossy, curled hair down to her elbows. Her fee was taking up the bulk of the budget on this job, which is why they had to shoot about two hundred outfits in nine days, on an industrial estate in Sutton instead of on the streets of Paris, or in that capital of all catalogue shoots, Miami. At a European size 10–12 she wasn't exactly enormous, but certainly larger than the pick-thin catwalk girls.

Justine picked up a tissue to wipe the stray gloss then poked the model across the chin with a blusher brush. Briefly released from the make-up artist's grip, Sharon snatched a bite of the croissant that Sally had left lying on the make-up station.

Sally glowered. 'Bloody plus-size models, you're like Hoovers. At least with the anorexic girls the rest of us never starve.'

'Doesn't pay to be too thin,' Sharon said. 'The fashion girls may get all the high-end mags but catalogue is where the money is and besides, nobody wants to have sex with them.'

'Too skinny,' said Sally.

'Too grumpy 'cos they never eat.'

'Too insecure – *bo-ring*,' said Sharon, breaking out of her lipstick prison again.

'Jesus, woman,' Justine screamed. 'You'd think you'd never had your make-up done before!'

Sally was holding up a wrap dress in an outrageously large size fourteen. 'I hope this bloody fits because we've got to do it in six colour ways.'

'Can't they just Photoshop it into different colours?' Lily asked.

'Apparently not, tech genius, so get steaming,' Sally said, throwing half a dozen multi-coloured nylon-mix dresses in her direction.

For the next six hours they worked flat out, photographing Sharon in no fewer than fifty different garments against a series of plain backdrops, strolling, smiling, and posing.

'Imagine you're in Paris, doll,' the photographer Simon said.

'Yeah,' Sally said, ''cos they're going to drop Paris into the background on the computer – which is, of course, great for us!'

'Did you get confirmation of the Cool Curves brochure through yet? It's a shoot in Miami, isn't it?' Justine asked.

Simon yelled, '*Powder!*' and she hurried over to run her brush across Sharon's face.

'No,' Sally said, holding a skirt open for Sharon to step straight into after she had torn off the dress she had just been photographed in, 'but you can talk to Lily about that – she's at the top of Jack Scott's hit list.'

'Lucky you,' Justine said, as Sharon struggled to get her long limbs through the arms of a white blouse without getting make-up on the collar.

'Can I have a dressed model *now* please?!' Simon pleaded. 'We are twenty shots behind today...and I am *not* running this into next week!'

The shoot did run over so the banter and the bitching carried on into early evening. By nine o'clock only Sally and Lily were left in the deserted studios, folding up the clothes, bagging them and putting them all back into their boxes.

'Thank God this job is over,' Sally said flicking the remaining pile of unfolded clothes. 'You coming for a drink?'

Lily folded the flaps over on the last box and picked up the masking tape gun. 'No I'm going to get home and do a bit of work.'

Sally looked at her. 'On this dress?'

Lily nodded. 'I know you think I'm crazy...'

'I just worry about you, Lils. It's so soon after losing Joe and, well, I don't want you getting all hung up on something that won't pay off.'

'Not everything is about money, Sally,' Lily said, then realized how stupid that sounded, given that she had rung Sally begging for work.

They hugged goodbye but for the rest of the evening Lily felt annoyed at Sally for not being more supportive.

The following day Zac skyped Lily again, but this time it was from his mother's house. Imogen was a plain, sturdy-looking woman in her fifties with grey, un-styled hair and huge glasses, the antithesis of her own elegant mother and camp, on-trend son. She came across as warm and friendly and was obviously really happy to meet a relative, even such a distant one by marriage.

'We have very little evidence of my Mom's life before she met Pops,' she said. 'We only know she was married to your great-uncle, Frank Fitzpatrick, from the magazine Zac found. Seems she was quite a socialite in her heyday but she kept all that under wraps when I was growing up.' Her voice trailed off, sad at the memory of her mother. 'It means such a lot to meet you, Lily. I'm so sorry about your grandaddy. I do so hope we can stay in touch.'

A few minutes after the call Imogen emailed through the interview with Honor Conlon from the trade drapery magazine. Lily printed it off and was excited to see it was a somewhat technical account of how The Dress had been made; the bodice structure, the button holes, the finer details of the dressmaking process were all here. However, as she read through Lily started to realize this was also, in effect, her shopping list. Twenty-five yards of specially-commissioned shot silk taffeta commissioned from Lyon, twenty pounds of crystals and pearls, ten yards of Carrickmacross Lace, and 100 yards of dyed silk tulle to give the 'cloud' effect to the billowing dress. Not to mention the hours of work by the skilled 'petite mains' who did the specialized embroidery and beading. Lily knew enough about sourcing vintage lace and silk to realize that these notions were all way above her pay grade. It was clear too, from the interview with Honor, that none of these elements could be skimped on while remaining true to the original design. In addition she would need time. It had taken Honor Conlon three months to make The Dress, but if Lily had to do all of the petite mains work herself, it could take her forever.

This garment had been, quite literally, made of money. If Lily was going to do this dress justice, she was going to need cash, a lot of cash, to make it.

Fifteen

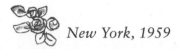 *New York, 1959*

After her experience with Breton's young designer Joy found herself getting back into her stride. Her clothes were her armour, her face was her shield, her fortune her protection. Those were the weapons her mother had taught her to use to get her through life, and now was the time she needed to use them.

Good clothes made Joy feel strong, and she *loved* her green dress.

She hadn't been sure at first – the colour had seemed rather gaudy and shiny to her when she took it out of the bag – but once it was on, with the wide cummerbund belt neatly fastened at the waist and the tweed jacket lined in the same shade as the dress, the whole ensemble felt elegant and refined. She decided to put it to the acid test and wore it to a ladies' luncheon at the Waldorf, where the most critical members of her set were always waiting to pull her down. Joy knew if she could survive them she would be OK.

Betsy Huntington was one, a notorious couture snob, who despite invariably being the first on the boat to the shows in Europe, always managed to look gauche and cheap. Today she was wearing a lavishly embellished Dior cocktail dress, built for a woman half her size.

Now she said, 'I'd recognize the cut anywhere, it's Jacques Fath. I discovered him, when he was here, in '48. I've had a few nice pieces from him since then. He was all the rage, but didn't he die a few years ago? That suit must be a few seasons old, Joy, you're slipping.'

Only Betsy would be cheap enough to price a dress by the date of its designer's death.

'Actually, it's not Fath,' Joy said.

'Well, *who* is it?' Amanda Hutton asked.

'Chanel?'

'Balenciaga? It's not Dior, anyway.'

'It *could* be Chanel…'

'Don't be stupid. Dessés? Ah, that Irish designer, Connolly? Sybil Connolly, that's it!'

'You're just guessing,' Betsy said, as if she were an expert on the matter. 'I tell you, it's Fath – Joy is just teasing us.'

'It doesn't matter,' Joy said, knowing that nothing mattered more to these women than *who* she was wearing, 'you won't know her. She's a new name…'

'She!'

'I told you it was Chanel…'

'Stop,' Joy said laughing. 'She's young, she's just starting out…'

'Well, she's bloody good,' Amanda said, sticking her cigarette in her mouth so that she could reach over and finger Joy's cuffs. 'Look at the finish on this jacket.'

'What's her name? Come on Joy…spill. Is she in New York?'

'Don't be stupid, there is no way that outfit was designed outside Paris,' Betsy said.

Joy had expected to be made to feel awkward over giving up drinking, but found that when she ordered soda and lime, instead of her usual Martini, nobody had passed any comment. In fact, many of the women chose not to drink at lunchtime. Joy was amazed at how much fresher and more confident she felt, how much more in control of things she was, when she wasn't drunk.

'She *is* in New York,' Joy told them, smiling. A flutter of excited shouts rang around the table. 'And I'm *not* being difficult, ladies, but let's just say she's something between a find and a protégé. As soon as she's open for business, I'll let you know.'

Joy excused herself to go the ladies' room and, as she turned her back on them, she could feel the gaze from a dozen pairs of eyes from her table follow her across the room. Women rarely went to powder their noses alone, but Joy did. She never asked for the company of the other women and they never volunteered it. Instead they would all stay back and talk about her. That was the price she paid for being a beautiful woman.

Despite her successful lunch, Joy did not become entirely convinced about the green dress and tweed jacket ensemble until later that evening.

Joy had taken to preparing dinner for her husband. Well, that was not entirely the case; Jones either prepared a simple meal himself or called something in from a local restaurant. He would leave the food in the kitchen, then Joy would don an apron and serve it up. Joy was a lousy cook, everyone knew that, but since Frank had given her this last chance, she was making an effort to be more domesticated for him.

It was late afternoon when Joy got in. Jones was out so she checked the food he had left out for dinner. They had discussed it that morning: two steaks ready to be fried (Joy could fry a steak) with the pepper-cream sauce in a saucepan on the counter, then a jug so it could be poured at the table. In the oven were some Dauphinoise potatoes heating and there was a Sara Lee cake in the freezer. A couple of weeks after waking from her drunken haze, Joy had begun to listen to Frank's tales from work and realized that all of the men in her husband's office went home to a hot meal cooked by their wives every evening. Joy became determined to give her husband that same experience and, in fact, found that she had started to rather enjoy the ritual of pulling the ribbons of a frilly apron over her head and pretending to be a perfect housewife.

'Hey, what's for dinner?'

Frank was early.

'Pepper steak. You want to sit while I cook?'

'Sure,' he said, and he went to the fridge and got himself a beer.

Joy felt an excited flutter of love. This was all going so well. Everything was all just so…easy. No arguments, no fighting, no sneaking around. If this carried on much longer, pretty soon she'd be able to go back to drinking in a nice civilized way again. It wasn't right Frank not being able to enjoy a glass of wine with his dinner, just because she couldn't join him.

'Where did you get this?' he asked. He picked up Joy's new jacket from the chair.

'Oh, it's new, I got it today. Do you like it?'

'It looks like Foxford tweed,' he said. 'It's…' and he tapered off. He was stroking the jacket. '…it's a type of wool, I haven't seen it for years – it's Irish.'

'It goes with this dress,' and Joy took off her pinny and did a twirl.

Frank smiled a big broad Irish smile and Joy felt impossibly sad, all of a sudden, as she realized she had not seen him smile like that for a long time.

THE DRESS

'It's so…green,' he said, laughing, 'but I really like it.'

Frank had never shown much interest in Joy's style. Many of the ladies' husbands accompanied them to the Paris shows every year, picking outfits they would like to see their wives in, checking the quality and provenance of the huge investments they were making in their wives' wardrobes. Joy had never even suggested Frank come with her. He placed little importance on her clothes and she was free to spend his money as she liked.

Nonetheless, Joy believed the pride she took in her appearance, the time and energy and money that she put into dressing to perfection was essential to the success of her marriage. If she let herself go physically Frank would leave her, there was no doubt in her mind about that. Her beauty was what she had brought to the party – always. What she lacked in reliability Joy knew she made up for with her looks.

Joy had been living with the fear that Frank didn't love her anymore since she had stopped drinking. He had not said 'I love you' for as far back as she could remember.

However, as long as Frank thought she was *beautiful* there was always a chance he could find the love again.

Frank reacting at all to an outfit was remarkable but the fact that he said he *loved* it? Well, that gave Joy the brief and delicious feeling that he loved *her*.

'It's beautiful,' he said, then seeming to check himself and think carefully he added, '…and you're beautiful in it.'

Joy was filled with a feeling that should have been love, but felt more like gratitude, as she walked over to her husband and kissed him full on the mouth.

Then Frank scooped the feather light frame of his beautiful, delicate wife up in his arms, and carried her into the bedroom.

131

Sixteen

'My husband has not the remotest idea about fashion, but he loved the day suit you made me,' Joy said to Honor at her first fitting for her dress.

'I am so pleased,' Honor said, brimming with confident pride. 'To be honest, I don't know what I would have done, if you hadn't liked it.'

She blushed then, wondering if she had gone too far.

'Well, I *loved* it,' Joy said, 'although I am still not so sure that green is my colour.'

'Well, your husband approved.'

'That's true,' Joy said, wondering if the girl could possibly know how important that was. She went behind the screen to strip down to her underwear.

'And anyway,' Honor said, getting into her stride, 'whatever colour we decide on, I want you to know that this won't just be a dress – it will be *The* Dress.'

'I certainly hope so, because it's a big birthday.'

'Thirty?'

Joy was behind the screen, getting undressed, so Honor could not see the shock on her client's face, that she had so easily guessed her age.

When Joy came out in her undergarments Honor was unable to help herself and smiled broadly, admiring the model-like figure in front of her. Her smile made Joy laugh a little. There was something warm about this younger woman that she really liked. Joy lit a cigarette and held her arms out, for Honor to take her measurements.

After Honor had made a note of every inch of Joy's body, she reached for the yards of muslin which she would use to help decide on the final shape of the dress. It was then that Honor started to get nervous. Although she had attended fittings before, with Sybil Connolly and Breton, it was usually nearing the end of the process, when she would be called in to pin and make alternations. Honor had never taken charge of a fitting with a real client before.

Honor's designs had all been on paper. Now she had to make a real dress, on a real woman's body and for a moment the idea of that overwhelmed her. This was not just any woman, either. Joy Fitzpatrick was one of the most demanding couture clients in New York. Honor tried to recall dressing the actors in her father's troupe, but the contrast between the portly farmer and the elegant vision in front of her just made her nerves buzz even more.

As Honor moved the fabric around Joy's body, she pretended to assess shapes in the mirror, moving her head from side to side and nodding, but in reality she was just terrified. She didn't know what she was supposed to be looking for and was afraid to touch the creamy, perfumed skin.

Joy, a seasoned hand at fitting, could tell at once that Honor was a bag of nerves, and it made her like the younger woman even more.

'You haven't done this before, have you?' Joy said.

Honor blushed, but said nothing, just kept mindlessly, pointlessly, moving the fabric around her shape.

Joy stuck the cigarette between her lips and grabbed the muslin from Honor's shaking hands. Quickly and adeptly she tucked the thin, dressmaker's fabric under and over her arms, pulling it tight across her flat stomach and slim hips, securing it under her bra straps and panty line, until it looked, to all intents and purposes, like a dress. Albeit a very cheap one.

'Now, if we like it, you can pin it, draw on it, or you can just take a good hard look at it and figure out how to make the toile to my measurements.'

'It's too high around the bust,' Honor said, her pride hurt.

As she moved the fabric, Joy put her long, manicured fingers around the dressmaker's plain, workman-like hand.

Joy knew what it felt like to try and bluff yourself through a situation where you felt out of your depth. She could see Honor that was intelligent but proud.

'You don't have to pretend with me, Honor, I know you are inexperienced, but I can also see that you are a gifted designer. Together we will get this dress right – no matter how long it takes.'

Honor felt something like an elated relief, as if somebody had looked inside her and, instead of revealing her darkest fears, had told her that they liked what they saw.

'This dress will be magnificent, I promise you,' Honor said, and then taking a chance added, 'I will make you the envy of New York.'

'My darling,' Joy said, sweeping her cigarette across her torso in a grand, glamorous gesture, 'I am *already* the envy of New York.'

For a moment, Honor wasn't sure whether Joy meant her

to laugh or apologize, but she laughed and with that, the beginning of a friendship was forged.

Joy was the most exacting client any designer could ever have. That first afternoon, Honor draped Joy twelve times, before they agreed on a basic shape. Honor didn't mind. It was a masterclass in couture fitting.

However, when Joy came back two days later, she did not like the toile Honor had made.

'The neckline is too high and it's too tight across the hip.'

Honor made the alternations, but at the next fitting was told: 'The neckline is too squared now, too loose around the hips.'

One week later: 'Honor, we need it deeper in the bust – the draping needs to be higher and on the hip...can you see this?'

Over the coming month, Joy came for two fittings a week; during each session, Honor showed her dozens of her drawings, which genuinely impressed Joy and she suggested modifications with which Honor mostly agreed.

Joy's demands would have sent a lesser designer half mad, but at no point did Honor lose faith, or get frustrated, as she imagined she might. In fact, every time Joy wanted a change, Honor could see its validity, and was happy enough to remake the toile. Although it meant that progress on the dress was very slow, she was enjoying the process. In just a few weeks, they had developed a strong working relationship. Honor had always put her passion for design over friendships, but now she had found someone who appreciated her talents and was helping her to develop. And Joy enjoyed Honor's company. She was clever and outspoken and the whole process of sharing this project made Joy feel not quite as alone as she had been.

However, Colette was becoming frustrated that her best

seamstress's time was being taken up on the idiotic whim of Joy Fitzpatrick. She had words with Breton and the two of them agreed, enough was enough. Joy's voice among the couture clientele was waning, they told themselves. She had not been to Paris in four seasons and Breton, who was an avid collector of gossip, told Colette, 'She drinks. I have not said anything before, because I don't like to spread gossip, but…'

Colette had heard it too, from Betsy Huntington, but hadn't liked to say.

At her next appointment, Colette (after imbibing a small brandy for courage) called Joy into Breton's office and told her that this had to be the last fitting with Honor.

'Mrs Fitzpatrick, our house has a policy of two design fittings per outfit: after that, fittings are for the finished garment to become complete.'

She politely explained that this should be unnecessary in a house of their repute and that, because she understood Honor was a junior designer, wondered if perhaps Joy would like a final fitting with herself and then they could start making the dress that week. Joy graciously declined her offer and assured her politely that this would certainly be her last fitting with Honor, in Breton's salon.

When Honor was told that Mrs Fitzpatrick would not be coming back and that she would not be finishing the dress, she was devastated. She bit her tongue because she could not afford to upset her employers, but she was fuming. That night she locked herself in her bedroom and cried tears of anger and frustration. She tore up two of her notebooks, in a fit of rage then sat, despondent, with her shredded drawings littering the carpet, like leaves fallen from the tree of dreams which she had planted all those years ago. It all seemed so pointless, somehow.

By morning, Honor had pulled herself together and told herself there was no point in creative dramatics. She would make it to designer status, eventually. Breton liked her and she herself knew that her work was good. However, there had been something about Joy, about the way they worked together, that had felt right. Joy was more than a client now, she was a muse. Honor wondered if there was some way she could contact her outside of her job. Some way of circumventing Breton.

It turned out that Joy had been thinking the same thing.

As Honor was about to enter Breton's studio, she saw Joy standing outside the building, next door. She was wearing her Balenciaga hounds tooth cape and an Hermes headscarf and dark glasses, smoking a cigarette in a dramatically furtive manner, as if she was hoping nobody could see her, but at the same time knowing that everybody would be looking. Honor smiled at her comical attempt to look conspicuously inconspicuous. She really liked this woman.

As soon as she saw Honor, Joy rushed over, looking around as if afraid.

'I have a proposal for you.'

Joy would pay her the same salary she was getting at Breton's and set her up in a room in one of Frank's office buildings, where Honor could work exclusively on the dress.

Honor was dumbfounded. Was Joy really proposing she leave her job just to design that one dress?

Straight away, Honor shook her head. 'I am a designer with Breton now – I won't go back to being a dressmaker...'

'Oh my goodness, that is not what I am suggesting at all!' Joy said, genuinely hurt by the implication. 'Breton's designs are no more than tolerable – you know you are so much better than him, Honor, and he knows it too. Do you really think he will let you shine? A couture house is only as good as its clients, and I am one of the richest clients in New York. You are talented and I like you, so, when you have finished my dress, I am offering to set you up with your own house and introduce you to the best-dressed women in New York.'

As Honor stood there with her mouth open, Joy continued, 'Just think of it. I will have first pick of your collections, we will all save on trips to Paris and you, my dear, will be a star in your own night. It's a given – you *must* say yes.'

Joy's talk was confident but Honor saw her face tell another story. She was nervous, afraid of rejection. Honor wanted to kiss her. She laughed and said, 'Yes, yes, yes!'

Joy shivered with delight and laughed, too. They arranged for Honor to call at Joy's apartment the following morning, bringing the latest toile with her.

'We can buy whatever fabrics and equipment you need and get your room set up then. We only have six weeks to the party – it's not long.'

After Joy left, Honor felt immediately nervous of what she had agreed to, working for some woman she barely knew. Monsieur Breton would go crazy – yet underneath her reservations was the certain knowledge that she had to complete the design and making of Joy's dress. This dress would be a big turning point in her career. It was meant to be.

Honor broke protocol, by not telling Colette first, but going straight to Breton. She explained quietly, saying she was sorry and offering to work her notice, even though she had promised Joy she would leave that day.

'You can leave today,' he said, although his tone was not angry. 'Joy will want you *now* – that is the whim of these women.'

He waved her away and as she was going to collect her

bag, he added, 'You are a fool, girl. Joy Fitzpatrick is not all she once was. I have a feeling you'll be back.'

Barbara was even less understanding.

'You hardly know this woman; all you know about her is that she's a crazy bitch, making you do all those fittings. She'll have you working day and night, like a slave, and who knows if she's as rich as she says she is, because if she doesn't pay you, Honor, you're still going to have to make our rent.'

She need not have worried. Honor moved into the one bedroom apartment that Joy had given to her as a studio. It was a furnished apartment, in a brownstone, on 48 East and 7th Street, that Frank had bought only a few months previously. All the tenants were very old and paying a peppercorn rent, so the building was more of an investment for Frank's portfolio than a profitable concern. Just after he bought it, one of the tenants died, leaving an apartment empty. Frank didn't want the other tenants to think he was waiting for them to die off before he renovated, so, as a non-paying tenant, Joy's dressmaker perfectly suited his needs. The place was still furnished, because although the old lady's family had picked up her clothes and personal belongings, they had no need of her furniture. Frank would have happily dumped the tatty Formica-topped tables and shabby wardrobes, but said that he would do an inventory and send the family money for the old furniture. It seemed the old lady had left little else behind and Frank knew what it was like to have nothing. While he could be ruthless in business, his investments as a landlord kept him in touch with 'real' people and he took his role as custodian of people's homes very personally, always erring on the side of generosity with his tenants. From Joy's viewpoint, the brownstone was an ideal, temporary place for Honor and her sewing machine. It was less than ten minutes' walk from the Fitzpatricks' home and it meant Honor could be available day and night.

Joy had thought the apartment a bit shabby and said she would happily redecorate, but Honor was content to move in right away. The most important thing was that it was hers alone, so she could cover the walls with her sketches and give over as much space and time as she liked to her work, without having to waste time commuting or talking to Barbara.

Within a few days, Honor had settled in. She had barely left the apartment: she was so happy drawing, and stitching yet another toile, while poring over the vast collection of art books that Joy had given her, seeking inspiration for embroidery panels and lacing. On the third day, she was going downstairs to put out the trash, when she saw a man flicking through some post, in the hallway.

She had not seen him before. All the other tenants seemed to be ancient, especially Mrs Mooney, the old lady who lived in the apartment on the ground floor. This man was certainly older than Honor but a good deal younger than her father. Tall and broad shouldered, with thick black hair, he was wearing suit trousers and an open collared shirt. No tie. Despite herself, Honor felt a flicker of attraction. Perhaps the change in her circumstances had brought about this sense of adventure, but instinctively Honor put her hand up to smooth her hair and she adjusted her skirt. As she descended the stairs, she heard Mrs Mooney open the door downstairs and say, 'There you are; I hope you've come to fix that broken shelf.'

'Not today, I'm afraid.' His voice was deep and there was something else…

The man had his back to her and didn't see her walk past. Mrs Mooney, who was half-blind anyway, didn't give her any excuse to introduce herself. Honor loitered at the trash area for a few moments but when she passed them again on her way back up the stairs they were still talking. Honor willed him to turn around, but he didn't. But then, she thought, he probably wouldn't have paid her any attention anyway. She was nothing special to look at. She stood at the top of the stairs for a few moments, fake-fumbling her key in the lock, and trying to eavesdrop, just so she could enjoy the timbre of his deep voice floating up the stairs.

His voice rose with laughter, then he said loudly, 'Mrs Mooney, you are a ticket!'

They were the words of an Irishman and now she identified the 'something else'. Beneath the New York twang was another, more familiar accent. It was the unmistakable slant of her hometown: Bangor, County Mayo.

Seventeen

Frank had not intended to lie. He had called around to the apartment to do an inventory of the deceased Mrs Kelly's furniture, for her family. Perhaps it was because Honor had not, unlike most of his tenants, expected that the business tycoon Frank Fitzpatrick, husband of Joy and darling of the social pages, would call around to his properties to attend to menial matters himself. However, the truth was that dealing with the ordinary people who lived in his properties made Frank feel normal and ordinary himself. So, every now and again Frank would give his buildings manager a day off, leave his suit jacket and tie in the office and wander around the residential apartments he owned in Manhattan, attending to his tenants' needs himself. These few hours when he pottered about the brownstones, talking to old ladies, changing lightbulbs, checking dead tenants' mailboxes, were the times when Frank felt most at home in himself.

Joy thought he was having after-office drinks with some colleagues and he knew she would have been horrified, to think of him mixing with the hoi polloi. Joy would never understand his desire to be ordinary and there was no point in his trying to explain it to her. She was playing the 'housewife' game at the moment – not drinking, pretending to prepare meals for him – she had even bought herself an Irish tweed jacket, like the rich women back home in Ireland used to wear to mass. In her own way, Joy was trying to be a good wife, but if Frank was totally honest with himself, it wasn't enough. It hadn't been enough for a while now.

When Honor opened the door, he had a vague feeling of familiarity. She was an ordinary looking girl, not much shorter than him with a sturdy, homely figure. Her kind open face was more practical than pretty and framed with mousy, light-brown hair.

'Are you the dressmaker?' he said.

'Designer,' she corrected him, although she was smiling.

Was she flirting with him? Joy's friends flirted with Frank all the time, but their manner of doing so was always arch and obvious, designed to embarrass rather than lure him. He could not tell with this girl: maybe she just had an exceptionally warm smile.

He should have introduced himself then, explained that he was Frank Fitzpatrick, Joy's husband, but some instinct held him back.

'I'm sorry, I don't really understand the difference,' he said.

She laughed. 'Neither do I, most of the time.'

She paused, smiling again and saying nothing, before holding out her hand. 'I'm Honor,' she said.

He knew her name of course, Joy talked of little else, these days, but her hand was warm and soft and she laughed when he took it. She was definitely flirting with him and it felt good. If she knew he was Joy's husband, the flirting would stop. Or maybe it wouldn't, but Frank didn't want to think about that, either.

'Can I help you with something?' she asked.

'I've come to do an inventory of the furniture.'

He let go of her hand, carefully, apologetically, as if he had picked up something in a shop he couldn't afford. He felt tongue-tied and silly, like a boy again.

'Well, you'd better come in, then,' she said. She was almost laughing at him again. Frank usually hated women laughing at him, Joy's crowd had done it a lot in the early days, before he had got into the swing of things, but he didn't mind the way this Honor did it. It was as if she was just happy, genuinely happy. It was as if she was glowing, from the inside out, and just to be standing near her made him feel warmer, more alive.

He took his pen out of his pocket and fumbled in his briefcase for a pad. He didn't have one with him. Why would he? His secretary took all his notes.

She was leaning against the flimsy glass partition to the kitchen, with her arms folded, wearing a cream shirt and short trousers. She stood with one leg crossed over the other to give her a casual balance. She had no make-up on that he could see, and her hair was tied back in a messy bun. Compared with the high artifice of current fashion she was practically naked.

'Do you need some paper?' she asked.

'Please, I seem to have forgotten…'

'Don't worry,' she said and handed him a notepad. 'I have dozens of them.'

Frank gathered himself and started to write a list of the contents in the apartment: *1 table: Formica top; 2 chairs: kitchen; 1 chair: upholstered…*

'So, you work for Mr Fitzpatrick?'

1 rug: worn; 1 clock: cuckoo.

He pretended he was concentrating hard on his list. 'Erm, I suppose, in a manner of speaking...'

'What's he like to work for? I work for his wife, but then, I suppose he told you that already...'

Frank coughed, to try to suggest that he was not fully listening. 'Does that cuckoo clock belong to you, or was it here when you came?'

'Do I *look* like the kind of woman who would own a cuckoo clock?' Honor made him look up from his pad, by staring accusingly into his face.

'I don't know,' he said, getting into his stride. Frank was enjoying himself – the flirtatious banter, even the stupid list. He should have been a building superintendent, then he could be married to a woman like this.

'I don't know what a woman who might own a cuckoo clock would look like. Is there a type?'

'Well,' Honor said, 'they don't look like me.'

He looked at her admiringly and for a moment too long, but didn't say anything. He didn't need to; she blushed.

'Swiss, maybe,' he said. 'Although what do Swiss women look like?'

'Statuesque and terrifyingly beautiful, like Katherine Hepburn.'

'Ah, yes,' he said, still making the pretence of writing on his pad. *Knives: loads; forks, spoons etc.* 'But *you're* not Swiss.'

'Are you saying I am not beautiful?' Honor said, arching her eyebrow.

He blushed and smiled and began counting cutlery. 'I'm just saying, I can tell you're Irish.'

'Indeed I am,' she said, 'a little town called Bangor, in County Mayo.' She filled the kettle and put it on the stove.

There's no better medicine than a cup of hot, sweet tea.
'Do you know it?'

Frank's hand was shaking, as he opened a cupboard and kept writing: *3 cups, plates, bowls, lots of bowls.*

'My name's Conlon, my father John was the local school-master. You might have known him?'

Frank collapsed inside. He wasn't sure that the words would come out, until he said then, 'Why would that be?'

'Well, you're from Bangor, aren't you? It's faint, but I'd know the accent anywhere. Sorry, I don't even know your name?'

She was Honor Conlon, John and Clare Conlon's baby. She looked like home, she sounded like home. The right kind of home; the one small shred of happy memory he had from that wretched place was the Conlons' kindness towards him, a brief moment of joy in fifteen years of brutality and hardship.

It was nearly twenty-five years since he had left that cruel, bleak bogland and yet it was still in him. He kept the boy hidden behind the hard shell of manhood; every man had his secrets, his vulnerabilities. Nobody ever asked, nobody ever questioned him and now, here was the Conlon girl who, by virtue of her birthplace and the sweet, warm nature she had inherited from her mother, was cracking him open like a breakfast egg.

He had to get out of there. Frank abandoned his inner building superintendent, picked up his briefcase with the starched efficiency of a chief executive and went out through the door.

He could see that Honor was confused and hurt and he, in turn, felt guilty about his rushed exit, so he turned at the door and said, 'My name is Francis.' He had not called himself that since arriving in America and he immediately regretted his weakness.

Frank's legs were shaking as he walked quickly down the steps of the brownstone. He shook the image of her round, happy face out of his head and told himself he hoped he would never see Honor Conlon again.

Yet in his heart Francis Fitzpatrick felt sick with an old longing.

Eighteen

'It's perfect.'

Joy was standing in front of the mirror in her dressing room. Honor had brought the toile over and it was their first fitting since leaving Breton. Joy picked at the fabric around her stomach and turned to the side, to check her profile.

'I think we've finally arrived, Honor, what do you think?'

Honor was elated. 'You look…amazing. It's beautiful already, even in the muslin. Honestly, you could wear it to a ball, as it is.'

Joy was beaming, too. For such an elegant and angular woman she became almost childlike when she was happy.

Honor touched her arm and said, 'Thank you for pushing me, Joy. I would never have got there without you…'

Joy flicked off the compliment, but she was delighted, not just with the dress but with the new friendship that was developing. Meeting Honor had come at just the right time. It felt strange at first, making friends with somebody not of her standing, but then Joy liked to do things differently. After all, she had chosen an entirely unsuitable husband. She had always feted artists and designers, so why should she not find herself wanting to spend time with, and confide in one?

Honor was honest and intelligent and fun and Joy felt she was a kind soul. Besides, she knew nothing about Joy's drinking past, or the struggles in her marriage. She only knew the new Joy, the fresh clean-out-of-the-box version. Honor made Joy feel as if she was special, as if she was a worthwhile and useful human being.

Once the shape was agreed, the real work on Joy's dress began. Choosing the fabric should have been straightforward, but it turned out to be one of the most difficult decisions Honor and Joy had to make. The silk they used would form the skin of the whole dress. Of course it had to be beautiful, fluid and able to move with Joy's body, but it also had to be strong. There would be so many complex embellishments layered on top of it, they had to be sure the raw material would be able to carry the load. They decided on the finest shot silk taffeta, in a deep shade of rose pink, from the French silk weaver, Tassinari et Chatel, in Lyon. It was as soft as a baby's skin, but so flexible you could build a circus tent with it, a very *expensive* circus tent. The fabric was so costly that the supplier had only four yards in stock and they needed twenty-five, so it would have to be woven to order. From the same place they ordered 100 yards of dyed silk tulle to give the 'cloud' effect they wanted for the billowing skirts.

'I know we want a light colour,' Joy said, when they were ready to put in their final order, 'but do you think navy, or even black, might be more, and I can't believe I am saying this, practical? God forbid we spill something on it. At least if it's dark, it wouldn't be *total* disaster.'

Honor flinched, remembering her coffee spill, then pulled herself together. 'Have some faith,' she said, determined not to compromise. 'Nothing bad is going to happen to this dress.'

So, although Joy continued to think Honor was being

somewhat foolhardy, they commissioned the delicate pink. As soon as they unwrapped the four-yard sample roll, and the delicious fountain of soft silk slithered out onto the table, Joy knew the designer had been right. Honor placed the pool of soft silk across Joy's shoulders, and it fell like milk down her back. Joy's pale skin came alive – it was the perfect shade.

Honor now had enough silk to start work on the bodice and a base on which to start transferring some of her best embroidery work. Now that they had agreed the fabric and shape of the dress, they had to work on the embellishments – on the embroidery, lace and beading. This dress, Joy told Honor, could be adorned to within an inch of its life. Money was no object. Every creative idea Honor had ever dreamed up could be put into it – beading, lacing, the finest fabrics and techniques – whatever it took.

Honor was in favour of not overdoing it. 'You must wear the dress and not have the dress wear you,' she explained, but Joy disagreed. She needed to send out a message.

It was because of the business, she told Honor. 'We want this dress to blow the minds of every woman in New York. It must be nothing less than magnificent: your career and my reputation depend on it.'

In truth, though, Joy needed the dress to be perfect for another reason.

The night before, Frank and she had had a row, of sorts. He had called ahead to say that he was having drinks with some colleagues. The novelty of preparing meals for her husband, without the lubrication of cocktails, had started to wear off. Joy had kept his meal warm, and after they sat down to eat, she asked him about his day.

'Who were you out for drinks with, darling?'

She could see he was agitated but had no idea why, until he blurted out, 'I lied. I wasn't out for drinks. I was over in one of my properties, sorting some things out.'

'What things?' she said.

Frank paused and said, 'Oh, just doing an inventory of some furniture – an old lady died and I promised her family that I would. Anyway, I decided to go around there and sort it out myself.'

Joy let out a little laugh. 'A furniture inventory for an old lady? What on *earth* is a furniture inventory? Sounds like something you'd do in a museum.'

Frank seemed embarrassed, then said, irritably, 'Forget it. It doesn't matter.'

'Well, it obviously *does* matter,' Joy said, 'if you felt you had to lie to me about it. Although I'm not surprised, because I *would* have told you off. You work too hard as it is. You have staff to deal with tenants, Frank. What's the point in paying someone to do something for you, if you end up doing it yourself?'

Frank pushed his food aside, got up from the table and said, 'I don't *have* to do anything, Joy. That's the problem. You may enjoy living on this higher plane of servants, mixing with privileged idiots. But an ordinary family needed my help, and I wanted to help them myself instead of sending someone else over. Is that so hard to understand?'

Joy apologized, but the small argument had got her thinking. She knew her husband was a man of simple tastes. She had tried being an ordinary housewife for him, but they both knew it just was a game. Frank had made a lot of money, but Joy had always had her own fortune to fall back on.

She thought about Betsy Huntington and Amanda and the way they deferred to their husbands. Joy never deferred to

Frank on matters of how they should decorate the apartment, or what designers she should consult for her wardrobe, but she knew he was happy about that. She had tried involving him more in decisions about their social life, but Frank never seemed to want to go to anything, anyway, unless it was likely to be useful for his business.

The more Joy thought about it, the more she came to realize that the problem with her marriage was that Frank thought she didn't need him. Of course, she did need him, desperately, and she was always telling him that. However, he believed it wasn't true. Her independent wealth stood in the way of him feeling truly close to her. This, she became convinced, was the cause of their problems. Her husband felt undermined, because she was financially independent. Now she was going to remedy that.

When she told Honor that money was to be no object in making her dress, she meant it. The garment was to be a statement of love to her husband; not only would it bring back the beauty of her youth, it would also cost Joy her inheritance, thereby proving her commitment to him, at last making her dependent on him.

She told Honor to call in the finest fabrics, the best crystals, ermine, marabou, feathers and fur, whatever she wanted. She could, Joy told her, hire other women to do the beadwork and the lacing, but Honor explained she intended to do as much of the work as she could by hand, herself.

'There is a belief that the spirit of the woman who makes the lace works itself into the fabric. That's why the only lace I would use is from the St Louis nuns in Carrickmacross. What they make is delicate, exquisite, but it's also pure in spirit.'

'Good, I can always use a bit of pure spirit.'

Honor laughed. 'They are *wildly* expensive, and work a long time in advance – months. You could wait up to a year for a bodice piece.'

Joy closed her eyes in irritation. 'Just draw up a design, Honor, and tell me where I can get hold of them. Everyone has their price, even daughters of God, and I can be *very* persuasive.'

Over the coming few days, Honor started work on the dress. She used silk organza as a backing fabric to the charmeuse, dipping it first in water and air drying it to prevent shrinkage later – then ironing both fabrics, wrong side out, with a steam iron, to be doubly sure. Making the bodice seemed endless but, as a seasoned couture dressmaker, there was never any question of Honor compromising on the process. Honor stitched the bodice by hand, breaking three ceramic thimbles, as she worked her fine needles through the thick webbing pockets that would hold the steel boning. She understood that, without this strong underpinning, the beauty of the beading and other embellishments would be meaningless.

'Will you be wearing gloves and a stole with it?' Honor asked, knowing that these accessories were usual for a strap-less evening gown.

'No,' said Joy decisively. 'They aren't obligatory and I don't want anything to clutter up the lines of the bodice.'

Once the bodice was ready Honor started to go through her notebooks, searching out ideas. There should be pearl buttons, from neck to waist at the back, she was certain of that. There would be embroidered panels and beading around the train and hem, but of what design she was not yet sure.

Honor sat in the small apartment and sketched, searching for interesting themes and ideas, but as her mind wandered, all she could think of was Francis. Why had he run off like that? She had been so sure that he would call on her again, yet it had been a week and there had been no sign of him in the building. She had thought of asking the neighbours about him, or even asking Joy if her husband knew him, although she doubted Mr Fitzpatrick would personally know the superintendents of the buildings he owned, but then she thought better of it. It was best not to chase these things, but leave them to fate.

There had been something between them, she was certain, but she was busy; she had her work and there was no urgent need for romance in her life. Nevertheless, she was sure that their paths would cross again. It was when she had mentioned Mayo that he had bolted. It seemed as if he had seen a ghost. Perhaps he had been in the Irish civil war as a boy, or was an Irish deserter from the Second World War. Perhaps he had been widowed from an early marriage and was afraid to love again. As glamorous possibilities surrounding her mystery man circled in her mind, Honor's pencil doodled the fairy tale fantasies of her childhood: a beautiful forest inhabited by unicorns, knights on white chargers, the spinning wheel in *Sleeping Beauty*, Rapunzel's tower, and the poison apple the wicked queen gave to Snow White.

The faster she drew, the more excited Honor got. As she laid her sketches out, for Joy to discuss the following day, Honor realized, with a kick of amusement and excitement that, despite herself, she was dreaming about a Prince Charming: in the shape of a rather ordinary building super-intendent, who may or may not have been from County Mayo, in Ireland.

Nineteen

 *London, 2014*

For the past two weeks Lily had got up early to get her online work out of the way so she could get to the dress toile by mid-morning. She worked slowly and meticulously and found that not working to her own design gave her more freedom, not less as Sally had suggested. Interpreting Honor's work gave her the joy of designing and sewing she had experienced as a student, yet none of the pressure of fearing failure. The only pressure Lily felt was in serving Joy's past and not, as it had been before, in creating her own future.

Lily had started costing it up and had nearly frightened herself out of the whole thing. She had stopped counting at £30,000 and that had not included the Carrickmacross lace.

There was hope on the horizon. Sally had got her that work gig in Miami and Gareth had sold all of her couture stuff in Birmingham. He had a cheque for almost £10,000 – four of it had come from the Chanel dress alone. Gareth didn't want to take any commission but Lily had insisted he take 15 per cent. She thought that would motivate him to sell the rest of her cheaper stuff through the shop.

When she called in to collect her money, Gareth asked how the project was going and Lily showed him the small notebook she was keeping, detailing all that needed to be done to bring The Dress back to life. It included her drawings and, at the back, the dreaded, half-finished shopping list.

Gareth found his hands going weak as he turned each page. Lily's drawings were so detailed, so meticulous; she was talented as well as totally gorgeous in absolutely every single way. Even further out of his league than he thought.

'If you come across anything you think would help, that would be great,' Lily said, as he handed it back.

'I picked up some brochures, actually,' he said, trying to keep his voice light and casual, 'for specialist fabrics. Also, I met a guy who deals in vintage corsets. He said he would keep an eye out for you. Plus, I picked you up a few remnants. Nothing fancy. Just because they were there.'

'Wow, that sounds great,' Lily said. 'Thank you! Can I see them?'

'Actually, I left them at home. Perhaps we could meet up later?'

'Oh, Gareth, I would love to but I'm leaving for Miami tomorrow, on a shoot. Maybe when I get back?'

'Great!'

I'm just getting better and better Gareth thought dismally to himself. Let me lure you back to my flat where we can rifle through some remnants and look at pictures of antique undergarments. How could a girl resist that offer? Well done, man.

As she left, Lily felt curiously vulnerable at having shown Gareth her work. She hadn't shown Sally the notebook or told her about Gareth's fundraising because she would have told her to forget it and Lily knew she could not do that.

Besides, Sally was all caught up with the Miami shoot on which they were now both going to be working.

'You have almost a million blog followers,' she told Lily. 'It didn't take much to persuade Jack we should have a vintage element to the shoot and pay you top dollar to come along and cover it.'

Sally had been pushing her idea for a 'Cool Curves' campaign to Scott's for months and had got them to agree to book the Size 12 Superstar, Sharon, to front the new brochure. In the planning meeting though, she had been slightly irritated at how eagerly Jack had fallen on the vintage idea.

'Vintage is huge right now,' he said. 'Lily would be perfect.'

'It's important we don't lose the Cool Curves angle,' Sally reminded him. 'We've planned this collection out very carefully.'

'Vintage Curves. I love it!' said Jack, already halfway out the door. 'Let's make it happen.'

Sometimes Sally wondered why she bothered. She doubted that her boss even knew she was there sometimes.

Nonetheless, Sally put together her crack team: Sharon as model and Justine on make-up. Lily's job was to record the whole trip 'pirate-style' for her own and Scott's blog – cross promoting both sites. Scott's had furnished her with a new high definition camera-phone so she could continuously tweet and vlog YouTube messages in virtual real time.

Lily felt like an ingénue next to Sally and Justine, with their special lightweight airplane pyjamas and bottled water and skin hydration routines.

'Thank you so much for this,' Lily said. She was enjoying every moment of this adventure, but there was still the niggling knowledge that, no matter how much money Scott's paid her for this gig, it wouldn't come close to covering the cost of the dress.

Sharon flew in from New York and met them at luggage reclaim in the arrivals hall. They were picked up in a black SUV driven by a cute Cuban and as they sped down the maze of broad highways Lily looked out at a crisp blue sky and palm trees so green and lush they looked too perfect to be real. As they approached Miami city, Lily stuck her camera out of the window and recorded cars and shops and people going about their ordinary everyday lives, with the excitement of a tourist seeing something for the first time. Maybe it was jetlag or just pure excitement but Lily felt alive in an exaggerated way; she felt utterly free.

Lily had only been to America once before, to New York for a long weekend with Sally. and she had loved it – from the vintage boutiques and the fashion buzz to the whole thing of just being in America – but never, *never* in her wildest dreams had she imagined a place could be as weird and as wonderful as South Beach, Miami.

The strip of art-deco candy-coloured hotels was pure vintage, with its doormen in old livery and classic cars parked casually around the place. Even the shop fronts were perfectly preserved. Lily felt as if she had stepped into an old Elvis Presley or Doris Day movie. In her red gingham blouse and retro-granny sunglasses, she felt as if she finally matched her surroundings.

As they stepped out of the car onto the shallow sandstone steps of the legendary old-school art-deco Raleigh Hotel Sally said, 'Welcome to the mad, bad capital of catalogue fashion.'

'Best location pool in Miami,' said Justine, the make-up artist. 'Impossible to get a bad shot. We'll have the week's work done by lunchtime.'

'Best burger and fries in the world,' said Sally.

'Thinnest population in America…' said Sharon.

'And oldest,' Sally added, saying to the barman with seasoned flair, 'Four mojitos please. Have them sent out to the pool.'

They followed Sally out to the pool and sat on soft uphol-stery seats under a fashionably art-deco awning, feeling conspicuous in their ordinary London travel clothes. The pool was a sheet of ice-blue glass shaped by smooth black and white tiles. Above them the sun beat down from an azure sky, making the green palm trees gleam. Everything seemed too big, too perfect. Lily felt high with the excitement of a brand new, born-again feeling, the feeling of stepping outside her own life. Sally began to explain Miami to her.

'While the body-type in Miami itself is clinically obese, here on South Beach everyone is either impossibly beautiful, because they work in fashion or film, or incredibly old and rich because they have retired here from the East Coast. So the first thing you need to be aware of as an ordinary mortal—'

'No surgery, under six foot, more than fifty pounds in weight...' Justine helpfully added.

'...is that after a few days, when your eyes adjust to the glittering, unfeasibly buff bikini bodies you will start feel like an ugly outsider. Do *not* give into this feeling or you will start being bothered by octogenarian men.'

'Ew!' Lily said. 'How does that work?'

'The really old guys like more standard-shaped women,' Sharon explained. 'Chicks with a bit of meat on their bones...'

'...like us,' Sally added even though Lily was as slim as most models.

'I guess they remind them of women in the 1950s, so they tend to leave the models alone and follow the regular girls around.'

'Old men? In their eighties? You're having me on.'

'Oh no,' Justine said. 'I am telling you straight, there is no cut-off point over here for those rich old boys, Lily. Money, Viagra and a tan – sure, what more could a girl want?'

'Don't think I haven't thought about it,' said Sharon.

'She's the most popular,' added Sally. 'They follow her around like a pack of small, yapping dogs.'

'They love my curves,' Sharon said, standing up and shaking her booty. 'Get one old enough then get him excited enough and you're set up for life.'

'You are *so* awful,' laughed Lily.

'OMG. They will *love* Lily in her vintage,' Sharon said. 'We'll need security!'

Across the water were a couple of women in bikinis lying on loungers, with their Jimmy Choo sandals and Gucci purses thrown idly at their feet.

'They look like models,' Lily said and nodded towards them.

'Tourists,' Sally said disparagingly. '*Nobody* comes to Miami to lie by a hotel pool.'

'The cool set are working, like us,' Justine said, standing up and draining her cocktail. 'Now, let's *go*.'

Their suite had an ocean view and was luxuriously furnished in perfect art-deco beach style; Lily had never been anywhere this plush before in her life.

'All thanks to you,' Sally assured her. 'Usually we'd stay in some flea-pit motel and just use this place as a location, but Jack Scott did this for you…'

Lily felt a little thrill and said, 'I'm sure that's not true.'

Sally looked at her suspiciously. '…so that when you were taking shots for the blog the backgrounds would be glam-retro and not seedy.'

The rest of the day passed in a whirlwind of fun and fabulousness.

Justine did Sharon's hair and make-up and the driver arrived with the photographer, an experienced professional in his fifties who Sally had worked with before. He had got them a permit to take pictures in an outdoor games park across town in an area called Little Cuba. As they drove up the wide, dusty streets it was if they had been absolutely transported to Latin America. Within moments of arriving at the park, the local men were performing for the camera and flirting wildly, not just with Sharon but with Sally and Lily too, although, true to form, Sally's curves attracted the attention of the local 'boss' and he took some persuading to let them go. Lily caught it all on film and when they got back into the SUV she was so hyper to get the blog started that she began writing it on her phone, sending tweets and instagramming images at the same the time.

Back at the hotel Lily checked her social media accounts for feedback and found it was coming so fast she barely had time to 'like' the comments before it was time for them to all get back out to the Raleigh pool and start shooting again.

At seven Sally called it a day. Chad was a top photographer out here and didn't 'do' unpaid overtime like Sally's English photographers, who could always be relied upon to squeeze in an extra shot at the end of the day.

They went up to the suite and Sally ordered food. They wolfed down 'designer' burgers and fries but Lily couldn't eat, she was too excited. Seasoned travellers, the other three took a power nap to help defer the jetlag until the following morning but Lily was wired. She sat on the balcony and looked down at the darkening hotel pool, where night lights were dropping like lit blooms from the lush foliage. She watched as the sky changed from burnished orange to warm purple and the clouds from white through grey to the dusty blue of a night sky. She never looked at the sky in London. Nature was something in the background of her life, like electricity – you knew it was there, serving an important purpose, but there was no need to pay it any attention, unless there was a power cut. Here, in this beautiful hotel, in this amazing place, Lily felt as though the changing colours of the sky were as much entertainment as she would ever need in a lifetime. Just sitting, alone, looking at the sky in this moment, the whole world looked shiny and new and perfect.

When the girls woke from their nap they got themselves spruced up and went down to the bar for a nightcap.

The art-deco Martini bar in the Raleigh had rounded furnishings and walls glimmering with glasses. It seemed like the private home of an old Hollywood film star.

Lily drained her glass. 'That was delicious. What was it?'

'Fifteen dollars' worth of rum, maple syrup and lime,' Sally said, smiling.

'It's called a Crown Colony,' said Sharon, 'which is maybe why you Brits love them so much.'

'Am I paying for it?' Lily asked.

'Started a room tab so it's on the job,' Sally said. 'I'll pretend I didn't know I wasn't supposed to until Jack arrives tomorrow.'

'In that case I'll have another one,' Lily said. 'Hell, make it two,' she added, as she grabbed and drained the glass that the barman had just put down in front of Sally.

'Ladies. Glad to see you are enjoying my hospitality.' Jack Scott's voice made them jump out of their skins.

Maybe it was because her system was fizzing with jetlag

or maybe it was the second Crown Colony (they really were quite strong) but Lily was suddenly furious with Jack for (a) sneaking up on them and (b) assuming they were robbing cocktails off him (which they were, but all the same...).

'How dare you assume that this delicious drink,' she said, picking up the third cocktail glass, 'is on a room tab and not on my...'

'Ouch, easy tiger,' was the last thing Lily heard before she felt her knees wobble and she collapsed to the ground.

When she woke up she was lying on a sun lounger with a man's jacket over her chest. Jack was on the lounger next to her smoking a cigar.

'What happened?'

'You passed out.'

'Oh my God...'

'Don't worry, you weren't that drunk. I persuaded the staff it was just jetlag jitters and not to call an ambulance.'

Lily tried to sit up but her body felt like lead. She was exhausted.

'Thanks,' she said. 'What time is it?'

'You've only been out for about five minutes.'

'Where are...'

'The others are inside getting drunk on my room tab – I carried you out here.'

Lily laughed. 'You carried me?'

'What?' Jack said slightly offended. 'You think I've never lifted a girl onto a bed before?'

'I doubt you've ever had to get one this drunk.'

'Is that a compliment?'

'Not really, I said she'd need to be drunk.'

'So how drunk would you have to be to go to bed with me? Hypothetically speaking.'

Lily turned to face him and let his jacket slip slightly from her shoulders. His arms were bare and brown, and the blond hairs on them were standing up slightly; the evening chill or another kind of excitement?

'Oh, I'd say I'd have to be *pretty* drunk, but not so drunk as I couldn't walk out when I wanted to.'

'You wouldn't want to walk out,' he said.

'Oh?' she said. Lily found she was grinning. Even though she shouldn't be flirting like this. Certainly not with notorious Jack Scott. Jetlag or South Beach or Raleigh Martini Bar cocktails or probably a combination of all three were making her feel reckless. 'So, what would I want to do, Mr Scott?'

Jack looked at her and smiled. It was not his usual broad Hollywood grin but softer; his grey-blue eyes glittered with mischief and he paused. For a moment Lily felt an embarrassed flush of fear, thinking he was going to lean over and touch her bare shoulder. But he said, 'You'd want to *run...*'

It was a deliberate tease.

'I never run,' she said, 'from anything.'

'Oh,' he said, 'I think you do.'

Then before she could ask what he meant he leaned over and pulled his jacket up over her shoulder.

'You rest there and I'll send Sally out with another cocktail.' Then as he was leaving he said, 'Unless you want me to carry you up to bed?'

Lily smiled charmingly, although inside she felt something closer to a peculiar laughing joy.

'No,' she said, 'but thanks for the offer.'

Lily leaned back on the lounger, drew Jack's jacket up to her chest like a duvet and looked across at the perfect scene in front of her. As she closed her eyes and descended into the deep sleep of the seriously jetlagged, Lily thought she saw the figure of Joy Fitzpatrick in her glimmering dress floating across the mirrored top of the Raleigh pool at midnight.

Twenty

 *New York, 1959*

'Do you really think this party is a good idea, Joy?'

The Fitzpatricks were having breakfast in their dining room. Jones was serving them pancakes. The butler was relieved that Joy was so occupied with this party that she had stopped taking such a keen interest in domestic matters. With his mistress not drinking, life in their household had gone back, in many ways, to how it had been when the Fitzpatricks first got married. Frank was working, Joy was buying clothes and being a society hostess and he was left to run their home in peace. The Fitzpatricks ate together, each evening; Joy pre-arranged the menu twice a week, and listed any purchases or specialist jobs that needed to be done around the apartment, like dry-cleaning the curtains or polishing the hardwood floors.

The same peaceful order had come back. No more wondering what state Joy would be in when he put his key in the lock. No more living under the black cloud of Frank's silent rage, as his boss struggled to stay polite. The only thing that was missing, now, in the Fitzpatricks' marriage, was the love. Jones felt sad about that. He had enjoyed those early days. Their flighty, flirtatious banter over the breakfast table, as they waited for him to step into the larder, so they could kiss, half knowing he could hear them. Just being in the presence of such happiness and hope had been uplifting. They still sat at the same table, at the same time and ate the same food as they did then. They even spoke many of the same words – 'Have a great day', 'Speak to you later' – but the love was gone. All that was left in their marriage was Joy's neediness and Frank's sense of duty. Jones knew all about answering the call for need and duty himself; they were enough to keep you in a job, but not in a marriage.

Joy had kept Jones and Frank abreast of all her plans. It was to be a sit down dinner at the Waldorf, so there were menus to choose, flowers to order, invitations to be drafted then sent, and seating arrangements to be made. She had tried to involve Frank, asking him to compile the guest list with her and help out with the job of choosing a band, but her husband was being impossibly surly about the whole thing.

That morning, for some reason, he seemed to be trying to persuade her to call the whole thing off.

'After all, it's not a twenty-first, Joy, you're *thirty*...'

Frank knew that he had said the wrong thing, but instead of feeling sorry, he just seemed to get more annoyed. He walked over to the bar and threw a measure of scotch into his morning coffee. Frank had instructed Jones to reinstate the bar a few weeks before, saying Joy's flower arranging station was ridiculous and adding that she would have to get used to being around drink like every civilized person. Joy was hurt by the implication that she was an alcoholic and by his refusal to help with her party, but then, almost everything Frank said hurt her these days.

Joy still clung to the belief that the party would change everything. When he saw the magnificent dress and how beautiful she looked in it, his heart would melt. When Frank understood what a fortune she had put into the dress, that she was sacrificing her inheritance for him, he would see how much she loved him and everything would go back to how it was. Frank would love her again, she was certain of it.

With the pressure of the impending party and a stocked bar beckoning to her from the corner of her drawing room, Joy found it easier to decamp to Honor's apartment during the day. She had a telephone installed there so that she could organize the party and oversee work on the dress at the same time. For some reason, this infuriated Frank, although he seemed at a loss to explain why.

'Thirty is not so old, Frank, and besides, the whole thing is arranged now.' As her husband threw back his coffee Joy felt a sort of longing tighten across her chest. For her husband's affection or the scotch, or both.

'What time will I tell Jones to fix dinner for? I'll be with Honor until six, at least...'

Frank snapped, 'I don't know why you are spending all your time with that woman.'

Joy felt defensive and hurt, but kept her voice steady. There was no point in arguing with Frank, when he got like this. In any case, if they did fight, there was nowhere for her to hide – no bottle in which to drown the wound of his words afterwards.

'She is not simply 'that woman', darling. She is a very talented designer who I am sponsoring and she also happens to be a lovely friend.'

'Well, I don't like it and I don't like her.'

Frank was being impossibly hurtful. What was wrong with him? What was wrong with her that, despite everything, she still could not seem to make her husband love her?

'But you've never met Honor, darling. You'd like her, I'm sure you would; she's Irish. Why don't I invite her round...'

Frank got flustered then and said it wasn't right, his wife being out during the day; he wanted her here at home, to look after him. It was all most unlike him.

His hand faltered over the scotch as if he wanted to have another, but then he grabbed his coat quickly and ran out of the door.

Joy told herself that Frank was under a great deal of pressure at work and resolved to leave the apartment after him in the mornings and make sure she was home before him at night. She would be careful not to mention either the dress or the party, any more than she had to.

After he left, Joy put on a Chanel two piece and asked Jones to book her a car to take her to her bank on Wall Street.

Once inside, the manager accompanied her to the vault and left her alone. Joy opened the box of her mother's gems: her inheritance. There were four long strings of the finest Japanese pearls, two of them antique; a large Chopard diamond choker with matching earrings; several breathtakingly intricate and expensive brooches by Van Cleef; and then a handful of assorted diamonds and gems that her mother had bought purely as investments.

'I don't trust bankers,' her mother had said, 'or stock-brokers, or men who move money around. Real gems never lose their value and they never go out of style.'

Joy had known, more or less, what was in the box, but had only looked inside once before, when removing the Chopard diamonds to wear on her wedding day. She had expected to feel something more, some sentiment for her mother, a feeling of power perhaps, or at least awe at the glittering gems. But all Joy felt was that these riches meant nothing to her. They were what stood between her depending on her husband and his believing that she needed him. Otherwise they were useless. Jewels had never made her happy. Drink made her happy. It was time she put them to some use.

Joy studied the jewels for a few seconds, then tipped the whole lot into her Kelly bag, and placed the empty box back in the vault.

'Are you sure about this,' her bank manager said.

Joy gave him a withering look and said, 'Of course I am sure.'

The banker knew she was emptying her fortune. He had seen dozens of women do the same, nearly always to give to some ruthless cad. He hoped to God that Joy Fitzpatrick knew what she was doing, because she was a pretty young thing and a good customer. However, it wasn't his job to interfere, and spoilt rich women like her were impossible to reason with, anyway.

The snow was abating and, as she left the bank, Joy could almost smell spring in the air. The bag was heavy with the weight of her fortune. Joy felt adrenaline pump through her system and she walked faster, her heart banging against her chest. Although Joy knew that what she was about to do was madness, she found herself grinning, as she walked up 5th towards 72nd and took the right hand turn towards Honor's brownstone. This, she decided, was what freedom felt like.

The Carrickmacross lace for the bodice overlay had arrived the day before, a few weeks ahead of time. Joy had rung the Irish convent almost daily, putting pressure on the nuns to deliver. In truth, she had been shocked at how much money they were demanding for their labour. In her naïveté, Joy had imagined these religious women would work voluntarily, while rich customers paid for the raw material and transport and perhaps made a small donation.

Honor laughed like a drain when Joy told her this.

'Nuns may be a lot of things, Joy, but they're certainly not cheap.'

She explained that they were paying, not only for the sisters' skilled labour but also for their creativity and their purity.

'They put genuine love into their work, and love doesn't come cheap. The Carrickmacross nuns tell stories through their lace. They take the finest details of love and nature and put them into your work. Their lives are so simple: eat, pray, sew; they have no other story except for what they invent for their lace. When you commission them, you are buying a piece of their soul.'

'I am not sure I want a piece of some grumpy old nun's soul on my dress,' Joy said.

Honor laughed, replying, 'Wait and see.'

When the lace arrived, in a simple brown postal package, Honor carefully moved back the tissue paper and placed the delicate material on the back of Joy's hand. It was like gossamer, so fragile that Joy was afraid it might melt into her skin.

'Will it be strong enough for you to work with?' Joy whispered, afraid the very sound of her voice might break it.

'Trust me,' Honor said, 'it might look as if it's made from butterfly wings, but actually it's unbreakable,' and she stretched the fabric tight between her fingers, making Joy cry out.

'Don't worry. Making lace is a delicate, precise process but once it's made, nothing can break it. As I said, it contains soul, and let's face it, there's nothing tougher than the soul of an old nun.'

With the dressmaking process really gathering steam, Honor worked day and night, embroidering the intricate panels she planned to sew into the fairy tale train. Each one was more opulent and detailed than the next and shaded with crystals and sequins. While the longer sections of the skirt could be machine sewn, most of the seams had to be to be done by hand. Honor did not know how she was going to get it all done in time – however, she was determined not to buy in any labour. This was to be entirely her dress, hers and Joy's. The longer she worked on the dress, the more she came to appreciate that Joy's input was essential.

'Look here, it's puckering at the waist. Can you see?'

Honor would struggle to see some tiny flaw during a fitting, then Joy would move her arm slightly and there it was – a glaring mistake, as obvious as a pulled thread. There was no criticism, no blame in Joy's observations, just the knowledge that, for a garment to be truly haute couture, it must be cut and finished to feel like a second skin.

'When I wear this dress,' Joy said, 'I must feel as comfortable as if I were naked.'

Honor sighed. She was already having trouble lifting the train alone from the table and had not fully figured out how she was going to structure the waistband of the bodice so that it could carry the damn skirt with all its embroidery and beading.

Honor was making tea when Joy arrived.

'Want some?' she asked.

'You know I can't drink that brown Irish muck.'

Honor laughed, then sat back down to her hand sewing, while she waited for the kettle to boil. She could not waste one single minute if this dress was going to be finished on time.

'Look what I bought you,' Joy said, spilling the contents of her bag over the Formica-topped table.

'I dug out a few trinkets; I thought they might be useful for decoration.'

Honor exclaimed, 'Jesus, Joy, they're beautiful, they're... tell me they're not *real.*' Honor's hand hovered over the diamond choker, afraid to touch it. 'They *are* real. Are you *mad?*'

Joy smiled enigmatically. 'A little, perhaps.' This was fun.

'Where did you get them?' Honor had picked up the pearls. Her hands were shaking as she ran the string gently across the back of her hand, studying it.

'The bank, of course.'

Honor dropped the pearls as if they were red hot.

'Joy, there is no way we can use these...on a dress? No, no way. Take them back...they must be worth a *fortune.*'

But now that they were there, spread out on the table next to the fabric, bringing it to life with their glittering splendour Joy knew that her mother's gems would make the dress beyond anything ever seen before. They would make this dress so special, so magnificent, that it would transcend all the ugliness, all the drinking, all the cruel words, and the heartache of her marriage. The jewels would turn the dress from a mere garment into something so valuable it would be like an act of God. Joy felt an act of God was what she needed.

'Of course they're not real,' she laughed. 'It's just some old paste of my mother's I had lying about the house. Can we use them?'

'Of course,' Honor said. 'If they belonged to your mother, we'll find a way of working them all in.'

Joy smiled and said, 'I'll make the tea.'

Honor might not realize the gems were genuine but Joy would know. Frank would know, because she would tell him; she would say, 'All my money means nothing, because when I am in this dress, I belong to you completely.'

When she came back with the tea, she found Honor looking thoughtful. She was sorting the jewellery into casual piles, according to colour and size.

'Are you all right?' Joy asked.

Honor thought about saying, 'fine', but then realized it had been a long, long time since anyone had asked her that question and the truth was, she wasn't feeling entirely all right.

'What is it?' Joy said. 'Is it me?'

'No, no,' Honor said. 'It's just...' then she trailed off. She couldn't say it out loud. It was just so stupid, so childish, and so girlish.

Joy lit two cigarettes and handed one to Honor. 'Come on, tell me.'

'It's nothing, really.'

'Now I am just going to *make* you tell me. You're pregnant? You owe money on the horses? Oh God, Honor, don't tell me one of your parents is dead and you have to go back to Ireland...'

'No, no, nothing like that.'

Joy dragged on her cigarette and narrowed her eyes expectantly.

Finally, Honor confided, 'Oh, all right, there's a man...'

Joy spun around on her heels and screamed, 'How thrilling! Tell me; tell me *instantly*, who is he? What's his name? Are you in *love*?'

Honor laughed. 'I've only met him once, and all I know about him is that his name is Francis and he's some sort of a builder or odd-job man.' She didn't mention she had met him in this very building. She didn't want Joy interfering and asking awkward questions.

'Oh, how thrilling. When are you seeing him again? When do you have *time* to see him? We must make time; you must invite him to the party!'

'No, Joy, sure, I don't even know if he likes me or not.'

'Silly woman, of course he likes you. How could he not like you? You are...' and before she spurted out the word unthinkingly she stopped to pause over it. '...you really are the most *wonderful*, kind, talented person.'

Honor smiled, touched by the genuineness of the compliment.

'I don't think it will come to anything, it is over a month ago since we met, but I think about him a lot. I don't know why. It's silly really. I've no time for any of that nonsense, anyway.' She stubbed out the cigarette, then went back to the table and picked up her sewing again. 'I'm married to my work; my passion is for dresses, any man will always come second to that.'

'That,' Joy said lighting another cigarette, 'is the most *awful* thing I have *ever* heard. A woman's passion for a man is the greatest passion she will ever experience. There is nothing else. Lord knows, I love my dresses, Honor, and my trinkets...' Her fingers lingered for a moment over her mother's diamond choker. '... but my husband? He's the only thing I have ever truly loved to distraction. I would trade everything, everything I own and everything I am, to make him happy.'

'You're lucky,' said Honor, 'to love someone that much.' Although in truth she thought it sounded rather frightening.

'Yes,' Joy said, and Honor saw a shadow cross her face, 'I am.'

Twenty-One

When Joy opened the door of the apartment later that week, she found Honor slumped asleep at the kitchen table. She was still wearing her spectacles, which were skewed sideways on her face. A large swathe of embroidered fabric was in her lap and the needle and thread she had been using were trailing across the floor. This was third time that Joy had found her like this. She had begged her to hire help, but Honor had insisted on doing all the work herself. She wanted complete ownership of the work and Joy understood that. The dress was not simply a garment; it was a labour of love. Joy's love for Frank and Honor's love of her work.

Joy opened the curtains, put the kettle and radio on, then gave her friend a sharp poke in the ribs.

'Quite apart from the fact that you could prick your finger in your sleep and get blood on the charmeuse, in which case we would have to start again, you really can't carry on falling asleep on the job like this, Honor. It's madness.'

'I know,' Honor said stretching, as she readjusted her glasses, 'but we've only got two weeks to get this finished.' Then, as if realizing it for the first time, she jumped with panic. *'Two weeks…!'*

Joy looked over Honor's shoulder. She was embroidering a panel of peony roses in shades of fuchsia, magenta and a deep, almost damson purple. It was exquisite.

The dress was standing in the centre of the sitting room floor on a tailor's dummy, and white cotton sheets were spread out on the floor all around it; it seemed to fill the whole room. The train still had several panels of embroidery to go on, but it looked almost finished. It certainly was a magnificent garment, but Joy had become so accustomed to looking at it that the dress's magic seemed lost to her now. Seeing it every day had made it as familiar as her own face. However, Joy found that she didn't mind. She had decided that, while the dress itself was wonderful, it was the process of making it, the routine of coming here every day, that she enjoyed. Hanging out with Honor while she worked and making herself useful. Joy ordered in the embellishments, beads and sequins, sourced the embroidery fabrics and threads and got the best price on everything. She scoured the museums and galleries for romantic images and brought catalogues and books to inspire Honor; she fed and watered her, encouraged and praised her. Honor herself would admit that, without Joy's help, she would not have been able to do what she did.

'What's left to do? It looks pretty much under control to me?'

The truth was, Joy was mooching about, looking for something to do. The party was completely organized. Everyone was coming, everyone had their seat allocated and now the whole thing was down to the manager of the Waldorf. All she had to do was turn up looking magnificent on the night.

'The skirt needs two more embroidery panels sewn in. Once they are done, then the whole skirt section can be steamed and pressed and all the final beads and crystals put in. The bodice has been pressed and is ready for the pearl buttons…' She nodded over at a pile of Joy's mother's pearls that had been de-strung and were sitting in a wooden button box on the table, in front of her. '…as soon as I get around to it.'

'Look,' Joy said, 'any idiot can sew on buttons, surely? Let me get somebody in. Surely one of the girls you used to work with could do that for you and let you get on with something else? Then you can take some time off and we can go out for lunch, like civilized women.'

Honor growled and said through clenched teeth, 'I am not feeling very civilized right now, Joy, and besides, that's *not the point*. Yes, there are other women that can do this work as well as me, but I don't *want* anyone else touching this dress. Do you understand? The only people who are allowed to touch this dress are you and me. Now, look what you made me do! I'll have to unpick it and start again!'

'Goodness, but you're grumpy,' Joy said. 'Pastry? Come on, you're hungry, I can tell.'

Honor put the sewing down and moved across to the kitchen counter where Joy had laid out a plate with pastries from the Jewish bakery. Honor hungrily wolfed back two while Joy picked at hers.

'Well, if I'm the only other person allowed to touch the dress, then I'd better give you a hand,' Joy said.

Honor nearly spat out her croissant.

'What?' said Joy. 'It's only *sewing*. We did sewing in finishing school, not that I paid any attention, but honestly, how hard can it be to sew a button on a dress?'

'Joy, it took me two weeks to teach you how to make a proper cup of strong tea.'

'That's not tea you Irish drink, it's *blood*, and besides, there are other people to make tea.'

Honor shook her head. 'Sorry, Joy, it will be quicker to do it myself.'

'Like sourcing the right embroidery threads? Like persuading a bunch of nuns to turn around a year's lace work in under two months?'

'This is different, Joy, this is sewing. It's a *skill...*'

Joy walked over to the kitchen table, grabbed an already threaded needle, one of her mother's pearls and marched over to the dress. 'If you don't show me how to do this, Honor, I'll just have a go at it myself.'

Honor shouted, 'No!' and flew across the room.

She had only finished sewing the bodice the night before, so this was the first time Joy had seen it. Her cheeks flushed with a mixture of shock and pleasure. The pearls and most of the smaller gems had been threaded, but some of the bigger stones had been too difficult to attach without holes so, where possible, Honor had left them in their settings and worked them in that way. In fact, Joy's heart had been in her mouth on many occasions over the past few weeks; once, when seeing a precious pearl slip from Honor's hands, then again, seeing her mother's diamond necklace, which had lived in a bank vault all its life, thrown carelessly onto a scruffy kitchen table. Sometimes Honor's manner was so intense that Joy wondered if she would have treated them any differently if she had known they were real. Looking at them now, on the dress, Joy thought she could not have created anything more beautiful out of them if they had been the Crown Jewels of England.

As a finished piece, the jewelled bodice was breathtaking, sparkling with the authenticity of its diamonds and pearls. Honor moved her working lamp across, so that it lit up the back of the bodice where the pearls would go. As she did so, the jewels sent out shards of magical light across the room.

'It looks incredible,' Joy said. Inside, her heart thudded as she realized the dress now contained all of her past, as well as her future.

'Come back here,' Honor said impatiently, pulling her over to the worktable. 'I'll show you how to sew the wretched buttons on.'

It took Joy three full hours, on a piece of scrap fabric, to perfect the pearl button technique, but she was determined to make her contribution. Honor was patient with her.

'First we have to wax and press the thread, and make a waste knot. Then, bring the needle out at the location of the button – the pearls must be just far enough apart from each other – then allow them be secured in the loop... Now make several tiny stitches to secure the thread and strengthen the button base, that's it... you need to make a stem to allow the button to sit in the buttonhole without denting; we'll need a shank of six threads to do this...'

Joy was astonished and frustrated to discover how complicated it was. Honor was right: this was much too hard for her to master. However, she had said she would do it, and pride would not allow her to give up. It was a slow process, gave her cramp in her fingers and split two nails. On her tenth attempt she got it right. Honor checked and rechecked, but Joy's pearl button was perfect.

'Can I do it on the dress, now?' she asked.

'If you mess this up I'll have to remake the whole bodice. You know that, Joy? You do it *exactly* how I showed you, and you have to work on the garment here, in situ.'

'Standing up?' Joy asked, shocked.

'Yes, Joy, standing up – just like a common shop-girl. It's already been pressed, so you need to be incredibly careful with it. Do not sneeze or yawn or drool...'

Joy looked at her, highly insulted.

'... place any part of your body too near the fabric. In fact, Joy, don't even breathe on it. Just sew the buttons on, one at a time and for goodness sake, take your time.'

'You go to bed,' Joy said. 'I'll call you when they're done.'

After two hours Joy had completed five buttons, but after three hours she had sewn fifteen of her mother's pearls onto the back of the dress. She woke Honor, with a cup of her disgusting Irish tea, then hurried her out of bed, to show her what she had done.

Honor was genuinely impressed. For the rest of the day she taught Joy how to do a lot of simple but time-consuming sewing, leaving Honor to get on with the one or two special touches. She was still designing a front panel for the bodice, to incorporate Joy's mother's diamond necklace which was too sturdy to take apart. Honor thought it was astonishingly well designed and constructed, for a piece of paste. She also had a small flower-shaped piece of antique lace. It had been given to her by her own mother and she had carried it around with her since childhood, as a luck talisman. Her luck had changed since meeting Joy and now Honor wanted to put something of her own into the dress. She felt it could perhaps work as the centrepiece of a wrist corsage, worked up with some tiny pearls and coloured crystals.

Joy sat on the floor beside the train, in her stockings. Honor had advised her to take off her skirt. 'You wouldn't be the first seamstress to sew herself into a piece of couture.'

Honor sat at the table, but they had barely started w hen it was teatime. 'Hell, I'll ring Frank and tell him I'll be late home.'

Honor didn't like the way Joy's husband insisted she be home to cook his dinner every night, although that was all men, really, and if there was one thing Honor knew, it was that Joy wasn't doing any actual cooking. The way Joy doted on her husband didn't entirely feel right to Honor, anyway. Either he was a tyrant, or she was afraid he had lost interest in her. Honor couldn't imagine any man losing interest in a woman as beautiful and funny as Joy.

Joy spoke quietly into the phone and Honor could hear from the tone of her voice that they were fighting. She sat down again and seemed to gather herself.

'How are things with you and that new man?' she asked. 'Have you heard from him again?'

'No,' Honor said. 'I don't expect he was that interested in me, really.'

'Well, if that's the case, he sounds like a rotten cad and you are better off without him. In any case, I told Frank you had a sweetheart. He was beginning to get jealous of all the time we were spending together.'

Honestly, Honor thought, Joy's husband sounded like a rotten bit of stuff altogether. They were better off without men at all, she thought. Both of them.

However, when Joy left later that night, Honor's curiosity was aroused. The telephone line had been put into her parents' house a few weeks before, so she dug out her mother's last letter and dialled the number. It was their first phone call, and the Conlons were enormously excited, her mother giddy about talking into the phone.

After a few minutes, Honor asked, 'Mam, do we know anyone called Francis from Bangor, who went to New York. A man in his thirties, well built...'

'You've met a man...'

'No, Mam, not like that, just someone I met. I think he's from Bangor.'

Her mother shouted to her father. 'She's met a *man*, John, in New York – from around here, a Francis...? What's his surname, love?'

'I don't know.'

'Well, that's not much use, then. Oh, here's your father, talk to him. Honestly John, it's amazing. It's like she's in the room with us...'

John came on the phone and asked how she was. She hadn't told her parents about leaving her steady job with Breton. She didn't want to worry them. She'd tell them when she was firmly set up on her own. As she was about to finish, John said, almost as an afterthought, 'The only Francis I know that went to America was that poor Fitzpatrick lad. He'd be nearly forty now. I heard he did very well – changed his name to Frank.'

Twenty-Two

Jones came to collect Honor and the dress at ten in the morning to take them all to the woods.

Vogue had heard that the beautiful Mrs Fitzpatrick had made a new fashion discovery and they wanted her to sit, in the dress, for Horst. Joy and Honor agreed that the magazine would have to wait until after the grand unveiling at the party, but the request gave Honor the idea that she would like to take some photographs of Joy in the dress herself. But she wanted to take them out in the area in Hastings-on-Hudson where her ideas had first been conceived.

'You want to take me out into a *rural* area?' Joy said, in her sharpest amused-yet-horrified voice.

'Yes,' Honor said. 'Nature is where I get all my ideas from and, in a way, the dress was conceived there. There is an amazing old oak—'

'I thought *I* was the inspiration for the dress, not some dirty old tree?'

'I think it would make a wonderful backdrop for you, in the dress. Please, Joy, it will be wonderful. I promise.'

'Oh, all right, I'll get Jones to do us a picnic hamper...'

'Great, and I'll eat it for you.'

THE DRESS

Honor had not told Joy that her husband had made a pass at her. Not, indeed, that he had made an actual pass at her but his intentions had clearly been, well, wrong, if not precisely dishonourable. Frank Fitzpatrick was an out and out cad: poor Joy. That was the story Honor kept telling herself, to drown out the nagging of the real truth: she had been deeply attracted to a stranger, with whom she had flirted wildly, without even checking if he was wearing a ring. Of course the man was Frank Fitzpatrick. It could only have been him. He hadn't wanted to say he was from Bangor because he was ashamed of where he came from. Her father had told her all about the terrible circumstances of his childhood – poverty, violence – of course he hadn't wanted all of that dredged up, that was why he had rushed off. The truth was that Honor could have seen all of that at the time, if she'd cared to stop and think. She had not done so, she saw now, because she had been selfishly following her own foolish desires. She had seen a man she was attracted to and had not looked beyond that.

Honor had wrapped the dress in a long, heavy cotton bag, then doubled it over. It was so heavy that she could barely lift it and was afraid to think of how Joy's slender frame would be able to support it. Jones spread it out in the large trunk of the Chevrolet and they headed out of the city.

There was more to this outing for Honor than just taking photographs. Joy had introduced Honor to her world, now Honor wanted to share some of hers with her new friend.

As the car quickly moved away from the cluttered, tall splendour of the island, over the bridge, to the seemingly endless suburbs, crammed with neat gardens and row upon row of identical low-rise housing, high streets with cheap shops and small churches, Joy could feel a kind of panic rise up in her. She felt uncomfortable being out of the city. They had a house in Aspen, and Frank, who hated hotels, insisted on keeping modest apartments in Boston and Washington, the two main cities where he did business.

Her parents had always kept a house in the Hamptons, but Frank hated it down there; a playground for the rich, he called it, as if that was a bad thing. Joy had no attachment to the place, so they sold the house and banked the money and, if Joy wanted to get out of the city for a summer, they would rent a place on the beach. However, in recent years Joy had found herself reluctant to travel anywhere in America outside Manhattan. She told her friends that this was because Europe was her true spiritual home, but in truth, she had developed a kind of fear of moving too far from the city, too far from Frank. When he went away she had more or less stayed in the apartment, drinking, waiting for him to come home. Since she had stopped drinking he had not left town at all. Joy thought maybe he was afraid she would drink again if he was not there to keep an eye on her, and she also thought that perhaps he was right.

As they passed through the suburbs, out into the broad, dusty stretch of highway, Joy reached over and took Honor's hand. It was a habit Joy had picked up as a girl. When her mother was taking her back to boarding school, holding her hand on the journey was an exclusive gesture of affection. The search for reassurance and comfort continued whenever she was in the car with Frank. Honor was surprised, but could see that Joy, who was gazing wistfully out of the window, was barely aware she had reached out. Honor recognized it as a peculiar gesture of vulnerability and enclosed her friend's manicured fingers in a comforting clasp.

They drove through the charming hamlet of Hastings-on-Hudson and came to a clearing at the side of the road.

'Park here,' Honor said.

'Really?' Joy said. 'Are we really getting out here?'

'Are you going to make this hard, Joy?' Honor said, and then, as she was unloading the dress out of the trunk, she turned, looked her straight in the eyes and added, 'This is *my* thing, Joy. These woods, nature, is where I get my inspiration; you're my muse and I want to share it with you.'

Joy nodded. She never knew what to say when Honor said honest things like that; it made her want to disappear, or cry.

'Will I bring lunch, ma'am?' Jones asked.

'No, thank you, Jones,' Honor answered before Joy had the chance. 'We'll be less than an hour, we can have lunch when we get back, if that suits.'

Jones gave her a disapproving look, then turned to Joy, who nodded approval.

Honor thought, her husband may be a womanizing pig, but that man, Jones, clearly adores her.

Joy followed her into the woods, picking through the bark and leaves on the dry mud path. She was wearing slacks, a sweater and flat leather brogues which she had bought in London years ago, but never had occasion to wear. Even though the air was more fresh than cold, Honor had told her to wear a warm coat because she might need something over her shoulders while she was changing into the dress. Joy was wearing a three-quarter length fur. They walked in silence for twenty minutes, before Honor veered off the path and into the woods proper.

'Is it much further?' shouted Joy.

She was getting frightened; it felt remote here, far away from everything. Joy told herself that Honor was with her, she wasn't alone, nothing bad could happen. She had promised Honor she would do this, but now she wished she had put her foot down and said no. Dragging her and the valuable dress out into the woods to be photographed was a stupid idea. She should have talked Honor into going to a studio. One phone call to *Vogue* and Horst could have been booked. Honor really was the most impulsive, silly person sometimes, and Joy was worse, for going along with her.

'Here we are.'

Joy stopped and looked up.

Honor was standing in front of a huge tree, its trunk as wide as four men and as gnarled as the face of an old wizard. On the ground all around it was a carpet of tiny yellow primroses and beyond it, a sea of bluebells.

'What do you think?'

Honor was standing in front of the tree with her arms spread, as proud as if she had grown it herself.

'It's lovely,' Joy said, although she was still unsure that there was any real point to this exercise.

Honor started to unpack, spreading cotton sheets out on the dry ground in front of her and laying the dress on top of it.

'Well, come on,' she said. 'Start stripping.'

'Here?' Joy said.

'Well, what did you think was going to happen? Come on, you agreed to this...'

Joy mumbled some objection and started to take her clothes off under her coat.

'There's never anyone here,' Honor said. 'We could both run around stark naked, for all it matters.'

'I'd rather not, if it's all the same to you,' said Joy primly, struggling to take off her sweater, while maintaining some modesty beneath her coat.

Honor walked over and held her coat while Joy stripped down to her underwear.

'Bra, too,' Honor said. 'It'll show under the dress.'

Joy groaned. 'Are you certain there aren't people lurking in those bushes?'

'None, I promise. Although I'll sell tickets, next time, if you don't get a move on.'

'There won't be a next time. This is such a stupid idea ...'

It was fighting talk, but Honor noticed that her friend was shaking. She was clearly afraid. For a second she felt sorry. In truth, she would never dream of stripping off here herself. It was a public wood and people might walk by at any moment, although Honor really, *really* hoped that they wouldn't.

As Joy bent to take off her lace bra, Honor looked at her friend's thin, pale body. Her spine was as delicate and defined as the string of pearl buttons on her dress and her breasts were tiny, negligible. Dressed, she was a strong, elegant powerhouse, but naked, her body had the vulnerable slightness of an underfed child.

Honor gently pulled the dress up over Joy's body. As her torso filled the strapless bodice and Honor buttoned the line of precious pearls up from the base of her spine, she imagined she could feel Joy's body grow into the dress. This was not, Honor felt, simply a small, shaking girl turning into a confident couture-clad woman; there was something more to it, although she could not have said what it was.

'Don't move,' she said to Joy.

'Don't worry. I am too terrified to move an inch. Are you sure nobody comes through here?'

Honor arranged Joy's train around her on the ground, then stepped back to adjust her camera, which she had set up on a tripod.

Dappled sunlight was glinting through the trees and illuminating the dress. Joy's carefully made-up face looked haughty, but her eyes were burning with a kind of tearful, feminine fragility. Honor saw that the fairy tale images she had embroidered on the train – the unicorn, the twisted roses, Rapunzel in her tower – all seemed to be coming to life, shimmering and dancing so vibrantly that Honor thought they would dance off the dress altogether and go skipping though the bluebell wood. The dress seemed to have, literally, come alive.

'My God,' she said.

'What?' Joy asked. 'What is it? Is there someone coming?'

'No, it's nothing,' Honor said. 'You just look beautiful, that's all.' The spell was broken, the dress had stopped dancing and Honor took her pictures.

On their way back into the city, Joy chatted, elated from her modelling adventure.

'You know it's a public wood?' Honor told her. 'People could have walked by at any moment.'

Joy gasped, but Honor could tell she was more thrilled than shocked.

'Now all we have to do is find you something decent to wear to the party.'

'Me?' Honor said. She honestly had not thought further than completing the dress.

Joy looked aghast. 'Of course, you'll be the guest of honour, darling. You'll be sitting with me and Frank. The ladies of New York will be enthralled by you; you'll be beating them off for commissions, although we'll have to find you a proper studio first…'

As Joy babbled, Honor looked out the window to hide the look of fear that she knew had swept across her face. She had been counting on never seeing Frank Fitzpatrick again. More frightening, still, was that in some small part of her, Honor Conlon wanted nothing more.

Twenty-Three

 *Miami, 2014*

The rest of Lily's week in Miami passed in a flutter of photography and pools, make-up and meals and lots of drinking cocktails late into the night.

Lily had been reluctant to leave The Dress behind but after a few days away she found she felt more alive, more creative, more connected than she had done in a long time. She was going home fresher and full of new ideas that would make her even more determined to see her dream through.

Lily loved being part of Sally's team. Justine and Sharon were great but the real surprise was Jack, who had stuck around for the full week, checking over and approving their pictures every afternoon, then entertaining them in the evenings with dinner and cocktails. It was clear to Lily that Jack Scott lived like this all the time, eating and sleeping in expensive hotels, in beautiful places and, undoubtedly, in the company of various interesting and/or beautiful women. Lily had always ridiculed and dismissed the playboy lifestyle but after a few days in the Raleigh, she had come around to thinking that, actually, this was not a bad way to live after all.

The one fly in the ointment was Sally. Lily was increasingly sure that Jack was a deeper and more considerate person than she had given him credit for. But Sally would have none of it and what is more, she strongly objected to Jack's encouragement of Lily's obsession with The Dress.

'I don't think Lily should be wasting her energy in remaking some dead woman's dress,' she said. 'I think she should concentrate on her own designs.'

'I'm not simply "remaking" a dress,' Lily argued. 'I am bringing a designer's legacy back to life. Besides, it's personal.' And, full of wine, she told them all about Joe and how Joy was married to the great-uncle they never knew.

'So you are trying to make your own history, as well as fashion history?' Jack said.

Lily blushed. 'Well, my own history maybe, but fashion history...might be a bit ambitious.'

'Might not,' he said, raising his glass.

Sally raised her eyebrows and muttered, 'Get a room.'

On their last night in Miami, Jack invited Lily to hold back after the others had gone to bed. Sally gave her a warning look, but Lily knew better. She actually now trusted the guy. Jack had not only encouraged her to talk about Joy's dress and all that would be involved in making it, he had also looked up her blog pages and read her article. She even showed him her notebook, with all her sketches and notes in it, and he seemed genuinely impressed.

'You must really believe in this dress,' he said, 'to want to replicate it. It sure will take a lot of work though, a lot of money too.'

Lily nodded and smiled. She didn't tell him that there was no way she could ever afford to make it. Desperate as she was, there was no way she would have Jack Scott think she was scrounging for money.

The journey home seemed longer and was more muted than the journey out because their adventure was ending rather than beginning. Lily had barely slept the night before, having stayed up late with Jack. Sally tried to give her a sleeping tablet on the plane but she refused, so that when Lily arrived back at her flat, late that afternoon, she was so miserable with jetlag that she simply crawled into bed and pulled the duvet up over her head.

She was woken up very early the next morning by her home phone.

'Hullo? Is that Lily Fitzpatrick? The blogger?'

The voice was clipped and business-like.

'Yes.'

'Good, hi, this is Karina Match from the *Fashion Daily* website. I am calling to ask if you can give me a quote about The Dress for today's edition?'

'Sorry?'

'Hashtag The Dress? The tweet you put up last night challenging PopShop to a frock-off?'

'I'm sorry,' Lily said, 'I have no idea what you are talking about...'

'Oh God, it's gone *viral* darling. Jack Scott has challenged Dave Durane of PopShop to create the most beautiful dress ever made, and you're the one making it!'

What the hell was going on?

'I'll call you back,' Lily said.

'Well, make sure you do because we've got readers online *right now* waiting to hear what you've got to say – remember we rang you first...'

As soon as she hung up the phone rang again immediately.

'Hullo, Lily Fitzpatrick? This is Radio 5. I was wondering if you'd be free to talk to Mike in about half an hour about The Dress?'

'Sorry, she's not here,' Lily said and hung up.

She left the house phone off the hook and reached for her iPhone. It was on silent with three dozen missed calls. It was currently buzzing with a new one, from Jack.

'What the hell is *happening*?' she said.

'Only the best publicity stunt ever,' he said. 'I was so impressed with all you were saying about vintage stuff, I retweeted you last night and challenged that prick Durane to a frock-off...'

Her heart was thumping. He had deceived her. Broken her confidence. Taken the private dreams she had to make this dress and made them very, very public. How dare he?! Was he mad?

Lily struggled to keep her cool, to keep her voice light. She still hadn't been paid for the Miami shoot and wasn't about to put the little income she was owed in jeopardy by annoying him. Too much, anyway.

'Well, I'm not making The Dress.'

'Of course you are. It's all you want to do. You have passion, Lily.'

'I can't afford it.'

'Lucky for you we pay for passion like yours,' he said.

'It's a *lot* of money,' she said.

'The way you were talking, I reckon about a hundred should cover it?'

Lily barely had her derisive laugh out before he added, 'Thousand, of course. What do you say? The Most Beautiful Dress ever made – you have complete creative control. You make it, I pay for it.'

Lily could barely believe her ears. Carte blanche and an unlimited budget? She would be mad to turn it down. She would also be mad to do it. She could fail in front of the whole fashion industry.

'Could you not just have challenged Durane to a duel or something?'

'Well, I do despise the guy but not enough to do jail-time for him.' Jack paused. 'Are you in on this Lily? No obligation. I'm serious, are you going to help me?'

'Let's meet and talk it through?' She made it sound casual but the adrenaline was pumping through her. Lily didn't know if she was terrified or thrilled.

They met in The Black Lion pub on Kilburn High Road. Lily was surprised Jack even knew where it was and that he offered to come up to her home turf. Somehow, although she lived around the corner, Jack got there before her. He had a tough-looking shaven-headed guy with him.

'Meet Eddie Masterson,' he said, 'my new driver. He got me here from Knightsbridge in … how long was it, Eddie?'

'Fifteen minutes, sir.'

'And how long have you been working for me, Eddie?'

'Two days, sir.'

'And who did you work for before that?'

'David Durane at PopShop?' Lily butted in.

'A thankless prick,' Eddie said, shaking his shaved head, 'and a nasty bit of work if you don't mind me saying so, sir.'

'I most certainly do not mind you saying any such thing,' Jack said. 'In fact, you can say it repeatedly and do call me Jack, for God's sake, especially in front of the ladies. And now you can take the rest of the day off, Eddie. I don't know how long I'll be.'

Lily annoyed herself by feeling slightly thrilled that he

was giving up his day to her, then he added, 'I can get the tube home,' and she smiled inwardly, knowing the ridiculous comment was also him showing off for her benefit.

After Eddie had left, Jack turned to her and said, 'Lily, I wanted you to meet my driver because I just stole him from Durane, along with an excellent PA and one of his knitwear designers. Durane's bound to try and get his own back and he might try and steal you, or Sally. The gloves are off; things might get mean and complicated. I want to know if you are up for this?'

'Up for what?' she said, finding it impossible to keep an element of flirtation out of her voice. 'For shafting Durane or making The Dress?'

'Hopefully both,' Jack said, then his face darkened. 'Although I need you to know I'll be going through with this challenge with or without you.'

Lily was shocked. 'How do you mean?' she said. 'The Dress is my idea.'

'No,' he said. 'The Dress is just something you are doing, Lily. It's me challenging PopShop that makes it an idea.'

'So what are you saying?' Lily felt like crying, being sick, but she held it together.

'You don't know it yet but this is going to be huge. PopShop is an international chain with endless resources and Durane hates me. He is going to pull out all the stops to win this thing. His money gives him access to the best designers London has right now and he is going to knock his team out to come up with something spectacular. I need to know we can match him. I need to know you are up for this.'

'Up *to* this you mean. I cannot believe you want to me persuade you to let me do *my own* project.'

She stood up, about to tell him where he could stick his

job, but he took her arm firmly, held her eye steady and gently pulled her back down.

'Lily, listen. I want you to do this but you have to understand there is a lot at stake.'

'Your pride,' she said.

'Which,' and his face was an impenetrable mask, 'is the pride of a very successful growing brand as well as a rather foolish man. If you make this work you will be the best-known designer in Britain. If you don't...?'

'I'm right where I am now,' she said, 'but I'll have made you look a fool.'

'Worse than that,' he said, 'I will find some other hotshot designer to make this damn dress for me and they will become the Next Big Thing because Lily, much as I like you...' he paused and gave a momentary melting look before snapping back into business mode, 'I am *not* going to lose this challenge.'

What Jack didn't know and she didn't tell him was that this was more of a challenge for her than it was for him. The chance to prove that she not only knew everything there was about vintage design, but could actually match it with her own vision as a designer and couture dressmaker. She had never done either of those things before at any level close to this.

Lily was petrified but her desire to see The Dress made was greater than her fear.

'I'll do it,' Lily said. 'I accept your challenge, Mr Scott.'

They shook hands on it and spent the next couple of hours mapping out a plan. Lily would merge her blog with Scott's website then write a running commentary on the progress of The Dress as it happened. Scott's would sponsor everything and give her all the resources she needed. She could commission the fabric, buy valuable antique lace and oceans of Swarovski crystal if needs be. Any additional craftspeople or labour she needed to employ along the way would be covered by Scott's, as would all travel expenses for research and sourcing.

Before they left the pub, they ran through the Scott's Twitter account on Jack's iPad and it was aflame with speculation as to who PopShop were going to employ to make #TheDress.

'If Durane has any sense he'll give it to an unknown like you,' Jack said, 'and make it an even fight. But he won't.' He opened up his huge golfing umbrella against the spring drizzle. 'He'll go for a big name. David is predictable like that; he doesn't deal with "nobodies".'

There was something about his phrasing that didn't quite sit with Lily but she was distracted by the fact that Jack was walking with her down Kilburn High Road.

'Where are you going?' she said.

'Back to your house,' he said casually.

She stopped and looked at him. 'Why?'

'You think I am going to get involved in some great Machiavellian scheme with somebody when I haven't even seen where they *work*?'

'I work from home, Jack.'

'I know. Tea and biscuits all round,' he said.

Lily had stopped and was staring at him.

'I don't know if I want you in my house…'

'Sorry? Where was it you said you *did* want me?'

She laughed. He was incorrigible but very funny.

As they passed Old Times, Jack swung into the off licence next door and Lily casually looked in the window. The mannequin was wearing one of her favourite tea dresses and she felt a pang of sorrow. She wondered if it was worth it, letting go of all these things she treasured, or was making

The Dress some sort of pact with the devil? She noticed that Gareth's mate Fergus was behind the till. Gareth must be away on a sourcing trip and she didn't know if she was annoyed or relieved that he wouldn't see her walking around Kilburn with Jack, who now came out of the off licence with beer and champagne and held them aloft saying, 'To celebrate our new *arrangement*.'

Jack knew just where the line was between tacky and sending himself up and Lily decided that whatever new adventure the afternoon brought, she was going to roll with it.

Sally was just turning into Lily's street when she saw them. Jack and Lily walking, arm in arm, towards her apartment. Jack swinging a bottle of champagne in his free hand and Lily laughing, clearly delighted with herself.

Sally had been furious when she received the *Fashion Daily* Twitter alert about #TheDress @LilyLovesVintage. They were all just back from Miami and she had dropped Lily off in Kilburn from the airport. But Lily had said nothing about Scott's involvement in her silly dress project. There was only one possible explanation: Jack and Lily had been having conspiratorial talks behind her back in Miami and had hatched this plan for a major campaign without consulting her.

Sally was stunned. How could they betray her like that? Jack was a scoundrel, although she had hoped he had *some* loyalty to her, but Lily? That really was a slap in the face. Her first instinct was to ring Lily and scream at her but as Sally brought the number up on her phone, she thought again. Maybe Lily didn't fully know what was going on? She was a bit of an ingénue when it came to business and Jack could be a manipulative bastard. It would be better to see Lily in person to thrash it out. Sally hopped in her car and headed up to Kilburn.

Now, as she sat there, with the evidence of their treachery in front of her eyes, she felt a raging fury sweep through her, coupled with a sense that her heart was breaking. If they thought she would take this lying down, they were sadly mistaken. They had picked the wrong girl to double cross in Sally Thomas.

Twenty-Four

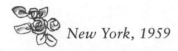 *New York, 1959*

'Is it all right if I leave now, Mr Fitzpatrick? I want to get ready – for tonight.'

'Of course, Nina.'

'Would you like me to fix you a drink before I go?'

She wasn't even sure why she said it, except that her boss had seemed so melancholy earlier, not at all like a man whose wife was about to throw New York's party of the year.

'No, Nina, I'm fine. You go.'

Frank's secretary smiled and said, 'I've left your tuxedo behind the door – you're not going home first?'

'My wife wants to meet me there. She wants her dress to be a surprise.'

Nina beamed. God, how happy he and Joy sounded.

'I am so looking forward to the party, sir.'

'Well,' he said smiling, 'so am I.'

What a good liar he was.

'I'll see you later, then,' she said.

Frank had insisted that all twenty people in his office be invited to Joy's birthday party.

'I don't know where I'll *put* them,' Joy had said. 'I mean, you know what snobs people are.'

'*Your* people are snobs,' he said.

'*Our* people, darling, don't forget that. I'll put all your office together, at one table – that way they won't have to mix until after the meal. By that time everyone will be so drunk no one will care *who* they are dancing with.'

Frank went to the drinks cabinet, poured himself a small whisky, then stood in the middle of his large office and drank it back. He had a whole floor of this building in Midtown, the headquarters for his various business interests: properties in Manhattan and Boston, the steel company in Washington, then there were his partner companies, two hotels, a department store and all the various stocks and shareholdings to be managed. Frank's companies were so diverse he couldn't put a name to what he did. He could no longer call himself a carpenter, a builder, or even a property developer, or landlord. Frank was in the abstract business of making money. This meant that he owned everything while, essentially, doing nothing; he was an important man who, despite his wealth, felt worthless. Frank Fitzpatrick was an illusion.

Meeting the Conlons' daughter had really thrown Frank. Honor Conlon – she had been a baby in a pram the last and only time he had ever seen her.

Most of the Irish who came to America stayed among their own. They married, often people from their own county – from their own town, if they could find them – they gave each other work and lived, as much as possible, as they had back in 'the old country'. Frank had expected to do the same. When there was business to be done, Frank could be as Irish as the next man, but when in Joy's world, he hid it well.

People speculated about Frank's background, but they generally guessed up. From the suave, confident way he carried himself, nobody would have suspected the rural destitution he had been born into.

This girl did, though. If she had not realized who he was, she would find out from her parents soon enough.

Rags to riches was the American dream and Frank was not ashamed of where he had come from: it was just that he did not like to think about it. This office, all the money, Joy, these were the things that occupied his mind now. His early years – his childhood, running barefoot across the black bogs of Bangor to fetch the doctor to his mother, after his father had beaten her in a drunken rage – were things he had left behind. He had locked the door on Bangor and built another, bigger, better life around it, so that he could believe his childhood had never happened.

Then he met Honor Conlon and the door flew open.

In the weeks since their flirtation, Frank had been haunted by his past, he had bad dreams at night and ugly memories popped into his head during the day. In business meetings he would look down at his hands resting on the leather desk and see his father's clenched fists, or his own knuckles and remember how bruised they were for weeks after he beat his father. Frank saw his young brother Joe in the face of every child that passed him in the street, his mother in every old woman, his father in every broken, raving street bum.

Mostly he stood in his big office, with its designer furniture, its deep carpets, its perfectly pretty secretaries and its deferential young executives and remembered that he didn't belong here. In truth, Frank had never felt entirely at home in the world of high-end business; his connection to the people around him was tenuous, built on a lie. Now it had been broken. Frank felt exposed and vulnerable and out of depth in his own life. He really did not want to see Honor Conlon again.

When Joy had told him, only a couple of weeks previously, that Honor was sweet on a man called 'Francis', who worked in one of his buildings, Frank's first reaction was one of dismay.

'Will your designer friend be at the party?'

'Of course, she is sitting at our table.'

So she didn't know who he was and if she did, she hadn't said anything to Joy.

'I may have to go to Washington on business, Joy... something really big has come up...'

He was never going to get away with it. Joy's face fell so fast, he was afraid she might start crying, or drinking, or both, there and then.

'You will be here, Frank, won't you? You *have* to be here.'

He heard the terror and panic in her voice and soothed her. So now, here he was, about to endure another one of his wife's showy parties and come face to face with his own troubled past, all in the same night. Frank poured himself another whisky and got changed.

The Waldorf had pulled out all the stops for the night. The ceiling of the ballroom was like a fairy tale, lit up like a warm starry sky. The crowd of two hundred or so guests was a who's who of New York society. Apparently. Frank seldom bothered looking around a room. If people wanted to talk to him, then they could come and find him. Unfortunately, the first person to do that this evening was Betsy Huntington. She always reminded him of a parrot, with her rich, fat bore of a husband, Geoff, who now came over to point out the great and the good to him.

'There's Jack Kennedy and the wife,' Geoff said, puffing on a cigar and pulling himself up to his full height, which was a little under Frank's shoulder. 'I don't know what *he's* doing here – really, this new-money Irish thing is all getting a bit much…'

'Geoff!' Betsy said.

'Sorry, Frank,' he said, only slightly deflated. 'Never think of you as Irish, somehow – married to Joy and all that.'

Even by Betsy's standards, her husband could sometimes be a very stupid man.

'Go and get me one of those champagne cocktails, Geoff – make it two, they look rather small.' As he trundled off, she apologized to Frank. 'Sorry, Frank, Geoff means well, but he can be a bit of an oaf.'

Frank gave her a withering smile and said nothing, but Betsy was not so easily deterred. 'I can't see Peggy Guggenheim. I'm sure Joy invited her but I think she said she was going to be in Miami this weekend but, oh, look, there's a Lesser Spotted Roosevelt – not one of the *real* ones, of course, but a relation. Well done, Joy, although I think he might be the trouble cousin – you know the one who *drinks*…'

Enough was enough.

'Excuse me, Betsy,' Frank said, 'I see some of my staff over there; I had better go and mingle.'

Betsy's face fell, then she rallied, 'Joy invited your staff? How very *egalitarian*.'

'Good evening, sir,' Nina said.

'Call me Frank tonight, Nina. You look nice.'

She blushed.

'Steady on, boss,' said Stanley, one of his young executives. 'Not too much fraternizing with the ladies, on your wife's big night.'

Nina gave him a slap on the arm.

'If I didn't know better, Stan, I'd say you're looking to keep young Nina all for yourself tonight.'

'Well, boss, she's certainly the best looking woman in the room, you'd have to agree…'

'Mrs Fitzpatrick hadn't arrived yet,' said Nina, and she looked at Frank. 'You do know they call her the most beautiful woman in New York? You must be so proud.'

'Ah, yes,' Frank said, taking a sip from his whisky. 'Very proud indeed.'

'Have you any idea what she'll be wearing, sir? I am so excited – the girls and I have been looking in the magazines for months, trying to imagine what it might be.'

Dear God, Frank thought, this is *worse* than Betsy Huntington.

'I honestly have no idea, Nina. Would you excuse me, I need to call home and see if she's left yet.'

As he headed through the room towards the hotel reception desk, Frank looked around for Honor. He wasn't even sure if he would remember what she looked like now, and that thought alone gave him some comfort. Perhaps she had forgotten him, would not recognize him. People come in and go out of our lives, he thought, nobody matters that much to each other. He looked at the faces of one or two women, asking himself, is that her, whilst knowing that it wasn't, then remembered that, of course, Joy had said Honor would be helping her get dressed. She would meet him in the lobby of the hotel at seven, and they could walk in together. It was now ten past seven. The fact that he had forgotten this arrangement sent a frisson of fear through Frank.

He lit a cigarette and asked the receptionist if he could use the phone. The Waldorf lobby was the grandest of all the New York hotels. That was why his Joy had chosen it; his wife liked to make an entrance. Every surface was adorned with a veritable forest of fresh flowers and the gleaming chandelier at the centre of the gold domed ceiling made the intricate floor tiles sparkle like jewels. It seemed, even in Frank's dark mood, that there was some strange magic in the air that night.

As he held the receiver to his ear and heard his house phone ring, Frank decided on his escape plan. He would tell Joy the Washington business was back on. He would ignore Honor, walk his wife into the room and then, after the second course, he would disappear. There was no need for him to engage in any way with the Conlon girl. When this stupid party was over, he would dissuade Joy from their friendship. Honor and her dressmaking was one of his wife's fads, like the decorating. She was too much of a snob to make real friends with an ordinary person. Honor wouldn't be hard to get rid of.

As the phone rang, Frank noticed that everyone had stopped what they were doing and had their heads had turned towards the door. His wife was making her big entrance. Even by Joy's standards, the dress she was wearing was extraordinary. Under the bright lights of the hotel lobby it glittered as if it was, literally, not of this world. The bodice was encrusted with shimmering gems that flicked shards of golden light across the room. The skirt beneath was a hill of fabric the colour of rose-petals. So soft and light it had the appearance of a cloud and was covered in images – unicorns and fairy tale towers and clambering roses – fine, complex drawings layered one on top of each other. Each image was meticulously decorated with diamonds and pearls and sequins – if you had a lifetime to look you would not be able to take it all in. As Joy moved through the parting crowd of awe-struck guests a long train followed her, its sequinned, beaded glamour as opulent and indulgent as a pool of pink champagne. The word dress or even gown did not begin to describe this feat of engineering. Even to Frank's uneducated male eye it seemed more like an elaborate piece of jewellery than a dress. It was certainly a work of art. The women in the room stood open-mouthed. Even the men were raising their eyebrows at this display of remarkable opulence. The dress was beyond beautiful; nobody could take their eyes off it, or Joy.

Except Frank. All Frank could see was Honor Conlon.

She was standing next to his wife and wearing a simple, long evening dress, with a single set of pearls. Her curled hair was loosely drawn back from her face, as if she had hardly had time to fix it, and her face was bare, except for a slick of hurriedly applied red lipstick. She was smiling at Joy. The girl looked happy. 'Happier than a person had a right to be' was something his mother used to say and, in seeing her happiness, he felt happy too. Joy's beauty and her extraordinary dress receded into the background and all Frank could see was the dressmaker.

Honor's gaze moved around the lobby and he knew she was looking for him. When she found him, Frank allowed his eyes to meet hers. He tried to keep his hands steady, but they were shaking so hard that he had to clench them into fists. When the girl looked at him, Frank saw something old and familiar in her eyes and he suddenly felt safe.

Twenty-Five

Honor had always known her dress was special, but it was not until the night of the party that she really saw it come to life. With its marbled walls and ornate pillars the exclusive hotel had a palatial monied elegance that usually managed to dwarf even the wealthiest, most overdressed crowd. However, this night, Joy Fitzpatrick filled it, turning the Romanesque palace and its furnishings into little more than a catwalk.

Joy wore the dress as if it was a second skin. The classic serenity of the jewelled bodice with its delicate lace panels flowed into a cloud of tulle from the waist down. Although the train was so heavy that Honor could barely lift it, Joy wore it with such grace that it seemed to glide in a glittering stream behind her. The intricately embroidered scenes around the skirt sprang to life with every step and as Honor followed her muse into the lobby of the Waldorf she felt she might explode with pride. Everything she had worked for all of her life was centred in that moment. All the beauty she had aspired to create in her was embodied in that one stunning woman and the magnificent dress they had created together.

Then she saw Frank.

He was looking, not at his wife, but at *her* and with such intensity, such *passion*, that she felt it like a kick to her stomach. Honor stood next to her great creation and smiled and smiled. She kept smiling and looking all around her at the people, cooing over Joy's dress, smiling for the flashbulb cameras, smiling at the women who gathered around to touch the train and exclaim over the jewelled bodice, but her eyes kept being drawn back to Frank's face, to where he stood at the reception desk. There he was, still looking straight at her.

Joy was incandescent with happiness and called her darling Frank over to stand by her side.

'Well, that is some gown, Joy,' a woman exclaimed.

'Everybody,' Joy announced to them all, 'this is the woman who made it – Honor Conlon. Remember her name; she'll be open for business soon.'

Honor kept on smiling, but she could feel Frank inviting her to hold his eyes. Her face was burning – with embarrassment or desire, it was impossible to tell.

They moved through to the ballroom, where large round tables were set out around the dance floor. Each table was decorated with an enormous bowl of cream roses and a tall candelabra, and was scattered with favours, scented almonds in pink and lavender silk purses. Honor had never seen anything like it before, the sheer lavishness of the decoration and the scale of the room were breathtaking and yet, all she could feel were Frank's eyes, still on her, not letting go.

When the accolades abated briefly, Joy finally had the chance to introduce her husband to her friend. Frank's face darkened and he looked around the room, agitated.

'Darling, this is the wonderful Honor. At last you meet. Now *be* nice, Frank.' Joy nudged him and said to Honor, 'Sorry about my husband, he *hates* parties. You entertain

Honor, she is *my* woman of the night. I've being summoned by *Vanity Fair* – I'll be back in a few moments, with the photographer.'

When she was gone, Frank smiled awkwardly at Honor and said, 'The dress is really beautiful.'

'Thank you,' Honor said.

They were standing side by side, looking at Joy as she walked across the room, gathering admirers in the wake of her regal, magical train.

'It must have taken a lot of work,' Frank said awkwardly.

Honor smiled. 'Yes,' she said, matching his understatement, 'it did.'

There was a pause, then Frank leaned down ever so slightly and said, 'I know you. You're John Conlon's girl.'

Honor got a fright at the mention of her father's name, but at the same time, could feel the warmth of his breath on her skin.

'And you're that guttersnipe, Francis Fitzpatrick, who stole money from my parents.' She tried to keep the tremor out of her voice, or at least hoped that it sounded more like anger than desire.

'Are you going to expose me?' he said.

It was a strange use of words. Honor realized Frank was, despite his bravado, vulnerable, but she did not want to engage in more intimate banter. It was wrong, so she changed the subject.

'Your wife looks beautiful tonight,' she said, then turned and, with all the decorum she could muster, looked him in the eye and said, 'Joy has been very good to me.'

Frank held her defiant stare, until Honor felt herself melt into a kind of hopeless passion. As she looked away, Frank reached down and firmly took her hand in his, holding it into the fold of her wide skirt so nobody could see they were touching. Then he said, quietly but clearly, 'I want you.'

That was when Honor knew she had to get out. Pushing his hand away, she walked quickly across the room. The huge ballroom was buzzing with people and unable to find the exit, Honor went into a ladies' rest room, where she locked herself in a cubicle and tried to gather herself.

Outside the cubicle a group of women was talking about Joy's dress.

'Well, you wouldn't expect anything less than spectacular, darling; after all, she *is* turning thirty.'

'I'll tell you something, I am getting the name of that designer and I'll be making an appointment this week.'

'You and every other woman in Manhattan, dear. I would try and nab her tonight, if you can, although there'll be some price tag on her work, after a debut with Joy Fitzpatrick.'

'It's still cheaper than flying to Paris.'

'You can say that again.'

Then they faded out through the door. Honor wanted to run, but at the same time knew it would draw more attention to herself. She took a deep breath and gave herself a good, old-fashioned Irish talking to. She tried to imagine what her mother would say. 'Frank Fitzpatrick is not the first man who tried to cheat on his wife and he won't be the last. He is a chancer, a fraud and a thief – don't walk away from this opportunity on his account. He'll give up trying to have his wicked way, soon enough, if you just ignore him and make it clear you're not interested.'

Except that Honor knew Frank Fitzpatrick wasn't really the problem.

Honor found Joy and stuck by her side for the rest of that evening and, as her inner mother had predicted, Frank did indeed back off. An hour into the party, when the band started up, Frank took his wife out, for the first dance. After stiffly leading her in a short waltz, he disappeared.

The rest of the evening passed in a whirlwind of introductions, barbed bitchy banter and congratulations. Once the dancing had finished and the cars started to arrive to take people home, Joy and Honor had a drink together.

'To the future of our dress!' Joy smiled and clinked the champagne glass filled with iced tea she had been carrying around with her all evening.

'The party was a triumph, Joy,' Honor said. 'The canapés were superb and that champagne fountain was magnificent.'

'Worth every penny,' Joy replied, 'and I am so pleased we opted for the late hot buffet, it allowed everybody to get nicely drunk, before eating. Wasn't that a marvellous idea?'

She was putting on a brave face but Honor was could see that her friend, client, muse and benefactor was deeply hurt that her husband had left. The dress, the party – all this had, Honor knew, been done for Frank, and he had left early, probably because of her.

'I am so glad you are here, Honor,' Joy said. 'I loved introducing you to everybody.'

They both knew Honor's presence had distracted her, and her guests, from her husband's absence.

'Thank you for staying with me. Frank had to leave early. A sudden work engagement, you know how men are.'

Honor smiled but she felt sick in her stomach.

'Of course, Joy,' she said. 'I'm your friend.' And even as she said it she felt guilty. 'I'll stay as long as you want.'

Maybe she should tell Joy about her husband. About what sort of man he was. About what he had done? No. Maybe one day, but not tonight. Honor offered to go back home with Joy in a taxi so she wouldn't be going home to an empty apartment on her birthday.

'That's sweet, Honor, but I've booked a suite here tonight,' Joy said. 'Frank will be back later and we'll have our romantic birthday together then.'

Honor smiled, and embraced Joy a little too tightly before leaving.

Joy was left alone, in the aftermath of her own party. She had been too upset to be angry with Frank when he rushed out earlier and had made him promise to come back to the party, after his stupid emergency merger had gone through. He had not made it back before the party ended, but then, Joy justified, maybe that was for the best after all. It would be nice to have some alone time together; a private party in the bar downstairs, before he swept her upstairs and helped her out of her magnificent dress. Frank hated parties, he hated crowds. That was why he had not made any fuss over her tonight, why he had been relieved to rush back to work.

The ballroom setting was all wrong. With just the two of them together, he would see the dress properly, the jewels, the Irish lace she had commissioned. He would see all she had put into it, the sacrifices she had made, he would see her again: Joy, the sad girl he was going to save.

Joy went through to the bar and ordered a soda water, then sat down in a booth. It was late, but this was the Waldorf and the bar was open all night and there were a few residents still up drinking. Joy sat and waited. After a half hour or so, the night porter came in and gave a note to the barman. He came over and asked if she was Mrs Joy Fitzpatrick and when she said she was, he handed her a hotel memo with her name scribbled on the front. Frank had called the hotel and left a message to say he had to go to Boston on urgent business. He would not be home until the following evening – at least.

Joy felt weak with disappointment. Sitting here alone in this magnificent gown, her husband had, in effect, stood her up. She picked up her clutch and quickly walked towards the door and then, as she reached it, Joy thought again. Turning back, she walked towards the long bar and sat up on a stool. Her train spread all around her on the floor looked like a melting ice-cream sundae. She clicked her fingers at the young barman and ordered a whisky on the rocks. If she had to wait the few moments extra it took to shake a Martini, she might change her mind. In any case, when the barman put the squat crystal tumbler down in front of her, Joy found herself hesitating to pick it up.

As her hand hovered nervously over it, a man she had barely noticed sitting next to her, spoke. 'Looks like you're making a decision, lady.'

She turned to him. He was an ordinary looking Joe in a very bad suit, clean shaven, with neat hair but the broad jaw and weathered features of a cowboy. Not bad looking. He was nursing a cup of coffee. What kind of a man drinks coffee in a bar?

'One's too many, a thousand is never enough. That's why I stick to the coffee.'

Joy gave him a withering look, but he just shook his head and smiled. 'Sorry for intruding,' he said. 'Just something about your expression, I guess, the way you're nursing that drink, reminds me of my last one, the I've-been-dry-for-a-while-maybe-I-can-handle-it whisky. Three days later, I woke up on a front lawn in White Plains – no idea how I got there.' Then he laughed, drained his coffee, tipped his hat at her and said, 'Enjoy your drink, lady.'

Joy was shaking, but she wasn't sure why. Here she was, in a priceless dress and this stupid, common man had made a comment on her expression?

One's too many, a thousand is never enough.

She knew what he meant, she knew what he was trying to say, the cheek of him. Two months off alcohol of any kind and she was a reformed woman, for God's sake. One drink was the least she deserved, to ring in her thirtieth birthday and settle her nerves, after being abandoned for the night by her husband.

She wrapped her manicured nails around the whisky tumbler and threw it back in two long gulps, then got down off the seat, to stop herself from ordering another.

Joy decided to not stay in the hotel suite, but lifted her heavy train and went into the street, where she flagged a taxi to take her home. One drink was plenty, and once she was back in her dry apartment, she could be sure it would be left at that.

That night she brushed her teeth more thoroughly than usual, slipped into her best Lucie Ann nightgown, then slept fitfully, waiting for Frank to come home. When he didn't, she moved into the drawing room and waited there. She snoozed, with the drapes closed for much of the day, holding onto the night and trying to convince herself that Frank would walk in the door any moment and resume her birthday date. She still wanted to believe he would move hell and high water to get home to her; she still wanted to believe he loved her enough to be with her. She still wanted him to see her in the dress. Last night he had been worried about this deal, distracted by work. Today he would come home, the deal would be done and things would be different.

When Jones came in with her breakfast pastries, Joy gave him the rest of the day and evening off. Then she went back into her dressing room, fixed her hair and make-up, put on her magnificent dress and waited for her husband to come home from Boston.

Nearly a full day later, Frank was still at work.

His secretary had called to say that the delay was because the merger in Boston had not gone through. Whatever it was, Joy was not in the least bit interested. He had let her down, that was all that mattered.

When Jones came in from work, Joy was still lounging on her Eames chaise wearing her bedtime silks. It seemed as if she had been sitting here alone in the dark for some time. Jones put the coffee down on the table in front of his mistress and handed her the *New York Times*. It was already open on the society pages.

'You looked magnificent, ma'am,' he said.

'Really?' She smiled up at him, her most fetching, charming smile, but it didn't reach her eyes. Jones was not given to sentiment, but nonetheless he felt sad for Joy today. The very air in the apartment seemed heavy with anti-climax. The butler opened the curtains and shook out a couple of cushions.

'It describes you as a goddess, ma'am, and...' He coughed discreetly. '...in my humble opinion – you were just that. I am not given to commenting on fashion but—'

'It was one helluva dress wasn't it, Jones?'

'It most certainly was,' he said, smiling. She returned it but again, there was no light in her eyes.

'Would you like eggs for breakfast, or will I send out for some pastries?' he said.

'I'm not hungry, Jones,' she said, but he called down for the bellboy to fetch some fresh croissants from the Jewish bakery, anyway. Joy would pick at something with her coffee and in any case, Frank would be back soon. Of course he would. The Fitzpatricks had their moments, but Jones believed Frank was a decent man. He wouldn't leave his wife alone for longer than he absolutely had to.

Joy picked up the papers and looked at a photograph of herself in the lobby of the Waldorf, flanked by Honor and Frank. Honor and Joy were smiling, glittering press-photographer smiles, but her husband looked distracted and worried. The rest of the pictures were of various guests, in the early part of the evening. There would be a bigger spread in the weekend papers.

Joy pushed the paper aside and felt the emptiness of her day, her life, echo inside her. She knew a drink would fill the crater of sadness but she would not have one – she would not. Frank would be home from his trip soon and when he came in the door she wanted to be sober.

Frank would make things right again. Only Frank could make things right.

Twenty-Six

 *London, 2014*

'Nice pad,' Jack said. 'Reminds me of my student digs.'

'I see,' Lily replied. 'Slumming it with the Great Unwashed.'

'If you say so,' he said, throwing himself down on the sofa. The cheap IKEA furniture looked suddenly more glamorous with his arm flung casually over the back of it.

His phone buzzed.

'Aha,' he said, picking it up. 'Here we go. PopShop announces Lucy Houston as their designer for The Dress. That was quick…'

They drank the beers and the champagne and made a start on a bottle of tequila she had brought back from a hilarious sun holiday with Sally five years ago. Lily opened up to him about how she had folded away her dreams of being a designer and Jack just listened. While Jack talked, mostly about work and about his dreams for Scott's, Lily sat across from him on the large, battered sofa and wondered if she fancied him. Jack was gorgeous looking and funny, so she certainly *should* and after all, here he was in her flat, drinking. Lily waited for that five second pause when they would be left looking at each other, then he would lean in. Men like Jack always got these things right; they didn't end up in awkward will-he, won't-he 'Gareth' type moments.

Lily had assumed Jack had brought her back here to seduce her, but as the night wore on and talk kept turning towards The Dress, Lily began to realize that her kissing moment might not happen after all.

'We need a story,' Jack said. 'Durane's dress has no back-story, that's what will give us the edge. You need to go to New York and find the woman who made the original dress and we'll get the whole thing on film.'

'The woman that was married to my great-uncle is dead,' Lily explained.

'What about the designer who made The Dress?'

'All I have is her name, Honor Conlon. She was never a big name or anything.'

Lily felt an affinity with Honor. A shadowy figure, featured only in one small photo in the drapery magazine, the designer who had made this extraordinary garment was clearly talented, yet had never made a name for herself.

'Well, let's find out if she's still alive,' said Jack, 'and if she is, let's get her on board. I have lots of people in New York, lawyers, investigators; I'll put them onto it.'

'No need, I have *one* Irish cousin,' Lily said.

'Well done, one Irish cousin is even better,' Jack replied. 'Look at Obama...'

By this stage the tequila bottle was nearly empty and the two of them were quite drunk.

'You might as well stay over,' Lily said, and when Jack nodded towards the open door of her bedroom she added, 'on the sofa.'

'Damn,' he said, jokingly. She knew he would follow her in to bed in a heartbeat if she invited him.

Lily slept badly, fizzing with the ridiculous fact that there was a world-class playboy sleeping on her put-you-up sofa.

She finally woke at seven to find Jack already up and getting dressed in her living room.

'Sorry if I woke you,' he said. 'Eddie's waiting in the car.'

'Do you not let him sleep?' Lily laughed.

'He works to my crazy hours,' Jack said. 'That's what I pay him for.'

'You can have a shower if you like,' Lily said.

It was weird looking at Jack's tanned, hairless torso. He must get himself waxed, she thought. When Gareth wore those awful comic-branded T-shirts in the summer, there was a little triangle of hair... Oh my God! Where did that come from?!

'No, I'll wait,' Jack said. 'I'll pop back home before work.'

Jack leaned down and kissed her gently and rather deliciously on each cheek then, as he reached her door he turned back and said, 'You really are very clever as well as gorgeous, Lily Fitzpatrick – we are going to do some great things together,' before running down the stairs to his car.

After he had left, Lily was so churned up with this crazy turn of events that she quickly threw off her hangover and got dressed.

It was as if her whole life had turned on its head overnight. Her dream job had suddenly landed on her lap and The Dress was going to happen. The best thing, she decided, was to just focus on work, starting with, as Jack had suggested, finding Honor Conlon in New York.

Zac had sent her a couple of Skype messages when #TheDress had started trending on Twitter so she got onto him and they talked excitedly about the competition.

Zac had never heard his grandmother talk about Honor Conlon but agreed he would help find her.

'Maybe she still has it?' he said. 'I have *no* idea where to start looking for her, but I've got a friend who's on internship at the Berg Fashion Library. I'll get her onto it, there must be some record of Honor somewhere.'

'If she's still alive she might be in an old folks' home,' said Lily hopefully.

'Forget it, cousin. I love you but I am not trawling through retirement homes in New York, there are *thousands* of them...'

'We'll both do some digging,' she said.

After she put the phone down she tried calling Sally. She was feeling overwhelmed with the mountain of stuff she had to do. Find an old lady in an old lady haystack (who may or may not still be alive), deal with the social media storm that was still surrounding her and, by the way, *actually make The Dress!*

Sally went straight to voicemail so Lily left a message pleading with her to call back. She put the phone down and spent the next three hours dealing with her Facebook admin; she couldn't even look at her Twitter mentions. People were 'taking sides' in the competition, pointlessly slagging off herself and Lucy Houston. She was a 'nobody wannabe'; Lucy was a 'boring has-been'. Even though it was stupid, infantile nonsense from idiots who had nothing better to do, it was still hard for Lily not to seize on the negative comments. Social media may have put her project on the world fashion stage but my goodness it was an ugly business. Lily checked through and 'liked' as much as she could, scheduled some posts for the following week so she wouldn't have to turn on her computer for a few days then sent out a tweet: *Looking for the original designer of #TheDress lady in her eighties called #HonorConlon worked with #JoyFitzpatrick #50sCouture.*

She went to the kitchen to make herself some lunch and as she picked up the empty beer cans from her coffee table she shuddered with excitement remembering all the plans she and Jack had for the project. She was desperate to share the news so she texted Sally: *Call me back – urgent gossip!*

When Lily got to the kitchen she realized she was so churned up inside that she couldn't eat.

She checked her phone. Where the *hell* was Sally?

Lily was getting hyped up and there was only one thing that could calm her down when she got panicky like this: bad daytime TV and sewing.

She went over to her worktable and picked up a skirt panel she had cut, planning that, one day, when she had the money, she would farm it out to a couture tambour beading workshop in Soho. She realized now that she did have the money and it made her feel so excited that she decided what she really needed was to start sewing herself. She picked up a box of simple glass beads and some sequins. As she threaded the crystals and sequins, securing and looping, Lily started to feel calmer, and quietly put all her concentration into creating delicate arrangements of minuscule patterns. Each tiny bead played its part, making up a beautiful whole, and this was how Joy's dress would come together. Bit by bit, bead by bead, one moment, one day at a time.

After a couple of hours' work Lily looked down on her tray and found she had created three delicate butterflies of intertwined crystals and sequins.

The room dusky and her eyes hurting, Lily carried the beaded fabric over to the window. As she held it up to check her work a shaft of sunlight caught it, sending sparkles from the crystals across the room. As a child her grandfather had told her that such tricks of the light were Irish fairies come to visit her; she wondered now if perhaps he was right. She had certainly just created something beautiful. In seeing the work she had done come alive like this Lily felt, Jack and the New York adventure and all the Twitter fuss aside, that she could do this; she could create the most beautiful dress ever made.

When the phone rang she did not rush to it, but seeing it was Jack she picked it up and said 'hullo' with a surprising sense of calm.

He sounded stressed.

'Lily, I've got some bad news. Your friend Sally has gone to work for Durane. She's PopShop's new Artistic Director.'

Twenty-Seven

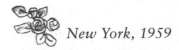 *New York, 1959*

When Honor got back to her apartment she barely had the energy to take off her make-up. She crawled into bed and thought to herself, it's over. The dress had been made and launched, the party was a huge success, now she could relax. Except that she could not relax. Because all she could think about, was him. The more she tried to push thoughts of him aside, the more Frank Fitzpatrick invaded her mind. With those three words, 'I want you', he had branded her. It was as if, by declaring his intent, he now owned her. Of course, such a thing would not have been possible had she not been attracted to him, for no matter how hard she tried to believe it was not true, Honor was drawn to him. Hopelessly.

For the next twenty-four hours, she locked herself in her small flat and devoted herself to quashing her rising feelings of longing for Frank Fitzpatrick. He was a rich rotter who wanted to cheat on his wife. He was a guttersnipe, from a bad home, who had stolen money from her parents. On and on she went, but all the time she just kept thinking of the certainty with which he had taken her hand and said, 'I know you.'

By late afternoon the following day, Honor was going stir crazy. The phone had rung a few times, but she hadn't answered it. It would only be Joy, asking where she was, wanting to catch up and Honor just couldn't face her. In truth, she could not face herself.

She made coffee and sat at her kitchen table. The floor was littered with sequins and discarded fabric trim; her sewing machine still sat at the far end of the table, threaded with the final barrel of what had seemed like hundreds of spools of pink silk thread. As she looked around, Honor realized that this was not her home, not really. It was the home of the garment she had launched the night before, the birthplace of what, from the moment they had walked into the lobby of the Waldorf, had become known in New York society as 'The Dress'.

The phone rang again and Honor jumped, spilling her coffee. She mopped it up with some discarded fabric and decided to get out into the fresh air and clear her head.

Twenty minutes later she was walking around the reservoir in Central Park, drinking in the sweet scent of the freshly blooming ornamental cherry trees. Her head was clear. This was what Honor needed – to reconnect with what she loved: nature. She sat on a bench and listened until, beyond the traffic and the bicycle bells and the laughing children, she heard birdsong. Life goes on, nature turns, the world was a bigger and more interesting place than a man who wanted her and a notion she might have of being in love. She wished for her sketchpad and, in just wanting that, was reminded of why she was here. Not for a man, this distracting, unexpected flash of foolish romance – but to work.

Already on her feet, she hurried back to the apartment to collect her book and her pencils, deciding she would spend the afternoon lying in the park, coming up with new ideas to wow the ladies of New York. She and Joy would continue with their plans to open a couture salon. Joy's husband was a busy man, as well as an impulsive idiot. Frank would forget her within days and in any case, he could easily be avoided. There was no way Honor Conlon was going to let some man get in the way of her dreams. Thank goodness, she thought as she walked up the steps to the brownstone, she had seen sense in time.

She opened the front door and saw him straight away, standing in the shadows under the stairs. Waiting.

'Honor,' he said moving towards her.

He looked dishevelled, shirt loose, unshaven, and irresistible.

Honor did not hesitate, but ran straight up the stairs, her heart banging against her chest, saying, 'I don't want to see you; get away from me.'

He followed and stood close behind her as she fumbled with her door key. As her shaking hands struggled to steady themselves in the lock, Frank put his hands over hers, then took the key from her and turned it. They stood chest to chest, next to the opened door.

Honor looked up into his face and said, 'I can't do this Frank, it's not right,' but she did not move away.

He leaned against her, until they both stumbled back into the apartment and fell against the wall, in a passionate kiss.

Both weak with longing, all finer feelings melted in the heat of their desire.

Powerless.

One night, not even a full night, that was all Honor had allowed herself to spend with Frank. Unable to help themselves, they had fallen onto and into each other, driven by forces of nature that seemed to pull Honor back to the bogs and the wild mountain landscapes of her home. Afterwards, as they lay wrapped around each other in her small bed, she knew that this feeling, this craving she had, this love she could feel rising in the pit of her stomach to a sobbing crescendo of want, would never let her go. She looked across at the clock and saw that it was 7 p.m. He had been in her bed for five hours.

'You had better go,' she said.

'I'm staying,' Frank said, his voice tender but firm. Even though she had not known him before, he felt so familiar to her; his voice sounded like home. But they had met once, he told her, when she was a baby.

'No,' she said, 'you can't do that – *we* can't do that. We have to stop this now, before it starts.'

'It's too late, it started the moment I laid eyes on you,' he said. His face was certain, confident; there was no guilt, no regret. Frank Fitzpatrick was right where he wanted to be.

'I love you, Honor.'

When he said those words, it seemed to Honor that her heart was suddenly cut loose from its mooring and began to float inside her, like some expanding balloon ready to explode in her chest; she had to grab onto it, hold it back, or it would lead her to places she did not want to go.

Honor knew that what they were doing was wrong, but when she looked at Frank she was overcome with a slow, soft emotion, that was somewhere between pity and desire. Frank was a powerful, wealthy man; yet here, naked, in her bed, he was just the boy who her father had rescued from his violent father, a lonely child reared on a diet of rage and meagre love, knocking on her door, looking for solace and a safe haven. Frank was a strong beautiful man and she longed to lie there forever and get lost in her desire for him; beyond that again there was the serendipity of how they had met. Two souls reared in the wilderness of the west coast of Ireland, both had made new lives, but in meeting one another, had opened up the door to home.

Frank said he loved her yet men said things like that all the time, just to get women to sleep with them. She wanted him, she felt compelled to be with him, but was that love? Whatever it was, Honor knew it was wrong. Aside from this being a terrible betrayal of Joy, it was a betrayal of everything she believed herself to be. She had already gravely sinned against God and herself, acted against every good judgement, every decent act her parents had ever taught her. This madness had to end; she would not be the cheap harlot who destroyed a marriage.

Honor untangled herself, grabbed a sheet to cover her body and said, 'Regardless of how you feel, this has been a terrible mistake. Please leave. Now.'

She wouldn't use his name. Hearing her own harsh words, she felt sickened by them, but she looked into his face with such a hardened determination that Frank's resolution wavered.

'I want you to leave, now. Please.'

He shook his head.

'I don't love you. I don't feel the same way. I need to you go home.'

'I know that's not true, Honor, I know this is happening very fast, but I have never felt surer of anything in my life. I know you feel it too. Let's talk this out, let's make a plan...'

She wanted to talk to him, reason things out, but knew that he would just try to persuade her to be with him. For a moment she considered it; then behind him, on the bedside locker, she saw a piece of fabric, a rejected piece of embroidery from The Dress, which her friend had fashioned into a small perfumed pillow. A piece of recreational foolishness that Joy had sewn for her, as a token. Joy had hurriedly presented it to her the night of the party, with no ceremony, simply taking it out of her purse before she thought better of it, saying, 'A small homage, from moi to toi.'

Caught up in the rush of getting ready, Honor had simply flung it on the locker. Now, Joy's husband's naked elbow was almost touching it.

'Get out!' she shouted. 'Now!'

Shocked, Frank reached for his clothes and began getting dressed.

'I'll go, then,' he said. 'This has all been a surprise, I understand that. You're thinking of Joy. You're a good woman, Honor.'

Honor closed her eyes and said, 'Just leave.'

Once dressed, he wavered briefly in front of her, hoping for a kiss, reassurance – the small boy again looking for a shred of hope, a promise of love.

'I'll call you later,' he said. 'We'll sort this out.'

The moment the door closed, Honor did not stop to consider his offer, did not allow herself even the most fleeting moment of regret. She worked through the night, packing up the apartment, then, in the morning, she got dressed and walked across town to Breton's studio.

Her old boss had read about The Dress in the paper; she was the talk of New York. He offered her a generous salary, to work under her own name, out of his studio. The readiness with which he made the offer made Honor realize that this was also a betrayal of Joy. Joy was responsible for Honor's name becoming established overnight. They had talked about opening a couture atelier together. However, she would get over it. She would think Honor was a bitch (she was right about that) and deride her name, but she would keep her husband and Honor knew that was the most important thing. Joy loved Frank, above all else. She would be angry, hurt, upset, but would find some other hobby to amuse herself; she would never find another Frank.

Neither would Honor, but she had her work to fall back on, so she threw herself into it. Breton allowed her to move into a loft room above the atelier where she was quite comfortable and had the solitude to work around the clock.

Within days, word spread and within three months, her slate of clients commissioning elaborate evening dresses meant Breton had to employ six more atelier staff to meet the demand. Honor kept herself too busy to think about anything, other than the job in hand. She was too busy to be happy, too busy to be pleased with herself, too busy to be proud of what she was achieving. Honor stayed still, at the centre of the whirlwind of her own life, not allowing herself the emotional luxury of engaging with the work and money and achievement, lest she be dragged into the potential maelstrom of betrayal and hurt and loss that had brought her here.

Until one day, while she was in the middle of fitting the toile on a wealthy banker's wife, she had to rush to the toilet to be sick. The worried client called in Colette, who finished the fitting and took Honor aside. This was the second time she had vomited like this at work, and she had missed two periods.

'When was the last time you bled?' Colette asked her.

'Seven, maybe eight weeks?' Honor reluctantly admitted.

'I know a woman,' Colette said. 'She's a trained nurse; I'll get you her number.'

Throughout the conversation, neither of them said the word 'pregnant' because that would make it real, and if the situation became real then there would be a choice to be made. The following day Honor locked the office door and telephoned the number Colette had given her. The woman said she had time that very afternoon.

'The quicker we get this done, the better,' she said. 'How far gone are you?'

'I'm not sure,' Honor said, shaking now with the reality of what was happening. There was a baby growing inside her. Frank's baby. Stop. Don't think about it. 'Two, maybe three months?'

'Well, which is it?' the woman said. 'A month can make a big difference, when it comes to dealing with these things. Best get in to me so we can have a look, anyway. Sooner the better – get it over and done with.' Then she gave Honor an address in Brooklyn.

Colette took over her work while Honor gathered up her things, left the studio and headed down towards the subway. She felt shaky and light-headed; she could feel it whispering inside her, this baby. Her mother had only produced one child, Honor. They had waited years and called her 'our miracle'. No more had come after her. Children were supposed to be a gift, not a penance, but this felt like punishment for the terrible thing that she and Frank had done. She had betrayed and she should pay, with the shame and hardship of motherhood out of wedlock, a destroyed career, the lifelong purgatory of being a parent to an unwanted child. Was this any better, though, killing the gift of fertility which God had proffered so meagrely to her mother? Honor had never thought she wanted a child, but then, she had never been particularly desperate for a man, until she met Frank. She did not want this baby, but she did not want to destroy it either. As she stood on the sidewalk, baulking at taking a step closer to her fate by descending the stairs, she felt the bile rise in her stomach again and leaned over onto the road to be sick. There was nothing in her stomach, but as she was retching, a man came and put his arm around her shoulder.

It was Frank.

Honor began crying, with the shame of being sick on the street, the pain in her gullet and the terrible truth of what was happening to her body.

'What are you doing here?' she sobbed.

'I am never far away, Honor. I'm always nearby. I know you want me to keep my distance, but I couldn't leave you like this. We need to get you to a hospital, you're not well, you're...'

Then before she could change her mind, without stopping to consider the consequences, Honor suddenly said, 'I'm pregnant, with your child.'

Twenty-Eight

He left the note on the Eileen Gray side table, where he knew she would find it as soon as she came into the room.

Joy's arms were weighed down with Bloomingdale's bags; she had been out shopping, trying to cheer herself up with ridiculous purchases: stockings, the same pair of wide-bottomed pants in three different colours, make-up, perfume, a ludicrous hat she knew she would never wear. Things had been awful between her and Frank in the few months since the party. Her expectation that he would notice all the effort she'd made with The Dress seemed ludicrous now, in the face of the distance between them. Frank was constantly distracted with work and barely ever at home. When he did come home for meals, he was surly and silent and made sure he came to bed hours after she did, so that she was already asleep.

When Joy had found out about that deceiving bitch, Honor, opening up her own label out of Breton's studio, Frank had offered her no support whatsoever, in fact if anything, he had seemed to withdraw from her even more. Joy felt so alone and depressed that she had started allowing herself one small tipple every afternoon and another before she went to bed. She kept it to just the two; she needed something to keep her going, something to look forward to, to make the dullness of her days more bearable. And her days were dull now. She couldn't face her contemporaries. She couldn't bear to hear about Honor's latest creation from the lips of her new clientele. Joy was still too angry; it was all still too raw. Now that the party and The Dress were behind her, now that Honor was gone, taking her ambitions to open a couture house with her, Joy found she had nothing to do except shop.

She called out for Jones to make her some coffee, then laid down her shopping bags and tore open the small sealed envelope. It was Frank's writing and on his office stationery. Probably telling her he was going away for a few days – again. Too angry with her, for some unnamed reason, to telephone. Still, a handwritten note was better than communicating through his secretary, Nina.

Dear Joy,
I'm in love with Honor and I am leaving you. We are planning to get married. Let's try to make this divorce as quick and painless as we can. My lawyers will be in touch with yours.
Frank

Joy read the note several times, trying to take it in. Her head told her it was a joke, a mistake, but a sharp whisper in her heart feared it might be true. She read the note once, twice, then with her jacket still on and her handbag still crooked in her arm, Joy went through to Frank's dressing room, where she saw that he had, indeed, taken a large suitcase, clothes and some of his shaving gear from the bathroom. In her shock, Joy noticed that he had left his particular brand of shaving cream behind and briefly worried he might get a rash. Remembering he was not simply away on a business trip, she reached behind the toilet rolls in the hidden utilities cabinet, pulled out the medicinal bottle of whisky and took a swig to settle herself.

As Joy stood looking at the gap in her husband's wardrobe, the dominoes started to drop. Frank's late night working, Honor's disappearance after the party – had she gone to meet him in Boston? Had he been to Boston at all? How far back did the affair go? Had Honor been teasing her, with talk of an Irishman? Could she have been audacious and cruel enough to taunt Joy with stories of having designs on her own husband? Did the whole of New York know about this already? Honor had opened her label with Breton within weeks of the party – perhaps this had been her plan all along? To use Joy's goodwill, her resources, her reputation as a stylish woman, to use Joy's money to make a dress that would secure her future then, to hell with it, take the woman's husband as well.

Then again, Joy knew her husband. Frank was not a man easily swayed; he was a man of character. No matter how difficult their marriage had become at times, he had never had an affair; he wasn't the type, she knew that. Frank would have to have strong feelings for another woman to leave his wife.

The bitch was no cheap floozy. She had turned Frank's head somehow. How and when was something she had to find out but, there was no way, Joy thought, necking back more of the whisky as her ire rose, that some jumped-up little Irish tart was going to get the better of her and steal her husband.

Divorce? Joy let out a cruel laugh, there was no way she was giving Frank a divorce. They would ride this out, like they rode out everything. Having Honor's name attached to a

New York so-called couture house was one thing, but taking Joy Fitzpatrick's husband from her was quite another.

Joy went back out to the drawing room phone and rifled through the small bureau for her lawyer's phone number, just as Jones came in with a tray of coffee.

She openly poured a shot of whisky into the cup, before he added coffee.

She picked up the note and waved it at him.

'Did you know about this?' she asked him.

Jones looked at her. 'About what, ma'am?'

'Don't you *ma'am* me, Jones. Did you know Frank was having an affair?'

He shrugged and said, 'It's not for me to say, ma... I mean...'

Jones looked crestfallen, shocked, hurt, but even as Joy formed the idea that it wasn't the butler's fault, the rage pumped through her. Everybody knew; everybody knew except her. Well, she was going to show them. He must have known and may have even helped hide the affair from her. The fact that he hadn't alerted her showed where his loyalty lay.

'If you know where my husband is, Jones,' she said coolly, 'I suggest you go and tell him that I would prefer you to stay in his service for the time being. You can also tell him that I will *not* be granting him a divorce.'

If Jones had had to choose between his two employers, he would have stayed with Joy. She was, for all her instability, a more charming and interesting employer than her husband and she needed him. Jones had guessed at the affair more than known about it. What Frank had done in leaving her this way was deplorable but it was, the weary butler thought, inevitable. Jones wanted to offer Joy some comfort, but he knew, regretfully, his own humble service could not soften this terrible blow. He bowed slightly and said, 'As you wish, ma'am.'

When he had gone, Joy spent a few minutes gathering herself. She would have to quell this rage and she must not drink. If – *when* – Frank came back, he would want her sober. He must not see she was drinking again. Drinking in front of Jones and flying off the handle like that had been a mistake. She had to calm down and be clever if she was going to get her husband back from this scheming bitch. She would explain to Frank that she was upset, naturally, and he would forgive her and everything would be all right.

Joy had one last shot of whisky, to centre herself, then threw the rest down the sink, gargled then swallowed some mouthwash, reapplied her lipstick and rang her lawyer. She told Daniel Cohen's secretary that she did not want or need an appointment, the girl was to simply to tell her boss that Joy Fitzpatrick was on her way in to see him, on a matter of some urgency. The girl said, 'Certainly Mrs Fitzpatrick,' almost as if she had been expecting the call. Did she know too? Of course she did. Everyone in New York knew. Joy put the thought out of her head, got herself out on the street, into a cab and drove the few blocks downtown to the offices of *Brand, Finkleton & Cohen.*

Daniel Cohen, himself, met her at the door and took her upstairs to his office. Daniel was a distinguished man in his fifties, and an old family friend of her father's. He had handled her parents' estate after they died, as well as many of Frank's early business transactions, before his company grew to a size where they needed a bigger, corporate firm. Joy refused coffee and dramatically shook out her chiffon scarf, before sitting down.

'Daniel, I'm afraid to say that some little bitch has got her claws into Frank and he is saying he wants a divorce. The whole thing is ludicrous. I need you to sort this mess out for me.'

Daniel raised his hands and said, 'Joy, before you go on any further, I should tell you that Frank has already engaged the firm on this matter.'

Joy felt her cheeks burn, as she tried to hold her composure. 'Already? I mean, he only left this...'

'Some weeks ago, Joy.'

'*Weeks* ago?'

'He has been talking to me about making divorce arrangements for some time, Joy. I'm sorry, I thought you knew.'

Joy felt sick. She was lost for words.

'No,' she said. 'I didn't know.' She rolled her scarf around her hands then held it up to her face; Chanel No. 5.

What was going on here? What did Daniel mean, he thought she knew? How could she have known? She had to focus, figure this out. She must make Daniel understand that this was all Honor's doing, then once he knew what sort of twisted woman he was dealing with, he would understand and he would advise Frank to leave her and go back to his wife.

'It's this girl, Daniel. She somehow wormed her way into my life, made me commission her to make an outrageously expensive dress so she could meet Frank and then...' As her story gathered steam, Joy began to believe it more and more. This was true, she and Frank has been duped. '...she got herself into Frank's path and, I don't know how, Daniel, because Frank and I are, as you know, devoted to one another, but she's manipulative and somehow, someway, she managed to steal him from me...' It felt good to be talking this way, it felt true, but before she could continue, Daniel cut her off.

'I'm sorry Joy, as I said, I can't really have this conversation with you. Frank engaged me weeks ago. I can find you another lawyer; I assumed you had already got somebody.'

He was stonewalling her. This was worse than she thought. Joy felt humiliated, then decided she had better ask straight out. 'Then why did you let me in, Daniel?' Joy said. 'Why am I sitting here? What does Frank want?'

'Joy,' Daniel said. Was that a trace of pity in his eyes?

'Go on, I'll engage another solicitor, as soon as I leave here, but you might as well tell me. What has the bitch got him to agree to?'

'He wants a quick divorce, so he can marry Honor…'

Joy felt the rage bubble up. 'Jesus, you've *met* her.'

'He brought her in here, yes.'

'So you can see what kind of a woman she is? You know what we are dealing with!'

The kindly old man remembered the ordinary, simply dressed young Irish woman, who had sat in his office two weeks ago, her worried face contorted with guilt, as Frank talked about settlements and assets. Her concern was only for Joy. Had it not been for Frank's promises to protect her from the guilt and shame of her pregnancy, Daniel Cohen wondered if she would have been there at all. It was clear to him that Frank loved this girl to distraction. The seasoned lawyer had seen his fair share of manipulative, scheming women, and this was as far from that as he could imagine. If anything, she was an innocent, who had somehow found herself caught up in the maelstrom of a poisonous marriage. Desperate to escape Joy's drinking, Frank had been to Daniel, looking for advice, well over a year ago. Frank was a good man, but Daniel regretted, now, getting caught up in this mess. Having said that, he was still better off on this side of the fight, rather than trying to reason with Joy. She had tried to cover the smell with perfume and pepper-mints, but he could smell the alcohol on her breath from across the room.

'The woman is deranged, Daniel. You're an intelligent man, you must have seen that. She deliberately set out to destroy my marriage, my reputation, my *life*, because, I don't know, she was jealous of me? The thing is what are we, what are *you* going to do about it?'

'Joy, please,' he said. 'Please don't do this to yourself. I knew your father, your mother; I hate to see you like this.'

Like what? What did he mean? What was the stupid old man talking about?

She observed the pity in his face now; he made no attempt to disguise it. Frank had talked to him about her drinking. He was going to use it against her.

'So,' Joy said gathering up her bag and folding her scarf carefully around her neck, 'as my oldest family friend and solicitor, you are betraying me, along with my husband.'

'Joy, please,' Daniel pleaded, although he did not get up from his chair to stop her from leaving.

'You have not heard the last of this,' Joy said, 'and you tell Frank and his whore that they will have a fight on their hands.' But even as she got into the open elevator of *Brand, Finkleton & Cohen*, then felt it shuddering down towards the lobby, even as she walked out into the harsh sunlight of Midtown, Joy knew that she did not have it in her to fight this.

She asked herself, did they both hate her that much? Had her marriage, her friendships, her dreams, really come to this end? Was it possible that the only two people she had ever really trusted could have betrayed her in this despicable way? Was she so unlovable?

The answer to the final question she could answer with impunity; the answer was yes. Frank didn't love her anymore because she didn't deserve his love; she had never deserved his love. Maybe Honor had played her, but it was no more than she deserved, shallow bitch that she was.

The pain shot through her with a physical intensity, like a stab to the chest.

Joy walked into the first bar she came across, an Irish joint on 4th Street, sat up at the bar and ordered a straight whisky and a chaser to follow.

Two regulars in the corner eyed the nice lady in the lemon suit and wondered what she was doing, drinking alongside them in the middle of the day. Joy noticed them looking but she didn't care anymore.

Twenty-Nine

'I'm pregnant.'

The words Honor had said to Frank, on the street next to the subway that day, had simply fallen out of her mouth. She did not think them through, they seemed thrown by some compulsion beyond her reason, perhaps a desire to save the baby, or herself, from the abortion? For whatever reason, once out, the words could not be unsaid and they set into motion a series of events that Honor had never wanted.

Frank melted, kissed her passionately, then said, 'This is wonderful, *wonderful* news, Honor,' whispering, 'I love you,' into her hair, as he held her close to him, right there on the street.

Honor felt safe and for a moment it seemed as if everything could be all right, even though they had betrayed Joy and now the evidence of that terrible betrayal was growing inside her. As she remembered that, Honor pulled away and said, 'Frank, we need to talk about what to do about this... I'm not sure that I want the baby, that I want all this...'

It was then that she saw Frank suddenly change. The gentle lover disappeared and gave way to the determined businessman she knew he was and yet had never seen before.

It was as if he had not heard her, had not wanted to hear.

'We'll get married at once. Don't worry, Honor, I'll stand by you. This child, our child, will have a proper family; *my* child will be well looked after, you can be sure of that. I have already talked to Cohen about divorce, but now I can get him to rush things through. We'll cite Joy's alcoholism and he knows a man who can help prove infidelity...'

Frank was talking with such manic certainty that there was no room for her own concerns and thoughts. Frank wanted to leave Joy and marry her and the pregnancy was his perfect excuse.

'No,' Honor wanted to say. 'You can't do that to Joy, Frank – *we* can't do this to Joy, it's wrong.' But she didn't.

She didn't say it, partly because she knew he wouldn't listen, but also because it wouldn't make any difference. This was what Frank wanted, *she* was what Frank wanted and men had to get what they wanted, unless a woman was smart enough to manipulate things to go their way which, clearly, Honor was not.

She had fallen for Frank, longed for him, but in the face of her friendship with Joy, she had found the strength and the moral fortitude to let him go. Now he was back and she knew that, in telling him about her pregnancy, she had become utterly powerless over her own destiny. Honor berated herself for her own stupidity, but she did not tell Frank he could not leave Joy, because it was what he wanted and thus was inevitable. In some very small secret part of her, perhaps Honor knew that it was what she wanted, too. Although Honor could not even say for certain that she loved Frank, her desire for him was like a virus. She had fought it, but it was in her bloodstream now and it seemed there was little she could do to rid herself of it.

On that afternoon, as soon as they got into the car, Frank instructed the driver to take them directly over to his lawyer's office, to make his divorce arrangements official.

'I know this is not your problem, Honor, but Daniel is a good man. Once he meets you and sees the predicament we are in, he will pull out all the stops to push this thing through really quickly.'

Honor was desperately uncomfortable, but Frank was taking charge, taking charge of this terrible situation she had found herself in.

They went straight from there to the Plaza, where Frank booked them both into a small suite. The staff knew him, but he put them both in under an assumed married name, Mr and Mrs Jones, and explained they would need the rooms indefinitely.

'We'll live here, until the divorce comes through. Then, after we are married, we can get a proper home,' he promised.

The whole thing was happening with such speed and Frank was so driven, so focused, so powerful in his intention, that Honor felt she had no other choice but to roll along with him. He left her alone in the luxurious hotel bedroom, where she sat, wondering how it was that now, she was here starting a new life with Frank Fitzpatrick, when she had left work that lunchtime, with the intention of going for an illegal abortion.

Frank returned two hours later with a large suitcase.

'It's over,' he said. 'Let's celebrate. Where would you like to go, darling? You just tell me and I'll take you there, we'll hit the town.'

Honor was shocked. It was one thing leaving his wife to be with her but how could he be so cavalier, so callous? It also made her angry that he imagined she would want to go out and celebrate at such a time.

'How is Joy?' she asked.

He shrugged, so she asked again. 'Joy? How did she take the news? Was she very upset?'

She knew it was a stupid question, of course Joy was upset, but she wanted to hear Frank say it, for him to face up to what they were doing.

'Tell me, Frank, I want to know what happened.'

Frank's face hardened. 'It doesn't matter,' he said. 'She doesn't matter.'

'You can't say that Frank, she's your wife.'

Frank's jaw set and his eyes, always so soft, turned steely grey. He looked at her with a coldness that made her actually shiver.

'Drop it, Honor.'

But she persisted. 'Joy has been very good to me, Frank, I feel terrible about hurting her this way. If we are going to be together, we have to do what's right for Joy too.'

As she was talking, she noticed a change come over Frank again. His whole body stiffened, his mouth hardened and his large hands curled into fists by his side.

'Don't mention that woman's name to me, ever again.'

Honor was about to reason with him, but as she opened her mouth, he said again, through gritted teeth, his body solid with rage, 'I mean it, Honor, don't push this.'

In that moment, Honor realized she was afraid of Frank. She had actually agreed to nothing he had asked of her that day; the trip to the lawyers, to arrange his divorce, his intention to marry her, even having the baby, and yet she had gone along with him, acquiesced in everything he wanted.

For a fleeting moment Honor thought it was not just Frank's certainty, or her powerful feelings for him, that frightened her, perhaps it was Frank himself that she was afraid of. In the past few hours, somehow, Honor, who had always stubbornly ploughed her own furrow, had handed her life over to this man.

Yet, she thought, perhaps this was the way things were supposed to be. She did not know of any woman who would not jump at the chance to be with a man as handsome and powerful as Frank Fitzpatrick, to be taken under his wing. Frank wanted her and she felt, if not compelled, well then, at least obliged, to give him what he wanted. After all, wasn't that what love was?

Her mother had always done what her father wanted and they were happy. Honor had thought she was happy on her own, but things were different now. She was in love and being in love meant putting your own thoughts and needs aside for the other person, so that's what she did for Frank.

Over the next couple of months, as Honor struggled to hide her expanding waistline at work, and continued to feel sick and weak with her pregnancy, Frank took over every aspect of her life.

When she expressed worry about taking time off work, Frank smoothed things over with Breton. He even agreed to invest in the Frenchman's business and the two men conspired to buy a small shop unit, next door to Breton's atelier where, once the marriage was sealed and made public, they could open as a place to sell the 'Honor Fitzpatrick' line of ready-to-wear clothes. All of this was presented to Honor as a fait accompli.

She would have preferred to plan all of this herself, but she felt too wretched to do anything, except the minimum amount of designing and some overseeing, while Colette took over her clients. Honor just counted herself lucky that she was marrying a man who would allow her to work, after they were married.

'I just want you to be happy,' he kept saying. 'What makes you happy, makes me happy.'

So Honor put all that she had known in her life aside, and hoped that the man who was to be her husband knew best.

Thirty

 *London, 2014*

'How much does Sally know about your dress?'

'Nothing, not much, a bit. Oh, I don't know, Jack, but I know Sally. She won't do anything bad.'

Lily didn't quite know why she was defending Sally to Jack. Shock, perhaps. She just could not believe that Sally would betray her like this. Perhaps there was some mistake?

'She already has, Lily.' Jack's voice was shaking with fury. 'Did you know she was talking to Durane about a job there?'

'Well, yes, I mean, no. She was talking to them a while ago I think.'

'Oh, Jesus Christ, Lily...'

'She turned him down. Are you suggesting this is *my* fault?'

'Of course not, it's just a real problem. I think they poached her just for the dress project.'

'Actually, I remember her saying they approached her about a job ages ago, Jack.'

'Really?' Lily thought he sounded hurt.

There was silence on the other end of the phone, then when Jack spoke again he sounded distant, business-like. 'I suppose you're right, there's no reason I should expect any loyalty, from either of you.'

'I didn't mean that Jack, I just meant that she wouldn't do anything to jeopardize this project. She's too professional.'

'I hope you're right,' Jack said. 'Anyway, I've a meeting now. We'll talk later, maybe have a progress report. Over dinner?'

'That would be great,' Lily said.

As soon as they hung up Lily tried calling Sally but her phone went straight to voicemail. Lily knew that Sally always had her phone on. She was blocking her calls. It was at that point that Lily herself became furious. What the hell was Sally thinking? She had always been ambitious, but *this*, betraying her boss and her best friend in one swoop? How could she do such a thing? How could her oldest friend turn on her like this? This was so bad that Lily wondered if she knew who Sally was anymore. The idea of that scared her more than anything. Sally was her rock, her oldest – her best – friend. It was too unsettling to think she could hurt Lily in this way.

Sick at the thought of what was happening, Lily decided to throw herself into the huge pile of work she had in front of her. There was a mountain of research still to do and hundreds of calls to make which was nothing if not a good distraction.

First on the list was getting hold of some vintage Irish lace. No matter how much money you had, good lace, the kind of lace she needed, was highly specialized and would take months to make from scratch. So, after much mooching around online Lily found a dealer with some beautiful old Irish lace working out of Westport in County Mayo. She booked herself a return flight (on her new Scott's credit card) for the following morning and spent ages looking for a nice, mid-range hotel. She picked one that was not too expensive but had a spa.

Lily tried Sally again. No reply. The thought crossed her mind that perhaps Sally was jealous of the friendship she had seen building between Jack and herself in Miami. Was it possible that Sally didn't want to see her friend succeed? That after all her nagging and concern for Lily 'wasting her talent' she was now put out that Lily seemed to be muscling in on her client?

Lily and The Dress were moving into a room that Jack's secretary had set up in Scott's London design studio for her the following week, so she kept herself busy with the task of reorganizing her apartment. As she packed away all her sewing things, ready for the moving van to collect on Monday morning, she kept thinking how Sally should be there, helping her.

When that was done, Lily got all dressed up ready for dinner with Jack. She showered, shaved and body creamed, blow-dried her hair and applied her make-up. Then she picked out a black silk 60s shift dress and strappy sandals ensemble that would look equally appropriate in a local Indian restaurant or West End high spot.

By 7 p.m. Jack still hadn't called so she rang him.

'Oh God, Lily, I am so sorry, I have a conference call with New York that I had completely forgotten about. Then there are two suppliers coming into town from China that I have to take out. I am so sorry; we'll do it tomorrow, yeah?'

'Can't do tomorrow,' she said, holding her voice breezy. 'I'm off to Ireland to buy some lace. I'm staying over in Westport, sounds like a nice place actually...'

'Ireland's great,' he said. 'You'll love it...' He sounded distracted already. 'Look, sorry, I have to go. Call when you get back, yeah?'

'Yeah,' she said. 'See you.'

After he hung up Lily got undressed and put her pyjamas on. With her day's work done and nothing left to do, she felt completely flat and a little sorry for herself. She had been abandoned by her oldest friend *and* her new boss, it seemed. This was the time when she would have wandered over to her family home. Grandad Joe would have cheered her up and her parents would have made a fuss of her. Now her parents were grieving and her grandad was dead.

She stuck on a pair of headphones and watched *Singin' in the Rain* on her iPad; old movies always cheered her up. When it was finished she was up getting herself tea when she heard the doorbell ring.

It was nearly ten o'clock, so she threw her head out the window and saw Gareth's friend Fergus at the door.

'Gareth asked me to drop this off,' he said, putting a package on the doorstep, before running off, obviously relieved she hadn't answered the door to him. If Gareth could be a bit awkward at times, his uber-nerd friend was the kind of guy who disintegrated as soon as a woman spoke to him. Lily felt disappointed that Gareth had not come himself. With all this nasty business with Sally, his comforting presence was just what she needed right now.

The package was about the size of a hatbox and as Lily carried it upstairs she was so curious that she started to peel off the brown paper and string immediately.

It was indeed an old hatbox, and inside that was a load of tissue paper, inside which was a beautifully preserved, 1950s couture corset.

She nearly cried. It was a perfect pale flesh colour with a clean, satin finish. This would save her making a bodice from scratch and thus, weeks of work. She could easily use this single vintage piece as a framework to build the rest of

The Dress around. It was exquisite and must have cost him a fortune. She looked for a note, but couldn't find one. Typical, laid back Gareth. So she called him. His phone went straight to voicemail. She thought about putting a coat on over her pyjamas and running up to thank him in person but then realized the shop would be closed and in any case he must be busy, otherwise he would have brought it himself.

She would call by and thank him in person as soon as she got back.

The Dress may have robbed her of a friend that day but it had also sent her a magnificent building block for its foundation.

The following morning Lily woke at the crack of dawn feeling excited. She was going to Ireland!

This was, she realized, the first time she had ever travelled by herself. Either Sally or her parents had always been with her before. New Lily had a sense of grown-up independence as she arrived at Luton airport by taxi. While she was getting a coffee in Pret A Manger she got a FaceTime call from Zac.

'OK, here it is,' he said without making any intro. 'You are not going to *believe* this. Honor Conlon made The Dress with my Granny then disappeared without a trace. But get this – in 1959 a new designer called Honor turns up working out of The House of Breton couturiers, except she's called Honor *Fitzpatrick*.'

Lily gasped. 'Oh my God, is it the same person?'

Zac closed his eyes, paused for dramatic effect then screamed, 'Yes! We weren't sure – like, how mad would that be? But *then* my friend had a deep, *deep* dig, we are talking ancient books of newspaper cuttings – did you know there is this stuff from *before* computers called microfilm? Anyway, she found an article from *Harper's Bazaar* citing Honor Fitzpatrick as the second wife of Irish tycoon Frank Fitzpatrick! I got her to scan it – I'll email it across.'

Lily was stunned. Her face moved away from the screen and across the airport concourse. People were drinking coffee, looking up at screens, running towards departure gates, clinging to their baggage and Zac had found another Irish relative she didn't know about. Honor Conlon was also her great-aunt by marriage.

'Is she still alive?' Lily knew it was a stupid question but it was the only one on her mind.

'There's a few designs featured in *Harper's*, kind of a cool dress and day-coat combo, so she must have made a name for herself, but then absolutely nothing about her at all after 1959. I don't know,' Zac added. 'Maybe she died… or retired?'

'She would have been too young to retire, or maybe…'

Or maybe she found it all too hard and just gave up, Lily thought. Realizing this about Honor made Lily determined that she was not going to give up this time.

Lily's gate came up on the screen, so she thanked Zac and said she would keep him posted if she tracked Honor down. She thought about Jack's offer of a private investigator, but decided it should be family alone looking for her.

While waiting at her gate she searched Facebook and Twitter. Although it was unlikely a woman in her seventies, her eighties even, might be searching social media, maybe she had grandchildren or great-grandchildren with the same name? Lily found four Honor Fitzpatricks in the US – all young, none in New York, but she messaged them anyway. She would check the death records for that period on the family archive website when she got back tomorrow and if that didn't turn up anything, she would have to let it go. Although she felt she should keep trying to find The Dress's co-creator and her great-aunt by marriage, Lily knew that she had to manage her expectations. If Honor were still alive, it would probably mean checking every single retirement home in New York State, and there wasn't enough time for that. She put out another tweet: *Urgently seeking #HonorFitzpatrick #50sDesigner #TheDress*. But even assuming it went viral, if Honor had stopped designing in 1959, it was unlikely anyone who might have known her was still alive.

It was raining at Knock, and even though they were only an hour west of London it was noticeably cooler. As she descended the steps of the plane Lily felt as if she was in a different world. The Ryanair plane had landed in what seemed to her like a wasteland of bog stretching on for miles. It didn't feel like summer and the landscape did not have the green hilly charm of the Irish countryside she had seen from television programs and films. Lily picked up the keys at the Avis desk and went to find her rental car.

She thought of trying to ring Sally again. It was an automatic thing. This was the first time in all the years they had been friends that the two women had let a day pass without speaking. As girls they had been at school then college together, running up their parents' landline bills in the evenings, and as adults they spoke once, sometimes twice every day. Lily felt hurt that Sally was not there to share her adventure. She was on her own; this was her journey, her escapade into unknown territory. It was weird being completely alone but, as she walked through the wet, packed car park into the car hire lot, a feeling of freedom swept over her. Lily suddenly had the urge to switch her phone, not to silent, but completely *off* and as she pressed the button and blanked the screen her feeling of excitement bordered on elation. She was beyond the reach of anyone – of her friends and family, the world of Twitter, Facebook, her work, of every expectation, every judgement anyone had ever made of her, including, especially, every expectation she had of herself. Lily could do what she liked; nobody was watching her. She found the Nissan Micra, settled herself inside and smelt that unique scent of freshly cleaned hire car. For the next twenty-four hours this was her vehicle and Ireland was her domain; she was like Thelma and Louise – but without Thelma (or Louise). Who knew what she might find out about herself? As she was setting the car's sat nav to the address of the lace dealer in Westport, Lily had a crazy idea.

Bangor, County Mayo, she tapped in and off she set in search of her great-Uncle Frank.

Thirty-One

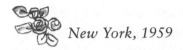 *New York, 1959*

After Frank left, Joy drank as if she had nothing to lose.

Jones gone, she sat in the apartment and ploughed through bottles of wine and whisky and listed her misfortunes.

Frank, the love of her life had left her. She had no husband and a woman with no husband was worthless. She was thirty, which meant she was too old to find another one and even if she weren't, Frank had spread a vicious rumour around town that she had a drink problem (the very idea!), so her reputation was in tatters, anyway.

Honor, a woman she had thought was a friend, had betrayed her and made a mockery of her name. Joy had no present and no future: drink was her only friend, now.

Hours passed, days passed, weeks, with Joy locked in her apartment. Even though she was ten floors up, she kept the drapes shut lest God Himself might look in the window and see the state of her. When she ran out of drink, she put on her long cashmere wrap coat, sunglasses and a headscarf and ran to the liquor store on 32nd and 3rd. Night and day ran into each other and Joy never knew if it would be midday, or midnight when she needed to scuttle past the doorman. Coming down in the lift, she would briefly hope he would not recognize her and pretend to herself that he couldn't know where she was going and why. Apart from the doorman, the man in the liquor store was the only person Joy saw for weeks. She was the richest looking drunk the man had even seen, but he'd been doing the late shift, selling liquor to truculent bums, for long enough to sense trouble, and he could tell she had enough in her to flare up, just by the way she walked in through the door.

'I am having a dinner party,' she said, the first few times, when she loaded up her basket with enough spirits to fuel a battleship, and one or two mixers, just to look polite. The man remained silent, never sarcastically saying what was on his mind. Another dinner party? So soon? After the third or fourth trip, Joy stopped making excuses, loaded up quickly and stayed grateful for his taciturnity and the speed with which he bagged the bottles and checked her out.

Aside from these trips, Joy's life became nothing but a routine of drinking, smoking and sleep. Sometimes she would wake up, her tongue furry, her head hurting and a gnawing pain in her stomach from not having eaten anything for days. Feeling wretched, she would be determined not to drink, to try and put some sort of shape back into her life.

One morning, she decided to stay sober long enough to call Frank's office. If only she could get through to him properly this time, reason with him, she was sure she could persuade him to come back. She had learned her lesson. He had been right, she was a drunk – but if he came back, all this could come to an end. With his help she could stop, but she needed him to be there. She would forgive him for running off with Honor. They were still married. They could make it work again.

Frank's new secretary said she would get him to call right

back. Joy paced the apartment, willing the phone to ring. If Frank called back, everything could go back to how it had been before. If only she had a friend to talk all this through with. Where were all her friends when she needed them? She remembered how that scheming bitch Honor had monopolized and manipulated her social life, so that old friends had been cut out of the picture; part of her vicious plan to set up her own couture business and steal her husband away. One hour passed, then two, and Joy became incensed that Frank was not calling her back. Her hands were shaking now, badly, she could feel the sweat building on her face, on the back of her neck, on her shivering palms. She could feel the panic rising, so she had a drink, just one, two – three to calm her nerves. Three. Three was enough to stop the shakes and the sweats, and then she'd be well enough to talk to Frank. She picked up the phone and, when the secretary asked who it was, she lost her temper and screamed at the woman to get Frank on the line, immediately. When the woman, with her snooty little English accent, said Frank was still in a meeting, Joy hurled a torrent of abuse at her. She slammed down the phone and drank until she passed out.

When she woke up again, vaguely remembering what she had done, Joy was flooded with the most crippling shame. How had she allowed herself to turn into such a wretched creature? Why did she do these terrible things? So she drank to make the pain go away – and when the pain went away, so did her inhibitions. She rang Frank's office all the time after that, as well as the offices of *Brand, Finkleton & Cohen*. It happened so often, over those few weeks, that the secretaries themselves grew used to it and knew not to hang up, but simply transferred her to an empty line, so she didn't jam the switchboard. Frank's office appointed a switchboard operator on a dedicated line, specifically to deal with his crazy wife.

Breton himself spoke with her, when she rang his salon, looking for Honor. Firstly, because the last thing his precious, pregnant designer needed was this type of abuse, whereas being French and artistic and a man, he was better able to handle it. Secondly, while he had some small sympathy for her, seeing such an elegant woman fall so low, he also could not quite help a slight flicker of schadenfreude after the way Joy Fitzpatrick had looked down her nose at him over the years.

Breton's attitude was echoed by New York society as a whole. Joy had fallen apart since Frank left, but the word was that she had been falling asunder long before that. Nobody called, nobody cared. Joy knew this and it just made her drink even more.

Joy thought she had lost everything, so she drank as if she had nothing left to lose. Except there was one more thing.

Her money.

After Joy had worked through the cash that Frank always kept in the house, for bills and the like, she started to get dressed up, to withdraw money from the bank. This necessity felt like a progress of sorts, to Joy. She needed a few drinks to steady herself, but the mere experience of making herself look respectable made her feel human, for a few hours at least. Withdrawing money from her own bank account, Joy would then buy drink, and perhaps a few groceries, then go back to the apartment.

One day, the bank teller looked up and said, 'I am sorry, Mrs Fitzpatrick, but there is no money in your account.'

The note of apology in her voice was so gentle that Joy did not make a fuss. She tried Frank's account, to which she had always enjoyed access but, unsurprisingly, it was closed to her.

She went to the liquor store and filled her basket, then, at the till, pretended that she had left her purse at home. She asked the store-manager for a line in credit and as he stood looking at the pride in her pursed lips, he tried to see the eyes behind her dark glasses. In the end he decided to give it to her. She might prove to be the best customer he ever had, but if she didn't pay her bill, at least he now knew who she was and where to find her.

When Joy got back to the apartment, she went straight into her closet to look for The Dress. She could cash in the jewels and get her fortune back. Perhaps then everything would start to fall back into place for her. The Dress had marked the beginning of her life falling apart; if she took it apart, things might return to normal – the spell might be broken.

But it wasn't in her closet. She ran over to Frank's closet, thinking that maybe Jones had moved it there, by mistake, and it was then that she saw her husband's closet was completely empty. Somebody had been into the apartment and taken things out. Who? When? Had they been robbed?

Shaking, she ran to the phone and called Frank's office. Before the girl put her on hold she managed to say, 'Tell Frank we've been robbed, my dress is gone.'

Half an hour later Jones, the butler, was at her door.

Joy was puzzled, but pleased to see him, nonetheless. She hastily looked around at the empty bottles and general mayhem and remembered the place had never been like this when Jones was living here, no matter how tardy her housekeepers might have been. Frank must have sent him around to help sort out the apartment and make sense of this mess with the money. He still cared about her; Frank must still care about her, if he had sent Jones to see that she was all right.

'The place is a bit of a mess,' she said apologetically, leading him in. 'You know I was never one for cleaning up.'

Jones, who had thought himself unshakable, was appalled at the scene of filthy squalor in front of him. Empty bottles everywhere, overflowing ashtrays, cigarettes stubbed out on the wool carpet, half-eaten containers of food that had been left open for days, weeks maybe. The place stank; there were surely rodents in here. Joy's long hair was matted into a lump on her head, as if she had not washed it for weeks, and she was skin and bone. She smiled at him and his heart broke.

'I would offer you coffee,' she said, 'but I don't know that I have any milk...'

The words trailed away as, suddenly, in his face, she saw what he saw. Living like this, she had been so focused on getting the next drink, making the pain go away, she had not noticed the mess; Joy's mess was always cleared up by somebody else.

She shouldn't have let him in, she now realized, until she had tidied up. But now he was in all she could do was mumble, 'Again, sorry about the mess.'

'Shall we sit down?' Jones said, his face inscrutable, picking his way across the floor as if the bottles weren't there and cleaning off a space on the stained Eames chaise.

Joy made a face, but humoured him and went and sat on the edge of the coffee table, hunched up, tense – she lit a cigarette and, to hell with it, rummaged around on the floor for an empty glass to fill with gin. She wouldn't drink out of a bottle in front of the butler; she wasn't a common drunk.

'I am sorry to tell you,' Jones said, 'that the rental and other bills have not been paid on the apartment for three months.'

What was he saying? This didn't make any sense? The bills just – got paid. This was ridiculous.

THE DRESS

'Mr Fitzpatrick sent me ahead of the bailiffs. He said he would pay them off and provide you with an additional monthly income if you were willing to move into a smaller apartment, somewhere more suitable to your needs.'

Joy closed her eyes. Move? From here? Focus. She needed to get some money. She needed to get her dress back.

'Where's my dress, Jones? I need my dress.'

She gathered her dressing gown over her bony shoulders. She looked desperate. Whatever depths she had sunk to of late, Jones still considered Joy Fitzpatrick to be a lady. She was born to it. That sort of breeding can never entirely leave you. He coughed an apology and said, 'I'm sorry, ma'am, but your husband instructed me to remove it from the apartment some weeks ago, when I came to pack away his things.'

'He sent you to come sneaking about the apartment when I wasn't here? Anyway, what did he want with my dress?'

For one glorious moment, Joy imagined Frank had taken it as a memento of her, that finally he had come to understand that The Dress was a testament of her love for him.

'He said it was the property of Miss Conlon. You were asleep on the settee, at the time. I did not trouble to wake you.'

Joy was speechless with hurt and shame. Stronger than that though was the knowledge that she needed the money embroidered in that garment; needed it to buy drink.

'I want that dress back, Jones, it is encrusted with my family jewels.'

She could tell that he did not believe her.

'You'll have to take that up with Mr Fitzpatrick, I'm afraid.'

The scheming bitch, Honor, had her husband and her fortune, now. The dressmaker had pretended she had not known the jewels were real, but she must have had them valued. Honor had won. Without The Dress and its jewels,

Joy had no income. Frank was obviously freezing her out until she agreed to give him a divorce. She could fight him, but she had no lawyer, and nothing to pay a lawyer and, in that moment, no heart and no energy for a fight.

'Jones, would you please go and tell Mr Fitzpatrick that I will give him whatever he wants.' Jones closed his eyes and nodded, and as he stood up she added, 'I have no lawyer, at present Jones. So would it be possible for you to come back and present Frank's proposal to me yourself?'

She could not even lift herself up from the sofa to see him out. Jones eyes filled up.

'I won't say it will be a pleasure, ma'am, but it will, as ever, be my honour to serve you.'

Frank was not in a generous mood when his butler relayed his conversation with Joy. She was bluffing, he was sure, and had her own fortune hidden away. However, he needed the divorce to go through quickly. He was surprised when Jones engaged him in a polite, but nonetheless firm negotiation, after which he agreed to give Joy a modest, liveable income, in exchange for her agreeing to sign the papers immediately.

Jones returned the following week to find Joy in an even worse state than the one he left her in. She was shaking so badly that he had to hold her hand steady while she signed the papers. In them she agreed to move from Fifth Avenue into an apartment in one of Frank's brownstones and live on a modest monthly income. It would be enough to keep her in drink, cigarettes and food and would cover the rent for the apartment, including utility bills.

Jones took a week's annual holiday, during which he secretly packed up all of Joy's things. While his mistress lay virtually unconscious, paralyzed with drink and grief, on her beloved Eames settee, Jones took all her personal belongings and moved his mistress into her new home – a small, but clean apartment in Midtown, or 'Social Siberia' as she would have called it in her heyday.

He left her sitting at a Formica-topped table with a bottle of whisky in front of her. It was all he could do to stop himself from staying there and looking after her, forever.

Thirty-Two

The day Frank Fitzpatrick married Honor Conlon was the happiest day of his life.

He flew her parents, John and Claire, over from Ireland and put them up in a suite at the Plaza a few days beforehand. Frank felt good that he had brought the family together and was thrilled by the look of sheer joy on Honor's face at being reunited with her parents.

She had been continually anxious, during the pregnancy, even though he had done everything in his power to reassure her that once they were married everything would fall into place. Honor was unhappy – about the pregnancy, about their betrayal of Joy – there was no getting away from it.

Frank knew Honor had no interest in money; it was one of the things that he loved about her. She had no desire for trinkets, or fancy furniture, or showing herself off around town in couture clothes. However, there were other ways in which money could buy happiness, and flying her parents in from Ireland, for the wedding, was one of them.

Honor had not wanted her parents to know about Frank, and she had told him that.

'This has been such a shock,' she said. 'I need time to think about all of this.'

Frank knew better. There was nothing to think about. It wasn't ideal that she was pregnant before they got married, but at least it had pushed things forward, to their inevitable end. Frank had become a success in life by seizing opportunities, by pushing things through. Honor was talented, creative, and ambitious and Frank admired all those things but, at the end of the day, she was a woman and women liked to sit around and ponder life. Men made things happen.

So, without consulting Honor, Frank had contacted John and Clare Conlon and told them of their plight. He and Honor were in love. He was divorced and she was pregnant, so it wasn't ideal. However, he loved their daughter very, very much. He was from Bangor himself; they might remember him as Francis Fitzpatrick. He had made good on his ambitions in America and was now a man of substantial means. He would welcome the opportunity to make good on his past behaviour towards their family and it was his intention to look after their daughter and grandchild, in great style. He had not told Honor about his plans, because of her delicate condition. The doctors were concerned, lest as an older first-time mother at almost twenty-five, she be caused undue stress.

'It would be a pleasant surprise,' he told the Conlons, 'for her to see you.' Then he thought and added, 'As it will also be a pleasure for me to pay you back, for the kindness you showed me as a boy.'

He enclosed tickets and details of how they could contact his secretary, who would iron out any problems. A week later he got a short acceptance note, cursory and impersonal but then, Frank reasoned, it was a lot to take in.

He only told Honor on the morning they were due to arrive and although she was furious at first, by the time they got into the car, she was excited by the thought of seeing them.

Frank knew then that he had been right to take control.

The Conlons looked older than he had remembered, and smaller. Frank felt an old familiar love, as he saw the bearded schoolteacher in his shabby corduroy jacket and his wife, in her simple woollen coat, come through the arrival gate. On seeing Honor, they both rushed immediately to greet her, with tearful embraces.

Frank was disappointed that John greeted him with no more than a handshake and a formal thanks, and even Clare, although she made more of an effort to smile at him, seemed aloof. He reasoned that they were obviously still in shock. After all, their only daughter had become pregnant by a married man and, even though he had left his wife to be with her, he was still a divorcee – a sinner. In time, they would surely come to understand the terrible suffering he had endured in his marriage and the deep gratitude he felt for their daughter in saving him. They would come to accept him as a son.

The wedding itself was to be small, no fuss – that was what Honor wanted. While Frank was ready to shout their love from the rooftops and to hell with the pre-emptive pregnancy and Joy, he didn't really care how they got married, as long as this woman pledged to spend the rest of her life with him.

The only guests, aside from the Conlons, were Breton, Colette and Frank's secretary, Nina, whom Frank had leaned on heavily during the last few months. Nina ran the office, kept Joy off the switchboard and even made sure that Honor went to her doctor's appointments.

'Frank loves you,' she kept saying to Honor. 'He wants to look after you.'

Honor heard a tone of reassurance in her voice. Nina probably knew Frank better than anyone else, and understood too, perhaps, that he could be controlling sometimes.

'He just wants what's best,' she said to Honor. 'Go with it, he's a good man. You're lucky.'

'I know,' Honor always said. 'I love him very much.'

Nina wondered, sometimes, from the way Honor looked at her, if that could really be true. There had been so much hurt, so much pain and confusion, so much drama around their meeting. Nina knew Honor was no gold-digger but at the same time, she didn't seem like Frank's type. Her boss liked to be in control and Nina could tell that Honor, although she seemed mild-mannered, was a career woman, which had to mean she was feisty. Joy had a mouth on her and she liked to drink, but she was always compliant with Frank's wishes. Joy was a trophy wife and Frank liked his trophies. Honor was the opposite of that and Nina, who was fond of Frank, worried sometimes, about how it might all pan out with this rushed second marriage.

They got married in City Hall. Honor wore a simple cream dress which Colette had run up for her a few days beforehand, and carried a specially commissioned bouquet of Irish wildflowers, that it had taken Nina half a working day to source from the best florist in New York, on Frank's instructions. Frank wore his collar open and a corsage of cornflowers, a plant he himself remembered, from growing up in the bogs of Bangor Erris, Mayo.

John and Clare Conlon did not notice or appreciate these touches, designed to impress them, but remained somewhat distant towards him, even after the register was signed and they were back at the Plaza for their wedding lunch.

Honor, however, was overjoyed her parents were there

and, as they were seated at their table in the Palm Lounge, she took Frank's hand under the table and whispered, 'Thank you,' to him.

Breton and Colette were charmed by the Irish guests and sat between John and Clare, flirting with them.

'I can see where sweet Honor gets her pale, exotic beauty from,' Breton murmured to plain-faced Clare.

'But my own father was a schoolteacher, in Provence,' said Colette, coquettishly, to a delighted John.

Meanwhile, Nina was ordering champagne from their waiter, making sure he understood that, although their wedding party was small and being held as a low key affair, in the public restaurant, their host, Frank Fitzpatrick, was nonetheless a hugely important man.

'So, Frank, you married your whore!'

Frank nearly jumped out of his skin. It was Joy.

'Surprise! Hey, Honor, sorry I didn't *formally* reply to the invite...'

Frank stood up suddenly, knocking over a glass of water, but Nina held his arm, reminding him not to act hastily.

'Glad to see you're not getting married in the dress that you stole from me.'

Clare Conlon flinched and reached over to her daughter, who was crying out, 'Joy, please, I'm sorry...'

'Ah, she's sorry,' she said, her voice a hiss of sarcasm, 'but not too sorry to steal my husband and my *fucking fortune, you whore!*'

Nina had to run to get the waiter and two large doormen who easily lifted Joy up and removed her, still spitting, cat-like, from the room.

Clare moved to sit next to her distraught, weeping daughter, while Frank followed the doormen and Joy out, his back stiff with rage. He returned a few moments later and apologized, with the kind of formality that implied he would never, ever recover from the humiliation he had just experienced. He could not even look at John Conlon. Well, at least his in-laws now knew what sort of a woman he had left for their daughter. In fact, he thought, while Joy had done her best to ruin their day, perhaps she had done him a favour, in showing his new family what a dreadful woman he had been married to. Maybe they would have more sympathy, now, for his loving of their daughter.

'What is an Irish wedding without drunkenness?' said Breton, lightening the mood.

'Joy always was a bit of a handful,' said Colette, to John Conlon, and then, 'So how do you celebrate weddings in Ireland?'

'Actually, by getting extremely drunk,' said John.

'Speaking of which,' Nina announced, 'here comes the champagne!'

They drank and laughed for the rest of the afternoon. Honor was shaken but after lobster, a large steak and plenty of champagne, she felt encouraged to put Joy's outburst aside. Having her parents there, Frank saw that his new wife seemed as happy as she had been the fateful first night, when they had met in Frank's redstone.

They were staying in a suite at the Plaza, until Frank found a new home, one suitable for all three of them. They made gentle, careful love, then, while Honor was sleeping, Frank stood and looked out over the city. He lit a cigar and thought how, despite everything, this, indeed, had been the happiest day of his life so far. His life had come full circle. At last he could look back, without fear, on his past, on his childhood, knowing that life had dealt him this strange second chance, by putting him in touch with the Conlons. Honor was his saviour and the giver of this new life, his legacy. His boyhood dreams of being part of a strong, stable family were finally coming to fruition and nothing was more important than that.

When he had smoked his Cohiba, Frank returned to the bedroom, planning to look at his new wife while she was sleeping, when he saw that the bathroom door was open and the light on. He moved towards it, hearing a strange muffled noise.

'Honor,' he called out.

When he opened the door, he saw his new wife lying on the bathroom floor, crying softly, her white silk robe covered in the sticky scarlet carnage of her own blood.

'You rest now, Mrs Fitzpatrick,' were the last words Honor had heard, as her new husband softly stroked her face.

She had been very shaken up by Joy's appearance at the wedding lunch, but gradually, with the help of her parents' reassurance and Frank's kindness, she had shaken off the terrible feelings of guilt and pain that contact with Joy brought up in her. She fell asleep, with the soft happy feeling that things were as they should be. A short while later, she woke, with a terrible pain searing through her abdomen, something pressing against her bowel, and she ran to the bathroom, all the time fearing, knowing, praying for it not to be...

'Dear God,' she said, 'dear God, don't let this happen – don't take my baby.'

The baby she had not known she had wanted, the baby that she had been going to get rid of, before Frank came along and rescued them both, was suddenly a reality. Until this point, six months into her pregnancy, she had still not considered the life growing inside her as any more than a catastrophic event, one that had pushed her and Frank into a shotgun marriage.

Now, as she could feel her own body scrabbling to release this tiny life, Honor realized that she wanted the baby more than anything, 'Please God, I'm sorry, I'm sorry for all I have done,' she pleaded. 'Don't do this...'

She ran to the toilet, but slipped on her own blood. As Honor collapsed on the floor, she felt the baby's head press against her cervix and her body push into the pain, until the foetus released itself, sliding on the end of the cord, across the polished tile. She cried out then reached down and gathered the tiny, bloody body up into her hands; it was a girl. The baby gave two short breaths, and then died. Honor cried out then and held it to her chest, enveloping it into the folds of her nightgown. When Frank came in and found her, Honor was in a sobbing heap on the floor, writhing and rocking in a pool of her own blood.

Frank roared, 'What happened? Honor, Jesus...' He moved towards her, then seeing the bloodied lump in her hands, he got frightened and ran from the room, to get help.

He returned, moments later, with a Plaza housekeeper, whom he had flagged down in the corridor. The older woman took a scissors from her apron, cut Honor's cord, then wrestled the dead baby from her sobbing clutches, to dispose of it. As she did so, Frank tore a sheet from the hotel bed. He gathered Honor her up in his arms and carried her himself, in the lift downstairs, to the waiting ambulance, holding her firmly, keeping her body steady, while she cried out, 'My baby, my baby, give me back my baby.'

The hospital staff were nice. Honor was given a sedative, cleaned up, fed tea and biscuits and told to go home and rest.

'Try again,' the doctor said to Frank, 'in a week or so, as soon as you can. She'll recover quickly from this, the female body is very strong.'

Over the following few weeks, Frank was kind and resolutely cheerful. He did not pressure Honor to try for another baby straight away.

'There's time,' he said. 'We're married now. We have all the time in the world.'

He moved his new wife back into the Fitzpatrick apartment on Fifth and Jones made the place perfect for her. Although he had eliminated all evidence of Joy from every room, Honor knew from the impeccably chosen furniture, the French imported Jean Prouvé pieces about which her friend had boasted so often, that she was a cuckoo in this nest. The child that had been conceived, through her callous passion for Joy's husband, had been taken from her and now Honor had to live with the guilt every day, living in the home of the woman whose husband she had stolen.

She went back to work, but her heart was not in design anymore. In truth, Honor could not find her heart; she seemed to have lost all feeling for Frank, even for her parents; she was numb. It was as though all the love in her had been disposed of, along with her dead child. Swept away into a hotel incinerator, like garbage.

Honor had no ill feeling towards the hotel worker who had wrenched the dead baby from her arms. It was as much as she deserved, after all the bad things she had done.

Thirty-Three

Joy knew that gate-crashing Frank and Honor's wedding had been a mistake – a horrible, humiliating mistake.

The doormen from the Plaza had thrown her to the ground harder than they needed to. As she fell on the sidewalk, Joy saw that Frank had followed them out; he stood over her with a look of such cold, cruel fury on his face that he did not even have to lower himself to speak to her, to get his point across. He looked ready to spit at her and, if he had been less of a gentleman or if the Plaza staff had not been watching, she was certain he would have done so.

But then, sometimes, even when things look really bad, they work out just as they are supposed to. If Joy had not found herself begging at her inflamed ex-husband's feet, if she had not felt so low that her greatest ambition was simply to get enough drink inside her to end it all, then she would not have managed to stagger as far as the bar of a small cheap hotel on West 58th, with the intention of drinking as much whisky as she could afford and blagging a bottle to take home with her. And if Joy had not walked into that bar, at that particular moment, she would not have bumped straight into a man, causing him to spill his coffee. 'Oh my goodness me,' he said.

'I am so sorry, ma'am.' Then, seeing she was not burnt or hurt, he smiled and added, 'Well, hullo, remember me?'

He looked vaguely familiar, although Joy had no idea where they might have met before. He was certainly not a business associate of Frank's, or indeed, a fellow socialite's husband, not in such a shabby suit. He had a pleasant, but forgettable, face and was looking at her with a curious mixture of pleasure and concern. Joy suddenly realized it had been a long time since anyone had looked at her with anything other than pity, or anger.

'Can I get you something?' the man said. 'Please, come and sit down, you look shaken.'

In the face of his kindness, Joy remembered the way the man in the liquor store looked at her, his cold detachment, Jones's pity and disgust when he had entered her apartment, the fearful irritation on the face of the security men who evicted her from the Plaza, the abject horror on the faces of the hotel guests, Frank's fury. She briefly looked over the stranger's shoulder and saw her own face, reflected in the mirrored window, distorted, ugly, her eyes filled with immeasurable sadness, yet glinted back at her with a kind of demented fear.

'Here,' the man said, holding the chair out. 'Let me get you something. What would you like?'

She could have a double shot now, to obliterate the pain and yet, looking across at her own reflection, Joy realized that, despite all she had drunk up to this moment, the pain was still there. The pain had always been there, even in her beautiful youth, even if nobody could see it except her, the lousy pain, the aching in her heart, the white noise in her brain which told her she was never good enough, never beautiful enough, never lovable enough, was always, always there. Drink used to be her medicine, it used to make the pain go away, make her feel happy and clever and light. Drink used to be her friend, but seeing herself in that moment, in that bar, she wondered what kind of a friend drink was to her, really, anymore. She had drunk a half bottle of Scotch before getting herself into the Plaza that morning and it hadn't made things better, it had made things worse.

One's too many, a thousand is never enough.

The words came into her head from nowhere and she said to the stranger, 'Coffee. I would like a cup of coffee, please.'

The man paused, the merest flicker of surprise in his eyes, then added, 'I'm having a sandwich, would you like me to order you one?' and Joy shocked herself again, by saying, 'Yes, that would be very nice.'

She sat at the table and, when the sandwich arrived, Joy, who had not eaten for as many days back as she could remember, toyed with it. Then, as she went to lift her coffee, her hand started to shake, sending a wave of the brown liquid splashing onto the saucer. She was mortified. This had been a mistake; she needed to get home, she needed a drink.

The stranger held out his hand and, putting it on top of hers, steadied the cup. Then he went up to the bar and came back carrying a drinking straw and a large glass tumbler.

He decanted the coffee into the glass, added a heaped spoon of sugar and the straw, then, gently placing it in front of her, said, 'Drink it like this. I'm sorry, I don't even know your name?'

'Joy,' she said. 'My name is Joy.'

She easily sucked the warm sweet coffee through the straw, her hands clasping each other firmly under the table. It felt soothing, like proper medicine.

'Your name suits you,' he said, then, as if pondering the meaning, smiled and said her name out loud, 'Joy.'

There was kindness in his face, but not a shred of pity.

'My name is Dan,' he said, 'and I'm a recovered alcoholic.'

Dan knew how to drink coffee through a straw when you had the shakes and he knew how to blag that final top-up drink out of a barman to get you home. Dan knew just how much drink he could take, without getting caught out in his job driving people around as a car salesman, and he also knew just how many drinks it took for a guy to wrap a brand new Continental around a lamppost and end up in the slammer. Dan lost a wife, a job and ended up in a mission downtown, before he rolled up at an AA meeting, where he found God, sobriety and enough work selling vacuum cleaners door-to-door to earn him the shabby suit on his back. He stayed away from places that served drink, mostly, but sometimes he stopped into a hotel bar, for a coffee, just so he could remember what it was like.

Funny how he had met her, both times, in a hotel bar and it was when he said that that Joy recognized him as the man she had met in the Waldorf bar, on the night of her party.

'I never forget a face,' he said, blushing, 'especially...' He trailed off and Joy knew that he had been going to tell her she was beautiful, then realized that she was glad he hadn't. Joy didn't want to be beautiful to anyone, anymore; she didn't want to be anything to anyone.

Joy did not know what to make of this man. She had let herself be picked up by him because she thought he would buy her drink, but instead, she was drinking coffee and listening to his life story.

By the time Dan had finished, Joy found she was feeling so settled, after the sandwich and the coffee, that she was ready for a drink. However, it didn't seem right, after all he had said, asking Dan to buy her whisky.

'Matter of fact, I am off to an Alcoholics Anonymous meeting now,' Dan said, 'if you want to come along...'

She looked at him, scandalized at the suggestion she was an alcoholic, but he stayed firm.

'The only requirement for membership is a desire to stop drinking,' he said, 'and if you'll pardon me saying, ma'am, it looks like you might be just about ready to stop.'

Joy did not know that she was ready. However, she didn't want to go home to drink alone, in her small, unkempt flat, so she said yes.

There were twenty other people packed into the small room, in a mission hall. The air was thick with smoke and, as soon as she entered the door, she was embraced warmly by several people and invited to sit and listen.

A man called Simon and a woman called Dolores sat at a long table, while a man, called John, introduced them and read from a big blue book that looked something like a bible.

As the two speakers told their stories, Joy felt herself open up. Although one was a carpet salesman and the other a barmaid, Joy felt as if they were talking about her.

'I always felt as if I was never enough.'

'Drink gave me confidence, it made me feel like I was a whole person.'

'Alcohol was the medicine I needed to help me cope with my feelings.'

'Everyone thought I had a drink problem, except me.'

As the meeting went on, she heard people confessing to things she did alone: hiding drink, not eating for days, waking up and not knowing how she had got home. Her secret thoughts seemed commonplace among these people.

I blamed my messy life, my bad marriage for my drinking; it never occurred to me that my life was messy and my marriage was bad, because I drank.

It was as if, in that one hour, Joy heard the truth of who she was and who she had become, for the first time. She had given up drink before, but never really with any genuine intent; it had only ever been to keep Frank happy, she had never really believed that drink was a problem. Life was the problem, Frank was the problem, Honor was the problem. Of course, they still were, but looking around the room, at these cheerful 'recovered drunks', as they called themselves, Joy realized that she was not alone. If these people had stopped, maybe she could, too.

After the meeting, most of the twenty people sat about, chain-smoking. Someone handed her a cup of coffee, just how she liked it – black and strong and as sweet as sherry.

Dan introduced her to the speaker, Dolores, and said, 'If you want to hang around and get sober, Joy, Dolly here will be your sponsor.'

Dolly explained, 'It's just a sharing partner, we call ourselves, someone you can call every day who can help you work through this thing we call the programme.'

'It's the only way,' Dan said. 'Most of us were hopeless alcoholics, but we all work through these twelve steps...' He nodded to a large poster on the wall. '...and that causes what we call a complete psychic change or spiritual awakening. My compulsion to drink was removed after my first meeting.'

'I had three weeks, craving a drink,' Dolores said, 'but after a month God removed my need to drink and I haven't looked back.'

'Are you ready for a change, Joy?' Dolores asked. 'Are you ready to start a new life?'

Joy looked into the face of this plain woman, who seemed to be in her fifties. Dolores was far from beautiful, but her lipstick had been neatly applied with a steady hand and that, Joy realized, was more than hers had been today. There was a certainty and a sense of peace around her new 'sharing friend' that seemed to her, in that moment, impossibly unattainable and yet Joy was being offered the chance to reach for it.

Not drinking alcohol ever again seemed, in itself, a ridiculous task and yet Joy knew she could not go back to the way things had been.

The poster of the Twelve Steps of Alcoholics Anonymous loomed over her.

Step 1: Admitted we were powerless over alcohol, that our lives had become unmanageable.

Joy's life was a mess and she was an alcoholic. Was that it after all? Had Frank been right all along?

'Can it really be that simple?' she said to Dolores.

The older woman smiled and said, 'It's simple, honey, but that don't make it *easy*.' Then she put her hands over Joy's and held them for a moment, before adding, 'If you don't mind me saying – you look just about beat to me.'

It was then that Joy began to cry. Tears streamed down her face until she took her shaking hands from under those of her new friend to wipe them away in large, messy swipes.

Dolores reached in her pocket for a handkerchief and handing it to her said, 'You ready to get to work, lady?'

Joy nodded silently, like a shy child on her first day at school.

'No time like the present. Dan can drive us where we need to go. You got a home, right now, or are you sleeping rough?'

Joy tried to hide her shock. 'I have a flat,' she said.

'Lucky you, more than I had when I came in. Is it dry?'

Joy laughed and said, 'Are you *kidding*? Do I *look* like someone who keeps a dry house?'

Dolores and Dan laughed and so did Joy. It was the first time she had laughed in months.

Dolores picked up her bag and said, 'Come on. Let's go and clear out your cupboards – then we can get to work on your head.'

As she sat in the back of a shabby car, with these two kind strangers up front, Joy thought about her life. At thirty, she felt as if she had been on this earth too long already, yet did not feel as if she had happily lived one single day of it. In the honesty of these strangers' stories and the certain, yet gentle, tone of their voices, Joy felt she was being handed, not simply a second chance at life, but the opportunity to begin her life all over again.

Thirty-Four

 *Ireland, 2014*

It took almost three hours for Lily to drive from Knock airport to the town of Bangor where her grandfather had been born. The sat nav had said two hours but the roads were so narrow in parts that Lily kept slowing down to allow the oncoming cars to whizz past her.

The weather was changeable. Leaving the airport it was warm with a fine misty rain, what her grandmother always described as 'a grand soft day'. As she passed through the small towns of Swinford, Foxford, Ballina, the sky cleared into bursts of sunshine with heavy intermittent shows. One minute the windscreen wipers would be going full lash, then after switching them off a rainbow would suddenly appear, so clearly and with such multi-coloured crispness on the horizon that Lily felt she was inside *The Wizard of Oz*.

'Ah, here,' she said, mimicking her grandfather's expression, when, just as she was passing through the small village of Killala, two rainbows appeared one after the other. 'That is *unfeasible*,' she said to herself out loud.

Lily felt happy, she realized. Despite being let down by Sally she was just happy being in her own head. Tears welled up in her eyes as she realized that the person she felt closest to right now was her grandfather, Joe; perhaps he was behind the rainbows, leading her on.

The sat nav guided her through a town called Ballycastle then on along a seemingly endless narrow road into the heart of a mountainous, sea-edged bogland that was so beautiful and remote it took her breath away. Although she had never been here before the mountains and cliffs and soft heathery purple bogs felt achingly familiar, as if their history was buried in her blood, like a splinter in her soul placed there by some ancient force. The sun moved like a spotlight across the vast landscape, lighting up sections of a mountain then sweeping across to another one.

In that moment, nothing mattered and Lily just drove and drove until the sat nav instructed her to turn left towards Bangor.

As she drove into the one street town, she saw a sign for the graveyard and headed towards it. It was barely two miles outside the town and Lily's stomach churned as she saw the white curved wall and the crosses behind it facing out into miles of remote boglands and mountain. Would her family be here, her grandfather's people?

She pulled the car up and, surprised by the sharpness of the wind, pulled her cardigan around her tightly. The front part of the graveyard seemed newer, with lots of marble and polished granite, so she walked to go over to the left hand corner where the grass was higher and the graves seemed older.

Her eye was drawn to it straight away, an ornate cross, taller than all the others, pushing up from a base of weeds.

Frank Fitzpatrick, 1920–1984,
of Bangor and New York.
A man is born alone, and dies alone.

He died in the year Lily was born, a man in his sixties. Lily felt impossibly sad. Frank Fitzpatrick was not alone in 1984 – he had a brother, living in London, and a nephew, her father. Yet he had chosen to stay away from his own family. Next to his gravestone was another, smaller grave. Lily pushed back the high weeds and was barely able to make out the wording carved into the cheap stone slab of a headstone: *Joseph Fitzpatrick and his wife Mary Fitzpatrick. RIP.*

Lily thought of all the people who had turned out for her grandfather's funeral and the vast crowd standing around eating sandwiches and drinking whisky and telling anecdotes about him. Joe had been a warm, happy man full of love and mischief and Lily wondered what kind of people his family must have been to have left the world behind them in this sad way. Her parents and grandparents had loved her. There had been no pain; problems were things that happened to other people. Sally's mother had had an affair when she was ten and run off with her lover to France, leaving behind her three small children and a devastated husband who developed a daily dope habit. Sally spent as much time as she could in Lily's house after that, lapping up her mother's home cooking and relishing the stability of regular mealtimes and TV squabbling. She kept telling Lily how lucky she was to come from an 'ordinary' home but secretly Lily sometimes envied the drama of Sally's house. Affairs and drugs and her actor father bringing home girlfriends barely older than Sally. Her own life seemed so staid, so boring in comparison. Standing here looking at the misery of her family history Lily suddenly felt a sense of gratitude that Joe had kept her away from this place and whatever dark history it held.

She was curious about what had happened to the Fitzpatricks; there was clearly some great drama playing out in the placing of these graves. However, the greater part of Lily understood that it must have been something so painful that her grandfather had had to escape it and keep himself and his family away from it all of his life. If there was drama in the emotions of a conflicted family, there was mostly just plain old pain and in that moment Lily came to understand that she was very lucky to have been spared the hardship of an unhappy family. In the past few months she had lost Joe and, standing by these cold gravestones, she felt her heart ache at the finality of death again.

As Lily turned and walked away from the Fitzpatricks' headstones it was this very thought that led her to look up as she walked past a headstone that was about the same grand height as Frank Fitzpatrick's, but the grave itself beautifully kept with flowers planted in a big terracotta pot on the carefully weeded white gravel.

Set into the front of the gravestone was a 1920s style wedding portrait of a couple and the words:

John Conlon, 1900–1990, schoolmaster of this parish,
and his beloved wife, Clare Conlon. 1910–1992.
Beloved parents of Honor Conlon of New York,
they will be sadly missed. RIP.

Lily could not believe her eyes. Could it be the same Honor Conlon? If it was, why was she not buried with her husband Frank Fitzpatrick? The fact that Honor was not buried here could mean she was possibly still alive. The grave was well kept so there must still be family or friends in the area. Lily looked at the old but surprisingly clear picture of the young couple. The Conlons' happy, friendly faces reminded Lily of her own parents and she was overwhelmed with a feeling of affinity with Honor. These must be the parents of the woman whose dress she was replicating. This is fate, bringing us closer together, she thought. She took out her iPad and snapped a picture of the smiling couple, then, fizzing with excitement, she drove back into Bangor and stopped at the first pub she could find.

There wasn't a soul in there and, despite the pine bar and booths, it seemed more like somebody's living room. A woman of around her mother's age came out from behind the bar and Lily, awkward about diving straight into an interrogation, asked if they did food. The woman said no but she could make her something small. She disappeared behind the bar and when she came back with a pot of tea and a ham sandwich Lily took a deep breath and asked her straight out, 'Did you know John and Clare Conlon?'

'The best people this town ever produced,' the woman said, sitting down. 'He taught me, and all belonging to me and he never raised his hand to a child in his life.'

She saw Lily looking slightly shocked. 'That was the way at the time,' the woman said, 'but John Conlon was a kind and compassionate man and so was his wife. Were they relations of yours?'

Lily thought of her dead relatives' unkempt grave and decided not to declare her connection.

'I'm looking for Honor Conlon,' she said, 'their daughter.'

The woman visibly bristled. 'She went to America when she was very young,' she said curtly. 'I never knew her.'

The woman's lips tightened in a disapproving pout but she didn't move away so Lily realized she was looking for more information. She felt herself feeling slightly hurt by the woman's chilly reaction to Honor.

'I don't know her myself, actually,' Lily said. 'I am just

trying to find her. I'm researching...something.'

'Well, you won't find her around here,' the woman said. 'She came home for her parents' funerals, but that was over twenty years ago now. She was here for three days for Clare's funeral and nobody has seen hide or hair of her since.'

'Oh,' Lily said, disappointed. All this way for a dead end.

The woman went back behind the bar then paused, turned around and said, 'Wait on here for a few minutes,' then left through the front door.

Lily sat alone in the pub, until ten minutes later the woman came back in and handed her a slip of paper.

'Honor Conlon left this address with the solicitor after her mother's funeral,' she said. 'I don't know if she's still there but as far as I know she sent some money over for the upkeep of the grave a few years ago.' Then she muttered, 'Not that she needed to. Everyone here loved the Conlons. The people around here look after their own...'

Lily thought of the Fitzpatricks again and for a moment she thought of asking the woman about them but then realized that she didn't actually want to know what had happened to them. She had seen the grave, and that was enough.

Lily thanked the woman then got back on the road to Westport for her lace. She kept her phone switched off and spent the journey looking out at the mountains and lakes of Mayo and thinking about what she had seen in the graveyard. This place was so beautiful but it felt sad too. The green fields were hemmed by glittering lakes and magnificent cliffs and the thin, winding roads were lined with purple rhododendron and pink-rose hedgerows. The sky lit up with shifting amber clouds and disco-rainbows. But the land was built on endless black bogs as deep as the earth's core. This place held secrets in its history, some of which were best forgotten, like her family, but some which she felt she was uncovering. The more she saw of this rich landscape the more Lily came to feel that Honor, the woman who had created that beautiful dress, was from this extraordinary place where its fluid light and shadows changed as rapidly as the shimmering of good silk and its graveyards held stories as complex as the finest Carrickmacross lace. There was something here that was connecting her to her dress, something connecting to her Honor, something this place was trying to tell her.

The rest of the day was busy. Lily found the lovely English woman, Sandra, she had contacted by phone and bought nearly her entire collection of Carrickmacross lace over tea in her small cottage on the edge of a mountain. Business was slow enough, Sandra said, out here in the middle of nowhere, but she had come there on holiday seven years ago and loved it so much she had stayed. Houses were cheap and as a dealer in vintage fabric she could work from anywhere. She could not believe her luck in finding a buyer like Lily and gave her a coin-sized brooch of stiffened antique lace as a gift to thank her for the business and 'as a good luck charm. Sounds like you'll be needing it to get that dress finished on time.'

Lily drove back to her hotel and used the spa, thought about ordering room service but then decided to get dressed up and go down to the restaurant. As she sat there, alone, at her table for one, Lily felt curiously grown up and content. As an only child Lily had always spent a lot of time alone, but this trip had given her a taste of what it felt like to be truly independent. Alone, but in a good way. At the grand old age of thirty, this was the first time Lily had eaten by herself in a restaurant and she thought to herself, how many more things are there out there that I haven't done? This had been an adventure; her life, she was starting to realize, *was* an adventure.

Back in her hotel room Lily switched on her iPad and emailed Zac the address she had been given for Honor (in Brooklyn), quickly switching off again before her social media alerts came up. She was enjoying being apart from her online life and decided to keep it going until she got back to London.

She wanted to savour her Irish adventure a while longer.

The spell was broken as soon as Lily opened the door of her empty flat and started walking up the stairs. She threw her bag down on the sofa and without taking her jacket off, distracted herself from the emptiness by checking in with her abandoned Twitter account. There were 500 notifications on her #TheDress stream with #ScottsSilent #PopShopMegaDress #VogueLOVESLucy and a link to a fashion news blog article about the challenge telling her that Lucy Houston had signed up for the cover of *Vogue* in anticipation of winning #TheDress and PopShop's artistic director Sally Thomas had released early sketches. In the meantime, they said, Scott's blog had gone silent and when Jack Scott was asked to comment, he refused. In the blogger's opinion Scott's was bluffing. Who and what was this 'Lily' nobody-person anyway, please? Was she a blogger or a designer? Lucy, with her clean lines, impeccable attention to detail and, hullo, her impeccable track record? She was *obviously* the clear winner.

Lily was disgusted. This was a direct slap in the face from Sally. She didn't even open the link to Lucy's dress. She wouldn't give them the satisfaction. Even so, Lily could feel the panic rising up in her. She told herself that all this bitchy Internet hearsay didn't matter, it would pass by as quickly as it came. As an established blogger herself Lily knew that better than anyone, but the truth was, Lily still doubted her ability as a designer to pull this thing off. After a few days away from it, the social media barrage itself felt intrusive and unsettling. The fact that it came from Sally made it too much.

She had to get out of the house. Out of her head.

Lily decided that a hot sweet drink in the company of her friend Gareth was just what she needed to settle herself. Besides, she still had to thank him for the corset.

As she was walking up the street, Sally rang. Lily didn't pick up, and then Sally's number came up again straight away. Lily was raging and hurt. Sally had taken the gloves off now and this was, truly, unforgivable.

As Lily stepped inside Old Times she noticed that Gareth had started growing a beard again. She was about the make a comment when he looked up at her briefly with a cool, detached expression instead of his usual warm smile, then went back to flicking through his catalogue.

'Hey,' she said, 'do you fancy a chai?'

Gareth shook his head, without looking up. What had she done?

Lily was furious. This was all she needed right now.

'Fine,' she said, and started towards the door. 'I don't know what's the matter with you but I'm not in the mood right now for hanging around to find out!'

As she was about to leave Gareth looked up and said, 'I didn't know you had a boyfriend.'

Lily stopped, then stood looking at him, open-mouthed.

'When I was going to drop off the corset the other morning, I saw him coming out of your gaff. Got into a big fancy car looking pretty pleased with himself.'

Lily continued to gape. Was Gareth for real?

'I didn't want to disturb you, and I couldn't just leave it there on the pavement so I got Fergus to drop it over later.'

Lily didn't know whether she was more dumbfounded that Jack had been caught leaving her house or that Gareth was behaving as if he was her boyfriend, which he wasn't.

'Well, I haven't got a boyfriend,' she said, 'and it's none of your business anyway whether I have or I haven't.'

Or is it? She asked inwardly, chastising herself then for being stupid.

Gareth looked as if he had been hit by a truck. *What* was going on here?

'Oh right,' he said, finally looking up from his catalogue at anything but her face. 'It's just I thought we might have had, you know...' He shrugged and held his arms out looking like he really wished he hadn't started this but knowing that, now that she was standing square in front of him he had to finish it, finally saying, '...a "thing"?'

Lily would have normally found this reluctant embarrassment sweet, but after Sally betraying her and all the Internet bad-mouthing she was feeling all riled up and confrontational.

'What, like a romantic "thing"?' she said. 'Like you and me, boyfriend–girlfriend, going out "thing"?'

It was not how Gareth had planned on asking Lily out but now that it was happening he had no alternative but to blush wildly and stammer, 'Well, I guess so, yeah.'

Lily was annoyed. She needed someone to help ease the pressure on her, not cause more of it with stupid dilly dallying and hint-giving.

So she said, 'Newsflash, Gareth, if you want a girl to go out with you, especially an old fashioned one...' She swept her hand angrily down the 1940s skirt–blouse ensemble she was wearing by way of a hint. '. . . you are *supposed* to ask her out first. Not send your mates out to spy on her.'

'I'm sorry, I—'

'Yes, well . . . Oh, forget it!' Lily shouted, no longer knowing if she was angry with Gareth or herself but knowing for sure that she had had enough upset for one day. She ran out of the shop.

As soon as Lily turned the corner she felt sick. She should go back immediately and straighten things out with Gareth, explain the whole situation with Jack and thank him for the corset properly. However, as she was turning on her heel, Lily felt the 'coin' of lace in her pocket and had a small, but very real epiphany.

She didn't need Gareth, or Jack or even Sally right now. What she needed was The Dress and, unlike Gareth, or Jack, or Sally, The Dress needed her.

Lily did not turn back to Old Times but instead ran towards her apartment, and as she ran, she felt a surge of inspiration pump through her veins. An idea had flashed into her mind. Her hands were shaking with excitement as she opened her apartment door. Lily bolted up the stairs, plugged in her iPad and printed off the Conlons' wedding picture from their Bangor grave. Then she laid it down on a piece of silk and began to trace the image of their faces onto the cream fabric.

This was what the trip to Ireland had been telling her; it wasn't the rainbows and the lakes, nor even the beautiful lace that was linking her to The Dress, it was the people. This was the place she was from, where her grandfather had been born.

This was the couple whose daughter had made the original dress and Lily was going to honour them by embroidering their images into the train of *her* dress.

For the next three days, nothing, not Twitter, not the Scott's competition, not her love life, or her family, or her friends or making things good with Gareth, was more important than doing that.

Thirty-Five

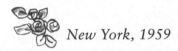 *New York, 1959*

Finding Joy

Step 8: Made a list of all persons we had harmed and became willing to make amends to them all.
Step 9: Made direct amends to such people, wherever possible, except when to do so would injure them or others.
(Twelve Steps of Alcoholics Anonymous)

Joy did not find getting sober easy.

The first few days were harder than she could have imagined. She had been drinking daily for some months now and the demons had taken hold of her system. She did not sleep on the night of that first meeting, shaking and shivering, as every inch of her body craved its familiar medicine. Her mind was telling her not to drink, but her body was screaming that this was *wrong*. It took every inch of resolve she had to get herself out of bed the next day, dressed and over to the AA Club for a lunchtime meeting.

'It'll pass,' one man told her, when she complained about feeling sick, and told her to just eat plenty of sugar.

She barely made it home from the meeting before she

began to vomit and sweat profusely. Joy felt so wretched that she rang her family doctor; was there something wrong with her to be running this sort of a fever? He would give her something good to calm her nerves – how stupid, stupid of her to have allowed herself to run out of Librium like that.

'Hullo, Doctor Allen's surgery, how may I help you?'

Joy's hands were shaking so hard that she could barely hold the receiver steady; panicking, she hung up. She couldn't tell the doctor what was going on – that would be too shameful for words – or turn up at the hospital like a common bum. It hadn't been like this before, giving up drink. How had she let it get this bad?

Then it hit her. Why was she putting herself through this? One drink would sort all of these terrible symptoms out. One half bottle of whisky and she would be able to get herself steady enough to get out to a meeting that night – she would wean herself off gradually, taper out, over a few days. As she stood up to get her purse and coat, Joy felt dizzy, fell to the ground and was so overcome with nausea that she could not stand up. She crawled to the bathroom and spent the next twenty-four hours crawling between the bed and the toilet. By the following morning she was managing to hold down water and by lunchtime, when Dolores called on her to check her progress, Joy felt the worst of her withdrawals were over.

From then on, things began to improve. Joy did everything Dolly told her to do, rising early each morning and saying a prayer before she even got out of bed, asking a God she did not entirely believe in to help her. Breakfast, an entirely new concept for her, was oatmeal generously sprinkled with sugar, which was fast becoming her addiction of choice, along with cigarettes.

Joy stuck rigidly to a routine. After breakfast, she spent

the next hour getting herself and her apartment cleaned up and ready for the day. She walked to the store and bought groceries for her evening meal, then went home and tidied them away, before spending an hour reading *The Big Book of Alcoholics Anonymous*. The rest of the afternoon was spent attending to any paperwork, or other business, before getting ready for her early evening AA meeting.

Joy was astounded at how much there was to be done, simply attending to the business of being alive and living what was called a 'good life'. She was mystified as to how she had occupied herself for all those years, without doing any of these ordinary things, like shopping, preparing meals, cleaning out one's own toilet pan and sweeping up one's own crumbs from the kitchen floor. She was amazed to find that each one of these chores now gave her a measure of satisfaction, because of the miraculous cycle of which they were a part. Joy had been unable to complete almost any task in her life, without reaching for a drink, or at least craving a drink, or thinking about a drink.

Joy had received her two-week chip the night before, and she was eating her breakfast as usual and looking around her apartment, thinking about what groceries she might need from the store, when it just struck her that she was feeling – she searched around for a word and all she could come up with was – *bored*. It was as if there was a spring inside her, that had relaxed for a few weeks and now it was beginning to tighten. She felt restless, fidgety, as if she wanted something to happen. Is this what I really want from life, Joy thought, chugging from meal to meal, meeting to meeting? It all just seemed so pointless, so grey, so boring, so... not *her*.

Who was this dull person, who ate oatmeal for breakfast and sat in small rooms, fraternizing with reformed drunks with badly dyed hair, wearing cheap pant suits? Tighter, tighter, the spring coiled, as the addiction imp, on her shoulder, whispered to Joy that she was taking this entire sobriety lark way too seriously. No drink, whatsoever, was ridiculous; no civilized person could be expected to forego their early evening cocktail. Joy looked at her watch; it was 5.50 p.m. If she was quick, she could get to the liquor store, buy a small bottle of vodka and some tonic. The addition of a fresh lime would cement her desire to bring her drinking habits back into line with 'normality'. She might even go along to the AA meeting later, just to prove, to herself and everyone there, that there were no hard feelings. Her new friends were well intentioned, but really, not her sort of people: she was not an alcoholic after all, just a woman unfortunate enough to have had her husband stolen from her by some devious bitch, and who had turned to the bottle, for a while, to soothe her nerves.

Joy put on some lipstick and ran down the hallway. She turned left out of the door, on an automatic route towards the liquor store, before she had the chance to change her mind.

As she was coming out, vodka bottle in the bag (they were clean out of tonic), she bumped straight into Dolores, who was on her way to call on her, for a pre-arranged supper, that Joy had forgotten about.

'It's not what you think,' Joy said defensively. 'I have guests coming and I thought I ought to get something in.'

It was an outright lie and they both knew it, but even so, Dolores did not react as Joy thought she would; she was neither disappointed, nor upset.

'Whatever is in that bag, why that's up to you, honey,' she said smiling, 'but I'm guessing it's a bottle and you ain't got no guests coming, save yourself, but there's no need to lie.'

Joy was shocked, not sure how to respond, so she just stood there. Should she be ashamed, contrite, apologetic?

'Really,' her sponsor said. 'If you want to drink, well then hey, there's not a person in the wide world will stop you, Joy – not me, not everyone in AA combined, not the Good Lord Himself. It's your call, Joy. You want a drink? You have it. Hell, I'll even ice the glass for you. We'll go and buy a lime, if you like...'

This was not the reaction she was hoping for. In fact, Joy had been relieved when she saw her sponsor because she did not *want* that drink. The truth was, she hadn't *wanted* a drink in a long time. It was just what she did, what her addiction compelled her to do.

As long as Dolores and Dan were around, they could keep her away from it. Joy felt sick at the idea that this was the way it was; nobody was going to save her from drinking herself to death, first not Frank, now not the kind people in AA either.

This was down to her. She looked down and the hand holding the bag was shaking almost as hard it had been during the first days of her withdrawal. Is that where she wanted to go back to? She held the bag out to Dolores.

'Hell, sugar,' she said. 'I don't want it – ain't no guest coming to my house got use for that, anymore.'

There was a trash-can a few yards away and Joy walked over and put the bag with the bottle into it, then she and Dolores went to the meeting.

Later that night, Joy thought of going back and retrieving her bottle from the bin; but she didn't, and for five full nights after that, she thought of going back to the same spot, just to check if it was still there. Even though she did not want a drink, even though she knew the bag would be long gone, she felt it calling to her, and every night that it called and she didn't go, Joy felt as a victory.

As the days passed, Joy started really to get to grips with her alcoholism. 'It's the demon,' Dolores warned. 'There's folks who drink too much and then stop. Once they stop drinking alcohol, they feel better and their alcohol problem goes away. Then there's folks, like us, who, even when we stop, still crave the crazy; it's not the alcohol that makes alcoholism a problem – it's the 'ism'.'

Joy's craving for drink didn't leave her but she came to recognize the whisper of her 'ism imp' and was able to drown it out with reason. With the help of her friends in AA and by working through the programme they set out for her, Joy began to embrace her simple life, and one day at a time, manage and tame the thirsty beast of her addiction. The greyness of life without drink lifted and became replaced by colourful friendships and the challenge of living her life, one day at a time.

'Do you have everything you need, here?' Dolly asked, when she called around to Joy's apartment one evening to collect her for the meeting. It had been eight weeks to the day since they had met and they were both excited about collecting Joy's two-month sobriety chip.

Joy was perplexed by the question and asked, 'How do you mean?'

Dolores looked around her, then back at Joy, apologetically and said, 'Sorry, I didn't mean to pry, it's just I thought you might want to brighten the place up a bit more? You know, given how well you seem in yourself.'

Joy looked around her apartment, a rather drab rental, in a brownstone, belonging to her ex-husband. The curtains were paper-thin, the wallpaper was peeling off in the kitchen and the rug, while it was clean, had seen better days. It was, in truth, as far away as Joy could imagine from the plush, designer glamour of their Fifth Avenue home. She had cleaned it up somewhat, since moving in, but Dolores was right, it still looked kind of grim. Joy had not minded that so much. In truth, she had barely noticed. She had everything she needed, shelter, food, kind people to help her, but Dolores had been talking about something else. Joy had not bothered to do anything with the apartment, because it was only her living there. The designer furniture, the silk drapes, the bespoke bedroom furnishings, they were, in part, a glamorous cover-up for the destitution she had felt inside. She didn't need to do that, anymore, to paper over the cracks with glamour and glitz; Joy was getting well, from the inside out. However, Dolores was right. Her apartment had a depressing, somewhat destitute air that did not reflect the contentment Joy was starting to feel in this new, simple, sober life of hers.

'Where would I start?' Joy said.

It seemed crazy, that a woman whose New York apartment had been considered one of America's most glamorous homes, was asking interiors advice from an ex-hooker from Brooklyn, but Joy still felt lost. Sobriety was like being born again; without drink to hold her up, Joy had to relearn how to do everything, including, especially, just being herself. This process of pulling herself back from beyond the brink of ruin, it was almost as if she had forgotten how to do all the things that had become second nature to her, one of which was decorating. Although, fixing up a bad rental, on a modest budget, was very different from decorating a palatial apartment with unlimited money.

'A lick of paint might be a good place, honey. Why don't we ask Dan to help out? He's pretty good with a paintbrush.'

Joy was surprised to feel herself getting a little kick when Dolores mentioned Dan's name. The two of them had become close friends in the last few weeks, going off for coffee after meetings, when she wasn't with Dolores studying the steps.

Tonight, after the meeting, they were working on Steps 8 and 9 – Joy's list of people she had harmed. Joy had already identified Frank, Jones and Honor and was dreading writing her apology letters to them. She did not know how she would endure the humiliation of it, but Dolores had told her it had to be done, and the quicker the better.

'The sooner you take full responsibility for your actions when you were drinking, the sooner you can put it all behind you.'

As was their habit, the two women found a corner of the smoky room, after the meeting was over, to talk through the work Joy had done on herself and discuss the following week's steps. Dolores always kept their chat to an hour and was uncompromising in her instructions.

'If you work the programme to the letter, you will be a recovered alcoholic in four more weeks and need never drink again. But you mustn't skimp, Joy; you must be brave and do everything, exactly as the *Big Book* says. It's simple but, as I keep saying, that don't make it *easy*.'

Dolores took out a pen and paper and made Joy draft her letters to Honor and Frank right there and then.

To Frank, she apologized for being a lousy wife, for embarrassing him, for not putting his needs before her own and for all the hardship and worry she knew he had endured being married to, as she was now able to describe herself, 'a drunk'.

However, when Joy started the letter to Honor, she could not think of a single thing she had done to wrong that woman. She had never even drunk in front of her!

'Think about it over the next few days,' Dolly said. 'You'll come up with something.'

'But I didn't treat that woman with anything but kindness,' Joy said.

'Well, you sure as hell hate her now,' Dolores reminded her, 'and hating-on somebody is just as bad in the eyes of the Lord as doing them wrong. Besides, when we hate, we hurt, lady. You've got to let go of the hate, Joy, for your own sake too.'

By the time she and Dolores had finished, Joy was emotionally exhausted and boy, did she feel like a drink!

Dan was waiting for her outside, smoking and talking with his own sponsee. Each of the more experienced members took on the task of being sharing partner to new members, giving them instruction after meetings. In four weeks' time, when Joy had been twelve weeks sober and completed the twelve steps, she would be expected to do the same.

'How did eight and nine go for you?' Dan asked, when Joy came out.

'Not too good, Dan. Frank was OK but why I have to apologize to Honor is still a mystery to me. Sorry I let you steal my husband, you conniving bitch?'

Dan shrugged and smiled.

'Yeah, I know – take responsibility,' she said. 'Dolly put me straight. It was all my fault and I've got to be nice but, goddammit, Dan, I hate that woman.'

Dan laughed. 'Goddammit, woman, you're starting to sound like me. I know what you mean, though; it nearly killed me, writing to my ex-wife. I hurt the woman, sure, but my God, she made me pay. Haven't seen my kids since the day she kicked me out seven years ago and she fixed herself up another husband pretty quick.'

'It wasn't Frank – I gave him an awful time, I know that, but she manipulated him, and me. She was my friend,' Joy said, building up a head of steam. 'I did so much for her, she shouldn't have betrayed me like that. Frank would never have left me, if it wasn't for her. Things would never have come to this...'

'Well, I'm glad they did,' Dan said, 'because I'd never have met you, if he hadn't.'

Joy suspected Dan was sweet on her, but he wouldn't make an approach until she had the twelve-week programme under her belt. Dan shuffled then and added, as a qualifier, 'And you should be, too, because you mightn't have got sober, if they hadn't pushed you to rock bottom.'

'I guess so,' Joy said, and it was then that it hit her.

Joy had spent her life guessing at being happy. She had been rich and beautiful, married to a dashing charismatic man, envied by every woman she knew and yet she had only ever been able to pretend at being content.

Why do you look so sad, when your name is Joy?

Frank had been attracted by her sadness, mesmerized by the air of tragic fragility that she covered up with her wit, social sophistication and, of course, drink.

Honor had known her for who she was; she had liked, maybe even loved her, for the ordinary person she knew existed, beyond the socialite façade. That was what she had always wanted, Joy realized; now and here, in Alcoholics Anonymous, she had found that. People who accepted her for the vulnerable, flawed person she was and, not only that, were helping her create a new life for herself.

She clicked a finger at her new friend Dan and he lit a cigarette off his own and handed it over to her.

As she stood on the doorstep of Mission Hall, with a man

in a bad suit, smoking a cheap cigarette, Joy dug down into herself, to the place that always frightened her, the empty black hole, and she realized that it was not the bottomless pit she had always feared. There was something there, after all; something warm and substantial was growing there. Joy wasn't afraid, anymore, in fact she felt...happy.

She had found Joy.

Thirty-Six

Frank could barely contain his own grief the night that Honor lost the baby, but contain it he did. There was no room for unseemly emotions in circumstances like that, certainly not for a man. There were no words to describe how he felt. Bereft? Cheated? It was the feeling that a rock had fallen from the sky and flattened his whole life, just as it seemed to be coming right.

When the anger came, he had a word for it, although he chose not to admit to it.

Frank was angry at everyone. At God, for first sending this baby and enabling him to marry Honor, then turning it into a cruel joke, by taking the baby away. Another dirty cosmic prank, like luring him into marrying a drunk disguised as a beautiful woman, to taunt him after the misery his wretched alcoholic father had put him through.

He was angry with Joy, furious at her for trying to destroy their wedding. Frank was determined to believe that the stress of her ugly scene had caused Honor's miscarriage. When Honor refused to go along with this theory, he was angry with her – although he was careful to hide it – and angrier still when she blamed herself.

Mostly, Frank was angry at himself, for not being able to make his wife's pain go away, but also for the fact that, after all the efforts he had made, he was still unhappy. Having escaped from his unhappy first marriage, Frank now seemed to be living in the centre of yet another tragic situation.

'Forget it and move on,' the doctors had told him, but Frank found he could not. Crucially, neither could Honor.

His rosy-cheeked, homely Irish wife was turning thin and wan and empty of joy and spirit. She had not returned to work in six weeks and spent her days sitting in the apartment, staring out the window across to Central Park.

'The only cure is another baby,' they had said, but Honor was adamant she did not want to try for another baby. Not yet, maybe not ever, that's what she said. Frank was angry with her about that, too, but he kept his counsel. He knew that, in time, Honor would come around. She would have to come around. It wasn't normal for a woman to not want a child.

In the meantime, he met with Breton, to talk about Honor going back to work. Frank did not want his wife to be working, but equally, he could see how desperately unhappy she was, sitting around the house all day, listless and depressed. To keep herself somewhat busy, Honor was also doing all the cooking and cleaning, making the loyal Jones all but redundant and unnerving him terribly.

After six weeks of Honor not working, Breton called Frank and said that, if his wife did not revive relationships with her clientele, shortly her name would become redundant. It was the men's decision and ultimately their responsibility to ensure that Honor got back to work.

The Frenchman approached this problem with his usual dramatic aplomb.

'Your wife is a creative person,' he exclaimed. 'An artist.

Her work is what she needs right now. Beauty! Design! These are the things that will save her from this malaise – not you, my friend. She needs to make some pretty dresses, fashion will be her cure! Of course, she is a woman and she must and will become a mother, but first, we must make her remember what a magnificent designer she is. We must remind her of her finest hour.'

Frank had already had Jones remove Joy's dress from their apartment, months ago, after receiving an anxious phone call from Breton, worried that the jealous ex-wife might try to destroy the masterpiece.

'Honor is too sweet to admit it,' he said to Frank, 'but her success as a designer rests on that dress – you must try and get it back from Joy.'

Jones had delivered The Dress to Breton's studio, where he had hidden it away from Honor, not wanting to rock the boat before she got married. Breton knew that Honor felt bad about Joy, although he could not imagine why. He was delighted to have the talented young designer back under his wing and dreaded to think what disaster would have befallen her, if Joy had gone ahead with her rumoured plans to start up in competition with him. With The Dress safely in his care, there was no hope of that happening now and he would keep it safe for Honor, until such time as she needed it.

He could see that time was now. So, with Frank's financing, Breton went ahead and opened the 'Honor Fitzpatrick' salon.

'I have something to show you,' Frank said. 'Get dressed up and I'll take the car around.'

Frank had been great, really, very patient with her, in the weeks since losing the baby. However, Honor sensed her ennui was now getting on his nerves. Her husband was trying to find a way of telling her it was time to move on.

'Where are we going?' she said.

'It's a surprise.'

'I don't like surprises,' she said, instantly regretting the curt tone of her voice.

'Well, you'll like this one,' Frank said, his voice more firm than playful. 'I am taking you to a wonderful new boutique.'

Honor went to the dressing room and flicked through her modest wardrobe. Frank had been trying to encourage her to fill it up, but she had no appetite for pretty things, never had, when it came to wearing them herself, anyway. She picked out a green cotton dress, brushed her hair back from her face, secured it at the nape of her neck in a loose bun, then applied some red lipstick.

Frank smiled at her and told her she looked beautiful. She was happy he was pleased with her and, for a moment, it seemed possible she could feel love again.

They had only driven a few blocks when Frank got out and said, 'We can walk from here.'

They were near Breton's studio and, as they came to the building where she used to work, Frank stopped.

'Here we are.' He was pointing to a window where her name was emblazoned across the shop-front: *Honor Fitzpatrick, Couturier.* Then, in smaller letters, underneath, as a reminder: *House of Breton.*

Honor gasped. It was her dream come true; except it was an old dream, from a life she barely recognized.

'Come in,' Frank urged. 'It's all ready for you.'

Inside, Breton, Colette and all the staff from the atelier were waiting with champagne. The shiny new rails were hung sparsely, with some of Honor's samples and her framed drawings lining the walls. The floor was fitted with plush cream carpet and, in the right hand corner, was an area curtained off, with elaborate pink velvet festoon blinds – presumably a fitting area. In the middle of all this was a glass cabinet, like the kind one would find in a museum and inside it, on a full size dressmaker's mannequin, with a spotlight trained on it, was the dress she had made for Joy.

Honor's immediate reaction was shock. Where had The Dress come from? Had Joy thrown it back to them, as a rejection of her? Had Frank and Breton *stolen* it from her? Everyone was smiling at her, Colette, the girls from the atelier. Frank was beaming and Breton even started a small round of applause. Honor caught sight of her own startled face in the mirrored wall behind the ornate counter, and saw how at odds she was with everyone else. Was this how her life was now, being out of step with the world around her? With her husband, her work – feeling estranged from her own life? In the past few months, everything had changed; she had gone from being a single woman, to a married one, pregnant to not pregnant, but she had also gone from being a good person, who had never harmed anyone in her life, to being the sort of person who betrayed a friend, in the worst possible way. Joy had commissioned that beautiful dress to please Frank, and now Honor had both. She had stolen not only her friend's husband, but her dream as well.

Honor smiled and said nothing, to Frank, to anybody. There was nothing she could say. The Dress was here now, whether Joy had wanted to throw her work back in her face, as useless trash, or if Frank had somehow stolen it back from his ex-wife, in some plot with Breton, to launch her design career – Honor felt both those options as having grown from a poisonous seed that she herself had planted, through selfish actions. Throughout her small party, Honor smiled and pretended to everyone that she was pleased with her new shop.

She was standing with Frank when Breton joined them. 'So, we have begun our new venture, Honor,' he said, looking very pleased with himself. 'You and I, young lady, we will dress the women of New York, in such style, in this magnificent little shop.'

'*Our* magnificent little shop,' Frank good-humouredly reminded him, 'and only when Honor is ready,' he added, closing his arm tightly around her shoulder. 'We don't want to wear out our most precious commodity, now, do we?'

They were talking about her as if she was their child, their possession, but then, this is what men did. It was why she had never wanted to get married. She had never wanted to be owned by a man, to be talked down to; men were in charge of the world. Honor did not hate Frank for his patronizing tone. She knew she was not simply a part of his world; she *was* his world. Just as he had been to Joy, she was now to him.

After the party, Honor told Frank and Breton she wanted to stay behind in the shop, by herself.

'Will you be OK here, on your own?' Frank asked, his face full of concern.

'Of course,' she said, 'I just need some time here, alone.'

Frank looked worried. 'You do like the place?' he said. 'You're happy, aren't you? I just want you to be happy.'

Honor's heart nearly broke for him. She wasn't happy and Frank knew it. She didn't even know if she loved him anymore; how could she, after they had both caused so much pain to Joy that God had punished them by taking their baby? How could she be happy in a marriage that had been created out of betrayal and hurt? The worry that Frank had felt about Honor's change in feelings, her coolness towards him, in these past few weeks, must have been how it had been for Joy. Frank's ex-wife had misguidedly commissioned a dress so beautiful that she thought it would make him happy, and now he had, bizarrely, tried to make Honor happy, by giving her back that very same bad talisman.

'Of course I'm happy,' she said. 'I love it.'

Frank's eyes flicked to the dress in the cabinet. Glittering and ornate, it was like a huge, bejewelled Indian elephant in the room. Nobody had yet referred to it directly and Honor did not want any mention of it now, certainly not from Frank.

So, Honor kept her eyes steadily on her husband and said, 'Go to the office, darling. I'll be fine, I just want to fix things up a bit more here.'

'Aha,' said Breton, catching the last of their conversation, 'the lady wants to put her own touches to the place – Breton's style is not sophisticated enough for the new Mrs Fitzpatrick's elegant Irish tastes?'

Honor laughed even though, inside, she could feel her heart turning to ash.

'You men go now,' she said, 'and leave me to my mysterious ways!'

Breton shooed Frank out of the door, joking, 'Vite! Vite! The women must be left to their tidying up.'

Frank laughed jovially, but as he closed the door behind him, Honor saw her husband glance back at her, his expression full of anxiety again.

'Thank you,' she mouthed, then gave him a reassuring smile to push him out.

Alone at last, Honor locked the door, pulled down the blinds, then opened the door of the cabinet, unzipped The Dress from the mannequin and laid it out on the new cream carpet.

It felt so familiar, spread out in front of her, less like a garment and more like the corpse of a dear friend. This piece of clothing had changed her life. Honor let her hands run over every inch of it – the tiny pearl buttons, the encrusted bodice, the lace panels, the embroidered skirt – the jigsaw of creativity that had resulted in what was, undoubtedly, a work of art. The hours, months of labour it had taken to create it were all here and yet, for Honor, the most important piece was missing: Joy. The Dress was, after all, the material manifestation of something that was, Honor now realized, far more important than the mere buttons and beads: their friendship.

Honor looked around and realized that the world she inhabited, the world of high fashion and its clients, would see what she had gained, a prestigious husband and a design label, with The Dress as the badge for all that. Honor could see only what she had lost – her friendship with her co-creator – and she knew she had to do something, anything, to try to make things right.

She reached into her bag (force of habit, Honor always carried a small sewing kit with her) and took out her stitch picker. Working quickly and meticulously, she deftly began to pick the pearl buttons from The Dress, laying them in a pile on the floor. Then she began to remove all the rhinestones and beads from the bodice. The very least Honor could do was return some of them to Joy. Honor wasn't naive enough to imagine this would put much salve on the wound, especially knowing how unreasonable Joy was, with her drinking, but it made Honor feel as if she was doing something. It would make her feel as if she was a good person.

As the jewels piled up, Honor put them in her pocket then went over to the shelved counter area to see if she could find something more permanent to put them in. The shelves ge Kerrigan

were empty; however there were a few congratulations cards, from the staff, and among them Honor noticed one small envelope that was lying flat, unopened. Honor lifted it, with the intention of ripping it open and using the empty envelope to store her beads, when she noticed the spidery handwriting scrawled across the front.

The envelope was addressed to her, care of Breton's studio, and the handwriting was unmistakably Joy Fitzpatrick's.

Thirty-Seven

 *London, 2014*

Gareth buttoned the purple, tweed 60s swing coat on his mannequin and tied the lime green silk scarf around her grubby neck. He was less self-conscious about being seen arranging ladies' clothes in his window these days. That was one thing that this whole experience with Lily had done for him, although he would trade it in an instant for a moment in her company again.

The purple coat was the last thing from the bag of clothes Lily had given him. Gareth had sold everything else. The money he owed Lily amounted to a few hundred pounds. He had originally planned to give it to her the next time she came in, but that was turning out to be 'never'. Lily was a big shot designer now. Gareth didn't follow social media, but his mate Fergus was into it and he said she was all over it with this dress project of hers. Turns out that bloke he saw coming out of her house was her boss, not a boyfriend, just like she had said. Why could he not have just asked her out when he had the chance? There had been so many opportunities he had let slip.

When the shop was quiet (which was most of the time) Gareth found himself sitting at his Formica table, rolling over in his mind all the times Lily had been sitting there with him, drinking chai, chatting away in the easy way they did. At any time he could have easily leaned over and kissed her, or at least tried to kiss her, but he never had. What he wouldn't give to get one of those ordinary moments back so he could reach over and touch her cheek and tell her how gorgeous she was. Whatever small hope he had had while they were friends was certainly gone now after his last, chronic display of geeky patheticness. He should have asked her straight out, ages ago instead of letting things slide along and hoping, what? That she would make the first move? As if! God, she had been so mad with him that day, her gorgeous cat-green eyes flashing at him. Just thinking about her shouting at him like that made him scarlet with shame but also, he couldn't help himself, desire.

Gareth had saved selling the purple coat until last because, frankly, it was hideous and he was certain nobody would want to buy it. Once he had got rid of all of Lily's stuff, Gareth knew it would be over. He would post a final cheque through her letterbox and there would be no excuse to see her after that.

In the six weeks since Gareth had sold all of her clothes, Lily had not been able to face him, although she thought about him every day. This was partly due to the fact that the sturdy, silk corset Gareth had given her had been used as a foundation for The Dress. Every time Lily worked on her creation she was reminded of Gareth's generosity and her own selfishness in not having thanked him properly for it. However, as each day passed, Lily found the idea of approaching him more and more difficult. Sending him a mere thank you note seemed too formal and somehow, not enough. In fact anything less than Lily flinging herself at him might appear like a snub now that he had (sort of) declared his feelings for her. There were times, when she walked past Old Times and saw her old clothes in his window, when Lily did consider rushing up to Gareth's counter and doing just that. Then she would remember that he owed her money and could have easily used that as an excuse to see her. That meant he was still angry or embarrassed, or more likely both.

In any case, Lily didn't have the time to wander up Kilburn High Road anymore for coffee.

The Dress was nearly complete and Lily herself was almost as transformed as her original toile. Life had changed. Firstly, she wasn't blogging any more. After the big Twitter fury she'd pulled herself completely offline.

She called Jack and told him that he needed to get someone in Scott's substantial marketing department to take over all her social media accounts until The Dress was finished. She was polite but firm, assuring him that she did not have time to do her work and tweet about it at the same time. Once that was done, Lily put everything else in her life aside and set about making The Dress happen.

During the day Lily liaised with lacemakers, tambour beaders, jewellers, embroiderers and couture seamstresses. She was uncompromising, a stickler for detail. Lily knew exactly what she wanted and what she wanted was perfection. Every inch of work produced went through her hands and every millimetre of it was meticulously studied. Misplaced crystals and loose threads, barely visible to the human eyes, were nonetheless noticed and sent back. After a month in the Scott's studio, Lily insisted the half-finished garment be transported back to her apartment. Her days were becoming hectic as the PR department started putting out press releases on the completion date and Lily wanted time alone with her masterpiece to concentrate on getting it absolutely right. Lily lived with her dress, often working on it through the night, doing all her finishing by hand.

Late into these nights, Lily thought about the women who had created the original dress, and most especially about Honor. Lily had resigned herself to never finding the old woman. She had given Zac the address she had been given by the woman in the pub in Bangor. He got a ferry across to the exclusive area of the Jersey Shore and tracked down the address. It was a large, rich-person's house, but it was all closed up, shutters down, gates locked and seemingly uninhabited. Zac left a letter in the mailbox addressed to Honor Conlon, with his details, asking that she contact him urgently.

Every few days Lily called to see if he had heard back, but he never did.

Eventually Zac said, 'The house was really locked up Lily. I think she might probably be dead or something?'

Reluctantly, Lily thought he was probably right.

While working on the embroidered panels of her parents' Bangor grave, Lily tried to channel Honor's spirit, but she could never get any sense of her. Joy and her elegant demeanour in those beautiful woodland pictures were more of an influence.

During her periods of evening isolation Lily also started to draw. In those last few weeks Lily found that in addition to having created a magnificent evening gown, she also had half a dozen sketchpads packed with designs that could easily be edited to create a decent collection.

She was sitting in her flat flicking through them one morning when the phone rang.

'I'm sorry. I made a mistake.'

Lily had picked up the phone in haste before she checked it for Sally's name. Her heart automatically melted at hearing her friend's voice for the first time in weeks.

'I thought they were taking me on because I was brilliant...'

Then Lily remembered how angry she still was.

'Bullshit. You could have gone when they first asked, but you waited until The Dress came up. You deliberately tried to sabotage the thing you knew was important to me. I can't believe I am even talking to you—'

'You're right, you're right!' Sally butted in, just before Lily hung up. 'I went to PopShop to get back at you and Jack. I was angry. I thought you had gone behind my back. Setting up your own private project without me.'

'Excuse me? You were the first person I told about it, and I think your exact words were, "if you want to get back to designing there are better ways than just copying some old frock". Besides, me and Jack were talking about The Dress the whole time we were in Miami. You could have joined in at any time, but you didn't. In fact, you were all eyes to heaven "yada yada" like it was the most stupid idea ever.'

'Well, you were all cosy, cosy with Jack with your notebooks and your *amazing* sketches which you had never even bothered to show me.'

'You had no interest, Sally, you made that clear... did you think my sketches were amazing?'

'Of course they were amazing...' She paused, and the two of them just sat in phone silence for a moment. Lily took a deep breath and welled up. She had missed Sally so much. She hadn't realized how much she still needed her. Still, Lily didn't know what to say. Sally had hurt her so much.

'I know I am a shite friend. The worst,' Sally continued. 'I was jealous...of the way Jack was with you.'

'Sally, there's nothing going on there.'

'Not *that* – just while we were in Miami I knew that he could see something in you; your light, your passion. I was always the one that pushed you, encouraged you and now – now you were listening to him and not me.'

'I always listen to you Sally.'

'No, Lily, you *never* do. And in this case you were totally right. I am a jealous bitch. Jack was *my* thing, you know? He was part of *my* world. I was this big success and you were just beautiful, floaty Lily – wasting her design gift on blogging and vintage – but then I saw he was going to make a big deal out of you and I got mad.'

'You've always pushed me, Sally.'

'No, Lily, I've always nagged you, it's not the same thing. I've held you back and pushed myself forward because the truth is...'

Then out it came.

'...the truth is you are so much cleverer and more talented than me, and you always have been. I was afraid of getting left behind. I didn't want to be in your shadow. God, Lily, I am so, so sorry. I am a vile horrible bitch and I don't blame you if you never want to see me again.'

'Oh, Jesus, Sally.' Lily was crying now too. 'Get in the car and come round here this instant.'

Half an hour later they were hugging it out in Lily's hallway, like it had never happened.

As Sally pushed her face into Lily's shoulder she muttered, 'I'm sorry.'

'It's no big deal,' Lily said, then added, 'Wanna see something that *is* a big deal?'

She took Sally's hand and led her into the sitting room to see The Dress.

As she stood in front of it Sally did something that Lily had not seen her do since Lee Gillespie snogged her in a Youth Club disco in 1997. She cried tears of pure joy.

The antique-rose bodice was inlaid with the finest lace and reached upwards in starched layered petals that were so fine they seemed to disappear into the air like breath on a winter's day. An elaborate display of crystals and pearls gathered at the waistline then crept down the hipbone in jewelled tentacles onto a huge skirt which was layer upon layer of soft silk and chiffon. It seemed so soft it could be mistaken for a cloud. Across sections of a lace overskirt were embroidered depictions of old wedding pictures, done with such painstaking accuracy they could have been screen prints. It was an original touch that pushed The Dress out of the realms of mere garment-making and into that of true art.

It was unlike anything Sally had ever seen before. She could barely believe Lily had made it but then, actually? Yes she could. She had always known Lils was super talented. 'That,' she said when she was finally able to gather herself, '*that* is the most gorgeous thing I have ever seen in my life.'

Lily was thrilled, not just at Sally's reaction, but because her dearest friend had been the first person to see the finished article. The person who had first told her she could be a designer, the one who had so wanted this for her all their lives and had gently pushed her back into it.

'You think it can win?'

'Oh, Lily,' she said, breathless. 'Win some stupid competition? Babe – this goes way beyond Lucy and PopShop and Scott's darling, this dress should be hanging in a museum. It's a masterpiece. It's a piece of couture history.'

They stood for a moment in silence, the figure of The Dress watching over them like some silent goddess.

'I left PopShop,' Sally said. Lily smarted, then smiled. Tough talking Sally was back.

'Nice. Is that why you called me?'

'Of course. OK, only partly. They sent me out to spy on you. I thought they actually wanted me because I was good, but it turns out all they wanted was for me to snitch out on you.'

'Which you did.'

'Which I didn't, actually.'

'Well, what was all that about releasing Lucy's designs to the press?'

'Dur? That was my final stand – to let you see what she was doing. Show her hand. Rather ordinary didn't you think?'

'The press loved her design...'

'The press love *anything* that's supposed to be a secret. Anyway, they fired me after that.'

Lily didn't know what to say. A small part of her thought she *should* be glad to see Sally suffer after how she had abandoned her but the greater part of her loved her friend so much and hated to see her treated badly. She muttered 'bastards' under her breath then took a deep breath and said, 'I suppose you want me to feel sorry for you and forgive you?'

'Absolutely. I've said I'm sorry, and anyway, I bet it gave you a kick up the behind. God knows, I'm sure you needed it you, lazy cow.'

'I suppose you want a job?'

'Friends first – work later. *Of course I want a job.*'

'I'll give Jack a ring.'

'He won't like it, he hates me.'

'Not as much as he hates David Durane.'

'And *loves* you…'

'Of course.'

'Plus, I have an *amazing* idea about how to promote the competition. It's huge, it'll take an act of God – but if anyone can pull it off, it's Jack and he'll love it.'

Lily rang her boss. He was not impressed and there was no offer to rush up to Kilburn and see them today. However, he was very curious, anxious even, to hear Sally's big idea, so he summoned them both into the Scott's boardroom.

Sally was petrified. She hadn't seen Jack since Miami. He was already sitting at the top of the table when they walked in, London's skyline stretched out behind him. He had his best intimidating-businessman face on. Although his expression was impervious he looked as gorgeous as ever. Sally determined she would find a way round him. She always did.

'Before you say anything,' she said before her bum hit the seat, 'I want to apologize, Jack. It was wrong of me to go to PopShop without telling you. Even if my motives were pure.'

Jack raised his eyebrows in cynical expectation.

'I went there as a spy, Jack, pure and simple. I can tell you everything you need to know about Lucy's dress.'

Jack raised his hand and was about to say he did not want to hear another word, when Lily butted in.

'It's true, Jack. Sally has told me everything about Lucy's dress – and it was really, *really* useful. I think we should get her back on the team.'

Nobody, least of all Jack, needed to know the nitty gritty of why Sally had left. She was back. That was all that mattered to Lily.

'I need Sally,' Lily said, 'to do the styling and art direction, if we are going to win this competition.' As she said it, Lily realized that actually, that was true. 'I need her input. Without her, I can't make it happen.'

Jack closed his eyes and when he opened them again the two women were giving him their most charming smiles. Lily, with her long red hair and scarlet lips and alabaster skin – she had Ingénue Creative written all over her but she was tougher than she looked. Sally, feisty, determined, full of great ideas and distractingly voluptuous, but she was not as tough as she pretended to be. Jack caved.

'Go ahead, then. Tell me your big idea.'

Jack held his stern expression but already he knew he would take her back. Sally was a great stylist, but besides that, there was just *something* about her. Nobody else put him in his place quite like her, and he liked it.

'Right,' Sally said. 'The best way, the *only* way you will win this competition is on a catwalk. I have seen Lucy's dress, and Lily's, hands down, is *the* catwalk dress. The Met Ball in New York is *the* fashion event of the year. Jack, you know the people in charge and if you don't, I researched their name and number from the PopShop files. I mooted the idea to Durane and he loved it but I persuaded him to hold off until I got some pictures of your dress – which, of course, I am not going to do. However, now if *you* make the approach to the Met people and mandate to charm them into hosting The Dress-Off, it will seem like *your* idea, which will drive Durane absolutely insane.'

She slid a piece of paper across the table.

'I like it,' he said, looking at the number.

'That last bit was just pure spite. A bonus. I thought you'd approve. Both dresses will be catwalked and voted on by the world's style elite. Publicity, publicity, publicity. Profile, profile, profile.'

Jack was all fired up. Lily was sitting back, letting them get on with it, enjoying the show.

'We have to get the old woman there,' Jack told Sally. 'That'll give us the edge.'

'We don't need an edge,' Sally assured him. 'I've worked both sides and you'll win hands down...*what* old woman?'

Lily filled her in on Honor, then put it to bed by saying, 'She's dead.'

It was easier than explaining everything, and it was probably the truth.

The meeting ended well. Jack got the Met Ball organizers on speaker phone. There and then he and Sally made the deal. They were resistant, as the event was only a few weeks away but between Sally persuading them of the editorial and historical value of the project and Jack throwing sponsorship money at the museum, they went for it.

'The tickets are $25,000 a head so we can't bring the whole team,' Jack said.

Sally gave him a look.

'Obviously you and Lily.'

Sally gave him another look.

'We'll negotiate. And let's have a party in London before we go.'

'It's a pleasure doing business with you, Mr Scott,' Sally said.

'And you, Ms Sally.'

Lily smiled, noticing that she might as well not be in the room.

Thirty-Eight

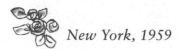 *New York, 1959*

Losing Honor

Dear Honor,
I am writing this letter to you, by way of an apology.

You have every right to be angry with me, nonetheless I beg of you to believe that my words are heartfelt.

I am sorry for all the vicious things I have said about you and Frank and I am sorry for ruining your wedding day.

In recent weeks I have come to understand how my behaviour, over the years, has affected those people I thought I loved.

In truth, I don't think I really understood what love was, until now. I was too busy, chasing away my fears and anxieties with booze, to fully give love to any other human being.

I wanted to be rescued from myself and I thought Frank would 'rescue' me. I confused that selfish need for reassurance and succour, with love.

Whether Frank ever truly loved me or not, is not for me to say, but I do believe that he is a good man and that he *deserves a better wife than I ever was to him and so, for what it is worth, Honor, I am giving your marriage my blessing.*

I am also extending those same good wishes to your business venture with Breton – you are a gifted designer and I have no doubt that you will succeed.

As for our friendship, I am deeply saddened by that loss, as I do feel there was a bond forged between us during the time you made me that beautiful dress. I know that the garment is back in your possession and, while I do miss its sublime beauty, I have no need of it in my life anymore.

With the help of some good friends and a Higher Power I choose to call God, I have finally come to understand that the greatest beauty I can ever achieve will come from inside my heart and I am concentrating all of my efforts on making that happen. Slowly, I am learning how to be a better person.

For the part you played in the drama that led me to this place, I thank you and wish you all the love, joy and happiness you deserve.

Warmest regards,
Joy

Honor stood for a few moments, trying to take the contents of Joy's letter in. Joy was forgiving her. Joy was saying sorry to her.

Joy had done nothing, compared with what she had done to Joy: taken her husband, stolen her dress, betrayed their friendship, reneged on their agreement to start a couture house together, destroyed her confidence and sent her life spiralling into a drunken mess. And yet here Joy was, apologizing to her? Begging her forgiveness for that one lousy outburst at the Plaza and saying bad things about her on the phone to Breton, while out of her mind in drunken grief. Was she being sarcastic? Talking about 'the part you played in the drama' and offering Honor and Frank her blessing – was Joy mocking her? If so, what an extraordinary act of cattiness, but then Honor read the letter again. 'Slowly, I am learning how to be a better person'. It rang true, all of the letter rang true. Once Honor realized that Joy was being sincere, she also realized that her paltry attempt to return the small pile of beads she carried in her pocket was a meaningless, shallow gesture. Frank's insistence that Joy was an unreasonable alcoholic seemed like a ploy, and believing him, a callous justification for their shallow marriage.

Honor was overcome with such a powerful feeling of anger that she did not know what to do with herself. Rage propelled her towards The Dress in a kind of slow motion and, as adrenaline pumped through her body, she began to rip at the seams of The Dress, tearing at the fabric with a heightened strength, ripping the silk with her bare hands, sending beads and sequins flying, as she screamed and roared her way into it, baying with fury like a wild animal, destroying her greatest work. It was as if, instead of a child, a terrible fury had been born out of all the bad things she had done. She was not destroying The Dress, she was destroying herself – turning the beauty she had created into the savage mess that was her own destiny. No matter how hard she tore at it, the beauty was still there in the corpse of The Dress – in the chunks of appliqué, the shards of lace, the scraps of fine silk. Screeching with frustration, she bundled the whole lot back into the glass cabinet and, with her hands shaking, took a box of matches out of her bag.

By the time Breton found her, Honor had set fire to The Dress. The women, who followed him down from the studio, wept when they saw the scene, some at the loss of such a beautiful dress, others simply with shock and fear at the transformation of their old workmate, but Honor's fury was not yet quenched.

It took the Frenchman, and his entire team of twelve women, to pull Honor away and keep her in a corner of the shop, until Frank could be called back to collect her. They managed to quench the fire and save the shop, but its centrepiece, The Dress, was nothing more than a smouldering pile of ashes.

Breton called an ambulance and Honor was taken to hospital, where she was sedated. As her mind wandered in and out of a drugged haze, Honor remembered her life before The Dress, before Joy and Frank, before her dreams of being a great designer became an ambition-fuelled reality.

Honor had always believed herself to be, fundamentally, her parents' daughter, a good, honourable person. She knew she was no nun; she had never especially pursued goodness, but she had taken for granted that it was there.

Honor now saw that her pursuit of beauty had altered that. Fashion pandered to women's vanity and wealth; her community-minded father had always viewed it as a shallow, meaningless pastime. She had thought that the goodness he and her mother had planted in her would always be there but now it seemed it wasn't. She had tried to make it right, but her efforts had been small and pathetic.

Joy, for all her alcoholic madness and her spoilt rich-girl upbringing, had proven to be a better person than she could ever be.

Honor hated herself, she hated Frank for loving her and, most of all, she hated Joy, for bringing this terrible flaw to light.

Anyone who had seen her destroy her finest work would say that Honor Fitzpatrick had lost her mind, but in actual fact the talented designer believed she had lost something much more important than that. After reading Joy's letter Honor felt that she had lost her soul. Without her soul, she was nothing; without her soul, she knew she would never design again.

After a week Honor was released home into Frank's care, under the supervision of a consultant psychiatrist.

Again, for three weeks, Frank and Jones found themselves nursing Honor – who was kept on a cocktail of soothing drugs – aside from the days when she was seeing Dr Rensch. Honor had no interest in talking to the rather cold German doctor but nonetheless, Dr Rensch reported their sessions, in florid detail, back to Frank. He explained that his wife was still suffering from shock after the miscarriage.

'In some women, the need for a child is so deep that they never recover. Be patient, another child will cure her. Bide your time.'

On the day she destroyed the shop, Frank found the letter Joy had written to her and knew it was at the root of Honor's fury. He had received one himself, the day before at work, and barely bothered reading it before throwing it in his wastepaper bin. Honor was different. She would have taken all Joy's manipulative ways to heart. He showed the letter to Rensch, but he said it was of no importance. It seemed that Joy had joined this cult of Alcoholics Anonymous – a ridiculous organization, in his opinion, with all its unscientific talk of God and such. She was being coy, she would drink again soon, and die. What a shame Frank had not known about him before, he himself ran a programme in a clinic in Switzerland that would surely have cured her. Still, she was in the clutches of these AA people now, so it was too late.

'You must concentrate on your second wife, Mr Fitzpatrick,' he assured Frank. 'She is the one we must deal with now, yes?'

Frank was, nonetheless, furious with Joy. He went to his lawyer and told him to cut her off entirely.

'Not a penny. Take the apartment back, too. Let her rot on the streets of New York, for all I care.'

Daniel Cohen, who had been so sympathetic when he came to him first with Honor, told him what he was trying to do was both illegal and immoral and said he could not help him.

'You have to let go, Frank,' he said. 'Wish poor Joy well, move on.'

As Frank's anger and animosity towards Joy deepened, so did his love for and patience with Honor. Although he was exhausted by her instability, he took only pleasure in looking after her, carrying in meals prepared by Jones on a tray, sitting at the side of the bed and feeding her, while she gazed out into space, in a silent, distant trance.

Rensch said the drug-calming therapy would end soon, that she was responding to the 'talking' therapy and would be well again. Dr Rensch was at the top of his field and very expensive. He assured Frank that his wife's insanity was temporary, although all women were delicate creatures and often need to be treated with care. He said it was wrong of Frank not to have protected his wife better, from Joy's outbursts. They had undoubtedly contributed to her current condition.

Rensch did not report back to Frank on the session when he asked Honor directly, 'Do you love your husband?'

There was a pause, then she said, 'No.'

It was the first and only time, the eminent psychiatrist noted, that he saw the sad, rather plain young woman cry.

Thirty-Nine

 *London, 2014*

Sally and Lily were packing up The Dress for New York when the Skype call came in on Lily's iPad.

Lily was unpicking some packing tape so Sally answered the call. All she saw was this kid with a bleached-blond quiff shouting. 'She's alive! She's alive! Honor's alive!'

'Hey, Lily, there's a crazy person Skyping you...'

Lily ran over.

'Zac! What happened?'

'So,' he said, dramatically spreading his hands in the air (Sally raised her eyes to heaven. She hated it when people were more dramatic than she was), 'that place I went to *was* Honor Conlon's house but she had sold it to some rich family from Europe. Because it's their holiday home, it's locked up for nine months of the year. They just got there for their annual vacation and they found my note to her. They contacted her first and sent my details on. It seems Honor is living in a nursing home and does all of her talking through a nurse called Emily. And get this – Emily the nurse emailed me just now with her Skype address and said to call her. I am *so* excited. It's like Honor was dead and now she isn't! How great it that?'

'Did you contact her yet?' Lily asked.

She saw an uncharacteristic shadow fall over Zac's face.

'No,' he said.

'Why not?' Lily asked.

Sally was standing in front of her making 'yada yada' and 'hurry up' signals.

'Truth is, I'm a bit scared.' He turned his eyes slightly from the screen. Sally grimaced and made another 'hurry up' sign as Lily waved her away.

'Firstly, they were both married to the same man, your Great Uncle which is *weird* and she might still be mad about that....'

'Zac, that was years ago,' Lily said, 'and your grandmother went on to be happily married. I'm sure it would be water under the bridge by now.'

Zac paused, looked down and said, 'I know it sounds silly, but I've never known any old people apart from Grandma Joy and, well, the whole thing of seeing someone that knew her just makes me feel a bit sad.'

He turned his face away and Lily knew he didn't want her to see him cry. Lily felt herself choke up in sympathy. They had both lost their beloved grandparents and those people were connected, somehow, through Honor.

'Send me her details and I'll take it from here,' Lily said. 'I'll call and let you know how we get on.'

'Yes!' said Sally punching the air. 'We have the old lady! Call the nurse, quickly, it's 10 a.m. in New York, she's just at work – call before she gets too busy.'

Emily the nurse picked up the call right away, as if she had been waiting. She was an attractive African-American woman, tall, slim, around their age. Lily told her she was impressed they had a Skype account in a nursing home.

'It's a pretty impressive home,' Emily explained. 'We have an exclusive clientele. Our residents are from all over the world and they like to stay in touch with what's going on. We're kinda out of the way here in Jersey, so we rely on video and Skype a lot, as a way of keeping in touch with the families.'

'Does Honor have much family?' Lily asked.

'No,' Emily said, her lips pursing. She seemed distracted.

'Well actually, it turns out I am Honor's great-niece,' Lily said, 'which is why I am so keen to get in touch with her. She was married to my great-Uncle Frank.'

'I see.' Emily had turned ice cold on her but Lily persisted.

'Also, the guy you contacted? Zac? He is the grandson of one of her oldest friends, Joy. Joy left pictures of a dress Honor made for her in the 1950s and so we thought Honor might want to—'

'Turn it off, turn the damn thing off...' A voice came from beyond the screen.

'I'm sorry,' Emily said, standing up. 'I have to go now...' and the screen suddenly went blank.

'What was *that*?' Lily said.

'That, you poor naive fool,' said Sally, 'was the old woman in the background, checking you out.'

'Of course it was,' Lily said. 'Why the hell didn't I think of that?'

Lily felt a pang of loss. She had been, to all intents and purposes, in the room with her great-aunt by marriage, the co-creator of The Dress, the one link to her grandfather's generation and she had blown it.

'I blew it.'

'Yes,' said Sally, 'you certainly did. So now it is down to me, as usual, to sort out this mess.'

'It's not sort-out-able Sally – there is no way she wants to see us. She's an old lady, leave her in peace.'

Sally sat down opposite her and said, 'Are you *joking*, Lily?'

Lily smiled. Sally was right. She had put so much of herself into making this wonderful garment but her dream was bigger than that. She had the opportunity to meet the woman who had created the original. Honor might not be willing to see her but she was still alive and…

'Where there's life there's hope,' said Sally, reading her mind. 'So let's finish getting this dress packed because we are going to get that old lady and we are going to bring her to the Met Ball!'

When Sally left, Lily walked over to her parents' house. Her grandmother's arthritis had worsened since Joe died and she was housebound. Lily's mother had given up work to look after her full time and her father was away in Sweden on a building job.

'I am so sorry we won't be in New York supporting you,' Mary said. 'You know how proud we are of you.'

Lily thought about all the love that was just sitting there, creating a constant cushion in the background of her life. She rarely stopped to appreciate it, yet it was the cornerstone of who she was.

'I hope Frank's widow is kind to you,' her grandmother, Eileen, said as she kissed her goodbye. Lily remembered the cold, unkempt grave of Frank Fitzpatrick and the standoffish attitude of the lady in the bar when she had mentioned Honor's name. 'You know not all old ladies are as nice as me.'

'Would Grandad disapprove of me digging up the past like this?' Lily asked her.

'Well, honestly Lily? He probably would,' she said. 'But he's not here is he? And I am just desperate to know what happened to Frank so be sure to bring me back the whole story.'

Lily smiled, but part of her felt her grandmother was just being diplomatic. She just hoped that she could close this family circle without opening any old wounds.

The following evening was their good luck, going away party. All the people who had contributed to the making of The Dress were invited to a soiree in Scott's design studio. Jack laid on champagne and sushi and everyone from the fabric suppliers to the tambour beading specialists joined the Scott's office staff in the converted Soho warehouse, including the lace lady from Westport who had given Lily the good luck charm.

Earlier that afternoon, Lily had called over to Old Things. Delivering a last-minute invite to Gareth had seemed like the perfect middle ground excuse to break the ice, except that he hadn't been there. So, Lily popped the invite in the door of the shop and walked away feeling flat and disappointed. She could not even be sure that Gareth would get it in time for that evening and even if he had, Lily felt pretty certain he wouldn't turn up.

So when Sally said, 'Ooh, look who just walked in. Your nerdy friend Gareth...' Lily got such a fright that she felt virtually propelled by fear towards the drinks table. As she was pouring a couple of glasses of courage down her throat, Jack came over and started bending her ear about something boring like travel insurance. By the time Lily got rid of him and had gathered herself enough to turn around and face Gareth, he was already gone.

'How could you have let him go like that?' she said to Sally. 'I needed to speak to him.'

'Didn't look like it the way you ran off. Anyway there was nothing I could do. He just scuttled off like a church mouse. Saw you were talking to Jack and got all weird. He said to give you this,' and she handed Lily a card.

She tore it open.

It was a generic 'Good Luck' card with her list of clothes neatly folded inside, all items ticked off, and a cheque for £497.56.

Lily's heart sank as she handed the card to her curious friend.

'Gee, this guy really knows how to woo a girl,' Sally said.

'It's not his fault; we had a sort of row.'

Sally gave her a withering look. 'A row?'

'Oh, all right, I had a go at him.'

'What for?'

'It's complicated.'

'Try me.'

'We had a sort-of-a-thing going.'

'A "thing"?'

'Yes, you know. Then he saw me with Jack and—'

'Aha. Jack would be pretty stiff competition for nerdy boy all right,' Sally said, acidly. Lily threw her a suspicious look.

'Me and Gareth had a bit of a "thing" for each other and now we don't because I blew it. OK? Subject closed.'

'Fine, fine,' Sally said, 'only if you don't mind me saying so...'

'I do.'

'...it looks to me like you still have a bit of thing going for him.'

'Drop it, Sally...Oh, look. There's Sandra. Really nice woman I bought the lace off in Westport. Sandra!'

Sandra came over and Lily forced herself to get distracted by talk of lace and Ireland, although the shadow of Gareth rushing off like that clung to her heart for the rest of the night.

The next day Sally and Lily and The Dress flew to New York.

They had packed The Dress upright in a tall box so they could squeeze it into the back of the taxi between them. Sally had insisted that The Dress have its own seat on the plane, it being too precious to go in the hold. Jack did not object. He had given Sally carte blanche. He had not even seen the finished dress himself yet, partly because, aside from transporting it to and from the specialist embroidery and beading studios in Soho, Lily had kept it under lock and key in her flat.

'Any word from Gareth?' Sally asked, as they settled into their seats.

'Why would I hear from Gareth?'

'I don't know, I just thought he might have followed up that amazing romantic card with a phone call?' Sally said.

'Ha, ha. He was trying to be polite in the face of my unbelievable stupidity. Can we leave it at that now, *please?*'

Sally took the hint and grabbed a passing hostess saying, 'Bring us a couple of glasses of champagne there love, will you? We're on a tab here.'

Lily drank her champagne and pretended she was excited about the Met Ball but talk of Gareth had quietened her adventurous mood.

Zac and his mother met Lily and Sally and The Dress at the airport. Zac was taller than Lily had expected, but she felt as if she knew him after all the Skype calls and drama they had shared up to this point. It was great to finally put her arms around him and give him a hug. Imogen, his mother, was warm and inviting.

'We are both so excited to see your dress. We don't have any other family except for each other, so this has been a really special experience for us – for Zac, especially.' Lily smiled and said it had been special for her too, until Sally, impatient as usual, bundled them all into the car.

Crammed into the back of Imogen Podmore's slightly scruffy saloon they headed straight to the address Zac had for Golden Acres nursing home in Jersey. Lily was on edge as she explained to Imogen that Joy's old friend, Honor, was living there. She had not explained that Honor did not want to see them, nor that that they were arriving on her doorstep uninvited and unexpected. To make things even more unsettling for Lily, Sally had refused to tell Lily what her 'cunning plan' to get in the door was – only that she had one.

'I can't wait to meet Honor,' Zac said. 'This is going to be such a buzz!'

Lily shot Sally a panicked look.

'Trust me,' Sally mouthed back at her silently. Lily tried, but she couldn't see how Sally was going to pull this off.

Golden Acres was a mock-Tudor manor with ornate gardens that suggested a wealthy, discerning clientele. Sally marched straight up to the desk and asked to see Honor Fitzpatrick's nurse, Emily, telling Lily, Zac and Imogen to wait in the large, lavishly furnished reception area. The five-foot tall dress box had a door at the front of it and looked somewhat like a coffin, so it got a few backward glances from the nursing staff as they scurried through.

When Emily came out Sally smiled as she noticed the pretty nurse was slim and six-foot tall, just as she had guessed from their stunted Skype call. Perfect.

Sally turned on full charm and explained that she was a friend of Honor Conlon's great-niece. Emily looked anxiously across at the group and Sally said, 'We've come all the way from London to see her.'

'I am so sorry,' Emily said, 'but she is adamant she doesn't want to see any family. She was quite insistent.' And she looked over Sally's shoulder again, smiling apologetically. The nurse had a conscience; this was going to be easier than Sally thought.

'Of course, we want to see Honor, but mostly, we have something to show her.'

'Oh, I don't know,' Emily said, and then Sally looked across and gave Zac a nod.

On her cue, Zac opened the door of the box and unpacked The Dress.

Its ornate, glimmering skirts swished out onto the polished parquet flooring, and the nurse gasped.

Forty

 *New York, 2014*

It was an ordinary day in Golden Acres; every day here was more or less like the last. Breakfast in her room was followed by her morning TV shows. Honor watched a lot of *Oprah* re-runs; she liked to see other people living out the complexity of their family lives in front of the nation, it made her feel grateful for her own simple, uncomplicated people-free existence. It wasn't much more than an existence, but she was happy with that. It was what she had chosen for herself a long time ago.

Honor had come to Golden Acres eight years ago after the arthritis began to take hold of her knees. She had been finding it hard to manage the stairs at home by herself and the regular day nurse had suggested this place. She liked it here although, in truth, Honor neither liked nor disliked any place. It was just food and shelter to her. The old woman was just keeping herself alive although, sometimes, she wondered why she bothered.

At around midday Emily, who Honor had decided was the only person she would have anything to do with in here, took her for a walk around the grounds. Sometimes she went in the chair if her knees were very bad, but if she was having a good day she would get out and walk part of the way. Then there was lunch, more TV and in the evening Emily insisted on taking her down to the lounge. They put entertainment on in there in the evening sometimes, but Honor always kept away from the other residents. She had no interest in making new friends at this stage of her life, especially not with boring 'old' people. In truth, Honor had been living in isolation for a long time and that was just how she liked it.

That was why she had got such a shock when she had learned that a great-niece of Frank's in London was looking for her. She had been curious when Emily mentioned it and got the girl up on the computer to talk but then when she had mentioned that Joy's grandson was also on her trail, that was too much, and she had told Emily to switch the damn thing off. The nurse had tried to persuade her to speak with them but, although Emily was acting with a good heart, she didn't know anything about Honor's past. She didn't know about what Honor had done, how she had lived, how she had come to have all this money and was able to live out her days in this expensive, if isolated, luxury.

The last thing Honor wanted was the past rearing its ugly head – not after all she had done to avoid it, not after all the sacrifices she had made to keep it at bay. So she had told Emily that on no account was she to let anyone in through her door, even family – especially anyone 'pretending' to be family, she emphasized.

'I was an only child,' she explained to Emily, 'and both my parents died long ago. There is nobody left. Anyone coming here looking for me now is only trying to steal my money.'

My money. Even just saying it felt wrong.

Oprah was a bit dull today and Honor was snoozing when

she heard Emily come through the door. When she turned around Honor thought she must be dreaming.

Emily's dark skin against the rose-coloured fabric made it seem to glow as she walked towards her, beaming, incandescent. Honor blinked. The Dress featured in her dreams often, even now. Beautiful dreams she had tried to hold onto in her sleep, where she was a child floating through the sky above Bangor on a cloud of chiffon, her parents smiling up at her. Nightmares then, where The Dress, blackened with fire, was sucked down into the bowels of the earth through the floor of that cabinet in the shop Breton and Frank had made for her. She never dreamed about Joy.

'The people that called you are outside Honor. They asked me to show you this. Isn't it beautiful?'

How could The Dress be here? She remembered destroying it before losing her mind that time and yet, this was surely the same gown, although it looked different somehow.

'The young woman we spoke to on Skype, Lily, she made it. She said it is a replica of a dress you made for a friend. She thought you might like to see it.'

This was real after all. Not a dream. It was really happening.

Honor wanted to turn away. It was too cruel, too painful, the past ambushing her in this way, and yet she could not. The last time she had seen The Dress it had been lying, like a corpse, on her salon floor. She had set fire to it, and with that act, her very life, and what was left of her heart after losing the baby had turned to ashes. Now here it was, The Dress, risen from the dead. The ghost of her past, the subject of her dreams. Except this dress wasn't a dream, or a ghost, it was real.

As Emily moved closer to her, Honor's hand instinctively reached out to touch the fabric. She noticed the lace was different, a more golden colour to her original white. Still dumbfounded, and overtaken with an old curiosity, Honor studied the jewelled bodice and saw that, while it had the same opulent structure and elements as her own design, this was, after all, a different dress. There was not quite the same placing of the jewels. It was a good copy, a very good copy of her own and a fine piece of design in itself. She would not see the girl. Honor had no desire to have her life overturned in this way. However, she would ask Emily to congratulate the young designer on her work.

She was about to impart this information, when she saw it.

On the front of the skirt there was an embroidered imprint of her parents' faces. In silk, shimmering into life, as the unicorns and fairy tale images had on her original, were John and Clare Conlon. They were smiling, serene, happy – like a beautiful mirage.

The same picture was on her mantelpiece. It was the only one she had of them, on their wedding day. The one she had asked to be embedded into their gravestone. The photograph was the only thing Honor had connecting them to her. It was the only evidence that she had ever had a family, that she had ever been close to anybody. The girl, this niece, whoever she was, must have seen their picture on the gravestone. Maybe when she was visiting her great-uncle's grave. She knew Frank was buried there. He was dead too now; they were all dead.

Seeing this Honor felt a sudden ache in her heart for her parents, but not just her parents, perhaps, Joy, Frank, somebody.

'Let them in,' she said to Emily, 'let them in and I'll tell you all a story.'

'You look a little like him – about the eyes.'

'Thank you,' Lily said.

'It wasn't a compliment.'

Silence again. The old lady was oppressively stern and the atmosphere in the room was heavy with her anxiety. Even Zac and Sally were stunned into an awkward silence. In the small but beautifully positioned bed-sitting room Imogen stood by the door ready to help Emily, who had taken off The Dress and laid it across the bed, before going to get some tea.

Lily took a deep breath, then reached into her handbag and pulled out one of Joy's pictures.

'Imogen and Zac found a set of these pictures...' She took one of the woodland pictures from her bag and tried to hand it to her, but Honor waved it away as if it was a hand grenade. Lily kept going. '...and a magazine article after Joy died. I am a designer myself and I felt inspired by a picture of this dress I had found when I was looking in old *Vogue* magazines online searching for my great-uncle, Frank Fitzpatrick. My name is Lily Fitzpatrick, you see. My grandfather was his brother and he died...' Honor refused to acknowledge her, but Lily continued, '...then I found out that Zac was my cousin and he's studying fashion, and then he got a friend to look you up in a library and we found you too...'

At this stage Lily just petered out. The old woman looked briefly over at the picture, but as Lily held it out tentatively to her, she kept her hands firmly in her lap then turned her face to the window. It was as if she was willing them to not be there and yet would not say anything directly to make them go away. Lily sensed Honor had something to say but the atmosphere was so tense she didn't know if she'd be able to stick it out long enough to hear it.

'So,' Honor finally said, 'I was working for the designer Breton when Joy Fitzpatrick came in and commissioned me to make a gown for her thirtieth birthday. The Dress took us months to make, I can't remember exactly how long. It caused a sensation. It was, as the press said, the most magnificent dress ever made.

'You saw the pictures, obviously or you wouldn't have been able to make that.' Her hands waved over the garment on the bed as if it were no more than a discarded dressing gown. 'So, I suppose you want to know what happened to Joy and I after that?'

Actually, Lily (and certainly Sally) thought, what we *really* want to know is are you willing to be scrubbed up and dragged along to a fashion ball at The Met tomorrow night to be a historical mascot for a high-street fashion label? A prospect, now that they had actually been confronted with this truculent old woman, that seemed so distant as to be laughable.

'Yes,' Lily said, raising her eyes and shrugging at the others out of Honor's eye line. 'Tell us what happened next.'

Honor kept her face pointed towards the window and spoke out into the middle distance as if they weren't there.

'Joy and I fell out over Frank. I won't go into why. For one reason and another, The Dress came back into my possession but I decided that, as Joy had given me some of her own mother's jewellery to work into the bodice work, I should return those trinkets to her, so I removed them from The Dress to give back to her. I thought it was only right I should return them.'

Honor briefly looked up at Lily for approval, but when Lily nodded it, the old woman seemed annoyed with herself for having 'asked' and looked out of the window, seemingly lost in thought for a while, before she went on.

'The Dress itself was destroyed in a fire in my studio – and after that happened I became rather ill for a time. Six months after that, Frank and I separated. I decided that, quite simply, I did not love him anymore. The business of how we had met, with his being married to Joy, had never...' She paused and closed her eyes. '...sat well with me, and after the fire in my studio and another...more personal matter that I won't go into, I decided I couldn't be married to him anymore.

'Before I left him I decided to make amends to Joy and return her mother's jewels. They were, I thought, of no value other than sentiment, but it was my way of saying sorry for having...' Another pause. '...stolen her husband from her, if you like.

'In any case, finding Joy was not too difficult. Frank had been cruel to Joy, trying to cut her off without a penny. I knew Frank's lawyer, Mr Cohen, to be a kind man, so I went to him, in confidence, and explained the situation. He gave me an address for her.

'I found Joy in a small apartment in Brooklyn where she had remarried, a car dealer of some kind according to Frank's lawyer, a strange name...'

'Daniel Podmore, my grandfather,' said Zac.

The old woman closed her eyes to indicate that she needed silence to talk and it was then that Lily realized she was not merely being unfriendly – she was making a confession.

'Joy answered the door. She looked well and, despite all that had happened between us, she was a madwoman for the drink, a raging alcoholic...'

Lily jolted at the revelation and saw Sally muffle a snigger. Imogen looked visibly riled and Zac curious as Honor continued. 'Anyway, she seemed quite well; obviously this man had straightened her out. I would never have had the guts to face her after stealing her husband except that she had written to me a few months beforehand apologizing for her appalling behaviour towards me and Frank, so I knew it was unlikely there'd be a scene. We had a nice exchange, although she didn't invite me in and before I had the chance to give her what I had come for, she cut me off and said, "I have a good life now, Honor, but I have had to leave my old life behind so I don't think it's a good idea for us to be friends anymore," then she turned and went inside.

'As I tried to give her the package her husband came out and saw me leaving it on the step. I explained they were some trinkets I was returning to her and he said, "Joy doesn't need anything from you or your husband. We are doing just fine, please leave us alone and don't leave anything behind you. My wife doesn't need any reminder of her past; she has a new life now." Then he closed the door in my face. So that was that.

'It wasn't as easy as I had thought it would be leaving Frank. He would not leave me alone, would not take no for an answer. In the end I had to cut myself off from him completely. I even distanced myself from my parents because I knew he would go asking them where I was too. I went back to being a seamstress, but not in a design house where Frank might find me, just doing alterations in a small drapery shop in the Bronx. Then the shop closed, I got laid off and when I couldn't make my rent one month I went digging around for something to pawn and that's when I found...'

Honor paused and Lily noticed that she was breathing very quickly. She was afraid, the old woman was afraid of something, at that moment Emily came in with the tea and Lily motioned to her some concern for Honor.

'...when I found Joy's jewels.' She paused and took a deep breath, closed her eyes and blurted out, 'The man in the pawn shop said they were worth in excess of $50,000.'

It didn't sound like that much now to any of them but at that time it must have been a fortune. Certainly from the look of abject terror on the old woman's face it was clear she thought she was going to be slung in jail for it.

Lily reached out and took the old woman's hand and tears began to well up in her rheumy eyes.

'I didn't take them back to her. I should have taken them back to her but I was so *angry*...'

Zac came over and knelt in front of her.

'Joy was so beautiful and now she had a good husband and she seemed to be happy and content, despite everything and I thought if I kept her money maybe I could be happy again too. But...'

Then the old woman broke down into terrible sobs.

'It's all right,' Zac said. 'We're just glad we found you.'

Lily looked across at Imogen, and she looked, actually, as if she did mind. This had been a painful episode for her and Zac.

'You look like her,' Honor said to Zac, touching his chin. 'So beautiful...' And she started to cry again – the tears she had not allowed herself to cry for some fifty years.

It was such a powerful relief that as the tears came, they almost turned to laughter. Had fifty years really passed with her locked inside that guilt, holding the terrible secret, knowing she was a bad person? The door had opened; she had confessed and now Honor was free. Could it really be that simple? Could the truth really have opened the doors of her guilty prison? Was seventy-nine too old for her to be given a second chance?

Emily went over to her and was about to usher them all out of the room when Honor gathered herself and said, 'No. I want them to stay. I want you all to stay. I don't want to be alone anymore.'

Forty-One

Emily brought them in tea and sandwiches and they stayed with Honor for the rest of that afternoon. After she had made her confession, the old woman was like a different person, full of anecdotes and chat. She seemed to become immediately fond of Zac, inviting him to come and sit next to her on the small settee and asking him all about his college course.

It was Zac who talked her into going to the Met Ball. 'You *have* to come,' he said. 'You'll be my date for the night. It's going to be the biggest night of my life, of all our lives. Please say you'll come.'

'I'm seventy-nine,' Honor laughed. 'My partying days are over.'

'Nonsense,' Zac said. 'We've just met so I can tell you now...' He did a Beyoncé click. '...your party days are just beginning, lady.'

Sally mouthed, 'Yo!' at Lily and gave her a fist bump. The kid was good. He had the old lady wrapped around his finger.

'Come for me, Aunt Honor. For Grandma Joy.'

Tears welled up in Honor's eyes. She wasn't Zac's aunt.

She wasn't anyone's aunt, or wife, or sister. Yet this young man was inviting her to be his family, in such a warm and casual way, after all she had done.

'I'll come,' she said, adding grumpily, 'but don't expect any great style, I've nothing to wear.'

'I took the liberty of putting a few frocks on hold for you,' said Sally. 'I'll have them sent here care of Emily in the morning?'

That Sally was a cheeky strap, full of herself. Honor looked across at her icily.

'I hope they're comfortable, otherwise I shall be wearing my pant-suit as usual. I think Emily has a clean one...somewhere.'

Honor and Emily exchanged a knowing look.

'I'm sure we can get one laundered before tomorrow.'

Sally looked suitably terrified. 'I'm sure, erm, there's a Carolina Herrera that will fit you. I'll make sure you get a good choice.'

Honor nodded her approval, and managed to give Lily a wink bringing her in on the joke.

They made practical arrangements for Honor to be collected by Zac in a limousine the following afternoon. While she and Zac became instant friends, Honor had noticed that Joy's daughter, Imogen, had remained aloof.

As they were leaving Honor reached out and took Imogen's hand. Imogen gave her a polite shake and was ready to pull away, but Honor held her grip.

'I was not a good friend to your mother...' Imogen flinched, but Honor held on. '...and perhaps I contributed to some dark times in her life. But I want you to know...' She faltered, her voice so quiet that Imogen had to lean down to hear her. '...that for the time I knew Joy, I loved her.' She paused again. 'Your mother was a most beautiful and lovable person.'

'I appreciate your honesty,' Imogen said, 'but it's a lot to take in.'

She tried to move her hands gently away from the old lady's grip but Honor was not ready to let her go.

She closed her eyes and, unable to open them for the pain in her heart, said, 'Please. Let me make amends.'

Imogen melted. Her own mother had been around this woman's age when she died. Whatever had happened between then, Honor and Joy had clearly once been close. She leaned down and kissed Honor warmly on both hands. 'Just having known and loved my mother,' she said, 'is amends enough for me.'

Lily and Sally were booked into the Plaza on Central Park. Jack Scott was staying there too, as was Sharon. Jack was bringing her as his 'official date' the following night so she could model Scott's new high-street plus-size evening wear collection. The theme of the Met Ball was How High Street Copies Couture and the Scott's–PopShop Dress-Off had earned such social media traction in the few weeks since it had been announced that the organizers had put the competition at the centre of the evening's programme.

On the day of the show, Lily and Sally had the task of finally choosing their model. They had already narrowed the girls down to twenty using look-books and video casting in London, and the New York agents understood this gig was a big deal so had put some of their best girls on first option. However, there had been a last minute glitch when the Met Ball production team insisted The Dress be delivered to them to be kept backstage twenty-four hours before the show. Something to do with insurance. Sally got into a huge fight with them insisting she needed it for the casting, but despite getting Jack's legal team involved, she could not wrestle it back off them. She managed to borrow a Vera Wang wedding dress sample as a stand in but it wasn't the same.

By lunchtime they had seen all of the models they had picked out and some that they hadn't. All of them beautiful but none of them quite right.

'Thank you!' Sally said, waving one girl out and grabbing a chocolate strawberry from the VIP food platter she had ordered to calm her frayed nerves.

'This is hopeless,' she said. 'They all just look so bloody *ordinary.*'

The last half dozen girls they had not even bothered putting into the Vera Wang.

'One more to go,' Sally said. 'She had better be good or we'll be picking off the reject list.'

The door opened and a young model walked in who made their jaws drop. Svetlana, Russian, stunning. But there was more. With her razor-sharp cheekbones, almond eyes, shiny black hair and haughty expression, she was the image of Joy Fitzpatrick.

'OMG. It's remarkable,' Lily said.

Sally nodded at the girl and said, 'Start stripping, dear, we've a lot of buttons to do up.'

In the Vera Wang dress, she was perfection.

'She looks exactly like Joy in the woodland pictures.'

'You're happy?' Sally said. Lily nodded.

'Then I'm happy.'

When Svetlana left, Lily was beaming.

'This was meant to be, the perfect girl turning up last. If we had booked any of the others, we might not have seen her and she is so right. Our dress is sure to win now. With Svetlana in it, it has to. It's fate.'

'Lils,' Sally said, 'I'm glad we got the model you wanted but to be honest we could put wheels under that dress and push it on a shopping trolley down the runway with no model in it, and it would still win – it's that good.'

Despite her relief in getting the right model, over the next three hours as they were getting ready for their big night, Lily could feel a terrible tension rising up in her. Sally had booked a hair and make-up artist and borrowed a selection of clothes for them. Sally wore a knockout 80s Azzedine Alaïa with a rubber corset bodice. Lily picked out a vintage Jean Dessès copper and navy evening gown for herself. But as the hairdresser was smoothing down her Audrey Hepburn bun, Lily had to get up and walk around the room. She could feel her heart start beating ten to the dozen and her palms were sweating as if she was having a panic attack. Lily calmed herself down, telling herself everything was in place; The Dress was safely backstage, the model was booked, the car was waiting outside and they all looked great. Despite this Lily could feel pre-show nerves taking over her. As Zac and Honor arrived Lily managed to hold it together enough to admire his custom-made gold suit and Honor's stunning Carolina Herrera evening gown. Sally was thrilled that Honor wasn't wearing a velour pant-suit. Everyone was so happy; she needed to be happy too.

However, on the short drive from the Plaza, around Central Park and up Fifth Avenue Lily's nerves started to spill over into panic. She felt overwhelmed with the pressure of what people would think of her work, what they would think of a lowly blogger slash vintage clothes dealer setting herself up as a big-deal designer against Lucy Houston. What had she been *thinking*, taking this on? What had *Jack Scott* been thinking?

When the car pulled up and the door opened, Lily looked out at the paparazzi-lined red carpet sweeping up the steps of the Metropolitan Museum New York and she felt like throwing up. Suddenly, the reality of her situation hit her. Inside that building were around seven hundred of the world's fashion and style elite and they would be voting on her dress. Online, Lily could deal with anyone. Every fashion journalist and style-celebrity had been retweeting #TheDress and #WeLoveLily but now she had to face them all in the flesh. Twitter was one thing, but this was real life.

'I can't get out of the car,' she said. 'I can't do this.' She turned to Sally and pleaded, 'It's too much. Honestly, you'll have to go in without me.'

Zac looked at Sally, worried, but she nodded across at him. 'You and Honor go first,' she said.

Zac took Honor's arm and, with the doorman helping her out of the car, Honor and Zac walked into the fray like they were born to it.

'I think I'm going to throw up...'

Lily looked genuinely pale and terrified. For a moment Sally baulked, then said, 'I don't care. There'll be no mess because you haven't eaten a scrap all day so your stomach is empty...'

'Oh God, Sally, suppose they don't like it. Suppose something goes wrong and—'

'They will love it – they will love you.'

'I don't want to look like some fake who just copied an old dress.'

'Lily.' Sally turned to her friend and gave her a soft look. She could have told her how much she loved and respected her as a friend and a designer, but that would make Lily cry and ruin her make-up. So instead, Sally gave her friend a sharp poke in the arm and said, 'Either you get your skinny arse out of this car in five seconds or I swear you'll go staggering up those steps with my stilettos up your behind!'

Lily knew by Sally's steely look that her friend meant business. She also knew she loved her and that if she didn't make this journey she would be letting down not just herself, but everyone else too. So Lily took a deep breath, swung one foot in front of the other and stepped out onto the red carpet. As soon as her heels hit the ground the photographers started shouting, 'Over here!' 'Look up!' struggling to call out to her without a name until one of them spread the word: 'Lily Fitzpatrick, one of the designers!' Then calls of 'Lily!' 'Over here, Lily love!' filled the air. While Lily channelled her best Dita Von Teese smile, Sally waved madly at all of them, blowing air-kisses as they walked.

Further up the steps, the paparazzi would not let Honor go. Zac held the arm of his grandmother's friend as if she were a prize. Honor looked like royalty in the lemon chiffon Herrera gown and, with her short white hair set back into an elaborate blow-wave, was every inch the 1950s fashion doyenne.

The atmosphere inside was of elegant elitism. The champagne was good, the canapés small but plentiful. The air was heavy with fashionista small talk and the smell of expensive cosmetics. Every bare back and shoulder was buffed to perfection, and every almost-bare bosom meticulously supported and arranged. These seven hundred or so people comprised the fashion and style elite of

America. Lily realized that she knew almost every face in the room. Hollywood A-listers, rock-stars, models and famous designers – no bloggers that she recognized. There was a lot of exquisite vintage. One quick scan revealed a fashion editor in Nina Ricci and a young actress who she could have sworn was wearing the little known Belgium designer, Maggy Rouff. A few brave souls wore outrageous costumes, but most of the men played it safe with Tom Ford. The crowd wandered around, pretending to look at the Costume Institute's exhibition while actually just looking at each other.

Lily, Zac and Sally were aware of Honor's frailty and managed to settle her into a corner chair which Zac had assertively demanded from a curator, and then they gathered around their charge in a protective little group.

'This is weird,' Lily said to Sally, still somewhat paralyzed with fear.

'Yes it is,' Sally agreed, 'but you know what? I think this is actually the greatest night of my life and I wouldn't be here if it wasn't for you so...' and she gave Lily the same sincere look she had given her in the limo except this time she meant it. '...thank you.'

Lily smiled and Sally was about to ask Honor if she wanted a drink when a production assistant, a young woman in black with an earpiece, rushed over and asked her in a firm voice, 'Is Lily Fitzpatrick here?'

'That's me,' Lily said.

'Great, I've come to take you backstage to fit your model – the show starts in less than thirty minutes.'

Sally and Lily followed the production woman as she cut a path through the crowded lobby and, waving her security pass at various beefy men in uniform, she led them through a few empty gallery spaces until they reached the curtained, chaotic backstage area. Among the half-naked girls, powder puffs, rails of clothes, shouting designers, iron-steam and hairspray, the woman sought out the corner where Svetlana was standing next to The Dress.

Lily's hands were shaking with excitement as the beautiful model stepped into her precious gown. This was the moment she had been waiting for, seeing her work worn by a beautiful woman, making it come to life. Sally came and took over buttoning up the pearl buttons but when Lily stood back and looked at Svetlana she felt such a crushing sense of disappointment she wanted to cry. It was nothing she could put her finger on specifically. While The Dress fitted well enough for her to walk down a catwalk, Svetlana's tiny frame was not filling it fully. Her tiny breasts were barely touching the bodice and her delicate arms seemed as thin as pins, next to the substantial beading and embroidery. The young woman was beautiful, but the opulence of The Dress seemed to swallow her up. It was a garment so ravishing it was making Svetlana's delicate beauty disappear.

Lily had chosen a model that looked like Joy but Joy didn't exist anymore. Lily had created a dress that was real, but she had chosen her model based on a dream. The Dress needed a woman of substance to do it justice.

'I'm sorry,' she said to Svetlana, 'it looks awful, I can't let you go on.'

'What?' said Sally. 'She looks...' Then stepping back to look at it herself she added, '...fine.'

'You'll have take it off Svetlana; it's just not right on you.'

Sally started to melt down. 'No, leave it on. You can't do this Lily. We've got twenty minutes to showtime. There *is* no other model...'

Lily suddenly remembered something. She checked her phone to make a call but there was no signal.

'Security blocks all phones,' the production woman told her.

Lily would have to do this in person.

'Take the dress off, Sally...sorry, Svetlana.'

Snatching the security pass from the shocked production woman's neck, Lily began to run. Back out through the gallery spaces, pushing past the beefy bodyguards and into the gallery. The crowd was thinning out. Looking around she saw that the guests had been called in to dinner and were moving towards the atrium. Her fingers shaking with adrenaline Lily pushed her way to the front of the seating plan chart and finally found the number of the Scott's table.

The dining room was stunning, the glass roofed atrium had fairy lights swooping down in a delicate curtain, and the tables were covered in crisp white linens and flowers. Lily frantically searched for table twenty-three where she found the place-name, but not the person she was looking for.

Beside the name card was a fancy pen and an envelope printed with gold writing that said 'Cast your vote for The Dress'. Lily grabbed it and wrote: *URGENT! Catwalk emergency! Come backstage as soon as you get this, Lily.* As she walked away her stomach tightened with nerves. What the hell had she just done?

Lily closed her eyes and took a deep breath, preparing to run back and beg Svetlana to stay, when someone tapped her on the shoulder and a honey-eyed American voice said, 'Hey, girlfriend, shouldn't you be dressing your model?'

It was Sharon.

Lily let out a sob of relief, 'Yes,' she said, 'I should be.' Then she grabbed Sharon by the arm and said, 'No time to explain, just put that drink down and run!'

Forty-Two

It was such a rush dressing Sharon that Lily barely had time to step back and look at her properly before she and Sally were ushered by the security staff to take their seats for the show.

All Lily knew was that Sharon more than filled her dress. There was some serious breath holding while the buttons were being done up, and her bosom spilled gloriously over the top like some modern-day Nell Gwynn. Once they got her into it, Lily could see that Sharon had not just the body, but the attitude that The Dress needed to walk it down a catwalk. Big and bold, Sharon was more than a match for its ornate grandiosity. She would *wow* them, Lily was certain of it.

Honor and Zac were already settled at the table. Jack was standing at another table talking with Claudia, a stunning nineteen-year-old eastern European model he had been seen in the papers with the week before.

'How predictable,' said Sally, sitting down next to Lily and nodding across at her. 'At least she's not sitting with us. He *will* be mine yet!'

'How can you even think about Jack's pants at a time like this?'

'Because,' Sally said, tucking into her starter, 'I haven't seen Jack's pants yet, therefore I am intrigued. Anyway, you'll be needing this...' She handed Lily a bread roll. '...to keep up your strength when you have to get up on that stage and collect your prize.'

Lily smiled, but inside she was shaking with fear again. Zac was sitting next to her and put his hand over hers on the table. She gripped his slim fingers and felt grateful to have this new person in her life, although his presence also reminded her of another man who should have been there, but wasn't.

Honor nearly jumped out of her skin when the bang-bang music started up. The Scott's table was near the front of a long catwalk running through the centre of the vast room. The shows today were so different from when Honor was designing. Back then the women would gather in the designer's studio and the models would simply walk past the seated women. Occasionally somebody might employ a pianist to play elegant background music, but more often than not there was no such distraction, it was just the clients and the clothes. Nowadays, Honor knew from her television shows, fashion was theatre. Sitting here, at the heart of this spectacle, Honor was not sure how she felt about that.

A floppy-haired American compere came out to announce the competition. His teeth were fluorescent under the lights, even whiter than that handsome Jack Scott who was flirting so earnestly with Sally. There was definitely something going on there. Lily was on her own, although Sally had confided in her earlier that there was a young man back in London that she was interested in. Honor smiled to herself at the realization that she was part of something again. Not simply involved with the competition and The Dress, but with the people who were making it happen.

The Dress had brought her back among people again although, in truth, Honor knew it had never been simply about The Dress. The friendship that had been born out of it had always been more important.

Joy would have loved tonight. She would have loved being at the heart of society, the theatre of the show, the spectacle of it all. Mostly, she would have loved Lily and her darling Zac. Yet Joy wasn't here – Honor was. She was the one Lily had found. She was the one who had survived to see their dress come to life again.

'Two of the world's biggest fashion brands,' the compere announced, 'backing two young English designers. Lucy Houston and Lily Fitzpatrick...' Honor noticed Sally give Lily's hand a squeeze – such a warm, easy friendship. '...fashion-fight it out for the title of Designer of the Most Beautiful Dress Ever Made. One uses the latest in high-tech fabrics and technology and the other draws its inspiration from the couture of the past. Which one will *you* choose?'

More modern bang-bang music started up as the PopShop dress appeared at the top of the catwalk. The model was painfully thin and wearing a sparsely cut dress that looked as if it was made from black liquid metal. It was cut to the navel and barely covered her breasts but comprised a long train that slithered along the ground after her like a live snake. It was an amazing garment but not terribly attractive. Then, Honor thought, women don't seem as bothered about looking elegant as they used to, although she didn't judge them for that. If she had continued designing, goodness knows what mad stuff she might have come up with.

THE DRESS

As the 'liquid' dress reached the end of the catwalk, Sharon came out on stage with the Scott's logo blazing behind her. The lights were so bright on the expanse of light fabric that Honor's eyes had to adjust before The Dress came into her view. It was now, with this Amazonian creature wearing it, that Honor could see Lily's dress was so much more than her original. It had not just the elegance and glamour of Joy's dress but substance and personality too. Where her original dress had been decorated with the romantic fantasies of little girls, Lily's train was embroidered with images of true love – marriage that had lasted a lifetime. This remarkable young woman had not, in fact, copied her dress but reinterpreted it in a unique way that only somebody who had a real passion for clothes and a genuine gift for design could have done. Honor had been a great designer but, she thought, Lily was better.

The lights went down and while the food was served each table voted on their favourite dress. Honor looked across at young Lily. Even though she was putting on a brave face for Zac, Honor could see how much winning this competition meant. This show was to Lily what Joy's party had been to Honor: her defining moment. Fail or succeed, win or lose. In her youth such concepts had seemed so simple, so black and white. Yet life turns everything into the grey stew of reality. Honor had won and lost all on that night, and she felt a tightening in her stomach as she hoped the same would not happen to her young friend.

The dinner ended. The lights went down. The compere with the dazzling teeth made a huge fuss about opening the envelope which contained the result. Five seconds. Ten. A lifetime of ageing. Honor saw Lily's hands restlessly clench and unclench as she tried to control her nerves.

'And the winner is...' Honor found she could hardly breathe. 'And the winner is...' How will she cope, thought Honor, if she does not win? She deserves to. She must. She surely will. My dress will win. 'And the winner is... Lucy Houston for PopShop!'

Honor felt all the energy which had sustained her till this moment drain away. The disappointment felt like the savage opening of an old wound. Even Jack's loud wolf whistling as he publically pretended there was no hard feelings could not distract her. She dared not look at poor Lily, utterly crushed by the verdict. They all sat for a few moments, subdued by defeat, until Honor broke the silence.

'How could we *not* have won?' Honor said.

Sally snapped back straight away, 'Simple. Because our dress was *too* good. The usual problem, they're looking at the girls not the clothes. Sharon is outsize. Its pure fashion-hag prejudice. Plain and simple. They didn't like the girl.'

'She could be right,' Honor said. 'Joy looked so beautiful in The Dress. But then, it was made for her – it was like an extension of her body.'

'So,' Sally said, 'it was like Joy was *literally* wearing her dream.'

'In a way,' Honor said. 'Her dream was love, and she wanted a dress that would make Frank love her. She wanted to be loved and that's what made her commission The Dress...'

'...and love is what motivated her when she wore it,' Sally added.

'And did it work?' Lily asked.

Honor was about to tell them that no, it did not work. In fact the opposite had happened because it was on that very night Joy's beloved husband had declared his love for

Honor, but before she had the chance to speak, Zac's face lit up.

'Granny once told me that she was wearing The Dress the night she first met my grandfather. She said it was just a chance meeting and they didn't get together until a long time after that. Grandad was having a coffee in the Waldorf really late one night, and there was a party on. This woman walked into the bar in this "astonishingly magnificent" dress and Grandad said she was the most beautiful thing he had ever seen. They only had a quick exchange. She rejected him, actually, but then he met her again, in another bar, a few months later. They fell in love and got married!'

Honor reached out and took the boy's hand.

'So,' she said, 'your grandmother found love in my dress after all.' Everything had come full circle at last.

As if that were not enough, the curator of the fashion museum now came across after the show to tell Lily that despite losing the competition her dress would be going on display. Thanks to the superb craftsmanship and its historical provenance The Dress warranted a place in their permanent collection. He then asked to be introduced to Honor. After kissing her hand deferentially, he sat and quizzed her about the time she had spent working with her old boss Sybil Connolly whom 'he had once had the pleasure of meeting', and her mentor, the lesser known but nonetheless highly-respected couturier, Breton.

Honor was puzzled to be of such interest and surprised to find how easily and comfortably she talked about her past.

Sally launched herself at the dance floor with Zac as soon as the meal was over, and Lily partied alongside them. Honor could see that despite the dancing, despite her dress being bought by the museum, despite all she had achieved that night, the feeling of having 'lost' the competition had not let her young friend Lily go. Sure enough, at 11 p.m. she offered to take Honor home. The old lady pretended she was feeling tired and the two of them went out to Scott's waiting limo.

At the top of the red-carpet steps Lily and Honor stood side by side looking across at the New York night sky, while a scattering of paparazzi waited at the bottom.

'I wish we had won,' Lily said, 'for you. I wish we had won for your sake.'

Honor laughed but didn't contradict her. 'You're a perfectionist,' she said to the young designer, 'like me.'

Lily laughed a little, then confessed, 'Yes I am,' before tucking Honor's arm into hers to start their descent. But the old woman held her back.

'The problem with being a perfectionist,' Honor said, 'is that life isn't perfect. Dresses can be perfect, because we can make them exactly how we want them. The perfect fit, the perfect finish, we can fashion couture to a standard that would satisfy the gods, but we can't do the same with life. The problem with those of us who make perfect things is that, sometimes, we think we can. The most imperfect things of all are people and love.'

She paused and Lily waited then said, 'I think I understand, but I find it hard when things don't go my way.'

'No way is your way and every way is your way, Lily. It takes talent and tenacity to make beautiful things but it takes courage to let them go. It takes courage to fail at love, not to be perfect. Beauty is only a temporary joy and it has tight boundaries. Love and friendship are the only things that can set people like us free from our perfectionist prisons but it's not easy. If I had understood that when I was your age, I would have had a much happier life.'

Then she paused again and, as if looking at a picture of her past on the skyline, she said, 'Joy understood what it was to fail and in the end, she had a much better life than me.'

'Not tonight,' Lily said. 'Tonight was your night.'

Honor smiled. 'Yes,' she said, 'it was.'

The old lady squeezed her hand and Lily now saw something of the Irish warmth she had seen in her parents' wedding picture, the Irish warmth of her grandfather Joe.

Honor's grip loosened to indicate she was ready to walk down the steps.

Lily gently helped Honor into the car and was about to get in beside her when the old woman stopped her. 'I'll be fine on my own,' she said. 'The driver knows where to take me.'

'I'll come with you,' Lily said. 'I'm done here anyway.'

'Not quite,' Honor said. 'I think there is someone waiting for you.'

Lily turned and there, standing alone on the steps of the Met, was Gareth. Lily's stomach did a somersault, part delight and part fear. She saw he was wearing a tuxedo, a very nice, slightly shabby vintage one. It was exactly what she would have chosen for him herself, but she knew that Gareth would have gone into a shop and simply picked out the first one that fitted him. That made it all the sexier.

'You scrub up nice,' she said, trying to keep the shake out of her voice. 'So what are you doing here?'

She didn't want to assume.

He looked nervous for a moment, coughed, and then said, 'Well, your friend Sally called me,' he said, 'from the airport, I think? She said I was to stop being such a wuss waiting for an invitation like some maiden aunt and that I was to man up and come and get you.'

Lily laughed. 'So this is you being a man?'

'I don't know about that...'

'Well, you came.'

'She sent me flight details and Fergus was free to mind the shop so...'

He paused.

'So?' she said, smiling. 'You're here. And?'

'Ah, right, here we go then.' Gareth took a deep breath and said, 'I really like you, Lily Fitzpatrick.'

'Is that it then?' she said. 'You flew halfway around the world to tell me that you like me?'

'Ah, right, no actually, it isn't...'

Then Gareth took Lily in his arms and kissed her with a thoroughness and passion that Rhett Butler would have been proud of.

When she managed to catch her breath, Lily said, 'That was...unexpected.'

'I don't know if that's a bad or a good thing,' Gareth said, 'but I've wanted to do that since we first met.'

Lily was smiling. 'Well,' she said, 'you took your time.'

'All the best things,' he said, 'are worth waiting for.'

And the best treasures, Lily thought, are hidden at the bottom of the basket where you have to rummage to find them.

Gareth looked deep into her eyes then smiled back at her and said, 'By the way, do you know where Bleecker Street is? There's a vinyl store there with a Bill Haley album I've been after for ages.'

'No,' she said, laughing, 'but I'm sure we can find it.'

Then Lily took Gareth's hand and the two of them headed off, to start a brand new adventure among treasured old things.

Epilogue

New Jersey, 1970

It was a beautiful sunny day in New Jersey and Joy was out in her front garden, pruning the roses. They really were magnificent this year. Since she and Dan had moved to this neighbourhood, seven years ago, just after Imogen's birth, Joy's rose collection had become something of a talking point. She had no fewer than fifteen varieties and some of them were such hardy breeds that the respectable street was more or less treated to a show of colour all year around. In the harshest winter last year, a magnificent scarlet Chrysler Imperial had bloomed on Christmas Day and Imogen and she had cut it, for their table centre-piece. They always had a full house at Christmas. There were so many lonely people in the world, especially at that time of year, alcoholics who had either lost their families, or who would struggle to get through the holiday season without a drink – they were all welcome at the Podmores' holiday table.

Joy loved the exquisite soft beauty of her flowers, but she also enjoyed the process of making things grow. The way the dirtiest, ugliest kitchen debris, eggshells and potato peelings fed the soil and made her flowers even more beautiful and vibrant. There was a justice in beauty born out of dirt that appealed to her.

Although the garden was where Joy got much of her creative satisfaction, these days her house too was immaculate. While she did most of the work herself, Dan's business was successful enough for her to afford a woman to come in, twice a week, to help her out. They were comfortable. Once a year, the three of them went to the Catskill Mountains on holiday; Dan had taught her to drive and they both had cars. Their mortgage was small, Dan was a hard worker and they were never short of money, for food or bills. Joy had lost her taste for couture and had taken very few of her old pieces with her into her new life. A couple of Chanel suits, her Nina Ricci gown and some beloved Balenciaga pieces, all of which she planned to pass onto Imogen. Those treasures aside, Joy still cut a smart figure. Her neighbours were vaguely envious of her, not least because of her reliable husband, Dan, who never got drunk or propositioned them at neighbourhood barbecues, who was always charming, but clearly, still madly in love with his wife and she with him. The couple had their work with Alcoholics Anonymous which kept them grounded and a circle of good friends, but mostly they had Imogen.

Joy had been astonished when she had found herself pregnant in her mid-thirties. She was worried at first, telling the doctor about her earlier struggles to conceive. He had assured her that, although her fertility might have been affected in the past by her alcohol consumption, when it came to making babies, the science was inexact to say the least. 'It's as much to do with the will of God as anything else,' he said, and Joy knew that to be true for most things in her life. He said the fact that she had stopped drinking might have helped.

Motherhood had been a revelation for Joy, from the pregnancy experience of carrying another human being inside her body, to her brave endurance of childbirth and the all-encompassing love she felt for her child. The complexities of her addiction were once and for all washed away in the great tide of emotion she had for the baby. Her craving for love was utterly sated; she loved every glorious moment of being a mother and it had confirmed her loyalty and respect for her husband, Dan.

The hunger for approval, the unstable feeling, the wanting in her stomach that she had mistaken for love during her time with Frank, had gone from her.

Until the day when, ten years after he had left her and thrown her out of his life, Frank Fitzgerald turned up on her front lawn.

He looked his age, fifty now. His hair was greying at the temples and he was slightly unkempt, but still handsome. Joy's heart gave a small jolt, out of some gone, but not forgotten, habit.

'Hullo, Joy,' he said.

Why do you look so sad?

'Hullo, Frank,' Joy said and smiled, but he didn't smile back. He looked worried and she had an old familiar flash of feeling responsible for his unhappiness.

Dan was out at work, Imogen was at school, so she said, 'Won't you come inside and have some coffee, Frank?'

He seemed to consider it, then looked at the house and shook his head, as if deciding the commitment to enter her new life would be too much. Joy tried to meet his eyes, but he kept his gaze trained on the horizon behind her, as if expecting something to fall out of the sky. There was something amiss. Was he was still angry with her? Had he not let go?

'I was wondering if you had heard from Honor, at all?'

Ah, Honor. Joy had read in the gossip columns, years ago, that she had left him. Although it was silly, Joy could not help but feel slightly disappointed that he had not come to see her.

'She called to our apartment in Brooklyn, just after we were married, maybe six months after you...' Kicked me out on the street, stole everything I owned? Joy was shocked that the old wound hadn't quite closed. '...after *we* divorced. She came to the door to say...'

What had Honor come to say that day? Joy remembered getting a fright when she saw her standing there, then fobbing her off. It was the last time she had seen Honor's face, her chin trembling slightly with defiant fear. It must have taken a lot of courage for her to turn up like that. Had she come to apologize, to recant, to ask for help? Perhaps she wanted to come and talk about Frank, about her plans to leave him. Joy would never know and, quite suddenly, ten years later, she was filled with regret for not having welcomed Honor into her home, back into her life. It had been too soon, back then; the pain had been too raw. If only Honor were to call on her here, now, today, what a different welcome she would give her; perhaps they might have become friends again.

'I don't know why she called on me, Frank, to be honest. It was too soon, after everything...I sent her away.'

Frank's face fell and Joy saw the hurt, vulnerable boy she had fallen in love with. The man who had seen the sadness beyond her name, the man who had fallen in love with the old Joy, the tortured, unhappy Joy she used to be.

'I can't find her,' he said. 'I've been looking for ten years.'

'For *Honor*?' Joy could not keep the shock out of her voice. Was it possible that he was still hanging on the past like this?

'She's my wife.'

The word wife hung in the air between them, in an untaken breath.

In that moment Joy realized that she still loved him. Not with the great untrammelled passion of her drinking youth, but with the deep humanity that had connected them in the first place. He had seen her sadness and Joy had hoped that loving him would chase that sadness away. She learned, the hard way, that only she could do that, that she and her God were in charge of holding her joy.

Joy could see that Frank was in pain and although she knew, through AA, that unasked for advice was rarely welcomed, she equally knew that she could not let him walk away without reaching out.

'You know, Frank, for years I thought I couldn't move on, until other people had forgiven me for all the terrible things I had done...'

Frank shuffled awkwardly and kept his head down. He had never responded to her letter. What was she trying to say?

'...But then, finally, I realized I had to forgive myself.'

He nodded, still looking down at the ground. His mouth was closed tight, as if he had nothing to say, or was trying to keep what he had to say from escaping.

'Let her go, Frank.'

In the face of his taut silence, Joy stopped.

Eventually he raised his head. His jaw had relaxed; his

eyes soft and sad. For a moment, Joy thought she had got through to him. Then he said, 'If Honor does get in touch, be sure to tell her I'm looking for her.'

Frank took a step towards his car, and as he did so the driver quickly got out and opened the passenger door. But then Frank hesitated and looked over at the house again. With its swept, suburban porch and worn, comfortable chairs, it seemed the antithesis of their elegant life in Manhattan, yet it belonged as much to Joy as the Fifth Avenue penthouse once had.

'I'm glad you have a good life,' Frank said. It was as much of an apology as she was ever going to get. Perhaps it's as much as I deserve, Joy thought.

'I hope you find her,' Joy called after him, then to herself, 'I hope you find what you're looking for.'

As Joy watched Frank walk towards his driver, his back tense and slightly hunched, she said a small prayer that he would.

Acknowledgments

For the first time in my writing life, I had no idea for my next book. I was starting to panic when, at a gallery show, I bumped into an old associate from my time working on fashion magazines. Eddie Shanahan engaged me in a conversation about the craft of couture that was so scintillating I suddenly woke up to the expression 'write what you know'. This book was conceived out of our shared passion for history and couture – so thank you Eddie.

In Spring 2014 I 'lost' *The Dress* when I left my unsaved draft on an iBook, in the back of a Dublin taxi. I took to Twitter and trended overnight as #TheLostNovel. I would like to thank the Irish media who moved hell and high water to get my book back for me – especially the Ray D'Arcy and Nicky Byrne radio show teams, P.R. Caroline Kennedy, the *Irish Mail* and fellow novelists Cecelia Aherne, Marian Keyes and Amanda Brunker for tweeting up a storm on my behalf. Also Eddie Masterson, the taxi driver who returned my laptop (and had Jack Scott's handsome driver named after him in return!).

For editing in the early stages, the brilliant Claire Bord. Your suggestion changed everything. You made such a difference, thank you.

My assistant Danielle Kerins. Editing, character development, proof-reading, comma police – you are the best publishing all-rounder any writer ever had. You blow me away every time – I am blessed. Thank you.

Also, thanks to Transition Year students, Catherine King and Elaine McHale, who joined me for part of the journey, and made themselves very useful indeed.

Lou Brennan – fashion designer, illustrator and muse for this book. Thank you for allowing me to draw on your expertise but mostly for designing the actual dress for me, then bringing it to life with your exquisite drawings.

Agents, Marianne Gunn O'Connor and Vicki Satlow for your unswerving support and belief in me. And, of course, Pat Lynch for always being on the end of that phone.

My wonderful editor Rosie de Courcy. At this stage of my career I never expected to work with such a game-changing editor. You have transformed the way I write. *The Dress* feels like the first book I have ever written – you have renewed my faith in both myself and the power of storytelling. This is your book as much as it is mine. Thank you. Thank you. Thank you.

Amanda Ridout and the Head of Zeus team, especially Emily Zinkin, Jessie Price, Kaz Harrison, Clémence Jacquinet and Claire Nozières. I feel very lucky to have such a talented, dynamic and passionate group of people publishing me.

My oldest friend Mary Keane Dawson for the love and life-coaching when it all got too much and fellow writer Ella Griffin, for keeping me sane with FaceTime calls.

My mother Moira, for being my rock and my first-ear, and my aunt, Sheila Smyth. Thank you both for cheerleading my writing skills, if not my appalling punctuation.

Lastly, always, my husband Niall, for enabling me to write and for allowing me to be 'the writer'. Thank you for continuing to live on the frontline of my dramas – I could not do any of this without you.